CONTENTS

D0040042

With utmost appreciation, I dedicate this Cardwell book to Kimberly Rocha, the craziest, most loving, generous, truly beautiful fan I've yet to meet.

CARDWELL CHRISTMAS CRIME SCENE

AND

SECRET OF DEADMAN'S COULEE

New York Times and USA TODAY Bestselling Author

B.J. DANIELS

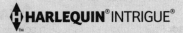

HARLEQUIN® INTRIGUE®

If you purchased this book without a cover you should be aware that this book is stolen property. It was reported as "unsold and destroyed" to the publisher, and neither the author nor the publisher has received any payment for this "stripped book."

ISBN-13: 978-0-373-83810-3

Cardwell Christmas Crime Scene
and Secret of Deadman's Coulee

Copyright © 2016 by Harlequin Books S.A.

Recycling programs for this product may not exist in your area.

The publisher acknowledges the copyright holder of the individual works as follows:

Cardwell Christmas Crime Scene
Copyright © 2016 by Barbara Heinlein

Secret of Deadman's Coulee
Copyright © 2007 by Barbara Heinlein

All rights reserved. Except for use in any review, the reproduction or utilization of this work in whole or in part in any form by any electronic, mechanical or other means, now known or hereinafter invented, including xerography, photocopying and recording, or in any information storage or retrieval system, is forbidden without the written permission of the publisher, Harlequin Enterprises Limited, 225 Duncan Mill Road, Don Mills, Ontario M3B 3K9, Canada.

This is a work of fiction. Names, characters, places and incidents are either the product of the author's imagination or are used fictitiously, and any resemblance to actual persons, living or dead, business establishments, events or locales is entirely coincidental.

This edition published by arrangement with Harlequin Books S.A.

For questions and comments about the quality of this book, please contact us at CustomerService@Harlequin.com.

® and TM are trademarks of Harlequin Enterprises Limited or its corporate affiliates. Trademarks indicated with ® are registered in the United States Patent and Trademark Office, the Canadian Intellectual Property Office and in other countries.

Printed in U.S.A.

www.Harlequin.com

Dear Reader,

When I moved to the small town in Montana where I now live, I couldn't wait to set a series of books here. I loved the open prairie after living most of my life in a completely different part of the state.

That series, the Whitehorse, Montana series, let me write about real small-town living in a place where there are more cows than people, more trucks than cars and more open space than most people can imagine.

There are nights the sky is alive with the northern lights in every color of the rainbow. Cloudless nights Montana's big sky is ablaze with stars. I love this place and I love writing about where I live.

So it's no wonder that I fell in love with my fictional town of Whitehorse. Which is why I'm delighted to see the first book in that series, *Secret of Deadman's Coulee*, return with my last Cardwell Ranch book.

I hope you enjoy it as there are now twenty-four books in the Whitehorse series—and more to come next year!

B.J. Daniels

B.J. Daniels is a *New York Times* and *USA TODAY* bestselling author. She wrote her first book after a career as an award-winning newspaper journalist and author of thirty-seven published short stories. She lives in Montana with her husband, Parker, and three springer spaniels. When not writing, she quilts, boats and plays tennis. Contact her at bjdaniels.com, on Facebook or on Twitter, @bjdanielsauthor.

Books by B.J. Daniels

Harlequin Intrigue

Cardwell Cousins

Rescue at Cardwell Ranch
Wedding at Cardwell Ranch
Deliverance at Cardwell Ranch
Reunion at Cardwell Ranch

Crime Scene at Cardwell Ranch
Justice at Cardwell Ranch
Cardwell Ranch Trespasser
Christmas at Cardwell Ranch
Cardwell Christmas Crime Scene

Whitehorse, Montana

Secret of Deadman's Coulee
The New Deputy in Town
The Mystery Man of Whitehorse
Classified Christmas
Matchmaking with a Mission
Second Chance Cowboy
Montana Royalty
Shotgun Bride

Visit the Author Profile page at Harlequin.com for more titles.

CARDWELL CHRISTMAS
CRIME SCENE

Chapter 1

DJ Justice opened the door to her apartment and froze.
Nothing looked out of place and yet she took a step back.
Her gaze went to the lock. There were scratches around
the keyhole. The lock set was one of the first things she'd
replaced when she'd rented the apartment.

She eased her hand into the large leather hobo bag
that she always carried. Her palm fit smoothly around
the grip of the weapon, loaded and ready to fire, as she
slowly pushed open the door.

The apartment was small and sparsely furnished. She
never stayed anywhere long, so she collected nothing of
value that couldn't fit into one suitcase. Spending years
on the run as a child, she'd had to leave places in the
middle of the night with only minutes to pack.

But that had changed over the past few years. She'd
just begun to feel…safe. She liked her job, felt content
here. She should have known it couldn't last.

The door creaked open wider at the touch of her finger, and she quickly scanned the living area. Moving deeper into the apartment, she stepped to the open bathroom door and glanced in. Nothing amiss. At a glance she could see the bathtub, sink and toilet as well as the mirror on the medicine cabinet. The shower door was clear glass. Nothing behind it.

That left just the bedroom. As she stepped soundlessly toward it, she wanted to be wrong. And yet she knew someone had been here. But why break in unless he or she planned to take something?

Or leave something?

Like the time she'd found the bloody hatchet on the fire escape right outside her window when she was eleven. That message had been for her father, the blood from a chicken, he'd told her. Or maybe it hadn't even been blood, he'd said. As if she hadn't seen his fear. As if they hadn't thrown everything they owned into suitcases and escaped in the middle of the night.

She moved to the open bedroom door. The room was small enough that there was sufficient room only for a bed and a simple nightstand with one shelf. The book she'd been reading the night before was on the nightstand, nothing else.

The double bed was made—just as she'd left it.

She started to turn away when she caught a glimmer of something out of the corner of her eye. Ice ran down her spine as she dropped the gun back into her shoulder bag and stepped closer. Something had been tucked between the pillows and duvet. Gingerly picking up the edge of the duvet, she peeled it back an inch at a time. DJ braced herself for something bloody and dismembered, her mind a hamster on a wheel, spinning wildly.

But what she found was more disturbing than blood and guts. As she uncovered part of it, she saw familiar blank eyes staring up at her. Her breath caught in her throat as tears stung her eyes.

"Trixie?" she whispered, voice breaking, as she stared at the small rag doll's familiar face.

On the run with her father, she'd had little more than the clothes on her back except for the rag doll that had been her only companion since early childhood.

"We should throw this old thing away," her father had said after a dog tore the doll from her hands once and he'd had to chase it down to retrieve what was left because she'd been so hysterical. "I'll buy you another doll. A pretty one, not some stuffed fabric one," he'd pleaded.

She'd been so upset that he'd relented and let her keep the doll she'd always known as Trixie. But she could tell that he would have been happier to get rid of the thing. She wondered if it brought him bad memories, since it was clear that the doll was handmade. Even the clothing. She liked to pretend that her mother had made it for her. If her mother hadn't died in childbirth.

Was that why her father wished she didn't care so much for the doll? Because it brought back the grief, the loss? That might explain why he had seemed to want nothing to do with anything from the past, including her doll. Not that she'd ever understood her father.

Life with him had been sparse and sporadic. He had somehow kept her fed and clothed and managed to get her into school—at least for a while until they were up-rooted again. But the incident with the doll now made her wonder.

From as far back as she could remember, she'd believed that the doll with the sewn face and the dull, dark stitched eyes needed her as much as she needed it.

Now she half feared all she would find was Trixie's dismembered head. But as she drew back the covers, she saw that the body was still intact. Someone had left it for her tucked under the covers almost...tenderly. With trembling fingers, she picked up the treasured rag doll, afraid something awful had been done to her that would spoil one of the few good memories she had of her childhood.

Cupping the precious doll in her hands, DJ began to cry—for herself and for Trixie. The doll was in incredible shape for how old she was, not to mention what she must have been through over the years. DJ thought of her being lost, someone discarding her in a trash can as nothing more than junk and that awful feeling she'd had that she would never see her again.

So how had Trixie miraculously turned up again?

Heart in her throat, she looked closer at the doll.

Something was wrong.

The doll looked exactly like Trixie, but... She studied the handmade clothing. It looked as pristine as the doll. Maybe whoever had found it had washed it, taken care of it all these years...

For what possible purpose?

As happy as she'd been to see the doll again, now she realized how unlikely that was. Why would anyone care about some silly rag doll? And how could someone possibly know she was the one who'd lost it all those years ago?

After being her constant companion from as far back as she could remember, Trixie had been the worse for wear before DJ had misplaced her. The doll had spent too many years tucked under one of DJ's chubby arms. So how—

With a jolt, she recalled the accident she'd had with the doll and the dog that had taken off with it all those years ago. The dog had ripped off one of Trixie's legs. With DJ screaming for help, her father had chased down the dog, retrieved the leg and later, at her pleading, painstakingly sewn it back on with the only thread he could find, black.

Her fingers trembling, she lifted the dress hem and peered under the only slightly faded red pantaloons. With both shock and regret, she saw that there was no black thread. No seam where the leg had been reattached.

This wasn't her doll.

It surprised her that at thirty-five, she could feel such loss for something she'd been missing for so many years.

She stared at the rag doll, now more confused than ever. Why would people break into her apartment to leave it for her? They had to have known that she'd owned one exactly like it. Wouldn't they realize that she'd know the difference between hers and this one? Or was that the point?

DJ studied the doll more closely. She was right. This one and Trixie were almost *identical*, which meant that whoever had made them had made *two*. Why?

She'd never questioned before where her doll had come from. Trixie was in what few photographs she'd seen of her childhood, her doll locked under her arm almost like an extension of herself.

Like hers, this one looked more than thirty years old. The clothing was a little faded, the face even blanker than it had been all those years ago, but not worn and faded like Trixie had been when DJ had lost her.

DJ felt a chill. So who had left this for her?

Someone who'd had this doll—a doll that was identical to hers before Trixie's accident. Someone who'd known there had been two identical dolls. Someone who knew this doll would be meaningful to her.

But why break in to leave it for her tucked under the covers? And why give it to her now? A life on the run had taught her one thing. The people who had left this wanted something from her. They could have mailed it with a note. Unless they had some reason to fear it could be traced back to them?

Regrettably, there was only one person she could ask, someone she hadn't spoken to in seven years. Her father.

She took a couple of deep breaths as she walked back into the living room. She'd left the door open in case she had needed to get out fast, but now she moved to close and lock it.

With her back against the door, she stared at the apartment she'd come to love. She'd made a life for herself here, and just the thought of being forced to give it up—

She was considering what her intruder might want from her when she felt a prick and dropped the doll. Sucking on her bleeding finger, she stared down at the rag doll. The dress had gaped open in the back to expose a straight pin—and what looked like the corner of a photograph.

Carefully picking up the doll so it didn't stick her again, she unpinned the photo and pulled it out. There were three people in the snapshot. A man and two women, one young, one older, all dark-haired. The young woman, the only one smiling, was holding a baby.

She flipped the photo over. Written in a hurried hand were the words: *Your family.*

What? She quickly turned the photograph back over and stared at the people pictured there.

She'd never seen any of them before, but there was something familiar about the smiling woman holding the baby. DJ realized with a start that the woman looked like her. But how was this possible if her mother had died in childbirth?

If it was true and these people were family...was it possible she was the baby in the photo? Why would her father have lied if that were the case? He knew how much she would have loved having family. He'd always said it was just the two of them. But what if that wasn't true?

Still, she thought as she studied the photo, if it was true, wouldn't they have contacted her? Then she realized they *were* contacting her now. But why wait all these years, and why do it like this?

The reason hit her hard. No one had wanted her to know the truth.

But someone had decided to tell her.

Or *warn* her, she thought with a shiver.

Chapter 2

"Are you sure it's the same doll? I thought you lost it years ago."

DJ gripped the utilitarian standard black phone tighter as she looked through the thick Plexiglas in the prison visiting room at her father.

Walter Justice had been a big, handsome man who'd charmed his way out of trouble all his life—until it caught up with him one night when he'd gotten involved in a robbery that went badly and he ended up doing time for second-degree murder. He had aged well even in prison, and that charm was still there in the twinkle of his blue eyes, in his crooked-toothed smile, in the soft reassuring sound of his voice.

She hadn't been able to wait until visiting day, so this was the best that could be done on short notice with the prison warden. But as surprised and pleased as her father had been to see her, he'd given the doll only a cursory look.

"It's the same doll," she said impatiently into the phone. "It's just not *mine*. Apparently someone made two of these dolls. The clothes are handmade—just like my doll. Everything is identical except the doll isn't mine," she explained impatiently. "So whose is it?"

"How should *I* know?"

"You have to know where *my* doll came from," she argued.

"DJ, you don't really expect me to remember where we picked up a rag doll all those years ago, do you?"

"Yes, I do." She frowned, remembering a photo she'd seen of when she was a baby. Trixie had been lying next to her. "I had it from as far back as I can remember. You should remember if someone gave it to me when I was a baby."

He glanced away for a moment. "Look, if you think it is some kind of threat, then maybe you should disappear for a while."

She hadn't said she thought it was a threat. Her eyes widened in both alarm and anger. What wasn't he telling her?

"That is all you have to say? *Run?* Your answer to everything." She thought of the cheap motels, the carryout food, the constantly looking over her shoulder, afraid someone would either kill her father or take him from her. First sign of trouble—and there was always trouble when your father is a con man—and off they would go, usually in the middle of the night. She'd spent too many years on the run with him as a child. This time she wasn't running.

"No," she said, gripping the phone until her fingers

ached. "This time I want answers. If you don't tell me, I'll get them on my own."

"I only want you to be...safe."

"*Safe?* So this doll *is* a threat." She cursed under her breath. For years she'd had to deal with people her father had swindled or old partners he'd shortchanged or screwed over. Half the time she didn't know who was after them or why they had to keep moving, always on the run from something. She'd felt as if she'd had a target on her back all her life because of this man. "What have you gotten me into now?"

"You can't believe this doll is my doing."

Why had she thought that her father, a man who lied for living, would be honest with her? Coming here had been a mistake, but then again, she'd had no one else to ask about the doll—or the photo.

She reached into her pocket. She'd come too far to turn around and leave without at least trying to get the truth out of him. "Who are these people in this photograph, and why would someone want me to have it?" she demanded as she pressed the crinkled photo against the Plexiglas between them.

DJ watched all the color drain from his face. Growing up, she'd learned to tell when he was lying. But what she saw now on his face was pain and fear.

His gaze darting away from the photo as he lowered his voice. "I don't know what this is about, but what would it hurt if you just got out of town for a while?"

She shook her head. "Stop lying to me. You recognize these people. Tell me the truth. Is this my mother? Don't you think I noticed that she looks like me? Am I that baby?"

"DJ, how is that possible? I told you, your mother died in childbirth."

"Then this woman isn't my mother?"

"On my life, you aren't the baby in that photo." He crisscrossed his heart. "And those people are not your family."

She'd been so hopeful. She felt like crying as she peeled the photo off the grimy glass and dropped it back into her bag along with the doll. She'd had to leave her gun in her car and felt naked without it. "But you did recognize the people in the photo."

He said nothing, which came as little surprise.

"I have no idea why I came here." She met his gaze. "I knew you'd lie."

"DJ, whatever you think of me, listen to me now," he pleaded.

DJ. That had been his nickname for her, and it had stuck. But hearing him say it had her fighting tears. She'd once thought her father was the most amazing man in the world. That had been a very long time ago.

She got to her feet, shaking her head at her own naïveté as she started to put the phone back. She'd fallen for his promises too many times in her life. She'd made a clean break when he'd gone to prison, telling him she never wanted to see him again.

Drawing the phone to her ear, she said, "It is clear to me that you've lied to me my whole life. What I don't know is why. But I'm going to find out."

"I did the best I could, just the two of us," her father said, his voice breaking. "I know I could have done better, but, DJ—"

She'd heard this before and couldn't bear to hear it again. "If I have family—" Growing up, she'd often dreamed of a big, boisterous family. Now, with Christmas coming, she felt nostalgic. If she had family, if that's why they'd left this for her now…

She'd seen an ad in a magazine of a family around a beautifully decorated tree on Christmas morning. That night she'd prayed to the starlit night that she could be that little girl in the ad.

But her prayer hadn't been answered, and now she no longer believed in fairy tales. If anything, life had taught her that there were no happy endings.

"DJ, you have to listen to me." He'd raised his voice. The guard was making his way down the line of booths toward him. "You don't know how dangerous—"

"Dangerous?" she echoed.

The guard tapped him on the shoulder. "Time to go."

"DJ—"

"Just tell me the truth." She hated how vulnerable she sounded. She'd seen his face when he'd looked at the people in the photograph. He *had* recognized them. But if they were her family, then why had he looked so… hurt, and yet so frightened? Because he'd been caught in a lie? Or because she had something to fear from them?

She'd had to become strong and trust her own instincts for so long… Growing up on the run with her father had taught her how to survive.

That was, until she'd found the doll and the photo of three people she didn't know, one of them holding a baby who, no matter what he said, was probably her. But what about that would put her in danger?

"Last chance," she said into the phone.

The guard barked another *"Time to go."*

Her father's gaze locked with hers. She saw pleading in his eyes as he quickly said into the phone, "There's a reason I lied all these years, but the truth is…you will be hearing from my family in Montana soon. Go to them until you hear from me." The guard grabbed the phone from her father's hand and slammed it down.

DJ stood staring at him, his words rooting her to the floor. Her father had family in Montana? *She* had family? A family that would be contacting her? If this was another lie…

Slowly she hung up her phone as she watched Walter Justice being led away. Frowning, she pulled out the photo. He's sworn these people weren't her family. Then who were they? Her mother's family? A cold dread filled her at the memory of her father's reaction to the photo.

The doll and the photo proved that they knew about her. That at least someone in that family wanted her to know about them. And now she was going to find them. That she was on her own was nothing new.

And yet the fear she'd seen in her father's eyes almost burned through her resolve.

In Big Sky, Montana, Dana Cardwell Savage braced herself as she pushed open the door to her best friend Hilde's sewing shop. Christmas music played softly among the rows and rows of rich bolts of fabric. For a moment she slowed to admire the Christmas decorations that Hilde had sewn for the occasion, wishing she had time to sew. She missed quilting and the time she used to spend with Hilde back when they were partners in Needles and Pins.

Seeing her friend at the back, she moved on reluctantly. She needed to tell Hilde the news in person. Her only fear was how her friend was going to respond.

Their relationship had taken a beating three years ago. Hilde had only begun to trust her again. And now this.

"Dana!" Hilde saw her and smiled, clearly pleased to see her. Raising four children, Dana rarely got down to the shop that she and Hilde had started together. Hilde had bought her out long since then, but Dana still loved coming down here, where it was so peaceful and quiet.

She moved to the stools by the cash register and pulled one up to sit down. There were several people in the shop, but fortunately, Hilde's assistant, Veronica "Ronnie" Tate, was helping them.

"Where are the kids?" Hilde asked.

"With Stacy." She loved that her older sister was so good about taking all of the children to give Dana a break. Stacy's daughter, Ella, was almost five now. Dana's twins were four, Mary was eight and her oldest, Hank, was nine. Where had those years gone?

"So, you're out on the town?" Hilde asked and then seemed to notice how nervous Dana was. "What is it? What's happened?"

"My cousin Dee Anna Justice, the *real* one. Except apparently she goes by DJ. I talked to my uncle, Walter, whom I was led to believe was dead." She didn't want to bias Hilde against the real Dee Anna Justice any more than she might already be, given the past. But she also couldn't keep anything from her. "Walter called from prison."

"Prison?"

Dana nodded. "He assured me that his daughter is nothing like him. In fact, she hadn't talked to him in years until recently. She doesn't know she has family, he said. She was never told about us. My uncle was hoping that I would contact her and invite her to come to Montana for the holidays so she can get to know her family."

Paling, Hilde's hand went to her protruding stomach and the baby inside her. Three years ago, a young woman claiming to be Dee Anna had come to the ranch. Dana, who had so desperately wanted to connect with a part of her family she hadn't known even existed, had fallen for the psychopathic, manipulative woman's lies, and they had all almost paid with their lives.

But Hilde had suffered the most. Dana still couldn't believe that she'd trusted the woman she thought was her cousin over her best friend. She would never forgive herself. The fake Dee Anna, it turned out, had been the roommate of the real Dee Anna Justice for a short period of time. The roommate had opened a piece of her mail and, since they resembled each other, had pretended to be Dee Anna. Dana had believed that the woman was the real Dee Anna Justice and almost lost everything because of it.

"Why would he keep something like that from her?" Hilde finally asked.

"Because his family had disowned him when he married a woman they didn't approve of. He thought his family would turn both him and his daughter away, apparently."

"But now?"

"Now, he said with Christmas coming, he hoped I would reach out to her and not turn her away as his family had done. She doesn't have any other family, he said." She saw Hilde weaken.

"I told my uncle about the woman who pretended to be Dee Anna. He was so sorry about what happened," Dana said quickly. "He said he'd never met DJ's former roommate, but that he was shocked, and his daughter would be, too, to learn that the woman was capable of the horrible things she did."

Hilde nodded. "So, you've contacted her?"

"No, I wouldn't do that without talking to you first."

Her friend took a breath and let it out. "It's all right."

"I won't if it upsets you too much," Dana said, reaching for Hilde's hand.

"You're sure this time she's the real Dee Anna Justice?"

"Hud ran both her and her father through the system. She has been working as a travel writer, going all over the world to exotic places and writing about them under the pen name DJ Price." One of the perks of being married to the local marshal was that he wouldn't let anyone else come to visit without first finding out his or her true identity.

"So Colt knows that the real Dee Anna has turned up?"

The only good thing that had come out of that horrible time three years ago was Deputy Marshal Colt Lawson. He had believed what Hilde was saying about the fake Dee and had ended up saving her life as well as Dana's and the kids'. Now the two were married, and Dana had never seen Hilde looking happier, especially since she was pregnant with their first child.

"I talked to Colt *first*. He said it was up to you, but none of us wants to take any chances with this baby or your health."

Hilde smiled. "I'm as healthy as a horse and the baby is fine. As long as we're sure this woman is the real Dee Anna and not a murdering psychopath."

The other Dee, the fake Dee Anna Justice, had set her

sights on Dana's husband, Marshal Hud Savage, planning to replace Dana. So Dana and her children had to go, and Hilde, the interfering friend in the woman's mentally disturbed mind, along with them. Dana shivered at the memory.

She had nightmares sometimes, thinking they were all still locked in that burning barn. "*That* Dee Anna is dead and gone."

Hilde nodded. "But not forgotten."

"No, not forgotten. It was a lesson I will never forget, and neither will Hud." She smiled and squeezed her friend's hand. "I'm just glad you and I are okay."

"We're more than okay. I know how much family means to you. Contact your cousin and tell her she's welcome. I would never stand in the way of you finding more of your relatives on your mother's side."

"I want you to meet her. If for any reason you suspect anything strange about her—"

Hilde laughed. "I'll let you know if she tries to kill me."

Chapter 3

Beau Tanner had always known the debt would come due, and probably at the worst possible time. He'd dreaded this day since he was ten. Over the years he'd waited, knowing there was no way he could deny whatever request was put to him.

The sins of the father, he thought as he stared at the envelope he'd found in his mailbox this morning. The return address was for an attorney in San Diego, California. But the letter inside was from a California state correction facility prisoner by the name of Walter Justice.

He wondered only idly how the man had found him after all these years, forgetting for a moment the kind of people he was dealing with. Beau could have ended up anywhere in the world. Instead, he'd settled in the Gallatin Canyon, where they'd first met. He suspected

Walter had kept track of him, knowing that one day he would demand payment for the debt.

The letter had been sent to his home address here on the ranch—instead of his office. So he knew before he opened it that it would be personal.

Telling himself just to get it over with, Beau studied the contents of the envelope. There were two sheets of paper inside. One appeared to be a travel article about Eleuthera, an island in the Bahamas. The other was a plain sheet of paper with a printed note:

> Take care of my daughter, DJ. Flight 1129 from LA arriving in Bozeman, Montana, Thursday at 2:45 p.m. Dana Cardwell Savage will be picking her up and taking her to Cardwell Ranch. I highly advise you not to let her know that you're watching out for her—and most especially that it was at my request.

It was signed W. Justice.

Under that he'd written, "Cell phone number for emergencies only."

Today was Thursday. DJ's flight would be coming in *this* afternoon. Walter had called it awfully close. What if Beau had been out of town? If he'd questioned whether Walter had kept track of him, he didn't anymore.

He read the letter again and swore. He had no idea what this was about. Apparently Walter's daughter needed protection? A small clue would have been helpful. And protection from what? Or was it from whom?

Also, he was surprised Walt's daughter would be coming to Montana. That was where their paths had crossed all those years ago. He thought of the dark-haired five-year-old girl with the huge brown expressive eyes and the skinny ten-year-old kid he'd been.

He remembered the way she'd looked up at him, how he'd melted into those eyes, how he'd foolishly wanted to rescue her. What a joke. He hadn't even been able to rescue himself. Like him, she'd been trapped in a life that wasn't her doing.

"Any mail for me?" asked a sleepy-sounding female voice from behind him.

He folded the letter and article and shoved them into his jean jacket pocket before turning to look at the slim, beautiful blonde leaning against his kitchen counter. "Nope. Look, Leah—"

"I really appreciate you letting me stay here, Beau," she said, cutting him off. "If this package I have coming wasn't so important and I wasn't between places right now…"

Beau nodded, mentally kicking himself for getting involved when she'd shown up on his doorstep. "Leah, I wish you hadn't put me in the middle of whatever this is."

"Please, no lectures," she said, raising a hand. "Especially before I've had my coffee. You did make coffee, didn't you? I remember that you always made better coffee than Charlie." Her voice broke at Charlie's name. She turned away from him, but not before he'd seen the tears.

She pulled down a clean cup and poured herself a cup of coffee before turning to him again. He studied her in the steam that rose from the dark liquid. He'd met Leah Barnhart at college when his best friend and roommate, Charlie Mack, had been dating her. The three of them had become good friends. Leah and Charlie had later married and both taken jobs abroad. Over the years, they'd kept in touch for a while, then just an occasional Christmas card. The past few years there hadn't even been a Christmas card.

No wonder he'd been so surprised and caught off guard to find her standing on his doorstep last night.

"And you're not in the middle of anything," she said after taking a long drink of her coffee.

"Why *are* you here?"

"I told you. I'm expecting an important package. I happened to be in Montana and thought about our college days…" She met his gaze and shrugged.

He didn't believe any of it. "Where's Charlie? You said he's still in Europe. I need his number."

She looked away with a sigh. "I don't have it."

He glanced at her bare left-hand ring finger. "Are you *divorced*?"

"No, of course not." She let out a nervous laugh. "We're just— It's a long story, and really not one I'm ready to get into this early in the morning. Can we talk about this later?"

He agreed, since he needed to get to work. DJ Justice would be flying into Montana in a few hours. He had to be ready. He had no idea what was required to keep her safe. It might come down to some extreme measures. Since he didn't know why she even needed protection— or from whom—now was definitely not the time to have a houseguest, especially one who knew nothing about his life before college. He wanted to keep it that way.

"You don't decorate for Christmas?" Leah asked as she looked around the large log home he'd built back in a small valley in the mountains not far from Big Sky. He'd bought enough land that he could have horses— and privacy. That was another reason he'd been surprised to find her on his doorstep. His place wasn't that easy to find.

He raked a hand through his thick, unruly mop of blond hair. "I've never been one for holidays."

She nodded. "I thought you'd at least have had a tree and some lights."

He glanced at his watch. "If you need anything, call my office and talk to Marge."

Leah made a face. "I called your office on my way here. Marge scares me."

He doubted that. He'd known Leah a lifetime ago. Was this woman standing in his kitchen the same Leah he'd toasted when she and Charlie had married? "Marge is a little protective."

"I should say. So you really are a private investigator?"

"That's what my license says."

She studied him with narrowed eyes. "Why do I get the feeling there is more to it?"

"I have no idea," he said. "Are you sure you'll be all right here by yourself?"

"I'll be fine." She smiled. "I won't steal your silverware, if that's what you're worried about."

"I wasn't. Anyway, it's cheap flatware."

She sobered. "I've missed you, Beau. Charlie and I both have. But I honestly do have a package coming here, and it's important or I wouldn't have done it without checking with you first."

"Then we'll talk later," he said and left. It made him nervous, not knowing what was going to be required of him over the next few days or possibly longer—and having Leah here was a complication.

Turning his thoughts again to DJ Justice, he realized

he was excited to see the grown-up DJ. He'd thought about her over the years and had hoped her life had turned out all right. But if she was in trouble and needed his help, then there was no way of knowing what her life had been like the past thirty years. He hated to think what kind of trouble she had gotten into that required his help.

Since her father was calling in a promise… Beau was betting it was the dangerous kind.

Andrei looked at the coin in his hand for a long moment. His hand shook a little as he tossed the coin and watched it spin before he snatched it from the air and slapped it down on his thick wrist.

He hesitated, mentally arguing with himself. He had a bad feeling this time. But the money was good, and he'd always gone by the flip of a coin.

Superstition dictated that he went through the same steps each time. Otherwise…

He knew too well the *otherwise* as he slowly lifted his palm to expose the coin. Heads, he went ahead with this hit. Tails…

Heads. A strange sense of both worry and disappointment filled him. But the coin toss was sacred to him, so he assured himself he should proceed as he pocketed the coin.

Stepping to the table, he picked up the information he'd been given on the woman he was to kill.

He noticed that a prison snitch had provided her whereabouts. He snorted, shaking his head and trying to ignore that little voice in his head that was telling him this one was a mistake. But he'd worked with the man who'd hired him before, so he pushed aside his doubts and picked up the photo of Dee Anna Justice, or DJ as she was apparently called.

Pretty. He wondered idly what she had done to warrant her death—but didn't let himself stay on that thought long. It had never mattered. It especially couldn't matter this time—his last time.

Maybe that was what had him on edge. He'd decided that this one would be it. With the money added to what he'd saved from the other hits, he could retire at forty-five. That had always been his goal. Another reason he'd taken this job. It would be over quickly. By his birthday he would be home free. He saw that as a sign, since this would be his last job.

Encouraged, he took the data over to the fireplace and lit it with a match. He would already be in Montana, waiting for a sign, by the time Dee Anna Justice arrived.

DJ leaned back into the first-class seat, wishing she could sleep on the airplane. Her mind had been reeling since finding the doll and the photograph. But now, to discover after all these years that she had family, a cousin...

She'd been shocked and wary when she'd gotten the message on her voice mail. *"Hi, my name's Dana Cardwell Savage. I'm your cousin. I live in Montana, where your father was born. I'd really love to talk to you. In fact, I want to invite you to the Cardwell Ranch here at Big Sky for the holidays."*

Instantly she'd known this call had been her father's doing. But how had he gotten her cell phone number? She mentally smacked herself on the forehead as she recalled the guard at the prison searching her purse. The only thing he'd taken was her cell phone, saying she could pick it up on the way out. She should have known her father had friends in prison.

She'd thought about ignoring the message. What if this was just some made-up relative? She wouldn't have put it past her father.

But the voice had sounded...sincere. If this Dana Cardwell Savage really was her cousin...would she be able to fill in the gaps about her father's family? What about her mother's family? Wasn't there a chance she might know something about the doll and photograph?

She'd always had the feeling there was some secret her father had been keeping from her. If Dana Savage had the answer...

After doing some checking, first to verify that Walter William Justice had been born in Montana near Big Sky and then to see if there really was a Cardwell Ranch and a Dana Cardwell Savage, DJ had finally called her back.

A few minutes on the phone and she'd agreed to fly out. "I can't stay for the holidays, but thank you for asking. I would like to meet you, though. I have to ask. What makes you so sure we're cousins?"

Dana explained about discovering an uncle she hadn't known existed until she'd found some old letters from him to her grandparents on her mother's side. "There'd been a falling-out. I hate to say this, but they'd disowned him. That's why I'd never heard of your father until a few years ago, when I found the letters."

His family had disowned him? Was it that simple, why she'd never known about them? "Do you still have those letters?"

"I do."

She had felt her heart soar. Something of substance she could use to find out the truth. She wanted answers so badly. "I've never known anything about my father's family—or my mother's, for that matter, so I'd love to learn more."

"Family is so important. I'm delighted that your father called. I'd heard he had died. I'm so glad that wasn't true."

Little involving her father was the truth, DJ thought. But if his family had disowned him, then maybe that explained why he'd kept them from her. She had a cousin. How many more relatives did she have that he hadn't told her about?

She tried to relax. Her cousin was picking her up at the airport and taking her to the family ranch where her father had been born. These people were his family, *her family*, people she'd never known had existed until recently. She wanted to pinch herself.

Pulling her purse from under the seat in front of her, she peered in at the rag doll. If only it could talk. Still, looking into its sweet face made her smile in spite of herself. It wasn't hers, but it was so much like hers...

She thought of Trixie and remembered leaving a motel room in the middle of the night and not realizing until later that the doll wasn't with her.

"You must have dropped her," her father had said as they sped out of town.

"We have to go back," she'd cried. "We can't leave her."

He'd looked over at her. "We can't, sweetie. If I go back there... We can't. I'll get you another doll."

She hadn't wanted another doll and had cried herself to sleep night after night until she had no more tears.

"It was just a stupid doll," her father had finally snapped.

"It was all I ever had that was mine."

Now, as she looked at the doll resting in her shoulder bag, she wondered where it had been. Had another girl had this doll as she suspected? But how would that girl know about DJ and Trixie? Trixie was lost, while this doll had been well cared for all these years. Why part with it now?

Her head ached with all the questions and a nagging sense of dread that she wasn't going to like what she found out.

It made no sense that people had given her this doll and the photograph unless they wanted her to find out the truth. But the way they'd left it, breaking into her apartment...

She had tucked the photo into a side pocket of her purse and now withdrew it to study the two women, the one man and the baby in the shot. The man and women were looking at the camera, standing next to a stroller. There was nothing in the background other than an unfamiliar stone wall to give her any idea of where it had been shot—or when.

With a start, she saw something in the photo that she hadn't noticed before. She'd always looked at the people in the photo, especially the woman holding the baby.

But now she saw something in the stroller that made her heart pound. A doll. The doll she now had tucked in her purse. Her father hadn't lied. She *wasn't* this baby, because it wasn't her doll in the stroller. But who was the baby, if not her?

Chapter 4

It had snowed last night, dumping another six inches. Fortunately Highway 191 through the Gallatin Canyon had already been plowed by the time Beau dug himself out and drove to his office on the second floor of an old brick building in downtown Bozeman.

"Good morning, boss," Marge said from behind her desk as he came in. Pushing sixty, solid as a brick wall and just as stout, Marge Cooke was as much a part of Tanner Investigations as the furniture.

"I'm on my way to the airport soon," he said, taking the mail and messages she handed him. "I'll probably be out of contact for a few days," he said over his shoulder as he headed for his office. He heard her get up and follow him.

As he sat down behind his desk, he looked up to find her framed in the doorway. She lifted one dark penciled-in eyebrow and asked, "Since you never take any time off and I know you aren't busy decorating for Christmas, I'll assume you're working. You want me to start a client file?"

"No, this is…personal."

Just when he thought her eyebrow couldn't shoot any higher, it arched toward the ceiling.

"It's not personal like *that*," he said, giving her a shake of his head.

"I have no idea what you're talking about."

He laughed. "I'll be checking in, but I know you can handle things until I get back."

"Whatever you say, boss. Far be it from me to suggest that you haven't been on a date since a Bush was in office."

"Clearly you forgot about that brunette a few months ago."

"That wasn't a date," she said as she turned to leave. "And she made such an impression that you don't even remember her name."

He sat for a moment, trying to remember the brunette's name. Sandy? Susie? Sherry? Not that it mattered, he told himself as he sorted through his mail and messages. He wouldn't be seeing her again.

There wasn't anything in the mail or messages that couldn't keep.

Taking out the letter and the article Walter Justice had sent him, he read them again, then flattened out the article, wondering why it had been included until he saw the travel writer's byline: DJ Price.

So was he to assume that DJ Justice's pseudonym was Price? He typed DJ Price into his computer's search engine. More articles came up, but no photo of the author.

From the dates on the articles it would appear she was still employed as a freelance writer for a variety of publications. If DJ Price was DJ Justice.

He returned the article and letter to the envelope, folded them into his pocket and shut off his computer. As he walked out of his office past Marge's desk, she said, "Shelly," without looking up as he passed. "Wouldn't want you straining your brain trying to remember the woman's name all the way to the airport."

Beau chuckled to himself as he made the drive out into the valley. He couldn't help feeling anxious, since he had no idea what he was getting himself into. Nor did he know what to expect when it came to DJ Justice.

At the airport, he waited on the ground floor by the baggage claim area. There were a half-dozen people standing around holding signs. Dana Savage was one of them. The sign she held up read, CARDWELL RANCH. DJ.

He hung back as the arrivals began coming down from upstairs. On the drive here, he'd told himself there was no way he would be able to recognize DJ. She'd just been a kid of five all those years ago. He'd been a skinny but worn ten.

But the moment he laid eyes on the dark-haired woman at the top of the escalator, he recognized her. Dee Anna Justice. That brown-eyed girl had grown into a striking woman. Her hair was long, pulled back in a loose bun at the nape of her neck. Burnished strands had come loose and hung around her temples.

Silver flashed at her ears and her wrists and throat. She was wearing jeans, winter leather boots that came up to her knees and a teal blue sweater. She had a leather coat draped over one arm, and there was a carry-on in her hand.

She looked up in his direction as if sensing him staring at her. He quickly looked away. This was not what he expected. DJ didn't look like a woman on the run. She looked like a woman completely in control of the world around her.

So what was he doing here?

DJ had still been upset as the flight attendant announced they would be landing soon. She'd stuffed her purse back under the seat. Out the window, she'd seen nothing but white. Snow blanketed everything. She'd realized with a start that she'd never felt snow. Or had she?

Now she surveyed the small crowd of people waiting on the level below as she rode the escalator down. She knew she was being watched, could feel an intense stare. But when she looked in the direction it came from, she was surprised to see a cowboy.

He stood leaning against the stone wall next to the baggage claim area. He was dressed in jeans, boots and a red-and-black-plaid wool jacket. His dark Stetson was pulled low, his blond hair curling at the neck of his jacket.

As he tilted his head back, she saw the pale blue familiar eyes and felt a shock before he quickly looked away. There had been a moment of...*recognition*. Or had she just imagined that she knew him? She tried to get a better look at him. Why had she thought she recognized him?

She had no idea.

He was no longer paying any attention to her. She studied his profile. It was strong, very masculine. He held himself in a way that told her he was his own man. He was no urban cowboy. He was the real thing.

She scoffed at the idea that she knew him. She would have remembered a man like that. Still, she couldn't take her eyes off him and was startled when she reached the end of the escalator.

Turning toward the exit, she spotted a woman about her own age holding a sign that said CARDWELL RANCH on it, and in smaller letters, DJ.

The moment her cousin saw her, she beamed with a huge smile. DJ was surprised how that smile affected her. Tears burned her eyes as she was suddenly filled with emotion. She had the crazy feeling that she'd finally come home. Which was ridiculous, since she'd never had a real home life and, as far as she knew, had never been to Montana.

She swallowed the sudden lump in her throat as she wound her way through the small crowd to the young woman. "Dana?"

"DJ?"

At her nod, Dana gave her a quick hug. "Welcome to Montana." She stepped back to stare at DJ. "You don't look anything like the last Dee Anna Justice."

DJ heard relief in her cousin's voice.

"I'm sorry. I shouldn't have said that," Dana said, then must have noticed that DJ didn't know what she was talking about. "Your father did tell you about your former roommate pretending to be you."

"No, I guess he failed to mention that."

"Well, it's water under the bridge… I'm just glad you're here and I finally get to meet you."

"Me, too," DJ said, feeling that well of emotion again.

"We'll get your luggage—"

"This is all I have." Traveling light wasn't the only habit she'd picked up from her father. She had stopped by the bank before she'd left San Diego. She took cash from her safe-deposit box, just in case she might have reason not to use her credit card. But that would mean that she was on the run and needed to hide.

Dana glanced at the overnight bag. "That's it? Not to worry. We have anything you might need. Ready to see the ranch?"

She was. "I'm looking forward to it." Again she felt someone watching her and quickly scanned the area. It was an old habit from the years when her father used her as a decoy or a lookout.

"Always watch for anyone who seems a little too interested in you—or the ones who are trying hard not to pay you any mind," he used to say.

She spotted the cowboy. He had moved from his spot against the wall and now stood as if waiting for his baggage to arrive. Except he hadn't been on the flight.

"Do you need anything else before we head out?" Dana asked, drawing her attention again.

"No, I'm good," DJ said and followed Dana toward the exit. She didn't have to look back to know that the cowboy was watching her. But he wasn't the only one.

Beau watched DJ leave, curious if anyone else was watching her. Through the large window, he could see Dana's SUV parked outside. DJ was standing next to it, the two seeming to hit it off.

No one seemed to pay her any attention that he could tell. A few people were by the window, several taking photographs. In the distance, the mountains that surrounded the valley were snowcapped against a robin's-egg-blue sky.

He watched DJ climb into the SUV. As it pulled away, there was the clank of the baggage carousel. The people who'd been standing at the window all turned, pocketing their phones. One man took a moment to send a text before moving to the baggage claim area. Everyone looked suspicious, and no one did.

Beau realized he was flying blind. He had to know why Walter Justice had hired him. He had to know what kind of trouble DJ was in.

Pulling out his phone, he stepped outside into the cold December afternoon. The air smelled of snow. Even with the winter sun shining against the stone wall of the airport, it was still chilly outside.

Beau was glad when the emergency number he'd called was answered. It took a few minutes for Walter to come on the line. He wondered what kind of deal the inmate had made that allowed him such service. Con men always found a way, he thought, remembering his own father.

"Have you seen her?" Walter asked at once.

"I have. But you might recall, I've seen her before."

"She was just a child then."

"She's not now," he said, thinking of the striking woman who'd come down those stairs. "That's just one reason I need to tell her the truth."

"No. That would be a mistake. You don't know her— she doesn't trust anyone."

"Whose fault is that?" Beau asked. "If you want me to get close to her, you have to let me do it my way. Tell me what kind of danger she's in."

"That's just it. I don't know."

Beau swore under his breath. "You expect me to believe that? I have to know what I'm up against." Walter knew enough that he'd "hired" Beau.

Silence filled the line for so long, he feared the inmate had hung up. "It could have something to do with her mother."

"DJ's *mother*?"

"Sorry, not DJ's mother. Carlotta is dead. Her grandmother Marietta is still alive. Marietta might have found DJ."

"Found her?"

"It's complicated."

"I'm sure it is. But if you expect me to keep your daughter safe, you'd better tell me."

There was a sound of clanging doors. Then Walter said, "I have to go. Call me tomorrow." And the man was gone.

Pocketing his phone with a curse, Beau headed for his pickup. He couldn't wait until tomorrow. He would have to do this his way—no matter what Walter Justice had said. He thought of the woman he'd seen. Years ago he'd yearned to save that brown-eyed girl. He was getting a second chance, but he feared he wasn't going to have any more luck than he'd had at ten.

What the hell had he gotten involved in?

Dana Cardwell Savage was a pleasant surprise. DJ saw at once the family resemblance in this cheerful young woman with the dark hair and eyes. She was so sweet that DJ felt herself relax a little.

"We are so happy to have you here," her cousin was saying. "Your father said that he's been wanting to get us together for years, but with your busy schedule…"

Dana glanced over at her and smiled. "I'm glad you finally got the chance. This is the perfect time of year to visit Cardwell Ranch. We had a snow last night. Everything is pretty right now. Do you ski?"

DJ shook her head.

"That's all right. If you want to take a lesson, we can certainly make that happen. But you ride, your father said."

"Ride?"

"Horses. It might be too cold for you, but it's always an option."

The SUV slipped through an opening between the mountains, and DJ was suddenly in a wonderland of white. Massive pine branches bowed under the weight of the fresh white snow. Next to the highway, the river was a ribbon of frozen green.

DJ had never seen anything like it. Or had she? At the back of her mind, she thought she remembered snow. The cold, soft flakes melting in her child-sized hand. That sense of wonder.

Dana was telling her about the Gallatin Canyon and some of its history. "I'm sorry," she said after a few minutes. "I talk too much when I'm excited."

"No," DJ said quickly. "I'm interested."

Dana smiled at her. "You are so different from the last Dee Anna Justice who visited us. Sorry. You said you hadn't heard about it."

"What happened?"

DJ listened and shuddered to think that she'd lived in the same apartment with someone like that. "I'm so sorry. I didn't really know her. We shared an apartment, but since my job is traveling, I was hardly there."

Her cousin waved that off. "Not your fault. That's why we're excited finally to meet the real you."

The real you? DJ almost laughed. She hadn't gone by her real name in years. She wasn't sure she even knew the real her.

Chapter 5

Jimmy Ryan could hardly hold still, he was so excited. He couldn't believe his luck as he saw the man come into the bar.

"You bring the up-front money?" he asked the moment the man took the stool next to him at the bar. The dive was almost completely empty this time of day. Still, he kept his voice down. This was serious business.

When the man had told him he was looking for someone with Jimmy's...talents, he'd never dreamed how perfect he was for the job.

"Montana? Hell, I used to live up there, you know, near Big Sky," Jimmy had bragged. He hadn't been there since he'd flunked out of high school after knocking up his girlfriend and being forced into a shotgun marriage, but that was beside the point.

"I remember you mentioning that. That's why I

thought of you. So maybe you know the area?" the man had said.

"Like the back of my hand. I might even know the target."

"Ever heard of the Cardwell Ranch?"

Jimmy had felt a chill as if someone had walked over his grave. This *was* too good to be true. "Are you kidding? I used to…date Stacy Cardwell."

"Well, maybe you won't want this one."

As desperate as he was for money, he would have killed anyone they asked, even Stacy herself, though not before he'd spent some quality time with her for old times' sake.

He'd thought it was fate when the man told him the hit was on a woman named DJ Justice, a cousin of the Cardwells. "Don't know her. Don't care even if I did. Just get me some…traveling money and then let me know how you want it handled."

The man had said he'd get back to him, but it had to be done soon. Jimmy had started making plans with what he would do with all that money.

Now, though, he felt his heart drop as he saw the man's expression. "I'm sorry. The client has decided to go with someone else."

"Someone else?" Jimmy cried loud enough that the bartender sent him a look. "Come on," he said, dropping his voice. "I thought I had it? I'm perfect for the job. Shouldn't it be a case of who gets her first? If it's the money—"

"They went with a pro, all right?"

"Excuse me?" Jimmy demanded, mad at the thought of losing the money and taking it as an insult. "I grew up in Montana. Do you have any idea how many deer I killed? You ever kill a deer?"

"A deer is a lot different than killing a woman." The man threw down some bills on the bar. "For your time." He slid off his stool and started to step away.

"You think that bothers me?" Jimmy had known some women he would have loved to have put a bullet in. He wouldn't even have flinched.

As the man started through the empty bar toward the back door, Jimmy went after him, trotting along beside him, determined not to let him leave without getting the job.

"I'll do it for less than your...pro."

"I don't think money is the issue," the man said without looking at him. "She just wants it done fast."

She? He was thinking jealousy, revenge, a catfight over some man. "So what did this DJ Justice do? Steal some broad's old man?"

The man stopped at the door. Jimmy could tell that he was regretting giving him the details. "Look, forget this one, and maybe the next time I have something..." The man pushed open the door.

"You want to see a pro? I'll show you a pro. I got this one," he called after him. "I'll find her first and I'll be back for the rest of the money."

Stacy Cardwell wiped her eyes as the movie ended. She couldn't help blubbering, not at the end of a touching love story. Maybe she was a sucker for a happy ending. Not that she expected one for herself. She'd picked the wrong man too many times.

But she was just happy to have her daughter, Ella, who was almost five years old. Ella had the biggest green eyes she'd ever seen and had stolen her heart even before she was born. Sure, Stacy got lonely sometimes, but she had her sister, Dana, and brothers, Jordan and Clay. Jordan just lived up the road. Clay was still in California but visited a couple times a year.

Years ago they'd had a falling-out over the ranch. Stacy still regretted it. But Dana had forgiven her, and now they were closer than ever.

"Hello?"

She quickly turned off the television as Burt Olsen, the local mailman, stuck his head in the front door of the main ranch house, where Stacy was curled up watching movies.

"Got a package for Dana," he said. "Need a signature."

Stacy waved him on into the house, smiling as he stomped snow off his boots on the porch before entering. Burt was always so polite. Dana was convinced that Burt had a crush on Stacy, but he was just too shy to ask her out. She was glad Dana wasn't here to tease her about him.

"How's your day going?" Burt asked, then quickly lowered his voice. "The kids asleep?"

She laughed and shook her head. "That would be some trick, to get them all to take naps at their ages. No, their grandpa took them sledding. I'm just holding down the fort until my sister gets back."

"Saw your car out front," Burt said. "Figured you might be sitting the kids. What'd ya think of that snow last night? Really came down. I've already been stuck a couple of times today. Glad I have chains on my rig."

She nodded as she signed for the package. "Can I fill up your thermos with coffee? I have a pot going."

"That would be right nice of you," Burt said, blushing a little. He was a big man with a round red face and brown eyes that disappeared in his face when he laughed. He wasn't handsome by anyone's standards, but there was a warmth and a sincerity about him.

"He will make some woman a fine husband," Dana had said more than once. "A smart woman would snatch him up."

Stacy had never been smart when it came to men, and her sister knew it. But she liked Burt. If she had been looking for a husband... But she wasn't.

When he returned from his truck with the thermos, she took it into the big farmhouse kitchen and proceeded to fill it with hot strong coffee. Burt had followed her only as far as the kitchen doorway.

"Having electrical problems?" Burt asked.

She turned to frown. "No, why?"

"I saw some feller up a pole not far from the house."

Stacy shrugged. "Here, I made sugar cookies. I'll put a couple of them in a bag for you."

"Oh, you don't have to..."

"Dana would insist if she was here," Stacy said.

"Well, thank you." He took the thermos and the plastic bag. "Shaped like Christmas trees," he said, holding up the bag to see the cookies. "You did a real nice job on them."

She felt her cheeks heat. Burt was so appreciative of even the smallest kind gesture a person did for him. "Thank you."

"Well, I'll be getting along, then." He nodded, not quite looking at her. "Might want to dig out some candles in case that lineman turns off your power. You have a nice day now."

"I'm going to try." She watched him drive away, wondering when Burt was going to get around to asking her out and how she was going to let him down easy.

In the kitchen, she got herself some cookies and milk. Going back to the television, she found another Christmas love story and hoped Burt was wrong about the power man cutting off her television. She didn't get that much time alone to watch.

But this show didn't hold her attention. She wondered when Dana would be back with their cousin Dee Anna Justice and what surprises this cousin might bring to the ranch.

As Beau climbed into his SUV and began the drive out of the airport on the newly constructed roads, his cell phone rang. The roads were new because Gallatin Field was now the busiest airport in the state. "Beau Tanner."

"What is your hourly rate?"

He recognized Leah's voice and imagined her standing in his living room. "You can't afford me. Seriously, what is this about?"

"I lied to you. Charlie and I...we're in trouble."

Beau wasn't surprised. "So, there isn't an important package?"

"There is, kind of. I hate involving you in this."

"I can't wait to hear what this is exactly, but can we talk about it when I get home?"

"Yes. But I insist on hiring you. I have money, if that's what you're worried about."

"That isn't it. I have something right now that is going to take all of my attention."

He got off the call, cursing under his breath. If this was about marital problems between her and Charlie...

He really couldn't deal with this right now. Ahead he could see Dana Cardwell's black Suburban heading toward Big Sky. Beau followed, worried about Leah and Charlie, even more worried about DJ Justice.

What kind of trouble was DJ in? Her father thought it might have something to do with her grandmother? That her grandmother had *found* her? He cursed Walter. Who knew how many skeletons the man had in his closet?

But what did that have to do with his daughter?

If Beau had to lay money down on it, he would have bet there was a man in DJ Justice's story. A man with a jealous wife or girlfriend? Or had DJ chosen a life of crime like her father? At least Beau's father had reformed somewhat after that night here in the canyon when Beau had made the deal with Walter Justice.

Since becoming a private investigator, he'd thought he'd heard every story there was. Where it got dangerous was when the spouse or lover would do anything to cover up an affair—or even a score. Usually money was involved. And passion.

So what was DJ's story?

Marietta Pisani stood at her mirror, considering the almost eighty-year-old woman she saw reflected there. *Merda!* She looked as cranky as she felt, which almost made her smile. When had she gotten so old? She didn't feel all that different than she had in her twenties, except now her long, beautiful, raven-black hair was gray. Her once-smooth porcelain skin was wrinkled.

She knew what had aged her more than the years— her only child, Carlotta. That girl had seemed determined to drive her crazy. It had been one thing after another from an early age. She shook her head, remembering the hell Carlotta had put her through, and then softened her thoughts as she was reminded that her beautiful, foolish daughter was in her grave.

Not that she hadn't left a storm in her wake. And now Marietta had to clean it up.

"Can I get you anything else, Mrs. Pisani?" asked a deep, elderly voice behind her.

She glanced past her reflection in the mirror to Ester, who'd been with her for almost fifty years. Ester had grayed since she'd begun working here as a teen. Sometimes Marietta mixed her up with her mother, Inez, who'd been her first housekeeper right after her marriage.

"No, Ester, I don't need anything."

"What about you, Mr. Douglas?" Ester asked Marietta's solicitor.

Roger shook his head. "I'll be leaving shortly."

"You can turn in," Marietta told the housekeeper.

"Just ring." The sixty-seven-year-old woman turned to leave. "Sleep well." She'd said the same thing every night for the past fifty years.

As Ester closed the door behind her, Marietta focused again on her own reflection. Nothing had changed except now her brows were knit into a deep frown. Ester hadn't been herself lately.

The thought caused Marietta a moment of alarm. Was the woman sick? Marietta was too old to train another housekeeper. Not that Ester kept house anymore. A housecleaning crew came in once a week, and she employed a full-time cook, as well. Ester's only job now was to see to her mistress.

Of course, Ester didn't see it that way. She resented the housekeeping crew and the cook and often sent the cook home early so she could take over the kitchen. She would then make Marietta's favorite meals, just as her mother had done.

The thought that Ester might leave her for any reason was more than she could stand. Ester was the only person in the world Marietta trusted—other than her granddaughter Bianca. She tried to put her worries aside, assuring herself that she'd be dead before Ester went anywhere.

Still, it nagged at her. Not that Ester had said anything. It was more of a…feeling that something was wrong. Unfortunately she knew nothing about the woman's personal life—or if she even had one. Ester had married some worthless man years ago, but she'd had the good sense to get rid of him early on. Since then, as far as Marietta knew, there was no one else in her life. Ester had doted on her and Carlotta and thought that the sun rose and set with Bianca.

When Carlotta had died a few months ago, Ester had taken it harder than Marietta. The housekeeper had loved that child as if she were her own. She'd helped raise her and was the first to make excuses when Carlotta got into trouble, which was often.

But the one Ester loved even more than life itself was Bianca.

It was her thirty-four-year-old granddaughter Marietta worried about now because of Carlotta's deathbed confession.

She clenched her gnarled hands into fists at the memory. The stupid, stupid girl. The secret she'd kept from them all could destroy the legacy Marietta had preserved for so many years—not to mention what it could do to the family fortune.

That was why the mess her daughter had left behind had to be cleaned up. For the family's sake. For Bianca's sake and the generations to come.

"I should go," Roger said.

She'd forgotten he was even still in the room. A slight man with an unmemorable face, he practically disappeared into the wallpaper. "You're sure you can handle this properly?" she asked as she looked past her own image to his.

He sighed. "Yes."

"I don't want Bianca ever to know. If that means paying this woman to keep quiet—"

"I told you I would take care of it. But it is going to cost you. Your daughter left us little choice unless you want to see your family's reputation destroyed by a complete stranger."

A complete stranger. That was what Dee Anna Justice was to her. Marietta had never laid eyes on this... granddaughter, hadn't even known she existed until her daughter's deathbed confession. "Just see that it's done and spare me the sordid details."

"Don't I always?" As he started to leave, she heard a rustling sound and looked up in time to see Ester skittering away.

Dana was telling her about the "canyon," as the locals called the Gallatin Canyon. It ran from just south of Gallatin Gateway almost to West Yellowstone, some fifty miles of twisting road that cut through the mountains. Sheer rock cliffs overlooked the highway and the Gallatin River.

The drive was breathtaking, especially for DJ, who'd never been in the mountains before—let alone in winter. The winding highway followed the river, a blue-ribbon trout stream, up over the Continental Divide.

"There used to be just a few places in the canyon, mostly ranches or dude ranches, a few summer cabins, but that was before Big Sky," Dana was saying.

DJ could see that luxury houses had sprouted up along the highway as they got closer to the ski resort and community that had grown around it.

"Our ranch was one of the first," her cousin said with obvious pride. "It is home. The only one I've known. And I have no intention of ever leaving it."

DJ couldn't imagine what it must have been like living her whole life in one place.

Dana slowed and turned not far past the sign for Big Sky Resort. Across the river and a half mile back up a wide valley, the Cardwell Ranch house sat against a backdrop of granite cliffs, towering snow-filled pines and bare-limbed aspens. The house was a big, two-story rambling affair with a wide front porch and a brick red metal roof. Behind it stood a huge new barn and some older outbuildings and corrals.

"Hud, my husband, keeps saying we need to build a bigger house, since we have four children now. But… well…"

"It's wonderful," DJ said and tried to imagine herself growing up here.

"You'll be staying in one of our guest cabins," her cousin said and pointed to some log buildings up on the side of the mountain. "I think you'll be comfortable there, and you'll have your privacy."

DJ was overwhelmed by all of it, so much so that she couldn't speak. As Dana parked, a dark-haired woman came out on the porch to greet them.

"Stacy," Dana called. "Come meet our cousin."

Chapter 6

DJ thought Stacy looked like an older version of her sister. She'd been prettier at one time, but her face told of a harder life than Dana had lived. Seeing how much she resembled both of her cousins gave DJ a strange feeling. For once, her father had told the truth. These people were her *family*.

Dana introduced them and then asked her sister, "How were the kids?"

"Dad came by and took them sledding," Stacy said. "He called just before you drove up to say he's decided to take them to Texas Boys Barbecue, since they say they're too starved to wait for supper. The café is owned by our cousins from Texas," she said to DJ. Turning back to her sister, she said, "I'm working this afternoon at the sewing shop, so I'd better get going, since I need to pick up a few things before then."

"Go, and thanks."

Stacy looked to DJ, who'd been taking in the ranch in a kind of awe. "It was great to meet you. I'll see you later?"

"You'll see her. DJ's staying for a while," Dana declared and climbed the porch steps to open the door and usher DJ in.

She stepped into the house and stopped. The decor was very Western, from the huge rock fireplace to the antler lamps and the Native American rugs on the hardwood floors. Even the Christmas decorations looked as if they'd been in the family for years.

There was also a feeling of déjà vu as if she'd been here before. Crazy, she thought, hurriedly wiping at her eyes.

"It's so...beautiful," DJ said, her voice breaking.

Dana laughed. "*My Christmas tree?* I know it's hard to put into words," she said, considering the misshaped evergreen in the corner, decorated with ornaments obviously made by children. "But I've always been a sucker for trees that would never have gotten to be Christmas trees if it wasn't for me."

DJ managed to laugh around the lump in her throat. "I meant your house," she said, smiling at the sight of the ungainly tree, "but your Christmas tree is...lovely. An orphan tree that you brought home. It's charming."

Her cousin smiled at her. "Let's have a late lunch, since I know you couldn't have gotten much on the plane, and we can visit."

She followed Dana into the large, cheery kitchen, wondering if she hadn't been here before. It felt strangely...familiar. Had her father brought her here at some point? Why else was she feeling so emotional about this large, rambling old house?

"I can't tell you how surprised I was when I found some letters from your father and realized that my mother had a brother I'd never known existed," Dana said as she opened the refrigerator and pulled out a large bowl. "I hope you like shrimp macaroni salad." DJ nodded and Dana continued. "It wasn't like my mother, Mary Justice, to keep a secret like that. Then to find out that he hadn't actually died…" Her cousin put the bowl on the table and got out plates, forks and what looked like homemade rolls. "Coffee, tea, milk?"

"Milk." She couldn't remember the last time she'd had milk, but it sounded so good, and it felt right in this kitchen. Everywhere she looked she saw family history in this house. One wall was covered with photos of the children, most atop horses.

"Sit, please." Dana waved her into one of the mismatched multicolored wooden chairs in front of the long, scarred table.

"I didn't know about you, either," DJ said as she pulled out the chair and sat. Dana joined her after filling two plates with pasta salad. DJ took a bite. "This is delicious."

They ate in a companionable silence for a while. The house was warm and comfortable. From the window over the sink, DJ could see snow-laden pines and granite cliffs. It was all so beautiful, exactly how she had pictured Montana in December. She hadn't thought she was hungry, but the salad and the warm homemade roll dripping with butter quickly disappeared. This felt so right, being here, that she'd forgotten for a while why she'd accepted the invitation.

DJ was running her finger along one of the scars on the table when Dana said, "I can't understand why my grandparents would disown their son the way they did. They were a lot older when they had your father. Maybe it was that generation...but not to tell us..."

DJ took a sip of cold milk before she asked, "Who told you he was dead?"

"I didn't speak to your mother personally, but her assistant—"

"My *mother's assistant*?" DJ asked, abruptly putting down her milk glass. "When was this?"

Her cousin thought for a moment. "That would have been in the spring three years ago. Her assistant, at least, that's who she said she was, told me that your mother couldn't come to the phone."

"I was always told that my mother's been dead since I was born," DJ said. "It's what I've believed all my life, so I don't understand this."

"I don't understand it, either. Then whose assistant did I speak with, if not Marietta Pisani's?"

"She told you my mother's name was Marietta?" She shook her head. "Where did you get the number to call her?"

"From...from the woman who'd pretended to be you, Camilla Northland. After she was caught, I asked her where the real Dee Anna Justice was. I thought she was telling me the truth." Dana put a hand over her mouth. "Why did I believe anything that woman told me? I feel like such a fool."

"No, please don't. So my roommate gave you the number?"

Dana nodded. "She said a woman had called the apartment asking for you before she left to come out here to Montana to pretend to be you. When your roommate asked who was calling, she said her name was Marietta."

"That's my grandmother's name, but she is also deceased. At least, that's what my father told me. But since he kept all of you from me…" Her life felt like one big, long lie. "My father told me that my mother's name was Carlotta."

Her cousin looked flummoxed. "Camilla seemed to think Marietta was your mother. Either she lied, or—"

"Or the person who called lied."

Dana nodded thoughtfully. "I believed Camilla, since she also told me that the reason my uncle had been disinherited was that he'd married a foreigner. The woman who said she was Marietta's assistant had an Italian accent. I asked about her daughter. I'm not even sure I called you by name. She said you were in Italy—or was it Spain?—visiting friends. Is any of this true?"

DJ shook her head. "I've been in San Diego all this time except when I was traveling for work. I have no idea where my former roommate could have gotten her information, but that she knew my grandmother's name… I don't think she was lying about the phone call. Do you still have that number?"

Dana shook her head. "I'm sorry."

"I was hoping you could help me piece together more of my family history. My father told me that he and I were the only two left. Until he told me that you might be calling, I had no idea that wasn't true."

"Well, you have me and Stacy, plus my brothers, Jordan and Clay, as cousins, plus our cousins from Texas. You'll meet Jordan tonight. Clay lives in California, not that far from where you live now. So, you never met anyone on your mother's side of the family?"

"No. All I knew was that my mother's name was Carlotta and my grandmother's was Marietta. My father's never been very…forthcoming with information. He let me believe I didn't have *any* family."

"Oh, DJ, I'm so sorry," Dana said, reaching across the table to take her hand. "Family is…my heart. My father and uncle, my father-in-law, are often…trying," she said and smiled. "I've fought tooth and nail with my siblings, lost them for a few years, but finally have them back. I can't imagine not having any of them in my life. I'm so glad that now you have all of us."

DJ's eyes burned as she squeezed her cousin's hand.

"All of us *and* Cardwell Ranch," Dana added and let go of her hand.

DJ picked at her lunch for a moment. Was it possible that her grandmother Marietta was still alive? Then wasn't it also possible that her mother, Carlotta, was alive, as well? She could see why her father might have kept her from his family, since they had disinherited him, but why had he kept her from her mother's family?

DJ remembered the night she'd finally badgered her father into telling her about her mother. He'd had too much to drink. Otherwise all he'd ever said was that her mother had died and it was too painful to talk about. That night, though, he told her that Carlotta had been a beautiful princess and the love of his life.

"She was too beautiful," he'd said. "Too spoiled, too rich, too much of everything. Her family didn't think I was good enough for her. They were right, of course." He'd let out a bitter laugh. "It cost me my family as well, but I will never regret loving her." He'd blinked back tears as he looked at DJ. "And I got you. I'm a lucky man."

She'd been full of questions. How could he have lost Carlotta and his family, too?

"Do you understand now why I don't want to talk about your mother? So, no more," he'd said with a wave of his hand. "I can't bear it." His gaze softened as it fell on her. "Let's just be grateful that we have each other, because it's just you and me, kid."

Even now, she couldn't be sure any of his story was true. Her heritage was a puzzle with most of the pieces missing. "I'm surprised that you'd never heard of my father before you found the letters," she said.

"I was shocked. Like I said, I still can't believe my mother would have kept something like that a secret."

"You said you still have those letters?"

"I can dig them out, along with that number—" At the sound of a vehicle, followed by the eruption of children's voices, Dana added, "After I corral the kids."

DJ cleaned up the dishes while Dana went to greet the children. She could hear laughter and shrieks of playfulness outside. She couldn't help but smile to herself.

Drying her hands, she pulled out the photo and studied it in the light from the kitchen window. With her cousin's help, she was going to find the family she'd been denied.

She gazed at the photo of the baby—and the doll in the stroller. If she wasn't the baby the smiling woman was holding, then who was, and why had someone wanted her to believe they were family?

Whoever had left her the doll and the photo knew the truth—and wanted her to know it. But what was the truth? And what was the motive? To help her? Or to warn her?

She felt a sudden chill. She would find out, but at what cost?

* * *

On the way to the small resort town of Big Sky, Stacy couldn't get DJ off her mind. There was a distinct family resemblance because of the dark hair and eyes, but still…she had the feeling that she'd met her when they were kids.

At the drugstore, she got out and was about to lock her car when she heard the sound of footfalls in the new snow behind her.

"Stacy?"

She started at the familiar male voice directly behind her. Turning, she came face-to-face with her old boyfriend from high school. *"Jimmy?"*

He grinned. "I go by James now. I'm surprised you remember me."

How could she not remember Jimmy Ryan? He'd dumped her right before her junior prom to go back to his old girlfriend, Melody Harper. He'd been the first in a long line to break her heart.

"Are you here for the holidays?" He and Melody had gotten married right after high school. Melody, it turned out, had been pregnant. He'd taken a job with Melody's uncle in California, and that was the last Stacy had heard or seen of him.

He was looking at her the way he used to, unnerving her. "I wondered if you were still around."

"I left for a while. How is Melody?"

"Wouldn't know. We're divorced. How about you?"

For a moment she couldn't find her voice. "Divorced." More times than she wanted to admit. "I have a daughter, Ella."

"Lucky you. It turned out that I couldn't have children."

She blurted out in surprise, "But I thought Melody was pregnant."

"Turns out she wasn't," he said bitterly. "She told me that she'd miscarried, so we spent a lot of years trying before the truth came out."

"I'm sorry."

His gaze met and held hers. He was still the most handsome man she'd ever known. His dark hair was salted with gray at the temples, which only seemed to make his gray eyes more intense. "Could I buy you a cup of coffee?"

Stacy felt that old ache. Had she ever gotten over Jimmy? Wasn't he why she'd jumped into one relationship, one marriage after another? "I have to get back to the ranch soon."

"Just a quick cup of coffee. I've thought about you so often over the years and regretted letting you down the way I did."

How many times had she dreamed that he would say those words—or at least words much like them?

She glanced at her watch. "I suppose a cup of coffee wouldn't hurt."

"You're tired from your long trip," Dana said after introducing DJ to all the children and her father, Angus Cardwell. "Dad, if you don't mind staying around for a few minutes, I'm going to take DJ to her cabin so she can get some rest."

"You're in good hands," Angus said. "Trust me."

DJ couldn't help but smile. Trust wasn't something that came easy for her. But Dana and this family inspired trust.

"The kids want to go see a movie in Bozeman,"

Angus said. "Maybe we'll do that and really make a day of it."

There were cheers from the five children. Dana laughed. "You haven't had enough of them? Fine. But we're all going to The Corral tonight. Stacy has agreed to babysit."

As they stepped outside, DJ on impulse turned to her cousin and hugged her. "Thank you for everything."

"I haven't done anything yet," Dana said. "But I am so glad you're here. Families need to stick together."

With that, her cousin walked her up to her cabin on the mountainside.

DJ couldn't believe the cabin as her cousin opened the door and ushered her in. Someone had started a fire for her. It blazed bright in a fireplace on the other side of a seating area. There was a small kitchen that she knew would be stocked with anything she might need even before Dana opened the refrigerator door to show her.

But it was the bedroom that stole her heart. "Oh, that bed." It was huge, the frame made of logs, the mattress deep in pillows and quilts. "I won't want to get out of it."

Her cousin smiled and pulled out a step. "This is how you get on the bed. I told them it was too high, but my brother Jordan made the beds, and so far everyone loves them."

"I can see why," DJ said, laughing. "This is amazing. Really, thank you so much."

"It's my pleasure. You'll get to meet Jordan and his wife, Liza. Clay, your other cousin, as I told you, lives in California. He'll be flying up for Christmas. But we'll get to all of that." She smiled. "I'm just happy you're here now. We can talk about Christmas later."

"I can only stay for a few days. With the holidays coming, I don't want to be in the way."

"In the way?" Dana exclaimed. "You're family. You'll make this Christmas even more special."

DJ couldn't help being touched.

"Get settled in and rest. We have something special planned for tonight. The Corral has the best burgers you've ever tasted, and the band playing tonight? It's my uncle and father's band—more relatives of yours I thought you'd enjoy meeting in a more casual atmosphere."

Dana was so thoughtful that DJ couldn't say no.

"I'll drop by some clothing and Western boots that should fit you before we go."

DJ started to tell her that this was all too much, but Dana cut her off. "You have to experience Montana and canyon life. I promise that you'll have a good time."

There was nothing more DJ could say, since she didn't want to disappoint her cousin. Dana had been so welcoming, much more than she should have been for a relative she'd never met before.

She watched Dana walk back down to the main house. Something in the distance flashed, the winter sun glinting off metal. She could see a repairman hanging from a power pole in the distance.

Emotional exhaustion pulled at her. The past few days had been such a roller-coaster ride. She closed the door and locked it. For the first time, she felt…safe.

The cabin was so warm and welcoming, she thought as she walked into the bedroom. The bed beckoned to her. Smiling, DJ pulled back the homemade quilt, kicked off her shoes and crawled up under the covers. She was asleep almost at once.

* * *

Marietta knew she wouldn't be able to sleep. She kept thinking about this granddaughter. She realized she knew nothing about her other than what Roger had told her. A father in prison. The young woman writing stories for travel magazines.

"Not married?" she'd asked.

"No. Lives alone. Stays to herself."

She tried to imagine the girl. Did she look like Carlotta or that horrible father of hers? What if she looked like Bianca?

Reaching over, she rang the bell for Ester. It was late, but she knew she'd never get to sleep without some warm milk.

"Is something wrong?" Ester asked moments later from her doorway.

"I can't sleep."

"I'm not surprised."

She stared at her housekeeper. "I beg your pardon?"

Ester shook her head. "I'll heat some milk. Would you like anything else?"

Marietta gritted her teeth as she shook her head. It wasn't her imagination. Ester was acting oddly.

When she returned with a glass of warm milk and a biscuit with butter and honey, Marietta asked, "Roger hasn't called, has he?"

"I'm sure you would have heard the phone if he had, but no."

"You don't like him." She realized she'd given voice to something she'd known for a long time. Not that she normally cared if her housekeeper liked her attorney or not. But tonight, it struck her as odd. Almost as odd as the way Ester was behaving.

"No, I don't like him. Nor do I trust him. You shouldn't, either." Ester started to leave.

"Why would you say that?" she demanded of the housekeeper's retreating back.

Ester stopped and turned slowly. "Because he's been stealing from you for years." With that, she left the room.

Marietta stared after her, dumbstruck. Was Ester losing her mind? It was the only thing that made sense. The woman had never talked to her like this. She would never have dared. And to say something so...outrageous.

She took a sip of the milk, followed by a bite of the biscuit, until both were gone. Neither was going to help her sleep tonight.

Chapter 7

The Corral turned out to be an old-fashioned bar and restaurant that looked as if it had been there for years. DJ liked the idea of a place having a rich history—just like the ranch Dana had grown up on. She couldn't imagine having that kind of roots. Nor could she imagine knowing the same people for years like Dana did—which quickly became obvious as they climbed out of the large SUV.

The parking lot was full of pickups and a few SUVs. Several trucks drove up at the same time they did. The occupants called to Dana and were so friendly that DJ felt a stab of envy.

"Do you know everyone in the canyon?" she asked.

Her cousin laughed. "Hardly. I did once upon a time. But that was before Big Sky Resort."

The moment they walked through The Corral door,

the bartender said hello to Dana, who quickly set them both up with light beers. "You're in Montana now," she said, clinking her beer bottle against DJ's. The band broke into an old country song, the lead guitarist nodding to them as he began to sing.

"You already met my father, Angus Cardwell, on lead guitar," Dana said as she led her to the only empty table, one with a reserved sign on it that read Cardwell Ranch. "And my uncle Harlan is on bass tonight. They switch off. They've been playing music together for years. They've had other names, but they call themselves the Canyon Cowboys now, I think." She laughed. "They're hard to keep track of."

They'd barely sat down and had a drink of their beers when Dana's brother Jordan came in with his wife, Liza, a local deputy still in her uniform. Jordan was dark and good-looking and clearly in love with his wife, who was pregnant.

"We came by to say hello, but can't stay long," Jordan said. "I'm sure we'll get to see you again while you're here, though."

"Is your husband coming?" DJ asked after Jordan and Liza had left.

"Hud's working tonight. But you'll get to meet him." Dana ordered loaded burgers as the band kicked into another song. "Oh, there's Hilde." Her cousin rose to greet her very pregnant friend. They spoke for a moment before Dana drew her over to the table.

Hilde looked reluctant to meet her. But DJ couldn't blame her after everything she'd heard about the pretend Dee Anna Justice.

"I'm so sorry about my former roommate," DJ said. "I had no idea until Dana told me."

Hilde shook her head. "It's just nice that we finally get to meet you. How do you like the ranch?"

"I love it, especially that four-poster log bed I took a nap in earlier."

Hilde laughed as she sat. Her husband came in then, still wearing his marshal's office uniform, and went to the bar to get them drinks.

A shadow fell across the table. When DJ looked up, she was surprised to see the cowboy from the airport standing over her.

"Care to dance?" he asked over the music.

DJ was so startled to see him here that for a moment she couldn't speak.

"Go ahead," Dana said, giving her a friendly push. "Beau Tanner is a great dancer."

Beau Tanner. DJ didn't believe this was a coincidence. "Did you have something to do with this?" she whispered to her cousin.

"Me?" Dana tried to look shocked before she whispered, "Apparently he saw you at the airport and wanted to meet you."

So that was it. DJ pushed back her chair and stood. Maybe his interest in her was innocent. Or not. She was about to find out either way.

He took her hand and pulled her out onto the dance floor and into his arms for a slow dance. He was strong and sure, moving with ease, and definitely in control.

"Dana told me you would be here tonight," he said. "I was hoping you would dance with me."

"Why is that?" she asked, locking her gaze on his.

His pale blue eyes were the color of worn denim, his lashes dark. Looking into those eyes, she felt a small jolt. Why did she get the feeling that she'd looked into those eyes before?

"I saw you at the airport. When I heard that you were Dana's cousin, I was curious." He shrugged.

"*Really?* You just happened to hear that."

"News travels fast in the canyon."

"What were you doing at the airport? I know you weren't on my flight. I also know you weren't picking anyone up."

He laughed. "Are you always this suspicious?"

"Always."

She lost herself in those eyes.

"You want to know why I was at the airport? Okay." He looked away for a moment before his gaze locked with hers. "Because of you."

"So much for your story that you just happened to see me at the airport and were curious."

"I don't like lying. That's just one reason we need to talk," he said as he pulled her close and whispered into her ear. "Today at the airport wasn't the first time I'd seen you. We've met before."

She drew back to look into his face. "If this is some kind of pickup line…" Even as she said it, she remembered thinking at the airport that he looked familiar. But she was always thinking people looked like someone from her past. That was normal when you had a past like hers.

"It was years ago, so I'm not surprised that you don't remember," he said as the song ended. He clasped her hand, not letting her get away as another song began.

"Years ago?" she asked as he pulled her close.

"You were five," he said next to her ear. "I was ten. It was only a few miles from here in this canyon."

She drew back to look at him. "That isn't possible. I've never been here before." But hadn't she felt as if she had? "Why would I believe you?"

He looked her in the eye. "Because a part of you knows I'm telling the truth. It's the reason you and I need to talk." Without warning, he drew her off the dance floor, toward the front door.

She could have dug her heels in, pulled away, stopped this, but something in his tone made her follow him out the door and into the winter night. He directed her over to the side of the building where snow had been plowed up into a small mountain. "Okay, what is this about?" she demanded, breaking loose from his hold to cross her arms over her chest. "It's freezing out here, so make it fast."

He seemed to be deciding what to tell her. She noticed that he was watching the darkness as if he expected something out there to concern him. "All those years ago, your father did me a favor," he said.

She laughed, chilled by the night and this man and what he was saying. "Now I know you're lying. My father didn't do favors for anyone, especially for ten-year-olds."

"Not without a cost," he agreed.

She felt her heart bump in her chest and hugged herself tighter to ward off the cold—and what else this man might tell her.

"Your father and mine were...business partners."

"So this is about my father." She started to turn away.

"No, it's about you, DJ, and what your father has asked me to do."

She stared at him. She'd come here wanting answers. Did this man have them? If he was telling the truth, she'd been to Montana with her father years ago. It would explain why some things and some people seemed familiar—including him.

She could see the pale green frozen river across the highway, the mountains a deep purple backdrop behind it. Everything was covered with snow and ice, including the highway in front of the bar.

"If our fathers were business partners, then I don't want anything to do with you."

"I wouldn't blame you, but my father got out of the... business after the night we met. I'm assuming yours didn't, given that he is now in prison."

She flinched. "How do you know that?"

"I told you. He did me a favor—for a price. He contacted me. It's a long story, but the night we met, your father and I made a deal of sorts. He helped me with the understanding that if he ever needed my help..."

"You said he did a favor for you? My father made a deal with a ten-year-old?"

"I promised to do whatever he wanted if he let my father go."

DJ felt a hard knot form in her chest. "I don't understand." But she feared she did.

"My father had double-crossed yours. Your father was holding a gun to his head."

"And you threw yourself on the sword, so to speak, by promising my father what, exactly?" What could her father have extracted from a boy of ten?

"He asked me to make sure that nothing happens to you."

She laughed, but it fell short. "That's ridiculous. Why would he think *you* could keep me safe?"

"I'm a private investigator. I have an office forty miles away in Bozeman. I'm good at what I do."

"And humble." She rubbed her arms through the flannel shirt her cousin had given her to wear. But it wasn't her body that was chilled as much as her soul. Her father, the manipulator. He'd gotten her here. Now he was forcing this cowboy to protect her? She shook her head and started to step away again. "I can take care of my—"

A vehicle came roaring into the parking lot. As the headlights swept over them, Beau grabbed her and took her down in the snowbank next to them, landing squarely on top of her.

Jimmy Ryan rubbed his cold hands together. He'd already spent several hours of his life sitting outside a bar, hoping to get a shot at DJ Justice. Finding out where DJ would be tonight had been child's play. Over coffee with Stacy he'd listened distractedly as she'd told him what she'd been up to since high school.

"So you're living at the ranch?" he'd asked. "How's that working out with family?"

"Fine. Another cousin has turned up. They seem to be coming out of the woodwork," she'd said with a laugh. "First my five male cousins from Texas. They opened Texas Boys Barbecue here in Big Sky. Have you been there yet?"

"Not yet. But you said another cousin has turned up?"

"Dee Anna Justice. DJ. I haven't gotten to spend much time around her and won't tonight. I'm babysitting the kids so Dana can take her out."

"Oh, yeah? Your sister taking her to someplace fancy?"

"The Corral. My father and uncle are playing there. You remember that they have a band, right?"

The Corral. "Sure, I remember. So what does this cousin look like?"

She'd described DJ. Sounded like he couldn't miss her, so to speak.

He'd glanced at his watch. "I'm going to have to cut this short. Maybe we can see each other again." If things went right tonight, that wouldn't be happening. But he hadn't minded giving Stacy false hope. And who knew, he'd thought, maybe they could hook up before he left. She was still pretty foxy, and he could tell she still wanted him.

Now, sitting across the highway in his rented SUV, his rifle lying across his lap, he just hoped he got another chance at DJ. Earlier she'd come out of the bar. But she'd been with some man.

He'd still been tempted to take the shot, but the man had stayed in front of her. When a car had come racing into the parking lot, the cowboy had thrown them both in a snowbank. What was that about?

"What in the—" DJ's words were cut off by the sound of laughter as several people tumbled from the vehicle.

"Shh," Beau said, pulling back to look at her. She saw a change in his expression. Still, the kiss took her by more than surprise. She pushed against his hard chest, but his arms were like steel bands around her.

Worse, she felt herself melting into him, into the kiss, into the warmth of his mouth and the taste of beer on his lips. She was vaguely aware of music and laughter and the sound of people as they entered the establishment before he let her go.

She was shaken by the kiss and everything he'd told her as he rose and pulled her to her feet. "What was that?" she demanded as she began to brush cold snow off her backside.

"A kiss. Apparently it's been a while for you, as well," he said with a cockiness that was downright aggravating. He began to help her with the snow, his big hand brushing over the Western shirt, vest and jeans she wore.

"I can do it myself," she snapped and took a step away from him. She wanted to tell him that she'd only kissed him back because he'd taken her by surprise. But he didn't give her a chance to lie.

"Don't look so shocked. It was just a kiss, right?" His blue eyes gleamed in the light from the neon sign over their heads. "It wasn't like you felt anything. Like either of us felt anything."

The man was exasperating. She hadn't come looking for any of this. "I was asking why you thought you could get away with kissing me like that. Or was that part of the bargain you made with my father?" she asked, hoping he caught the sarcasm.

"I wasn't sure who was driving up just then. I was merely doing my job. Protecting you, since the one thing your father didn't make clear is whom I'm protecting you from. As for the kiss, it just seemed like a good idea. It won't happen again."

"You're right about that, because I don't need your so-called protection." With that, she pushed past him and started for the bar as Dana opened the door and called, "DJ, your burger's ready."

Jimmy Ryan wasn't the only one watching some distance from The Corral. Andrei had learned to be patient, studying his mark, waiting for a sign that the situation was perfect.

He would get only one chance to pull the trigger. Rushing it would put the mark on alert and make his job next to impossible. That's if he didn't get caught trying to get away after blowing it.

He'd seen Dee Anna Justice, or DJ, as she was called, go into the bar with her cousin. He wasn't even tempted to take the shot. Later everyone would have been drinking and that would add to the confusion about where the shot had come from.

He'd been surprised when DJ had come back out so soon—and with a man. They seemed to be in an intense conversation.

Who was this cowboy?

What happened next turned Andrei's blood to ice. A vehicle came roaring into the bar's parking area. The cowboy with Dee Anna threw her into the snowbank next to where they had been talking.

Andrei sat up straighter, tightening his grip on the binoculars. Why was the cowboy so jumpy? It made no sense.

He swore. Had there been another contract out on her—one that had failed? How else could he explain why the man with her had reacted like that?

What had he gotten himself into?

Beau stood next to the snowbank, cussing under his breath. Walter had warned him not to tell her. Now he understood why. The woman was stubborn as a danged mule.

He touched his tongue to his lower lip and tasted her,

smiling as he thought of the kiss. No matter what she'd said, he'd felt her kissing him back.

Another vehicle pulled into the parking lot, dragging him back to the problem at hand. DJ Justice. How was he going to keep her safe? And safe from what? Or whom? He cursed Walter Justice. Tomorrow he would call him back, but in the meantime, all he could do was keep an eye on the man's daughter.

Good luck with that, he told himself as he went back into the bar. She was sitting again with her cousin. He went to the bar, taking a stool where he could watch her in the mirror behind the counter. She looked up and their gazes met for a moment.

She touched her tongue to the corner of her mouth and licked away a dollop of ketchup. Then she smiled as if she knew exactly what that had done to him. It was clear that she understood how their kiss had affected him. Because it had affected her, as well? Not likely.

He pulled his gaze away to nurse his beer. This woman was going to be the death of him.

Chapter 8

Jimmy cursed and told himself to stay calm. He was going to get his shot. He'd been ready, but the damned man kept blocking his shot. He'd decided to try to take them both out when he got his chance.

He put the crosshairs on her head. His finger teased the trigger. He took a breath. He couldn't blow this.

A semi roared past between him and the bar, kicking up a cloud of snow. When he looked through the scope again, the woman had pulled away from the man and gone back into the bar, the man right behind her. Who was this guy, anyway?

Jimmy swore, hauled his rifle back in and closed his window. He tried not to be discouraged. He had Stacy, which meant he had a standing invitation to Cardwell Ranch. Why rush it? What was another day?

He was getting cold and tired by the time the door of

the bar opened again. He put his window down, lifted the rifle and looked through the scope. Two women. He recognized Stacy's sister, Dana, leading the way. Right behind her was… DJ Justice.

His heart began to pound. His finger on the trigger began to shake. Before he could get the crosshairs on her, the door of the Suburban opened and she was gone.

He beat the steering wheel with his fist, then whirred up the window. He'd get his chance. He had to. A thought struck him. He'd find out where DJ was staying on the ranch and take her out quietly, he thought as he tested the blade with his thumb. A bead of blood appeared on his skin at the mere touch.

The idea of cutting her throat appealed to him. He was good with a knife. It would be better this way. Better chance of killing her and then making a clean getaway before anyone was the wiser.

He just had to make sure that the pro didn't get to her first. Maybe their paths would cross. He sheathed the knife, smiling at the prospect of surprising the pro.

DJ watched the winter landscape sweep past under a full moon. "I really like your friend Hilde."

Dana smiled as she drove them toward the ranch. "I'm so glad. Hilde liked you, too. So, what did you think of Beau Tanner?"

She shot a look at her cousin. "How long have you known him?" she asked, avoiding the question.

"Not all that long. His family is from the canyon, but he returned only about five years ago. You two seemed pretty close when you were dancing."

DJ smiled. "You aren't playing matchmaker, are you? You know I'm going to be in town only a few days."

"You'll be here a lot longer than that if I have my way," Dana said and laughed.

When they reached the house, the porch light was on, but everyone appeared to have gone to bed hours ago.

"I should probably go on up to my cabin," DJ said, getting out of the Suburban.

"I saw that my sister made sugar cookies. I'm thinking cookies and hot cocoa. Interested? It's not that late."

DJ couldn't resist. "If you're sure we won't wake everyone up."

"The kitchen is a long way from the upstairs bedrooms. Come on," she said, leading DJ inside.

A few minutes later, nibbling a sugar cookie, DJ watched her cousin make hot cocoa. Her mind kept returning to Beau Tanner and what he'd told her earlier, not to mention the kiss. That she'd felt something—not just something, but *something*—made her angry with herself. Worse, he'd known she felt it.

But she suspected he had, too. She smiled to herself as she recalled his expression as he'd watched her lick the dab of ketchup from the corner of her mouth.

"DJ?"

She realized she hadn't been listening. "I'm sorry?"

"Do you want me to get out the letters or is it too late?" Dana asked.

"No, I would love it, if you can find them."

"I found them earlier and put them in the desk down here," she said. "I know you're anxious to learn everything you can about your family. Me, too. Pour us each a cup and I'll get them."

DJ filled two mugs with hot cocoa and, with a plate of cookies, sat down at the table. Dana returned, sat down next to her and pushed a bundle of letters toward her.

The envelopes were yellowed with age and tied together with a thin red ribbon. DJ looked at her cousin as she picked them up with trembling fingers. "They must have meant something to your grandmother for her to keep them like this."

Dana nodded. "I thought the same thing. I can't imagine turning my back on my children, no matter what they did."

"You haven't met my father," she said with a sad smile. "I'm sure he sounded charming on the phone. But he was a born con man. He never did an honest day's work in his life. That's how he ended up in prison."

"My grandparents were hardworking ranchers, up before dawn, so they must have been horribly disappointed that their only son wasn't interested in staying on the ranch," Dana said with such diplomacy that DJ loved her all the more for it.

"You don't mind if I open these and read them?" she asked.

"Of course not. They're from your father. If they can help, please. I just don't want them to upset you."

DJ laughed, thinking of all the things she'd been through tonight, Beau being one of them. "I was raised by my father. Nothing about him would surprise me." She knew that wasn't quite true. When he'd mentioned Montana, what she'd heard in his voice—longing, regret, love—*that* had surprised her.

She opened the first letter. Something about her father's precise handwriting made her ache inside. It was clear even before she read the first few words that he was trying hard to make amends. He wanted his parents to get to know his wife.

DJ put that letter away and picked up another. This

one was along the same lines as the first. He talked about
wanting to return to the ranch, to raise a family there.

The next letter was even more heartbreaking. He was
pleading with his parents to forgive him. She saw that
the letters had been written only weeks apart.

DJ wasn't sure she could read the last letter. The writing was so neat, so purposeful, so pleading. In this letter, he said that he desperately wanted his family to meet
his baby girl, DJ.

> Don't punish her for my mistakes. Please don't
> deny your grandchild because of mistakes I've
> made. I will do anything you ask of me. I'll do
> it for my child… I'd do anything for DJ. All she
> has is me.

As she read the last lines, her eyes burned with tears,
the words blurring before her. She quickly closed the
letter and put it back into the envelope. He had pleaded
for their forgiveness and asked if he and his baby could
come home. Clearly they hadn't forgiven him, since her
cousin had never met him.

But she and her father must have come to Montana
later, when she was five. How else could she have met
ten-year-old Beau Tanner? How else could her father
have forced such a promise out of him?

He'd tried to give her family. She didn't think his
words could break her heart any further and yet they
had. He'd poured his heart out to his parents and yet
they hadn't budged. No wonder he'd never told her about
his family. But what had he done to make them so cold
to him?

"He must have done something they felt was unforgivable. I can't believe it was simply for marrying a woman of Italian descent," she said and looked at her cousin.

"I don't know. I never really knew my grandparents. I was young when they died, but they were very strict, from what my mother told me. However, I'm with you. I don't think it was the marriage. I think something else happened. Maybe if you asked your father—"

"He isn't apt to tell me, unfortunately, since I knew nothing about any of this," she said quickly and got to her feet. "There is something I'd like to show you." She picked up her bag from the chair where she'd dropped it. "Do you recognize this?" she asked as she held out the doll to her cousin.

Dana took the rag doll so carefully, holding it gingerly as she looked into its innocent face. "It's old, isn't it? Was it yours when you were a child?" she asked as she studied the construction and clothing.

"You've never seen it before?"

"No, I'm sorry. I can tell that it is handmade." She pointed to the small embroidered red heart, almost like a birthmark, on the doll's chest, under the collar of her dress. "Did someone make the doll for you?"

"That's what's so…frustrating. I had an identical doll, but I lost it years ago. When I first saw this one, I thought it was mine. It's not, though. Mine had an accident with a dog."

"How odd. So, how did you come to have this one?" Dana asked.

"I recently found it in my bed in my apartment."

Her cousin quickly rubbed her arms as if chilled. "That is spooky. And you have no idea who could have left it for you?"

She shook her head. "None. But this was pinned to the rag doll's body, under her dress." She took out the photo and handed it to her cousin. "What about the people in this photograph? Do you recognize them?" DJ asked hopefully.

Dana studied the old photograph for a long moment before shaking her head. "I'm sorry, but I've never seen them before."

Taking the photo back, she felt a deep sense of disappointment. She'd hoped that her cousin would have the answers she desperately needed.

On the table was one of the first letters she'd opened. "Did you see this part?" she asked her cousin. "There was another woman my father had been in love with that summer. Apparently it was someone his parents adored. If he broke that woman's heart..." She looked back through the letter. "He mentions a Zinnie." Glancing up at Dana, she asked, "Do you know anyone by that name?"

Her cousin thought for a moment. "Could be Zinnia Jameson. Well, at least, that's her name now. She married a local rancher. She would be about the right age. They live about ten miles up the canyon. It's too late to ask her tonight."

"But we could go tomorrow?"

Dana smiled and rose. "Tomorrow, though if your father broke her heart, she might not want to talk about it."

"It was more than thirty-five years ago."

"As if that makes a difference when it comes to a broken heart," her cousin said. "Maybe Zinnia is why Walter's parents couldn't forgive him."

Roger Douglas had just poured himself a drink when his phone rang. He couldn't help being nervous. If he didn't get rid of Dee Anna Justice… Paying her off wasn't an option. That would mean opening up the financials. He couldn't let that happen. All he needed was a little more time to win the money back. There was a poker game tomorrow night. High stakes. With a little luck…

The phone rang again. He pulled it out of his pocket, expecting it would be Marietta. He really wasn't in the mood to talk to her tonight.

With surprise, he saw that it was the man he'd hired to find him a killer. Was he calling to say the deed was done? His heart soared. With Dee Anna Justice dead, he would have the time he desperately needed to cover his tracks.

"Tell me you have good news," he said into the phone without preamble.

"We have a problem."

"I don't want to hear—"

"He thinks you put an earlier hit out on her."

"What? That's ridiculous."

"Well, something's wrong. He says there's this cowboy dogging her like he thinks someone is going to try to kill her."

"I have no idea what that's about, let alone who this cowboy might be. You said that other man you talked to about this…contract could be a problem."

"It's not him."

"You sure about that?"

"Look, I'll talk Andrei down. He's a pro. He'll complete the contract."

"What about the other guy?"

"Jimmy? Who knows? He might get lucky and take

her out. He's cheaper, and with the pro getting cold feet, this could work out better for both of us."

"It had better."

"Easy, Roger. The only reason you and I are pals is that you owe my boss a potful of money. So remember who you're talking to." He hung up.

Roger downed his drink and poured himself another. If this blew up in his face...

Beau wouldn't have been surprised to find his house empty when he finally got home. Leah had shown up like a ghost out of the past. He half expected her to vanish the same way.

The house was dark as he entered. As he turned on the light, he was startled for a moment to see a shadowy figure sitting by the window.

"You could have turned on a light," he said, annoyed with her for showing up, for only hinting at whatever was wrong and now for startling him.

"I like the dark," she said, turning to look at him. "Also, you can't see the northern lights with a lamp on. Didn't you notice them?"

He hadn't. He'd had too much on his mind.

"Rough night?" she asked as he hung up his Stetson and coat.

"You could say that. Look, I'm not staying, so now probably isn't the best time for you to tell me what's going on with you and Charlie."

She nodded, making him wonder if she was ever going to tell him. "Is everything all right?"

"Just work."

Leah nodded as if to say she knew he was putting her off and it was okay. She got up and followed him into the kitchen. In the overhead light, he could see that she'd been crying.

"Once I finish this job—"

"It's all right. But I do appreciate you letting me stay here."

He nodded as he made himself two sandwiches and bagged them with a couple of colas. "I'm going to grab a quick shower."

"I was just headed for bed. I didn't realize how late it was. Beau, if there is anything I can do—"

"No. Thanks for cleaning up after yourself."

She laughed. "I didn't mean in the house. I have some experience with undercover operations."

He stared at her. "As what?"

"An operative. But we can talk about that when this job of yours is over."

An operative? He realized how little he knew about her and Charlie as he watched her head for the guest bedroom. He'd thought that she and his former best friend were having marital problems. Now he didn't know what to think.

He didn't have time to speculate. Right now, his number one problem was DJ Justice.

Chapter 9

It was after midnight. The snow-covered mountain-side shone like day in the light of the huge white moon hanging overhead.

"Let me walk you to your cabin," Dana said as DJ started to leave.

"No, it's late and I can get there just fine on my own." She smiled at her cousin and gave her a hug. "But thank you. For everything."

"I'm sorry I wasn't more help with the doll and photo. Tomorrow, though, we'll pay Zinnia a visit."

"We'll get it figured out," DJ said, hoping it was true. At least she knew more now than she had before coming here. Her father's letters still broke her heart. What had he done?

"So you liked Beau?" Dana asked almost shyly.

DJ chuckled and shook her head. "The truth is, my father asked him to look after me while I'm out here."

"Really? What did he think might happen to you? Or," she said, smiling, "was he trying to throw the two of you together?" From the glint in her cousin's eyes, it was clear that she thought Walter was also playing matchmaker.

DJ shrugged. She really had no idea. If she hadn't seen her father's fear... "Again, thank you for everything. See you in the morning." As DJ stepped out on the porch, closing the door behind her, she caught movement out of the corner of her eye. For a startled moment, her hand went to her bag. Unfortunately she'd had to leave her gun behind in California.

Beau Tanner rose from the chair he'd been sprawled in, his boots scraping the wood porch as he tipped his Stetson. "Didn't mean to scare you."

"What are you doing here?" He *had* scared her, but she was trying hard not to show it.

"My job. I told you. Your father—"

"And I told you. I can take care of myself. I release you from any promise you made when you were ten." She started off the porch but heard his boots right behind her. She spun on him. "What are you planning to do? Follow me everywhere?"

"If that's what it takes to make sure you're safe."

She thrust her hands on her hips. "This is crazy. Look, I'm fine. There is nothing to protect me from."

"You sure about that? Well, I'm not. And until I am..."

"Fine. Follow me if it makes you happy." She started up the mountainside, breathing hard from her anger and just seeing him again. The last thing she needed right now was some man who...who irritated her. Her heart was beating faster at just the sound of his long strides as he easily caught up to her.

"Let's just keep to the shadows of the pines," he said, pulling her out of the moonlight.

She indulged him and his paranoia, filling her lungs with the cold night air as she tried to ignore him. The cowboy wasn't the kind who was easily ignored. She caught a whiff of his scent, a mixture of the great outdoors, fragrant soap and a powerful maleness.

DJ hated the effect it had on her as her body betrayed her. She felt an ache inside her like something she'd never felt before. Maybe it was from years of not feeling safe, but she wanted to be in his arms again. She wanted to feel again like she had that moment in the snowbank when his mouth was on hers. She wanted to feel…protected, and she had in his arms.

Which was why she couldn't let herself give in. She would be here only a few days, and then she would be returning to California and her life there.

"This is where we part company," she said as she climbed the steps to her cabin and started to open the door.

He'd taken the steps in long strides, and now his large hand closed over hers. "Not until I make sure the cabin is secure."

She opened the door, turning on the light as she stepped inside, Beau right behind her. She couldn't believe how far he was taking this. "It's late and I need to get some rest."

He didn't seem to be paying any attention to what she was saying. She hadn't wanted him in her cabin. Earlier the place had felt spacious, but it didn't now. "This is silly. You can see that there is no one in here."

He turned to look at her. "I think you have some idea

who might want to harm you. That's information I need. Tonight. Before this goes any further."

She heard the determination in his voice and sighed inwardly. *Let him have his say and then send him on his way*, she thought. "Fine."

It had been a long day, but after the nap earlier and everything that had happened, she felt more wired than tired, in truth. She moved to the small kitchen and opened the refrigerator, remembering the variety of beverages and snacks her cousin had shown her.

"Wine or beer?" she asked, knowing the only reason she was asking was that she needed the distraction.

"Beer." He had moved to the small breakfast bar and taken a seat on one of the stools. She handed him a bottle of beer and took one for herself. Twisting off the top, she took a drink. It was icy cold and tasted good.

Leaning against the kitchen counter, she studied the handsome cowboy. It was his eyes, she thought. She had remembered them because they were so unusual. Worn denim. Maybe also because there was kindness in those eyes that she would have recognized even as a child of five.

"I'm sorry you got involved in this," she said as she picked at the label on her bottle for a moment. When she looked up, she realized he'd been studying *her*.

"Why does your father think you need protecting?" Beau asked and watched her take another drink of her beer as if stalling. He understood she was holding out on him. He'd been in this business long enough to know the signs. DJ was running scared, but she was trying damned hard not to show it.

"You say you met me years ago?" she finally asked.

"Did you know anything about my family before that? Or after that?"

He had removed his Stetson and tossed it on one of the other stools. Now he shrugged out of his coat, the same one he'd worn to the airport. He could see that this was going to take a while.

"Are you going somewhere with these questions? Or just avoiding mine?" he asked after draping his coat over a stool. He locked gazes with her. "I have to wonder why you aren't being straight with me. I hate getting myself killed without knowing why."

She looked chagrined as she put down her beer and turned to him. "I'm not sure what this has to do with anything, but before I left California, my apartment was broken into. The intruder left something for me."

He held his breath as he waited, imagining all kinds of nasty things.

"It was a doll with a photo pinned to it." She nodded as if she could tell that wasn't what he'd expected. "I used to have a rag doll identical to it. It wasn't a commercial doll. Someone had made it. Made two, apparently. Because as it turns out, this one wasn't mine. But it is so much like mine…"

"…that you wondered whose it had been."

She smiled. "Glad you're following along."

"And the photo?"

She reached into her shoulder bag and took out the doll and photo. She handed him the photo. "I don't recognize any of them or have any idea who they might be. I asked my father, but…"

"He said he didn't know them."

"But from his expression when he saw the photo, he knows who they are. He suggested I get out of town."

Beau studied the photo. "You think you might be this baby?"

"My father swore I wasn't."

"But you don't believe him."

She sighed. "I don't know what to believe. For years he told me I had no family. A couple of days ago I find out about the Cardwells—and the Justices. My father was born here, apparently. His family disowned him after he married my mother. He wrote a few letters trying to get back into their good graces. He must even have come here if you and I met all those years ago."

"You think he was here trying to make amends?"

"It doesn't sound like making amends was the only reason my father came here. Otherwise I doubt we would have met."

Beau nodded as he picked up the doll she'd set on the breakfast bar. "I called your father after I saw you at the airport today."

That surprised her. She took a drink of her beer and seemed to be waiting for what was coming.

"I told him that in order to protect you, I needed to know what I was protecting you from," he said. "Your father swore that he didn't know, but when I pressed him, he said it might have something to do with your mother's family. He said they might have…found you."

She shuddered. *"Found me?"*

"That's what *I* said. Unfortunately he had to go before he could tell me anything further. I thought you might know why he would say that."

DJ stepped past him to move to the window that looked out over the ranch. As she drew back the curtain, he said, "I wish you wouldn't do that."

She let the curtain fall into place and turned to look

at him. "You think this has something to do with my *mother's* family? Why would they leave me the doll and the photo if they didn't want me to know about them?"

"Maybe they didn't leave them. Maybe some well-meaning person did." He shrugged. "I got the impression that your father thought you had something to fear from them."

She took another sip of her beer. "Well, that's interesting, given that all my life he's told me I didn't have any family. Not just that," she said as she walked back to the counter where she'd been leaning earlier. "I always felt growing up that we were running from something, someone. A few times it was one of my father's...associates. But other times..."

"You think it might have been your mother's family?"

She shrugged and toyed with the label on her beer again. He saw her eyes fill with tears. "That would be something, if the people I have to fear are...family."

"We don't know that." He got up, moved to her and took the nearly full bottle of beer from her. He set it aside. "You should get some rest."

He expected her to put up a fight, but instead she merely nodded. "It has been a long day." Her gaze met his. He did his best not to look at her full mouth.

Stepping away from her, he reached for his coat and hat.

"As it turns out, my father had a girlfriend before he married my mother," she said behind him. "Dana and I are going to visit a woman named Zinnia in the morning. I have a bad feeling he broke her heart. Still, I'm hoping she might be able to help me put another piece into the puzzle that is my father."

"I'm going, too, then."

"I told you. I release you from any promise you made my father years ago."

He nodded as he shrugged into his coat. "Just the same, I can go with you or follow you. Your choice." Beau snugged his Stetson down over his blond hair. His boots echoed on the hardwood floor as he walked to the door, opened it and turned. "I'll be right outside if you need me." He tipped his hat to her.

She opened her mouth, no doubt to argue the point, but he was out the door before she could speak. As he settled into the swing on the porch, he listened to her moving around inside the cabin and tried not to think of her in that big log bed he'd seen through the open bedroom doorway.

"Stacy? Did I wake you?" Jimmy knocked over the bottle of whiskey, swore and grabbed it before most of it ended up in the motel carpet. "You still there?"

"Jimmy?" she said sleepily.

"James. I told you, I go by James now." He took a drink and pushed aside his irritation at her. Tonight hadn't gone as he'd planned, and he felt the clock ticking. Who knew what the pro was doing tonight, but getting into the ranch wouldn't be easy for him—especially at night. There were hired hands, ranch dogs, lots of people living there. Unless they knew you... He told himself he still had the upper hand.

"What do you want?" Stacy asked, sounding irritated with him now.

He quieted his voice. "I was thinking about you. Thinking about old times. You and me." He could almost feel her soften at his words. Whatever he had back then, he still had it—at least where Stacy was concerned.

"So you decided to call me in the middle of the night?" She didn't sound irritated anymore. Maybe she was a little touched by the gesture.

"Yeah, sorry about that. I just couldn't get you off my mind. I wanted to hear your voice."

"You didn't say what you were doing in town. Are you living here now?"

He'd been vague, letting her think he was looking for a job, a place to live, letting her think he might be staying. "We can talk about that sometime, but right now I want to talk about you."

"What about me?"

"I still remember the way you felt in my arms."

"You do?"

"Uh-huh. Do you remember…me?"

She made an affirming sound.

He could imagine her lying in bed. He wondered what she had on. Probably a flannel nightgown, but he could get that off her quick enough.

"You are the sexiest woman I've ever known," he said and took another sip of the whiskey. "You said you live on the ranch now. In one of those cabins on the mountainside that I can see from the road?"

"Jim—James."

"I was thinking maybe—"

"My daughter. Ella, I told you about her. She's here in the cabin with me."

"I would be quiet as a mouse." There was just enough hesitation that it gave him hope, but she quickly drowned that idea.

"No. If that's all you wanted, I really need to get some sleep."

He realized that he'd come on too strong. He cursed

under his breath. "No, that's not all I want. I shouldn't have called tonight. But after seeing you… I want to take you out to a nice dinner. That is, if you're free."

Silence, then, "When?"

"Tomorrow night. I figure you'll know a good place to go. Nothing cheap. I want to make up for this call."

"Okay."

He shot a fist into the air. "Great. I'll pick you up. What time? And hey, I want to meet your daughter." He'd almost forgotten about the kid again.

"Sure," she said, sounding pleased. "Tomorrow, say, six? My sister will babysit Ella."

"See if she'll take her for the night, because I want to get you on a dance floor after dinner. I can't wait to get you in my arms again."

Stacy laughed. "I've missed you."

He smiled to himself as he hung up and picked up the hunting knife from the bed. "Tomorrow night." He would mix a little pleasure with business.

Chapter 10

The next morning, just after sunrise, Dana found Beau on DJ's porch. She handed him a mug of coffee and a key. "Go over to the cabin next door. I can stand guard if you think it's necessary."

He smiled at her, glad to have Dana for a friend. "I don't think you need to stand guard." He figured DJ should be safe in broad daylight with so many people on the ranch. And he didn't plan on being gone long.

"Thanks for the coffee—and the key. But I think I'll run home and get a shower and a change of clothing. DJ said the two of you are going to visit Zinnia Jameson. I'd like to come along."

"Fine with me. I'm glad you're looking after her." Her smile seemed to hold a tiny surprise. "She's special, don't you think?"

He laughed. "You're barking up the wrong tree. It

isn't like that." He thought about the kiss and quickly shoved the memory away.

"That's what they all say—until love hits them like a ton of bricks."

Beau left, chuckling to himself. He'd heard that Dana Savage was one great matchmaker. She'd helped all five of her cousins find the loves of their lives. But she'd apparently failed with her older sister, Stacy, he thought.

And she would fail with him.

On the way home, Beau put in another call to the number Walter Justice had given him. A male voice answered just as before. He asked for Walter Justice.

A moment later another male voice came on the line. The gravelly voice informed him that Walter couldn't come to the phone.

"I need to talk to him."

"Not sure if that is ever going to happen. He got shanked last night. They've taken him to the hospital."

"Is he going to be all right?"

"Don't know." The line went dead.

Beau held his phone for a few moments, listening to the silence on the other end. DJ's father was in the hospital, possibly dying? There might never be any answers coming from that end.

He pocketed his phone, telling himself that he needed to let DJ know. She said she didn't care about her father, but having been through this with his own, he knew it wasn't true. When the man was your father, no matter how much he screwed up, his loss…well, it hurt. He remembered feeling racked with guilt because he hadn't kept in touch with his father. For years he'd wanted nothing to do with him.

Ultimately it all came down to blood and a built-in love that came with it.

Reaching his house, he climbed out of his pickup, thinking about the Walter Justice he'd known years ago. He wondered how he'd aged since he'd been in prison. He doubted he'd changed, which could explain why he was in the hospital now.

Beau swore under his breath. He didn't know what to do. He had to keep DJ safe. It was a debt that he wouldn't renege on—even if Walter didn't survive. He wasn't the kind of man who went back on his word. But he also knew there was more to it. He kept thinking about that brown-eyed little girl and the woman she'd become.

He would tell her about her father. But not until after their visit to Zinnia Jameson's house. He wasn't sure how she would take the news. Maybe there was no connection between what had happened to her father and whatever Walter feared might happen to his daughter.

Either way, Beau was even more concerned for her safety.

Andrei sniffed the wind, waiting for a sign. He clung to the utility pole, careful not to attract any undue attention.

This job had turned out to be harder than he'd thought. For some reason Dee Anna had picked up an overprotective cowboy. Because of that, he was having trouble getting the right shot.

That alone should have made him quit the job.

But his birthday was coming, and he'd planned this for too long. His last hit. He would feel incomplete if he didn't finish. Also, he never quit a job once he'd flipped the coin and it had come up heads. It felt like a bad idea to do it now. He never liked to test luck.

So he would finish it and celebrate his birthday as he hung up his gun.

All he had to do was kill Dee Anna Justice. But not today, he thought as he sniffed the wind again. She and the cowboy had to feel safe. Then they would make the mistake of letting him get a clean shot. He would bide his time.

"This couldn't wait until a decent time of the day?" attorney Roger Douglas demanded as he joined Marietta in the library. He stepped to the table where Ester had put out coffee and mini citrus muffins. He poured himself a cup and took two muffins on a small plate before sitting down.

"I wanted an update on the…situation," Marietta said. She felt calm and in control, more than she had in the few months since Carlotta had confessed.

"It's a little early to—"

"I assumed you would be handling this yourself and yet here you sit."

He picked up one of the muffins. She noticed that his hand shook as he popped it into his mouth. Clearly he was stalling for time.

"Have you even found her?" she demanded.

"Yes, of course. She's at a place called the Cardwell Ranch near Big Sky, Montana. She's staying with a cousin on her father's side of the family. I've had her apartment bugged for several months—ever since you asked me to find her."

"But you haven't gotten around to offering her money?"

"What is this really about?" Roger asked patiently, as if she was a child he had to humor.

"Have you offered Dee Anna Justice the money or not?"

He studied her for a moment before dragging his gaze away. "Maybe we should discuss this when you are more yourself."

"Actually, I am, and for the first time in a long time. I am going to want to see all the financials on the trust funds." He paled, confirming what she'd feared. Her nosy housekeeper knew more than she did about what was right in front of her eyes. "But on this other matter…"

Roger rose. "I don't know what's gotten into you, but I told you I would handle it."

"How much are you planning to offer her?" She saw something in his eyes that made her heart drop. How much money had he stolen from her? Was this why he was dragging his feet? Because there wasn't enough money left to bribe Dee Anna Justice?

"What did you do?" she demanded.

He began to pace the room. "You're not thinking clearly, so I had to take things into my own hands. Trying to buy off this woman is the wrong approach. She would eventually bleed you dry. You know what kind of woman she is given that her father is Walter Justice. I told you I'm taking care of it and I have. I've hired someone to make sure she is no longer a problem."

For a moment Marietta couldn't catch her breath. "You did what?"

He dropped down into a chair next to her and took one of her hands. "It is the only way. I've kept you out of it. I—"

She jerked her hand free. "You stupid fool." Her mind raced. "Is it done already?"

"No, but I should be hearing from him—"

"Stop him!" She shoved to her feet. She was breathing hard, her heart thumping crazily in her chest. She tried to calm down. If she had a heart attack now… "You stop him or I will call the police."

Roger looked too shocked to speak. "You wouldn't do that."

"Try me. Call him now!"

"My job is to protect you."

She shook her head. "Protect me? Give me your phone. I will stop the man myself." She held out her hand.

"You can't do that, Marietta." He sounded scared. "You don't know what this man is capable of doing if he feels you're jerking him around."

"You think he is more dangerous than me?" She let out a chuckle, feeling stronger than she had in years. "Roger, get your affairs in order. You're done, and if I find out what I suspect, that you've been stealing from me, prepare for spending the rest of your life in prison. You're fired, and if you try to run, I'll send this man after you."

All the color had drained from his face. "You don't know what you're saying."

"I do, for the first time in a long time. I've depended on you to make decisions for me because you made me question myself. But I'm clearheaded now, Roger." He started to argue, but she cut him off. "Make the call."

She watched, shaking inside. But whoever he was phoning didn't answer. She listened to him leave a message calling off the hit.

"This is a mistake," Roger said as he pocketed his phone. "I've been with you for years. I've—"

"Get out." She pointed toward the door. "Don't make me call the police to have you thrown out. And you'd better pray that the man you hired gets the message."

As he left, Marietta heard a floorboard creak. Ester. The nosy damned woman. She thought about firing her as well, but she was too upset to deal with another traitor in her midst right now.

The woman who answered the door later that morning at the Jameson house was tiny, with a halo of white-blond hair that framed a gentle face. Bright blue eyes peered out at them from behind wire-rimmed glasses. "Yes?" she asked, looking from DJ to Beau and finally to Dana. She brightened when she recognized her.

"Sorry to drop by without calling," Dana said.

"No, I'm delighted." She stepped back to let them enter.

"This is my cousin DJ."

"Dee Anna Justice," DJ added, watching the woman for a reaction to the last name. She didn't have to wait long.

Zinnia froze for a moment before her gaze shot to DJ, her blue eyes widening. "Wally's daughter?"

DJ nodded. She'd never heard anyone call her father Wally.

"And you know Beau Tanner," Dana said.

"Yes," Zinnia said. An awkward silence fell between them, but she quickly filled it. "I was just going to put on a pot of coffee. Come into the kitchen, where we can visit while I make it." Her eyes hadn't left DJ's face.

They followed her into the kitchen. DJ had been so

nervous all morning, afraid that this might be another dead end. But now, from Zinnia's reaction to her, she had little doubt this woman had been the one her father's parents had hoped he would marry.

"Dana is helping me piece together my past—and my father's," DJ said, unable to wait a moment longer. "You were a part of the past, if I'm not wrong."

Zinnia had her back to them. She stopped pouring coffee grounds into a white paper filter for a moment. "Yes." She finished putting the coffee on and turned. "Please sit."

DJ pulled out a chair at the table. Her cousin did the same across from her. Beau stood by the window.

Zinnia came around the kitchen island to pull up a chair at the head of the table. When she looked at DJ, her expression softened. "I loved your father. Is that what you wanted to hear?"

"And he loved you."

The woman nodded, a faraway look in those blue eyes. "We'd been in love since grade school." She chuckled. "I know that sounds silly, but it's true. We were inseparable. We even attended Montana State University in Bozeman together. Everyone just assumed we would get married after college."

"Especially my father's parents," DJ said.

"Yes. I had a very good relationship with them. I was like another daughter to them, they said." She smiled in memory.

"What happened?" DJ asked, even though she suspected she already knew.

Zinnia straightened in her chair as if bracing herself. "Wally got a job as a wrangler taking people into Yellowstone Park. His parents were upset with him because they needed him on the ranch, but Wally was restless. He'd already confessed to me that he didn't want to take over the ranch when his parents retired. He wanted to travel. He wanted…" She hesitated. "That's just it. He didn't know what he wanted. He just…*wanted*." Her gaze locked on DJ's. "Then he met your mother. She and some friends were touring the park." Zinnia shrugged, but her voice cracked when she added, "Apparently it was love at first sight."

The coffeemaker let out a sigh, and the woman got up. DJ rose, too. "May I help?"

Zinnia seemed surprised. "Why, thank you. There are cups in that cabinet."

She took out four cups and watched as Zinnia filled each. DJ carried two over, giving one to Dana and the other to Beau as he finally took a seat at the table. She'd expected to see him on her front porch when she got up this morning, but to her surprise, he'd come driving up, all showered and shaved and ready to go wherever she was going.

He'd been so somber, she wondered if he wasn't having second thoughts about getting involved with her father—and her. She couldn't blame him. It seemed ridiculous for him to tag along, since she seemed to be in no danger. Maybe her father had overreacted.

She'd said as much to Beau, but he'd insisted that he had nothing else planned that day except spend it with her.

Because of some promise he'd made a con man when he was ten? What kind of man would honor that?

Beau Tanner, she thought, turning her attention back to Zinnia.

"My grandparents must have been horribly disappointed," DJ said after taking the cup of coffee the woman handed her and sitting back down.

Zinnia sat, cradling her cup in her two small hands. "They were as brokenhearted as I was," she said with a nod and then took a sip of her coffee, her eyes misty.

DJ wanted to tell her that she'd dodged a bullet by not ending up with her father. But even as she thought it, she wondered what kind of man her father might have been if he'd married Zinnia and gotten over his wanderlust.

"I had no idea that my mother had a brother," Dana said into the awkward silence. "Then I found some old letters. That's how we found you."

Zinnia nodded. "Wally's parents did everything they could to get him not to marry that girl, to come back to the ranch, to help them, since they were getting up in age. Mostly they wanted him to marry me." She smiled sadly. "But in the end…" Her voice broke. "Sadly, I heard the marriage didn't last long." Her gaze was on DJ again.

"My mother died in childbirth."

The older woman seemed startled to hear that.

DJ stared at her. "That is what happened, right?"

"I only know what Wally's parents told me."

"It would help if you could tell us what you do know," Dana said.

Zinnia hesitated for a moment and then spoke quietly. "As you might have guessed, I stayed friends with Wally's parents. They were such sweet people. They were devastated when Wally didn't come back." She took a sip of her coffee as if gathering her thoughts. "Wally called at one point, asking for money. I guess he thought they would give him what he felt was his share of the ranch." She scoffed at that. "He always made things worse."

Seeming to realize that she was talking about DJ's father, Zinnia quickly added, "Forgive me for talking about him like that."

"There isn't anything you can say that I haven't said myself. I know my father. He didn't get better after he left Montana."

"Well," the older woman continued. "When he called for money, he told them that Carlotta—" the name seemed to cause her pain even after all these years "—had left him to go spend time with an aunt in Italy."

DJ reached into her shoulder bag and took out the photo. As she passed it over to Zinnia, she asked, "Do you recognize any of these people?"

Zinnia studied the photo for only a moment before she put it down. "The young woman holding the baby is Carlotta Pisani Justice. Or at least, that had been her name. I saw her only once, but that's definitely her. You can see why Wally fell for her."

Picking up the photograph, DJ stared at the young woman holding the baby. This was her *mother*. "My father swears that the baby she's holding isn't me."

Zinnia looked at her with sympathy. "We heard that her wealthy family had gotten the marriage annulled somehow and threatened that if she didn't go to Italy, they would cut off her money. It seems she met someone her family liked better in Italy, quickly remarried and had a child with him."

"So this child would be my half brother or sister," DJ said more to herself. When she looked up, she saw Zinnia's expression.

The older woman was frowning. "But if her family had the marriage annulled… Why would they have done that after your mother and father had a child together?"

DJ felt an odd buzzing in her ears. She thought about what Beau had told her. Her father feared that her mother's family had "found" her.

"Is it possible they didn't know about me?" DJ asked, finding herself close to tears. Her gaze went to Beau's. She saw sympathy in his gaze but not surprise. All those years on the run. Had they been running to keep the truth from her mother's family?

The doll and the photo meant *someone* knew about her. Not only that, they also wanted her to know about them.

Beau drove DJ and Dana back to the ranch after their visit with Zinnia. Both were quiet on the short drive. The sun had come out, making the snowy landscape sparkle like diamonds. As he drove, he chewed on what they'd learned from Zinnia. He felt for DJ. Apparently her mother had walked away not only from her father but also from her.

But what part had her father played? He could only guess.

He hated that the news he had to give her would only make her feel worse. But he had no choice. He couldn't keep something like this from her. She had to know.

As he pulled into the Cardwell Ranch and parked, Dana's children all came running out. They were begging to go see Santa at the mall in Bozeman.

Stacy was with them. "I didn't put it in their heads," she said quickly.

Dana laughed. "Looks like I'm going to the mall," she said as she started toward the kids. "DJ, you're welcome to come along. You, too, Beau."

Beau shook his head. "Thanks, but DJ and I have some things we need to iron out."

Dana shot her cousin a mischievous look.

"Tell Santa hello for me," DJ said.

Beau said to Dana, "Mind if we take a couple of horses for a ride?"

Dana grinned. "Please. I'll call down to the stables. DJ, you can wear what you wore last night. You'll find a warmer coat just inside the door of the house."

"You do ride, don't you?" he asked her.

"I've been on a horse, if that's what you mean. But whatever you have to tell me, you don't have to take me for a ride to do it."

A man came out of the house just then, wearing a marshal's uniform. Dana introduced them. DJ could tell that something was worrying him and feared it might have to do with her.

"Have you had any trouble with the electricity?" he asked Dana.

"No, why?"

"Burt came by with the mail and told me he'd seen a lineman on one of our poles. By the time I got here, he was gone. Just thought I'd ask. Burt's pretty protective, but still, it did seem odd. Maybe I'll give the power company a call."

As Hud drove away, followed by Stacy and Dana and the kids, DJ turned to Beau. "Seriously, we can't talk here?"

He smiled and shook his head. "Let's get saddled up. We can talk about who's taking whom for a ride once we're on horseback and high in the mountains."

"I'm not going to like whatever it is you need to tell me, am I?"

He shook his head. "No, you're not, but you need to hear it."

When he'd seen Dee Anna and her cowboy saddling up horses, Andrei had known this was the day. Several things had happened that he'd taken as signs. He would have good luck today.

He'd made arrangements the night before to procure a snowmobile. He'd been stealing since he was a boy and still got a thrill out of it. He'd always liked the danger—and the reward. His father had taught him how to get away with it. He smiled to himself at the memory. He missed his father and hoped that he would make him proud today.

Andrei felt good. He was going to get his chance to finish this. He didn't plan to kill the cowboy, too, but he would if he had to. He could tell that the two felt safe here on the ranch. As they rode toward the mountains behind the ranch house, he smiled to himself.

Today would definitely be the day. Last night after stealing the snowmobile, he'd traversed the logging roads behind the ranch. He would be waiting for them on the mountain. He had an idea where they would be riding to. He'd seen horse tracks at a spot where there was a view of the tiny resort town of Big Sky.

He would be waiting for them. One shot. That's all he needed. He would be ahead of schedule. Still, he wanted to get this over with. He knew that feeling wasn't conducive to the type of work that he did. But he couldn't help the way he felt. He was anxious. Once he finished this, he couldn't wait for the future he'd planned since his first job when he was fourteen.

His cell phone rang. He ignored it. He could almost taste success on the wind as he climbed on the snowmobile and headed up one of the logging roads toward the top of the mountain behind Cardwell Ranch.

From the window Marietta watched her granddaughter come up the circular drive and park the little red sports car that had been her present for her thirtieth birthday.

"She can buy her own car," Ester had said with disapproval. "She has a job. It would be good for her and mean more to her."

Marietta had scoffed at that. "I have no one else to spoil." Which was true—at least, she'd believed that Bianca was her only granddaughter at the time. "She is my blood." Blood meant everything in her family. It was where lines were drawn. It was what made Bianca so precious. She was her daughter's child with a nice Italian man whose life, like her daughter's, had been cut short.

At least, that's what she'd told herself, the thing about blood being thicker than water and all that. But that was before she'd found out her daughter had conceived a child with…with that man.

Bianca got out of her car and glanced up as if she knew her grandmother would be watching. Her raven hair glistened in the sunlight as her gaze found Marietta at her window. Usually this was where her granddaughter smiled and waved and then hurried inside.

Today she stood there staring up, her face expressionless, her manner reserved. After a few moments, she looked toward the front door, brightened, then rushed in that direction.

Marietta knew then that Ester must have opened the door. Bianca loved the housekeeper. Maybe even more than she loved her grandmother.

That thought left a bitter taste in her mouth. She turned away from the window. Out of stubbornness, she thought about staying where she was and letting Bianca come to her.

But after a few minutes had passed, she couldn't stand it any longer and headed downstairs.

She found Ester and Bianca with their heads together, as she often did. The sight instantly annoyed her. But also worried her.

"I thought you would come upstairs," she said, unable to hide her displeasure.

Both women turned toward her but said nothing. Marietta looked from Ester to Bianca and felt her heart drop.

"What's wrong?" she demanded. "Has something happened?"

"I know, Grandmother. *How could you?*"

Chapter 11

DJ rode alongside Beau through the snow-covered pines until behind them the house could no longer be seen. The world became a wonderland of snow and evergreen below a sky so blue it hurt to look at it.

She didn't think she'd ever breathed such cold air. It felt good. It helped clear her head.

The cowboy riding beside her seemed to be lost in the beauty of the country around them, as well. What was it about him? She felt drawn to him and his cowboy code of honor. Yet all her instincts told her to be careful. He was the kind of man a woman could fall for, and she would never be the same after.

She'd spent her life never getting attached to anything. This man, this place, this Cardwell family all made her want to plant roots, and that terrified her. For so long she'd believed that was a life she could never have. But maybe, if the doll and photo were her mother's family reaching out to her and not a threat…wasn't it possible that she could finally live a normal life?

They rode up a trail until the trees parted and they got their first good view of Lone Peak across the valley and river. This late morning it was breathtaking. The stark peak gleamed against the deep blue of the big sky. No wonder this area had been named Big Sky.

"It's incredible, isn't it?" Beau said as he stopped to look.

DJ reined in beside him to stare out at the view. The vastness of it made her feel inconsequential. It wasn't a bad feeling. It certainly made her problems seem small.

"Beautiful," she said on a frosty breath.

"Yes, beautiful."

She felt his gaze on her. Turning in the saddle, she looked into his handsome face. He looked so earnest… "Okay, you got me out here. Why?"

"I thought you'd like the view."

She shook her head. "If you're trying to find a way to tell me that you're stepping away from this—"

"I don't break my promises." He pushed back his Stetson and settled those wonderful blue eyes on her. His look was so intense, she felt a shudder in her chest. "We need to talk about what Zinnia told you. But first I've got some bad news. I called your father this morning." She braced herself. "He was attacked at the prison. He's in the hospital."

DJ wasn't sure what she'd been expecting. Not this.

The news was a blow. For years she'd told herself that she hated him, that she never wanted to see him. She blamed him for her childhood. She blamed him for keeping her family from her. She bit her lip to keep from crying. "Is he—"

"It sounds serious."

DJ nodded, surprised how much her chest ached with unshed tears. "You think his attack..." She didn't need to finish her sentence. She saw that he thought whatever she had to fear, he suspected it was connected to her father's attack. "Why?"

"I don't know yet. But I will find out."

He sounded so sure of himself that she wanted to believe him capable of anything. Wasn't that why her father had cashed in on the promise? He must have believed that if anyone could keep her safe, it would be Beau Tanner.

"You think I'm in danger?"

"I do. We need to find out what is going on. We need to find your mother's family."

"But nothing's happened. Yes, I was left a doll and photo of people I didn't know at the time..."

"They broke into your house to leave it."

"But what if it's my mother's family trying to let me know about them?"

He shook his head. "DJ, if that was the case, then why wouldn't they have simply picked up the phone or mailed the doll and the photo with a letter?"

"You see the doll and photo as a threat?" Hadn't she at first, too?

"I agree, someone wants you to know. The question is, why? Given what we learned from Zinnia Jameson..."

She saw where he was going with this. "It could explain a lot about my childhood. I always felt as if we were running from something. What if my father was trying to keep my mother's family from finding us? You don't think he might have…kidnapped me, do you?"

Stacy wasn't surprised when Jimmy showed up at her part-time job at Needles and Pins, the shop that her sister's best friend, Hilde, owned. He pushed open the door, stepped in and stopped dead.

He was taking in all the bolts of fabric as if realizing he was completely out of his element. Stacy watched him, amused. James Ryan afraid of coming into a quilt shop. It endeared him to her more than she would have liked.

"Jimmy?" she said as if surprised to see him. Actually she wasn't. After she'd run into him yesterday, it had been clear he was hoping to see her again. That he had tracked her down… Well, it did make her heart beat a little faster. She'd always thought of him as the love of her life.

He came in, moving to the counter where Stacy was cutting fabric for a kit she was putting together. "James."

"Right. Sorry. Old habits… Do you like the colors?" she asked as she finished cutting and folded the half yard neatly. "Tangerine, turquoise, yellow and brown."

"Beautiful," James said without looking at the fabric. "So, this is where you work?"

"Part-time. I help Dana with the kids and work some on the ranch."

"Busy lady," James said. "I just wanted to make sure we were on for tonight."

She felt her heart do that little hop she'd missed for a long time. "Tonight. Right." She hesitated, torn. Then heard herself say, "Sure, why not?" even though a few not so good memories had surfaced since his call last night.

"Good. I can't wait." He sounded hopeful, and the look in his eyes transported her straight back to high school, when he used to look at her like that.

Stacy felt a lump in her throat. Was it possible they were being given a second chance at love? It seemed too good to be true. "I never thought I'd see you again."

He grinned, that way too familiar grin that had made her lose her virginity to him all those years ago. "Neither did I. Life is just full of surprises. Great surprises. So, I'll pick you up on the ranch. Which cabin did you say was yours?"

"The one farthest to the right on the side of the mountain. You remember how to get to the ranch?"

He laughed. "Like it was yesterday."

Marietta had to sit down. She moved to a chair and dropped into it. Her heart pounded in her ears and she feared it would give out on her. She'd feared something like this might happen and had told Roger as much.

"Maybe the best thing would be to tell Bianca," she'd said.

"Have you lost your mind? Once you do that, you're basically admitting that this…woman has a right to part of your estate," Roger had said. "No, there is a better way to handle this, and Bianca never has to know."

Why had she listened to that man?

Bianca brushed back her long, dark hair and glared at her grandmother. "What have you done?"

Marietta's gaze shifted to Ester. She'd never seen such determination in the woman's expression before. Her lips were clamped tightly together and her eyes were just as dark and angry as Bianca's.

"What have you *done?"* she wanted to demand of her housekeeper. Yes, Ester was nosy. And yes, she'd been acting odd lately. But Marietta had never dreamed that she would go to Bianca. She'd trusted the woman. A mistake, she saw now.

Bianca crossed her arms over her chest. "Isn't there something you want to tell me, Grandmama?"

Use of that pet name was almost Marietta's undoing. She lived only for Bianca. Everything she'd done was for this precious granddaughter.

"Tell you?" she echoed, stalling for time.

"Tell me the truth," Bianca demanded, raising her voice. "Do I have a sister?"

Marietta had known when her dying daughter had confessed she'd conceived a child with Walter that this day might come.

Now she realized how foolish she'd been to think she could keep something like this a secret. Although her daughter and Walter had certainly managed. It was clear that Ester had known about the other child, probably from the beginning. That realization hurt more than she wanted to admit.

It would be just like Carlotta to have shared this information all those years ago with the woman who'd practically raised her. Suddenly she recalled Ester at the sewing machine in her tiny room. She'd been startled and tried to hide what she was doing. Marietta had thought she was trying to disguise the fact that she wasn't working like she was supposed to be.

But now she remembered what the housekeeper had been working on. Dolls. There'd been two identical dolls! Two rag dolls, and yet Bianca had always had only the one.

Betrayal left a nasty taste in her mouth. Her gaze darted to Ester. "I want you out of my house!"

"No!" her granddaughter cried, stepping in front of the housekeeper as if to shield her. "Do not blame Ester for this. If you fire her, you'll never see me again." The ultimatum only made the betrayal more bitter. "If it wasn't for Ester, I might never have known that I have a sister you've kept from me all these years."

"I wasn't the one who kept it from you all these years. That was your mother—and Ester." She could see now that Ester had been collaborating with Carlotta for years. Had she been stronger, she would have strangled the woman with her bare hands. "It's Ester who has known for so long, not me. Your mother didn't bother to tell me until she was near death. If you want to blame someone—"

"I'm not here to place blame. My mother had her reasons for keeping it from me. I suspect those reasons had something to do with you. But I won't blame you, either." Bianca stepped toward her. "I just want to know about my sister."

"She isn't your *sister*. She's only half—"

Her granddaughter waved a hand through the air. "She's my *blood*."

That it could hurt even worse came as a surprise. "Your *blood*?" she demanded. "Watered down with the likes of a man…" She sputtered. Her contempt for Walter Justice knew no words.

Bianca dropped to her knees before her grandmother and took both of Marietta's hands in hers. "I want to know about her. I want to know all of it. No more secrets. Grandmama, if you have done something to hurt my sister…" She let go of Marietta's hands. The gesture alone was like a stab in her old heart.

"Get me the phone!" she ordered Ester. She called Roger's number. It went directly to voice mail. She left a message. "Fix this or else."

Beau couldn't help but laugh. "Kidnapped you?" He shook his head as he and DJ dismounted and walked their horses to the edge of the mountainside to look out at the view. "I think anything's possible. But I got the impression from your father that somehow your mother's family didn't know about you. And now they do."

"And that puts me in danger?"

He turned to gaze into her big, beautiful brown eyes, wanting to take away the pain he saw there. He'd been trying to save this woman in his dreams for years. Now here she was, all grown up, and he still felt helpless.

"DJ." His hand cupped the back of her neck. He drew her closer, not sure what he planned to do. Hold her? Kiss her? Whatever it was, he didn't get the chance.

The sound of the bullet whizzing past just inches from her head made him freeze for an instant, and then he grabbed and threw her to the snowy ground as he tried to tell from which direction the shot had come.

"Stay down! Don't give the shooter a target," he ordered as he drew his weapon from beneath his coat. Nothing moved in the dark woods behind them. Only silence filled the cold winter air for long moments.

"The shooter?" she repeated, sounding breathless.

In an explosion of wings, a hawk came flying out of the pines, startling him an instant before he heard the roar of a snowmobile.

"Stay here!" he ordered DJ as he swung up into the saddle.

"Wait. Don't…"

But he was already riding after the snowmobiler. He crested a ridge and drew up short. The smell of fuel permeated the air. Below him on the mountain, the snowmobile zoomed through the pines and disappeared over a rise. There was no way he could catch the man. Nor had he gotten a good look at him.

He swore under his breath as he quickly reined his horse around and headed back to where he'd left DJ.

She'd gotten to her feet but was smart enough to keep the horse between her and the mountainside.

"Are you all right?" he asked. He'd been sure the bullet had missed her. But he'd thrown her down to the ground hard enough to knock the air out of her.

Clearly she was shaken. She hadn't wanted to believe she was in any kind of danger. Until now. "Did you see who it was?" she asked.

"No, he got away. But I'll find him or die trying."

Andrei couldn't believe he'd missed. It was the cowboy's fault. If he hadn't reached for her right at that moment… But he knew he had only himself to blame. He'd been watching the two through his rifle scope, mesmerized by what he saw. They were in love.

He'd found something touching about that. He'd been in love once, so long ago now that he hardly remembered. But as he watched these two through the scope, he'd recognized it and felt an old pang he'd thought long forgotten.

Fool! Andrei was shaking so hard he had trouble starting the snowmobile. He'd never really considered that he might get caught. As long as the coin toss came up heads, he'd known his luck would hold.

Now, though, he feared his luck had run out. He ripped off his glove and tried the key again. The snowmobile engine sputtered. He should have stolen a new one instead of one that had some miles on it.

He tried the key again. The engine turned over. He let out the breath he hadn't even realized he'd been holding and hit the throttle. He could outrun a horse.

As he raced through the trees, he felt as if his whole life was passing before his eyes. All his instincts told him to run, put this one behind him, forget about Dee Anna Justice.

But even as he thought it, he knew it couldn't end this way. It would ruin his luck, ruin everything. He would make this right because his entire future depended on it.

He was almost back where he'd started a few miles from the main house on Cardwell Ranch when he lost control of the snowmobile and crashed into a tree.

Chapter 12

DJ couldn't quit trembling. It had happened so fast that at first she'd been calm. She'd gotten up from the ground, staying behind her horse as she watched the woods for Beau. Had someone really taken a shot at them? Not them. *Her.*

She'd never been so relieved to see anyone as Beau came riding out of the pines toward her and dismounted. He'd given chase but must have realized there was no way he could catch the man. She'd heard the snowmobile engine start up, the sound fading off into the mountains.

Still, she didn't feel safe. "You're sure he's gone?" she asked now as she looked toward those dark woods.

"He's gone. We need to get back to the ranch and call the marshal. I can't get any cell phone coverage up here."

Her legs felt like water. "If you hadn't tried to kiss me again…"

He grinned. "Maybe next time… That's right. I told you there wouldn't be a next time. I'm usually a man of my word."

She could tell he was trying to take her mind off what had just happened. "I guess you have a kiss coming."

"Glad you see it that way." He looked worried, as if what had almost happened hadn't really hit her yet. Did he expect her to fall apart? She was determined not to—especially in front of him.

She could tell he was shaken, as well—and worried. His gaze was on the trees—just as it had been earlier.

"Why would someone try to kill me?" she demanded. This made no sense. Nor could the same person who'd sent her the doll and the photograph be behind it. That had to be from someone in her family who'd wanted her to know about them.

But she remembered her father's fear when he'd seen the photo. Who was he so afraid of?

"All this can't be about something my father did over thirty years ago," she said, and yet it always had something to do with him. She thought about what Zinnia had told them. "Apparently this person really carries a grudge." She could see that Beau wasn't amused.

"We're going to have to find your grandmother."

"Marietta Pisani. You think she's hired someone to shoot me? Why now?"

"I wish I knew. But maybe it's what your father said. They didn't know about you and now they do."

She shook her head. "They don't even know me. Why would they want to kill me?"

He shook his head. "From what Zinnia said, it could involve money."

"If that's true, no wonder my father told me my

mother died in childbirth. He was actually trying to spare me. How do you like that?" She let out another bitter laugh as she turned to look at the cowboy. "So now they want me dead."

"If your mother died a few months ago, maybe that was when the rest of the family found out about you. It must have come as a shock."

"My mother chose her family and their money over me."

"I'm sure it wasn't an easy choice."

She hated the tears that burned her eyes. "I am their flesh and blood. Wouldn't they want to meet me before they had me killed?"

He reached for her, drawing her into his strong chest. She buried her face in his winter coat. "Let's not jump to conclusions until we know what's going on, okay?"

She nodded against his chest. "Why didn't my father tell me the truth when I showed him the photo?" she asked, drawing back.

"I'm sure he regrets it. He swears that when you came to him, he didn't know what was going on."

She pulled away. "My father lies."

Beau stared at her slim back as she swung up onto her horse. She was reasonably hurt by what she'd learned from Zinnia, but she was trying so hard not to show it. "I don't think he's lying about this."

"Someone else knew about me." She turned to look at him. "That person sent me the doll and the photo."

He hated to tell her that maybe the doll and the photo might merely have been a way of verifying that she was indeed Walter Justice's daughter. When she'd received the items, she headed straight for the prison—and her father, whom she hadn't acknowledged in years.

"But now they're afraid I'll go after the money." She shook her head. "After years of believing I had no family other than my father, now I have so much that some of them have put a price on my head. I don't know what to say."

Beau didn't, either. "You could contact them, possibly make a deal—"

"I don't want their money!" She spurred her horse.

He had to swing up into the saddle and go after her. The woman could handle a horse. He rode after her, sensing that she needed this release. Her horse kicked up a cloud of snow that hung in the air as he caught up and raced like the wind alongside her.

Her cheeks were flushed and there was a steely glint in her eyes that told him of a new determination.

"You'll help me find out who is behind this?" she asked as they reined in at the barn.

"You know I will. But first we have to report this." Swinging down from the saddle, he called the marshal's office. Hud told them to stay there. Good to his word, he was there before the horses were unsaddled and put away in the pasture.

Hud sent several deputies up into the woods to the spot Beau told him about. They'd be able to find it easily enough by following the tracks.

Once inside, he steered them both into the kitchen. "Here," Hud said, shoving a glass of water into DJ's trembling hands. "I have something stronger if that would help."

She shook her head and raised the glass to her lips, surprised she was still trembling. She'd believed she could take care of herself. Now she was just thankful that Beau had been there. What if it had been she and Dana who'd ridden up into the mountains?

"I'll take that something stronger," Beau said to Hud, and he poured him a little whiskey in a glass. Beau downed it in one gulp but declined more.

"This doesn't make any sense," DJ heard herself saying. "It had to have been an accident." She wanted the men to agree with her. But neither did. She could tell that Beau was convinced this was what her father had feared.

She listened while Beau told Hud in detail what he knew. Then she said, "If I brought whatever this is—"

"We'll get to the bottom of this," Hud said. "I'll tell you what Dana would. You're with family. We aren't going to let anything happen to you."

But even as he said it, DJ could see that he was worried. The last Dee Anna Justice had come here and brought trouble. The real Dee Anna promised herself that wouldn't be the case this time. She had hoped she'd find the answers she needed in Montana. Now she worried that she was endangering the family she'd just found.

She would leave as soon as she could get a flight out.

But even as she thought it, she had a feeling she wouldn't be leaving alone—if Beau had anything to do with it.

Andrei grimaced in pain as he finished bandaging his leg in his motel room. The snowmobile accident was just another bad sign, he told himself. And yet he had survived it with minimal damage.

He'd managed to push the wrecked snowmobile off into a gully where it wouldn't be found—along with some of the debris that had been knocked off it when he'd hit the tree. He'd gotten away. That alone should have been cause for celebration, since it was the closest he'd come to being caught.

Had he not missed, the cowboy would have been trying to save his beloved instead of racing on horseback in an attempt to catch her would-be killer.

He stood now to test his leg and, groaning in pain, sat back down. He wouldn't be climbing any more power poles, that was for sure. But he wasn't going to let this mishap change anything. He'd be fine by tomorrow, he assured himself.

The problem was that now DJ and her protective cowboy would know he was out here. They would be even more careful than they had been at first. He would have to wait—and watch. In good time, he told himself. And he still had time. He could complete this before his birthday, and he would.

He checked his phone. There were two messages from the man who'd hired him. Andrei didn't bother to listen to them. Whatever the man wanted, it didn't matter. This had become personal. Nothing could stop him now.

Marshal Hud Savage leaned back in his chair in his den on the ranch to look at Beau. Dana, Stacy and the kids had returned. Not wanting to upset them, he'd suggested the two of them talk in his den. They'd known each other for years—just not well. Their cases had never overlapped until now.

"So, Dee Anna's father hired you?" Hud asked.

Beau liked to keep things simple. He'd learned that years ago when dealing with his father—and the law. He nodded. "He asked me to watch over his daughter."

"He wasn't more specific than that?"

"No."

"And how exactly did he know about you?"

"I guess he could have looked in the phone book under private investigators," he said, dodging the truth.

Hud nodded. "Seems odd, though, asking you to keep an eye on her while she's here where her cousin's husband is the marshal."

"Not really." He softened his words with a wry smile. "Walter Justice is in prison. It could be he doesn't trust law enforcement."

The marshal chuckled at that. "Point well-taken, given what we know about Walter." He studied Beau openly for a moment. "You had taken DJ for a horseback ride."

"To talk. DJ's trying to find out more about her family."

"Dana said the three of you went to visit Walter's high school girlfriend, Zinnia Jameson?"

Beau nodded. "DJ knows nothing about her father's past. We were hoping Zinnia could provide some answers."

"That's what you had to talk to DJ about?"

He could tell that Hud was suspicious, since it had been Beau who'd taken her to a spot where a shooter had almost killed her.

"We needed to talk about what we'd learned, but also, I had to give her some bad news. Her father was shanked in prison."

"I'm sorry to hear that. I get the impression from Dana that DJ and her father aren't close."

"No, but he's still her father."

Hud sighed. "There's something about your story... Tell me again what the two of you were doing right before you heard the shot and felt the bullet whiz past."

Beau laughed. He had great respect for the marshal. The man had sensed he hadn't told him everything. "I was about to kiss her. I'd pulled her closer…"

The marshal nodded smiling. "You were trying to kiss her?"

He grinned. "Unfortunately the shooter took a pot-shot at us before that could happen."

"So, this is more than a job for you?"

Beau didn't want to get into the whole story of the first time he saw DJ and how he'd never forgotten her. "There's been some attraction from the start."

"I can understand that. It's those Justice women." He turned serious again. "You didn't get a good look at him?"

"No. Nor the snowmobile. Earlier I thought I heard one in the distance, but I didn't think anything about it. It's December. Everybody and his brother have one of the damned things, and the mountains around here are riddled with old logging roads."

"But you're convinced the bullet was for DJ?"

"Depends on how well the man shoots. If he was aiming for me, he can't hit the side of a barn. But if he was aiming for DJ, he's good. Really good. If I hadn't drawn her toward me when I did…"

"You're thinking a professional?"

"I am."

"You have any idea why someone would want Dee Anna Justice dead?"

Beau hesitated. He understood why Hud had wanted to talk to him alone. DJ was Dana's family. Hud would have done anything for his wife.

"It might have something to do with her mother's family," Beau said after a moment. "I'm going to shadow her until we find out what's going on. I don't have much to go on." He told the marshal the names of both mother and grandmother.

Hud wrote them down. Marietta and Carlotta Pisani. "Why would her own flesh and blood want to harm her?"

Beau shook his head, thinking of Cain and Abel. He couldn't help but wonder about DJ's half sister. "There might be money involved."

"Grandmama, you're scaring me. Tell me what you've done," Bianca demanded as her grandmother hung up the phone. "I'm assuming that was Roger you called. He hired someone to find my sister and then what?" She shook her head as if too disappointed in her grandmother to talk for a moment.

Ester had dropped into a chair across from them.

Marietta looked at her precious granddaughter. Her heart was in her throat. What if the man Roger had hired had already accomplished what he'd paid him to do? Now she realized that she could lose the one person who mattered to her.

"Do you have any idea how much I love you, how much I have tried to protect you—"

Bianca's look stopped her cold. "What have you done?"

"It might not be too late."

"Too late for what?"

Marietta waved that off and tried to rope in her thoughts. Roger would already have called if it was done. Of course he'd stopped it. Roger was too smart to go against her wishes on this. She reminded herself he was so smart that apparently he'd been stealing from her for years. She was the matriarch of this family, but Roger was a man she'd leaned on since her husband had died all those years ago.

"Listen to me. I'm trying to make this right." Her fear of losing Bianca's love, though, was a knife lodged in her chest.

"Tell me everything you know about her," Bianca said, sitting down next to her.

There was no keeping it from her now. "I don't know very much, just what your mother told me. Her name is Dee Anna Justice."

"So after Mother told you, did you try to reach her? You just said it might be too late."

So Ester *hadn't* told her everything. Marietta thought she still might stand a chance of regaining Bianca's love, her trust. "You have to understand. Your mother was very young. She fell in love with this man from Montana who was all wrong for her. Fortunately she realized her mistake…" She almost said, *"before it was too late,"* but that had been what she'd thought at the time.

Now she knew that it *had* been too late. Carlotta had given birth to Walter Justice's child—and kept the truth from nearly everyone.

On her deathbed, Carlotta had cried, saying it was Marietta's fault that she'd had to keep Dee Anna a secret all these years.

"I wanted my child with me. I needed my child with me. But you had made it clear that if I didn't come home, forget about Walter and go to Italy to stay with my aunt…"

"You are going to blame me for this?" she'd demanded.

"I had to give up my child because of you."

No, Marietta had argued. "You gave up your child for *money*. You knew I would cut off your allowance if you stayed with that man. It was your choice."

Had her daughter thought that one day she could just come home with the child and all would be forgiven? Or had she given up on that foolish idea when she'd met the nice Italian man she'd married and become pregnant with *his* child?

"Surely Walter Justice would have gladly given up the child had you demanded it," she had pointed out to her daughter.

"You're wrong. He loved me. He loved Dee Anna. He would never have let you get near her, knowing how you felt about him. But, Mother, now you can make up for the past. Now you have a chance to know your *first* granddaughter."

Carlotta must have seen her expression, because her own hardened. "Or not. Whatever happens, it's on your head now, Mother."

Marietta realized Bianca had asked her a question.

"Why did you hate my sister's father so much?" Bianca asked again, accusation in her tone.

"He was a crook. All he was interested in was our money."

"*Money*. Why does it always come back to that with you?"

"He's serving time in prison. I think that tells you what kind of man he is." She hated that her voice rose, that she sounded like a woman who'd lost control of her life. A woman who was no longer sure of the stand she'd taken. A woman who would die drowning in regret.

Bianca rose. "I want to meet my sister."

"Stop calling her that!" Marietta snapped irritably. "She is merely your mother's mistake."

Her granddaughter looked horrified at her words.

She regretted them instantly. "You don't understand," she pleaded. "This woman isn't one of us. If she is anything like her father, she'll demand part of your inheritance. I know you think you don't care about the money, about the family legacy—"

"It is the family *curse*," Bianca said. "That's what mother called it. She used to wish her family was dirt-poor."

Marietta wanted to laugh. Her extravagant daughter would not have liked being poor, let alone dirt-poor.

Bianca's eyes narrowed. "So this is about money. You're afraid she will want money."

"No, I was willing to give her money. It's about you, Bianca. I don't want you to be hurt. Contacting this woman can only—"

"Tell me how I can find her," Bianca said, cutting her off.

She swallowed and looked to Ester. "Why don't you ask *her*?" she said, pointing to her housekeeper. "She seems to be well-informed."

Ester's gaze met hers, unspoken secrets between them. The housekeeper hadn't told Bianca about the hit man. But she'd hinted at it. Did Marietta really want her to tell everything she knew?

"I'm asking *you*," her granddaughter said.

Marietta sighed. She knew when she'd lost. Wasn't it possible that Dee Anna Justice could already be dead? If so, Bianca would never forgive her. And the family legacy could already be gone, thanks to Roger. She had only herself to blame for all of this. But to lose both Bianca and her fortune would be unendurable.

"She's at the Cardwell Ranch near Big Sky, Montana, but—"

"I'm going to find her," Bianca said with more determination than Marietta had ever seen in her.

As she started to leave, Ester said, "I'd like to go with you."

Bianca shot a look at her grandmother and seemed to hesitate. "Can you manage alone with your bad heart?"

"I've been on my own before," Marietta snapped, wondering how she *would* manage. "Don't worry about me."

"I'll call when I find her," Bianca said.

Everything she cared about was walking out that door. She didn't think her heart could break further. She was wrong, she realized as she saw Ester's suitcase by the door and knew that she might not see either of them again.

"We have to find out who's behind this," Beau told DJ before they left Cardwell Ranch. "I thought we'd go by my office in Bozeman. I should warn you about my assistant. She's… Well, you'll see soon enough."

He wasn't surprised when Marge did one of her eyebrow lifts as they walked in. What did surprise him was how quickly she took to DJ.

Like a mother hen, she scurried around, getting coffee, offering to run down to the cupcake shop for treats.

"We're fine. We won't be here long," he told her with an amused and slightly irritated shake of his head. He ushered DJ into the office, saying, "I'll be right back," and closed the door behind her.

Turning to Marge, he said, "What is going on with you?"

"Me?" She gave him her innocent look.

"This isn't a *date*. DJ is a *client*, of sorts. This one is…off the record, but it is still work. Nothing more."

"DJ, huh?"

He shook his head. "Why do you take so much interest in my love life?"

"*What* love life?" she said, fiddling with some papers on her desk.

Beau ignored that jab. "Are you hoping to get me married off?"

"I never said a word."

"You don't have to." He started for his office, but something was bothering him. Turning back to her, he said, "I have to know. DJ walks in and you instantly like her. You've never liked any of the women I've dated, and you've never done more than share a few words with them on the phone. What is different about this one?" he demanded, trying to keep his voice down.

Marge smiled. "You'll remember this one's name."

Chapter 13

DJ pulled up a chair next to Beau as he turned on the computer and began his search. She felt surprisingly nervous sitting this close to him. It brought back the memory of being in his arms, of his mouth on hers. There was something so masculine about him.

"You all right?" he asked as she moved her chair back a little. "Can you see okay?"

She nodded and tried to breathe. "How long has Marge been with you?"

"Since I started. She's like a mother hen." He shook his head. "But I couldn't run this office without her." She heard true admiration and caring in his voice. She also sensed a strong loyalty in him. Look how he'd agreed to protect her based on a promise he'd made so many years ago.

"I like her."

He glanced over at her. "And she likes you. Believe me, it's a first." Their gazes locked for a moment. She could feel the heat of his look and remembered how he'd almost kissed her up on the mountain.

At the sound of his assistant on the other side of the door, he turned quickly back to the computer. "Okay, let's see what we can find out about your grandmother. Marietta Pisani. There can't be that many, right?"

DJ thought about how this had started with the doll and the photo. Her father's letters had led them to Zinnia, who'd told her more about her father—and mother—than she'd ever known. Leave it to her father to tell Beau that the doll and photo might have something to do with her mother's family. Why couldn't he have told her that?

Because he'd been lying to her since birth, she reminded herself. She felt a stab of guilt. He was in the hospital, badly injured. She'd called but hadn't been able to learn much—just that he was in stable but serious condition. She told herself he was tough. He'd pull through. She hoped it was true.

"Your father told you that your mother was dead, but that your grandmother Marietta is still alive, right?" Beau was saying. "Marietta Pisani. Is there any chance she's related to the noble Pisani family of Malta? Descendants of Giovanni Pisani, the patrician of Venice?"

"I have no idea," DJ said.

"Maybe you'll get a chance to ask her," he said and motioned to the screen. "I found only one in the right age group. A Marietta Pisani of Palm Desert, California."

DJ swallowed the lump in her throat. This was the woman who'd had her daughter's marriage to Walter Justice annulled. "What do we do now? You can't think that my grandmother..." Her words faltered. She could see from his expression that he could think exactly that.

Her father had also thought it. Why else would he have asked Beau to protect her? But surely she didn't need protecting from her own grandmother?

"We call her," Beau said and reached for the phone.

It took Marietta a while to calm down after Bianca and Ester left. At first she was just scared. Scared that she'd lost everything. Then she was furious with Ester for butting into her family business. She'd tried to reach Roger but suspected he was not picking up. The coward.

At some point, she'd have to find out if there was any money left. But right now, it was her least concern. Her daughter would have thought that funny, she realized. The joke was on her, she realized. Roger had stolen her money. All that worry about the family legacy and now she realized that if she lost Bianca, nothing mattered.

When a middle-aged woman arrived with a suitcase in hand claiming to be Ester's younger sister, May, she almost turned her away.

"I'm not like Ester. I'll see to you, but don't think you can browbeat me the way you do her."

Marietta was offended. "I don't browbeat anyone."

May huffed and slipped past her. "Just tell me where my room is. Then I'll see about getting you fed. I cook whatever I can find to cook and you eat it. That's the deal."

With that, the woman had sashayed off in the direction Marietta had pointed.

This was what her life had come to? She almost wished that she'd died this morning before she'd seen that little red sports car drive up.

But then she wouldn't have seen her precious grand-daughter. Not that their visit had gone well.

She tried Roger's number again. Again it went to voice mail. It was in God's hands, she told herself. God's and Bianca's and Ester's and whomever Roger had hired.

She prayed that Dee Anna Justice was still alive. She just didn't want Bianca hurt. But who knew what this Dee Anna Justice was like? She couldn't bear the thought of Dee Anna rejecting Bianca. If there was any money left, she knew her granddaughter would gladly share it with her...sister.

Marietta made the call. She had to take control of her life again, one step at a time, until her old heart gave out.

As Stacy dressed for her date, she felt torn between excitement and worry. Did she really believe that she and James could start over again after all these years? Maybe she was hanging on to a first-love fantasy James, one who had never existed.

"What has he done for a living since high school?" Dana had asked. She didn't know. "What does he do now?"

"I think he said real estate."

Her sister got that look Stacy knew only too well.

"You remember him," Stacy said. "You liked him in high school, didn't you?"

"I didn't know him," Dana said. "But I do remember that he broke your heart."

"It wasn't his fault. He thought his ex-girlfriend was pregnant..." She stopped when she saw Dana's expression. "He did the right thing by her. He married her."

"I suppose so," her sister said. "Just...be careful. It's not only you now. You have to think of Ella."

She'd thought only of Ella since her daughter's birth. There hadn't been any men, not even one date. But now she could admit that she felt ready. She wanted a husband and a father for Ella and said as much to Dana.

"There is nothing wrong with that," her sister said, giving her a hug. "Maybe James is that man. Maybe he's not. Give it time. Don't let him rush you into anything."

She knew what Dana was getting at. James had rushed her into sex in high school. She hadn't been ready, but she'd feared that she would lose him if she didn't give in to him.

As she finished dressing, Stacy told herself she wasn't that young, naive girl anymore. If James thought she was, then he was in for a surprise.

Roger swore when he saw how many times Marietta had called. He didn't even bother to check the voice mails. He knew she'd be demanding to know what was going on. He'd called the man who'd hired the hit man and had finally heard back.

"He rushed the job and missed," the man told him. "Now he has to fix it. So back off. These things take time. Worse, now she knows someone is trying to kill her. Also, the marshal is involved."

Roger felt sick to his stomach. "You told me that he would make it look like a shooting accident. This isn't what my boss wanted at all. Call him off."

"I'll do what I can. He isn't answering his phone."

Could this get any worse?

"He's going to want the rest of the money. You'd best have it ready for him," the man warned.

"Of course." Roger hung up, sweating. His phone rang again. He saw that this time it was the accountant he'd been working with. Marietta. She was checking the trust funds. He was dead meat, he thought as he let her call go to voice mail.

He decided he'd better listen to Marietta's message. What he heard turned his blood to ice.

"Bianca knows! She and Ester are headed for Cardwell Ranch in Montana. If anything happens to them, I'll have you killed in prison, and you know I can do it. I might not have as much money as I once did, but I still have power."

He disconnected, not doubting it for a moment. He looked around the room. He couldn't wait any longer. She knew that he'd been embezzling money for years from the family trust funds. He'd hoped that he could win it back, but his gambling debts were eating him alive. If the thugs he owed didn't kill him, then Marietta would.

His cell phone rang again almost instantly. He put it on mute, telling himself he would throw it in the ocean the first chance he got and buy a new one. Then he stepped to the suitcase. His passport and the plane tickets were on the table by the door. He picked them up, took one last look at the house he had mortgaged to the hilt and, suitcase in hand, walked out.

Marietta let out a scream of pain when she heard an estimate of how much money was missing from the trust funds.

May rushed into the room. "If you're not bleeding, this had better be a heart attack or a killer snake in the room."

"I want to die."

May shook her head. "Let me get a knife."

"I've made a horrible mess of things."

"Haven't we all? If you don't want your supper burned, die quietly while I get back to the kitchen."

Marietta could hear her heart pounding and welcomed death. What had she done? Her mind wouldn't stop racing. All she could think about were the mistakes she'd made. She had another granddaughter. Bianca would have loved having a sister. She used to ask for one all the time. It broke Marietta's heart.

The irony was that Carlotta's second husband hadn't been much of a step up from Walter. Gianni had some shady dealings before his death. But at least he'd come from a good Italian family with money.

She had wanted so much for her daughter.

And yet Carlotta still hadn't married well.

"Playing God wearing you out?" May asked as she brought in her dinner tray.

"Do you always say whatever you think without regard to whether or not it is proper?" Marietta demanded.

May smiled. "Not much different from you, huh?"

"I'm not hungry," she said, trying to push the tray away.

"Too bad. I'm going to sit right here until you eat. Ester said all I had to do was keep you alive. I figure you're too mean to die, but just in case…" May pushed the tray back at her and sat down, crossing her arms.

Marietta glared at her for a moment before picking up her fork. If she had to eat to get the woman out of her room, she would.

"You know nothing about any of this," she said.

May chuckled.

"If I thought Ester was talking behind my back—"

"What would you have done? Fired her?" May shook

her head. "Ester didn't have to tell me anything about you. I saw it in the sadness in her eyes. She's been loyal to you, just as our mother was. You don't realize how lucky you are that she put up with you all these years. Anyone else would have put a pillow over your face years ago."

"I feel so much better knowing you'll be staying with me until Ester comes back," she said sarcastically.

"You think Ester is coming back?"

Marietta stopped, the fork halfway to her mouth. She didn't want to acknowledge her fear that Ester was gone for good. "She won't leave me alone. Not after all these years."

"Because of your sweet disposition? Or because you pay her so much?"

She felt her face heat but said nothing as she concentrated on her food again. This was what her life had come to, she told herself. She was an old woman alone with an ingrate who had nothing but contempt for her. She half hoped the woman had poisoned her food.

Chapter 14

The phone rang. Marietta snatched it up, hoping it was Bianca calling. Maybe she'd changed her mind about going to Montana, about meeting her half sister, about... everything.

"Hello?"

"Is this Marietta Pisani?"

"Yes." Her heart pounded.

"My name is Beau Tanner. I'm a private investigator in Montana. I'm calling about your granddaughter."

"Bianca?" Montana? Was it possible Bianca and Ester had gotten a flight out so soon and were now in Montana?

"No, Dee Anna Justice."

She gripped the phone so hard that it made her hand ache. She held her breath. Hadn't he said he was a private investigator? Shouldn't it be the police calling if Dee Anna Justice was dead?

"What about her?" she asked, her voice breaking.

"You recognize the name?"

"Yes. She's my granddaughter. What is this about?"

"I was hoping you would tell her," the private eye said. "I'm putting her on the phone."

"Hello?"

Marietta heard the voice of her first granddaughter and felt the rest of her world drop away.

"Hello?" the voice said again.

Marietta began to cry uncontrollably.

May came in, saw what was happening and took the phone. "I'm sorry. She can't talk right now." She hung up the phone. Turning, she demanded, "Where do you think you're going?"

Marietta had shoved away the food tray, gotten to her feet and gone to her closet. Pulling out her empty suitcase, she laid it on the bed and began to throw random clothing into it. "I'm flying to Montana."

May took in the suitcase the older woman had tossed on the bed. "Do you really think that's a good idea given your…condition? Let alone the fact that you might be arrested when you land."

So Ester had shared information with her sister. Marietta knew she shouldn't have been surprised. "You've been in on all this?"

May smiled. "It was my son who left the doll and a photo of her mother, grandmother and Carlotta's second husband for DJ." She sounded proud of what she'd done. "Ester was afraid of how far you would go. She said DJ couldn't be brought off. She wouldn't have wanted a cent of your money. So all of this was a huge waste on your part."

Marietta finished throwing a few items in, slammed

her suitcase and zipped it closed. She'd been surrounded by traitors. "You couldn't possibly understand why I've done what I have."

"Why you used money to keep your daughter away from a child that she loved?" May demanded. "Did Carlotta tell you how she cried herself to sleep over that baby you forced her to give up?"

"Forced her? It was her choice. Just like it was her choice to marry the man. So easy to blame me, isn't it?"

May put one hand on her bony hip. "What would your daughter think now if she knew that you were trying to kill that child?"

Marietta swallowed. She wanted to argue that it was all Roger's doing. But she'd trusted him to handle it. Her mistake. All she'd thought about was erasing the existence of Dee Anna Justice to save the family.

"Help me with my suitcase."

May didn't move.

"I'm going to save the woman. Does that make you happy?" she barked.

"*The woman?* She's your grandchild. She's your blood. She's Bianca's sister."

"I don't have time to argue with you." She shook her head. "None of you know this Dee Anna Justice. What if she wants nothing to do with our family? What if she rejects Bianca? What then?"

"Bianca is a strong woman. She will survive. I think you might underestimate the connection they have," May said. "Ester kept in touch over the years with Dee Anna's father. She saw the girl grow up."

"My suitcase."

May stepped forward, slid the suitcase from the bed

and began to wheel it toward the front door. "You best hope that you're not too late."

It was already too late in so many ways.

"Some woman took the phone and said she couldn't talk. Before that it sounded like she was…crying," DJ said as she saw Beau's anxious expression.

He took the office phone and replaced it in its cradle. "At least now we know that she's the right one."

"I guess. She was definitely upset. But upset to hear from me or to hear that I'm still alive?" She could see he was even more convinced that her grandmother was behind what had happened earlier today on the mountain.

"What now?" As if she had to ask. "The would-be assassin will try again, won't he?" She didn't give him time to answer. "I can't stay at Cardwell Ranch," she said as she pushed to her feet. "I can't endanger my cousin and her family—"

"That's why I want you to move in with me."

She blinked. "No, I couldn't."

"If it makes you feel any better, I have a…friend staying with me. Leah."

"I see." A friend, huh? Was that what he called it? She realized how little she knew about this man.

"I can protect you better on my home ground."

"I think everyone would be better off if I just left Montana."

"You're wrong. But if you leave, I'm going with you. Sorry, but you're stuck with me until this is over."

She stared at him even though she'd expected this. "You can't be serious, and for how long?"

"As long as it takes. But if you could just give me a few days and not leave, it would be better. If whoever shot at you is still here, it will give me the chance to catch him."

She didn't like the sound of this. She'd come to care about this man. She didn't want to see him get killed protecting her and said as much.

"Have more faith in me," he said with a grin. "Let's go get your things." They drove in silence to the Cardwell Ranch.

Dana put up a fight when Beau told her his plan.

"Christmas is only a few days away," she argued. "DJ is family. She should be here with us."

"With luck, this will be over by Christmas," he told her. "Hud thinks it is best, too."

"Hud." With that one word, Dana looked resigned.

DJ hugged her. "I'm so sorry. I would never have come here if I thought it might be dangerous for your family."

"You have nothing to be sorry for," Dana said. "You take care of her," she said to Beau. "I'm depending on you."

"I hate this," DJ said as he drove them off the ranch. "I hate that I involved them and, worse, you. You're only doing this because of some stupid promise you made when you were a boy to a man who had no right to ask anything of you."

Beau was quiet for a long moment as he drove. It almost surprised her when he finally spoke. "The first time we met, I wished that I could help you," he said without looking at her. "I've regretted it ever since."

She spoke around the lump that had formed in her throat. "I don't want you to get killed because of me."

"I don't want that, either," he said with a chuckle. "But

I'm not that ten-year-old anymore." He finally glanced over at her. "I can help you. I know what I'm doing."

She looked away, fighting back tears. All this was because of her father falling in love with the wrong woman? Now he was in the hospital possibly dying and she was... She was in Montana with a cowboy who was determined to save her.

They hadn't gone far when Beau turned off the highway and crossed a narrow bridge that spanned the Gallatin River before driving back into the canyon. At the heart of the valley was a large log house. Behind it was a red barn and some outbuildings. A half-dozen paint horses raced around in a large pasture nearby.

"This is where you live?" she asked, a little awed by the beauty of the scene.

"Do you like?" he asked and glanced over at her.

"I love it." She felt a lump form in her throat. She could see Beau here. "You're a real cowboy."

He laughed. "You're just now realizing that?"

She turned to look at him. She was just now realizing a lot of things, she thought as she stared at his handsome profile in the last light of the day.

Jimmy was late picking her up, making Stacy have even more second thoughts. But he seemed so glad to see her that she pushed them aside and tried to have a nice time.

He took her to one of the local restaurants, ordered them both a cocktail and drained half his glass before letting out a sigh. He actually looked nervous, which made her laugh and forget her own nervousness.

"So tell me about this cousin staying on the ranch," he said.

"Dee Anna Justice. She's the daughter of my mother's brother, whom we didn't know anything about." She really didn't want to talk about DJ, though. "So, what did you say you're doing in Big Sky again?"

"Working. A brother no one had ever heard of?"

"Working at what?" she asked, wondering why he was so interested in the Justice side of the family.

"This and that." He drained his glass. The waiter came over and before Stacy could look at her menu, James ordered for both of them, including more drinks. "You don't mind, do you?" he asked after the waiter had already left.

She shook her head, although she did mind. "How long did you say you've been back?"

"Did I say? A few weeks. Actually, I'm looking for a job. Anything opening up on Cardwell Ranch?"

She couldn't help but laugh. "What do you know about working on a ranch? As I recall, you hated helping on your uncle's."

"I forgot what a good memory you have." That didn't sound like a compliment. The waiter came with their drinks and he downed his quickly.

"Jimmy—"

"But you can't seem to remember that I go by James now." He was clearly irritated and not trying to hide it.

"Sorry. Why did you ask me to dinner tonight?"

He leaned back, giving her a what-do-you-think look. "I thought for old times' sake…" He shrugged. "You dating someone?"

Fortunately their meals came. They talked little. Jimmy ate as if he hadn't had a meal in days. He devoured his steak and then asked her if she was going to finish hers. She'd lost her appetite early on in the date, so she gladly slid her plate over and let him clean it.

What had she been thinking? Her sister was right. The Jimmy Ryan she'd been in love with all those years ago wasn't the man sitting across from her.

"Ready?" he asked as he signaled the waiter for his bill.

Turning, she spotted Burt Olsen, their mailman. He nodded and smiled at her. He appeared to be picking up something to go.

Stacy just wanted this date to be over. When Jimmy saw her looking at Burt, he threw an arm around her waist and propelled her toward the door.

"Maybe I should drive," she said as they started toward his truck.

"I don't think you should think." He still had hold of her as they neared the pickup. He opened the driver's-side door and practically shoved her in, pushing her over to get behind the wheel.

"Jimmy—James."

"I remember you being a lot more fun," he said, gritting his teeth.

And vice versa, but she said nothing as she saw Burt getting into his vehicle. He'd been watching the two of them. And she knew that if she said anything to Jimmy, it would turn into a fight. Burt was the last person she wanted seeing her and Jimmy fighting. She told herself that Jimmy hadn't had that much to drink—and it was only a short drive to the ranch.

Neither of them spoke during the drive. As they crossed the bridge, he glanced over at her. "You hear me?"

She hadn't realized he'd said anything. "I'm sorry?"

"I'm sure you are." He drove on into the ranch and pulled up in front of her cabin. "So which one is this cousin of yours staying in?"

She pointed to the last one at the other end of the row. She knew what was coming, but Jimmy was out of luck if he thought she was going to invite him in.

"Thanks for dinner," she said as he shut off the engine. She reached for her door handle. But before she could get it open, he leaned over and grabbed her hand to stop her.

"I'm sorry about tonight. It wasn't you. I got some bad news right before I picked you up. I should have canceled." He drew back his hand.

"What kind of bad news?" she asked out of politeness.

"An investment. It fell through. I was counting on it."

She hoped he didn't ask her for money. "I'm sure you'll be able to get a job."

"A *job*." He said the last word like it tasted nasty in his mouth. "Just not on your ranch, huh? You don't even know what I do for a living."

"A little of this and that is all you told me." She reached for the door handle again.

This time his hand came around the back of her neck. He clamped down hard enough to take her breath away. "You're kind of a smart mouth. I do remember that about you."

Stacy tried to wriggle out of his grasp. "Stop!" she said as he pulled her toward him as if to kiss her. "I said *stop*!" That feeling of déjà vu hit her hard. This was what had happened in high school, only then she'd thought that he was so crazy about her he just couldn't help himself. She knew better now.

Chapter 15

Leah looked up expectantly as Beau entered the kitchen. She smiled quickly as if covering her disappointment. Who had she expected? Her husband? Or someone else?

Her gaze went to DJ, her expression one of surprise and something else. Jealousy?

"This is DJ. She's going to be staying with us. DJ, Leah."

"No last names?" Leah asked, pretending to be amused.

He walked to the stove. "You cooked?"

"Don't sound so surprised. I'm a woman of many talents."

Beau could believe that somehow, even though he hadn't been around Leah in years. She'd always seemed...capable.

"Looks like you made enough for three," he said, lifting the lid on one of the pots and glancing into the oven, where what looked like a Mexican casserole bubbled. Looking up, he said, "You must have been expecting company."

She shook her head, but not before he'd seen that moment of hesitation. Her laugh wasn't quite authentic, either. But he wasn't about to get into it with her now.

He turned to DJ. "Let me show you to a room."

"It was nice meeting you," Leah called after them.

"You, too," DJ said over her shoulder, and then added only for his ears as they climbed the stairs and rounded a corner, "She doesn't want me here. Wouldn't it be better if I—"

"She isn't my *girlfriend*. She's the wife of my former best friend. I have no idea what she's doing here, so what she wants is really of no interest to me."

DJ was surprised at his words. He'd been so protective of her, and yet he seemed angry at the woman they'd left downstairs.

He saw her surprise as they reached the end of the hall, and he started to open a door but stopped. "I don't mean to seem cold, but it's what she's not telling me about her and her husband that has me worried."

"It's none of my business."

He studied her openly. "Come on, let's hear it. I can tell there is something on your mind."

"Did the two of you ever—"

"No. She was always Charlie's girl, and before you ask, no, I was never interested in her."

"It's odd, then, because she seems very possessive of you."

He shrugged and pushed open the door to a beautiful room done in pastels.

"What a pretty room."

He didn't seem to hear her. "I'm right next door if you need me. Leah is downstairs in the guest room."

"Who's room is this?" She realized her mistake at once. "I shouldn't have asked."

"I was engaged to a woman with a young daughter. This was going to be her room, but it didn't work out."

"I'm sorry."

He shook his head. "Looking back, I loved the thought of having a child more than I loved having her mother as my wife." He took a step toward the door. "Get unpacked if you like, then come downstairs. Let's find out if Leah really can cook or not."

After he left, DJ looked around the beautiful room. He'd made it so pretty for the little girl. There was such love in the room. She felt sad for him. How lucky that child would have been in so many ways.

She took her time unpacking what little she'd brought, giving Beau time with Leah. Whatever was going on between them, she didn't want to be in the middle of it. She had enough troubles of her own.

Taking out her phone, she put in a call to the prison. Her father was still in serious condition at the hospital.

She withdrew the photo of her mother from her purse and sat down in the white wooden rocker to study it. This woman had been her mother. She hadn't died in childbirth. No, instead, she'd apparently given up her first child to make her family happy, then married another man and had another child.

But what, if anything, did this have to do with the man who'd shot at her? According to what Beau had been able to find out, her mother really had died recently. So who wanted her dead? The grandmother who'd refused to talk to her? Zinnia had said that her mother's family had money. Surely it couldn't be that simple.

But her father had known the moment he looked at the photo. Her mother's family had found her, and that had terrified him enough that he'd pressured Beau Tanner to protect her.

But what about the other daughter? The one who'd had the doll? What about her half sister?

As Jimmy grabbed at her, Stacy swung her fist and caught him under the left eye. He let out a curse. His grip loosened and she shoved open the door, only to have him drag her back. He thrust his hand down the front of the dress she'd bought for the date. She heard the fabric tear as he groped for her breasts.

With his free hand, he grabbed her flailing wrists and dragged her hard against him. "You like it rough? You'll get it rough," he said, squeezing her right breast until she cried out.

Stacy hardly heard the driver's-side door open. Jimmy had been leaning against it and almost fell out as the door was jerked open.

"She said stop," a familiar male voice said.

Jimmy let go of her, pulling his hand from inside her dress to turn angrily toward the open door—and the intruder. All he got out was "What the he—" when a fist hit him between the eyes.

Stacy saw it only out of the corner of her eye. The moment Jimmy let go of her, she slid across the seat and climbed out of the pickup. That was when she saw who her savior was. Mailman Burt Olsen's face was set, his voice dangerously calm. "You go on inside now, Ms. Cardwell. I'll take care of this."

She hesitated only a moment before scurrying up the steps. Once on the porch, she turned back. Just as she'd feared, Jimmy was out of the truck and looking for a fight. He took a swing, but Burt easily ducked it and caught Jimmy in the jaw with a left hook. He toppled back toward the open truck door. Burt doubled him over as he fell, shoved him back into the truck and closed the door.

"He won't be bothering you anymore tonight," the mailman called over to her. "But if you need me to stay..."

She almost couldn't find the words, she was so surprised. "No, I'm fine now. But thank you, Burt."

He tipped his baseball cap. Past him, she could see where he'd parked his car and walked up the mountainside. He'd come to her rescue after seeing what had been going on at the restaurant, and all she could think was that he'd let his supper get cold to do it.

Inside the cabin, she locked her door just in case Jimmy—*excuse me*—James, didn't get the hint. The man was a fool, but he wasn't stupid, she told herself. Glancing out the window, she saw that Burt was waiting for Jimmy to leave. She was relieved when a few minutes later she heard his truck start up and drive away.

In the bedroom, she saw that her dress was ruined. She tossed it into the trash. Thinking about Burt Olsen, she had to smile. She'd never seen this side of him before.

Jimmy had never been so furious. Who the devil had that man been? Stacy's sweetheart? Nice of her to mention, if that was the case. But he'd called her Ms. Cardwell. Must have been a hired man.

Not that it mattered. He'd sat for a moment, stunned

and bleeding and planning his revenge. The lights went out in Stacy's cabin. He considered breaking down the door but realized he wasn't up to it. There was always another day. The woman would pay.

As he started the truck's engine to drive out of the ranch, he thought about the dude who'd hit him. If he ever saw him again…

He hadn't gone far when his headlights flashed over someone in the shadows of one of the outbuildings. For a moment he thought it was the man who'd attacked him. He slowed and saw his mistake. This man, who ducked behind the barn, was much larger, dressed in all black. He was carrying something. The moonlight had caught on the barrel of a rifle.

Jimmy sped on by, pretending not to have noticed. As he drove down the road to where it dropped over a rise, he realized he'd seen the man before. It was the lineman he'd seen on one of the power poles when he'd driven in earlier.

"Lineman, my ass," he said to himself as he quickly pulled over and cut the engine. He pulled his hunting knife from under the seat.

It was time to take care of the competition. He quietly opened his door and stepped out into the winter night. He could see his breath as he started back toward the barn. The pro must be waiting for DJ Justice to return. Stacy had said earlier that she thought DJ had left with some neighboring cowboy.

Well, Jimmy had a surprise for the man, he thought with a grin. He'd take care of the pro, and then maybe he'd double back for Stacy. He was feeling much better suddenly. And if the bitch thought she would get rid of him that easily, she was sadly mistaken.

* * *

Beau found Leah setting the table for three. "So, what's going on?"

She looked up as if she'd been lost in thought and he'd startled her. "Supper is almost ready. I made a casserole. I'm not much of a cook, but—"

"I'm not talking about food. What are you really cooking up?"

Leah gave him a blank look. "I told you—"

"You were expecting a package, but…" She started to interrupt. He stopped her with an angry slash of his hand through the air. "What are you really doing here? Earlier you told me that you and Charlie were in trouble and you needed my help."

"I was wrong. This is something that will have to work itself out on its own. I can't involve you."

"You've already involved me. I'm tired of whatever game this is that you're playing. Tell me what the hell is going on."

She slowly put down the plate she'd been holding, straightened the napkin and silverware and then finally looked up at him. "There is a lot I can't tell you. Charlie and I…we've become involved in some…covert work. Our latest…assignment didn't go so well. I got out. Charlie…" Her voice broke. "We made a pact years ago that if we ever got separated, we would meet here." Her eyes glistened. "Because you were always our one harbor even in college."

"Why didn't you tell me that right away?" he asked quietly as he considered what she'd told him.

"Because I didn't come here to involve you in anything. You and your friend aren't in any danger. Charlie's and my work is done far from here. No one knows I'm here except Charlie. I made sure that I wasn't followed."

He had a million questions, which he suspected she wasn't going to answer anyway, but the creak of the stairs told him that their conversation was over. At least for now.

He'd never been a trusting man—thanks to his father. He hated the way his mind worked. He questioned what most people told him. Leah was at the top of the list right now.

The knock at the door made them both jump. Beau had taken off his shoulder holster and hung it by the door. He stepped to it now and motioned for Leah to go into the den. DJ had stopped on the stairs. One look at him and she'd frozen in midstep.

Another knock, this one harder. Beau strode to the door and pulled his weapon. Stepping to the side, he opened the door, the weapon ready.

He felt a moment of shock when he looked at the rugged, clearly exhausted man standing there. *"Charlie?"*

Chapter 16

Andrei heard the car engine as someone left the ranch. He frowned as he waited for the sound of the vehicle crossing the bridge and didn't hear it. He listened. A chill moved up his spine. He had been watching the house from his hiding spot. But now he stopped at the edge of the barn and sniffed the air.

The vehicle had definitely not crossed the bridge. Nor had it turned back. He would have heard it. That meant that it had stopped. The winter night was so quiet he could hear the ice crack on the edge of the river. He heard the soft click of a car door being closed and readied himself.

The driver had seen him. That rattled him enough. But the driver was also trying to sneak up on him. That meant the person would be armed with some kind of weapon.

All Andrei had was a rifle. But he didn't want to shoot

and call attention to himself. So he would wait until the man reached the corner of the barn and then he would jump him. He was ready.

He pressed his back against the side of the barn at the corner and waited. This would complicate things, he thought, on a job that was already complicated as it was. But since his accident, he'd been frustrated. Maybe this was exactly what he needed to let out some of that anxiety.

It had always been more satisfying to kill someone with his bare hands than shoot them from a distance. Given that his leg still hurt like hell, he probably should have walked away. But it was too late now. A twig under the snow snapped close by. No time to make a run for it even if he could have run. This could end only one way. One of them was about to die.

The man came around the corner of the barn. The large knife blade in his hand caught the winter light.

"I'm afraid we won't be joining you for dinner," Charlie said after he and Beau had hugged like the old friends they were. His gaze met his wife's. She stood a few feet away, tears in her eyes and relief etched on her face. She hadn't moved since Beau had opened the door, as if to give the two men some time.

"We need to get going, but it is great seeing you," Charlie said.

"That's it?" Beau demanded as Leah scurried down the hall to the guest room, returning moments later with her overnight bag. She stepped to her husband's side and pressed her face into his neck for a moment, his arm coming around her. The hug was hard and filled with emotion. Clearly this was the package she'd been waiting for.

Charlie had always been good-looking. Now, even though he appeared a little haggard, his smile was infectious. "It is so good to see you. One of these days, we'll be back permanently. I hope we can get together then, have a couple of beers and talk. But right now…"

Beau shook his head. He'd been angry at Leah for not telling him what was really going on. But he couldn't be angry with Charlie, his old friend. "Just be careful." He shook Charlie's hand and watched as the two disappeared down the road. Beau saw car lights flash on and heard the sound of an engine, and then they were gone as if they'd never been there.

He turned to look at DJ.

"Are you all right?" she asked.

He gave her a quick nod. "I hope you're hungry. We have a lot of casserole to eat."

She moved toward the kitchen. "I'd better take the casserole out of the oven, then."

"Maybe we could just sit in front of the fire and have a drink while it cools down a little. I could use one." He moved into the living room and stepped to the bar.

"Wine for me," she said when he offered her a bourbon like the one he'd poured for himself. "You don't have to say anything."

He ran a hand over his face and let out a bitter laugh as they sat in front of the fire. "I didn't trust her. Leah was one of my best friends years ago, and when she showed up…" He met DJ's gaze. "I hate how suspicious I am of people. I question everything."

DJ was silent for a moment before she said, "Your father was a con man, right?" He nodded, making her smile. "And you expect us to be trusting?" She laughed at that. "We grew up with no stability, no security, no feeling that everything was going to be all right. How did you expect us to turn out?"

"You might be the only person who understands. But you seem to have it all together."

"I *do*?" She laughed again. "It's just an act." The wood popped and sparked in the fireplace. Golden warm light flickered over them. She took a drink of her wine and felt heat rush through her.

"You think we will ever be like other people?" he asked.

"Probably not. But maybe at some point we won't have so much to fear."

"I remember the first time I saw you. Those big brown eyes of yours really got to me. I wanted to save you. I told myself that if I ever got the chance, I would do anything to help you."

She met his gaze and felt a start at what she saw in those blue eyes. Thinking of how it had felt to be in his arms, she yearned for him to hold her. It wouldn't change anything. There was still someone out there who wanted to kill her, but for a while...

Except she knew that just being held wasn't enough. He made her feel things she'd never felt with another man. She would want his mouth on hers, his body—

"We should probably eat some of that casserole," she said, getting to her feet. She no longer wanted temporary relief from her life. Could no longer afford it. Tomorrow morning would be too hard on her. Too hard to let go of this cowboy and the connection between them that had started so many years ago.

Beau seemed to stir himself as if his thoughts had taken the same path as her own. "Yes."

They ate in a tense silence, the fire crackling in the living room, the kitchen warm.

"This is good," she said, even though she hardly tasted the casserole. She was glad when the meal was over and wished that Beau hadn't insisted on helping her with the dishes.

"I think I'll turn in," she said as soon as they'd finished cleaning up the kitchen.

He looked almost disappointed. "See you in the morning."

She watched him go to the bar and pour himself another bourbon. When she headed up the stairs, he was standing in front of the fireplace, looking into the flames.

Her steps halted, but only for a moment. She *did* understand him. They had a bond that went back all those years. She felt as if she'd always known him. Always… felt something for him.

That thought sent her on up the stairs to her room. But she knew she wouldn't be able to sleep. She felt lost, and she knew that Beau did, too.

She lay in bed, remembering the older woman's voice on the phone. Her grandmother. And hearing the woman crying so hard that she couldn't talk. Was this really a woman who wanted her dead?

Beau had just put the coffee on the next morning when he heard DJ coming down the stairs. The phone rang. He'd had a hell of a time getting to sleep knowing that DJ was only yards down the hall. He couldn't help worrying about what the day would bring. A phone call this early in the morning couldn't bode well.

"Beau Tanner," he said.

"It's Marshal Savage, Beau. I've got some news. A man by the name of Jimmy Ryan, a suspected small-time hit man, was found dead on the ranch this morning. Based on the evidence we found in his vehicle, we believe he was the shooter yesterday. He had a high-powered rifle and a photo of DJ with a target drawn on her face."

"You said he's dead?"

"His throat was cut. Earlier last evening, he'd gotten into an altercation with a local man here on the ranch. We suspect the disagreement ended on the road on the way out of the ranch. Jimmy Ryan was found some yards off the road by one of our barns."

He couldn't believe what he was hearing. "So, it's over?" he said and glanced at DJ.

"It certainly appears that way."

"Do we know who hired him?"

"Not yet. We'll continue investigating. I'll let you know if anything new turns up. Dana wanted to make sure that DJ knew. She has her heart set on her cousin staying until after Christmas, and since it is so close…"

"I'll tell DJ and do everything I can to keep her in Montana until after Christmas." He ended the call and found himself grinning in relief. It seemed impossible. The hit man had gotten into an argument with someone and it ended in his death? He wouldn't have believed it if it wasn't for what the marshal had found in the man's vehicle.

"That was the marshal," he said. "They think they have your hit man."

"They caught him?"

Beau didn't want to get into the details this early in the morning, so he merely nodded. "He's dead, but they found evidence in his vehicle that makes it pretty apparent that he was the shooter. I don't know any more than that."

"I heard you ask if they knew who'd hired him."

He shook his head. "I'm sure they'll check his cell phone and bank account. But all that takes time. Hud did say that Dana would be heartbroken if you didn't stay for Christmas. He begged me to get you to stay." He held up his hand as he saw that she was about to argue. "Whatever you decide, I'm sure you don't want to leave until we know more. So...while we're waiting, I have an idea. Have you ever cut your own Christmas tree?"

She looked surprised before she laughed. "I've never even had a real tree."

He waved his arms toward his undecorated living room with Christmas so close. "Never bothered with it myself. But this year, I feel like getting a tree. You up for it?"

DJ had a dozen questions, but she could see that they would have to wait. To her surprise, she was more than up for getting a Christmas tree. "After that amazing news, I'd love to go cut a tree."

"Great. Let's get you some warm clothes, and then we are heading into the woods."

She loved his excitement and her own. Clearly they were both relieved. The man who'd shot at her was dead. It was over. She had planned on being gone by Christmas. She still thought that was best. But what would it hurt to help Beau get a Christmas tree?

Dressed as if she was headed for the North Pole, DJ followed Beau through the snow and up into the pine trees thick behind his house. They stopped at one point to look back. She was surprised again at how quaint his place looked in its small valley surrounded by mountains.

"You live in paradise," she said, captured by the moment.

"It is, isn't it?" He seemed to be studying his house as if he hadn't thought of it that way before. "Sometimes I forget how far I've come." He glanced over at her. "How about you?"

She nodded. "We aren't our parents."

He laughed. "Thank goodness." His gaze lit on her.

DJ saw the change in his expression the moment before he dropped the ax, reached out with his gloved hand and, cupping her neck, drew her to him. "I believe you owe me a kiss."

His lips were cold at first and so were hers. The kiss was short and sweet. Their breaths came out in puffs as he drew back.

"You call that a kiss?" she taunted.

His gaze locked with hers. His grin was slow, heat in his look. And then his arms were around her. This kiss was heat and light. It crackled like the fire had last night. She felt a warmth rush through her as he deepened the kiss. She melted against him, wrapped in his arms, the cold day sparkling around them.

When he pulled back this time, his blue eyes shone in the snowy light in the pines. Desire burned like a blowtorch in those eyes. He sounded as breathless as she felt. "If we're going to get a tree…" His voice broke with emotion.

"Yes," she agreed. "A tree." She spotted one. It was hidden behind a much larger tree, its limbs misshapen in its attempt to fight for even a little sunlight in the shadow.

"Dana has this tradition of giving a sad-looking tree the honor of being a Christmas tree." She walked over to the small, nearly hidden tree. "I like this one. It's..."

He laughed. "Ugly?"

"No, it's beautiful because it's had a hard life. It's struggled to survive against all odds and would keep doing that without much hope. But it has a chance to be something special." There were tears in her eyes. "It's like us."

He shook his head as if in wonder as he looked at her, then at the tree.

"Okay, you want this one? We'll give the tree its moment to shine."

"Thank you." She hugged herself as she watched him cut the misshapen pine tree out of the shadow it had been living under.

He studied the tree for a moment before he sheathed his ax. "Come on, tree. Let's take you home."

Bianca didn't ask until they were both on the plane and headed for Montana. "You knew about her? My sister? Since the beginning?"

Ester nodded. "Your mother couldn't keep anything from me."

"But you didn't tell Grandmama?"

The housekeeper sighed. "Your mother made me promise, and what good would it have done? I'd hoped that in time... Marietta sent your mother to Italy to stay with an aunt there while she quietly had the marriage annulled. The next time I saw your mother, she was married and pregnant with you."

Bianca shook her head. "How could she have just forgotten about the baby she left behind?"

"She never forgot. When I made that rag doll for you, your mother insisted I make one for your…sister."

"That's why you left my doll and a photograph in her apartment."

"I had a nephew of mine do it. I wanted to tell her everything, but I was afraid."

She turned to look at the older woman. "Afraid my grandmother would find out."

"Afraid it would hurt you. I'd done it on impulse when I realized your grandmother was trying to find DJ."

"DJ? Is that what she calls herself?"

"It was a nickname her father gave her."

"So you saw her occasionally?"

Ester sighed. "Only from afar. Her father insisted. I would tell your mother how she looked, what she was wearing…" Tears filled her eyes. "It was heartbreaking."

"She was well cared for?"

"Well enough, I guess. Her father wouldn't take the money offered him by your grandmother's lawyer at the time the marriage was annulled."

Bianca scoffed. "So maybe he isn't as bad a man as Grandmama makes him out to be."

"Your grandmother had good reason given that he never amounted to anything and is now in prison. But he raised your sister alone and without any help from the family. I admire him for that, even though it was not an…ordinary childhood for DJ. I know he feared that the family would try to take her. I was the only one he let see her—even from a distance."

"I always wanted a sister," Bianca said more to herself than to Ester.

"I know. And I always felt sad when you said that growing up, knowing you *had* a sister. But it wasn't my place to tell you."

"Until now. Why *did* you tell me now?" Bianca asked, turning in her seat to face Ester.

Ester hesitated. Bianca could tell that the housekeeper didn't want to say anything negative about her grandmother.

"Because you were afraid of what my grandmother might do," Bianca said, reading the answer on the woman's face.

"No, I was afraid of what Roger Douglas would do. I knew I couldn't stop him, but you could."

"But did I stop him in time?" Bianca looked out the plane window. *She had a sister.* Her heart beat faster at the thought. How could her grandmother have kept something like this from her? Worse, her own mother?

She'd seen how her grandmother had used money to control Carlotta. She had always told herself that she wouldn't let Marietta do the same thing to her and yet she had taken all the gifts, the Ivy League education, the trips, all of it knowing that she'd better bring the right man home when the time came.

"Do you think she'll be all right by herself?" she asked Ester.

The housekeeper smiled. "Your grandmother is much stronger than any of us give her credit for. But I called my sister while you were getting our tickets. She can handle Marietta."

"Thank you. No matter what she's done, she's my grandmama."

"She is that."

Bianca closed her eyes. She'd lost her father at an

early age, so all she'd had was her mother, grandmother and, of course, Ester. It was Ester who had kissed her forehead each night, who got her off to school, who doctored the scrapes and lovingly applied the medicine. Her mother had always seemed lost in thought. She assumed that no one noticed how much wine she had at night before she stumbled to her room in the huge house overlooking the ocean.

Now Bianca wondered if giving up her first child had haunted her. When she'd often had that faraway, sad look in her eyes, was it Dee Anna Justice she was thinking about?

If so, she knew she should have been jealous of the hours her mother had been off—if even in her mind—with her other daughter. Had she loved her more? It didn't matter. She felt no jealousy.

Opening her eyes, she looked out the plane window again. They were almost there. She wasn't going to let anything—or anyone—keep her from her sister.

Bianca had always felt as if there was something missing from a life in which she seemed to get anything she wanted.

What she'd really wanted, though, was a sibling. She remembered asking her mother once if she could have more children. She'd wanted a brother or sister so badly.

"Don't be ridiculous," her mother had snapped.

"I know Daddy's dead, but can't you find another man—"

"Stop it, Bianca. Just stop it." She'd sent her to ask Ester about dinner. As Bianca had left the room, she'd looked back to see her mother go to the bar to pour herself a large glass of wine. Her mother had been crying.

She'd never seen her mother cry before, so she'd made

a point of keeping her desire for a sibling to herself after that.

Now she understood those tears. Had her mother ached for that other daughter just as Bianca had ached for her?

The captain announced that they would be landing in the Gallatin Valley soon.

"Maybe we should call this ranch," Ester said, but Bianca shook her head.

"I don't want them to know we're coming." When Ester seemed surprised by that, she added, "If you were my sister, would you want to meet us? I can't take the chance she might leave to avoid us, especially if Grandmama has...done something."

Ester nodded.

Bianca reached over and took the housekeeper's hands. "I hope she likes me."

Ester's eyes filled with tears. "She will love you."

Stacy was in shock. When she'd told her sister what had happened last night, she hadn't heard yet about Jimmy. "Burt wouldn't kill Jimmy. He wouldn't kill *anyone*."

"You said yourself that you'd never seen him so angry and that he hit Jimmy twice," Dana argued after she had told Stacy about Jimmy's body being found out by the barn, his throat slit. "Anyway, Hud has only taken Burt in for questioning based on what you told me."

Stacy got up from the kitchen table to pace. She'd lived around her brother-in-law long enough to know how these things worked. Hud would have to go by the evidence. "Burt hit him. Jimmy fought back. Of course there will be some of Burt's DNA on him, but that doesn't mean Burt killed him."

She couldn't believe this was happening. Jimmy was dead. But that wasn't as upsetting as Burt being blamed for it.

"Hud will sort it all out." Her sister eyed her with a mixture of pity and concern. "I thought you weren't interested in Burt."

Stacy hated to admit that she'd felt that way until last night. But she'd seen a different side to him. "He rescued me from Jimmy. He followed us from the restaurant because he was worried about me. And with good reason. I don't know why I agreed to go out with Jimmy. I made excuses for him back in high school when he forcibly took my virginity. He said he was so turned on by me that he couldn't stop himself and it was my fault."

Dana shook her head in obvious disgust. "All while you were saying no?"

She nodded. "I tried to push him off...but I didn't try hard enough back in high school. Last night I would have fought him to my dying breath."

Her sister didn't look pleased to hear that. "I told Hud what you told me, but he will want your side of the story," Dana said, picking up the phone.

Stacy shook her head as her sister started to hand her the phone. She realized that Hud would have questioned her earlier, but she had taken the kids to school. "I'm going down to his office. He's questioning the wrong person."

"I should warn you, he'll want to know where you were last night," her sister said behind her.

She turned slowly. "You can't think *I* killed Jimmy."

"Of course not."

"If I was going to kill him, I would have done it years ago after he raped me. I think until last night, I was still blaming myself for what happened—just as he let me do all these years. Now that I think about it, if Burt hadn't shown up when he did…" She looked up at her sister. "I would have killed him before I let him rape me again."

She went out the door, knowing that she'd made herself look guilty. Better her than Burt.

Chapter 17

Andrei heard the news at breakfast in a small café at
Meadow Village. He had tried to go about his day as
usual, pretending to be one of the many tourists at the
resort for the holidays. No one paid him any mind, since
he wasn't limping as badly as he had been.

It wasn't like he could go to Cardwell Ranch. The law
was crawling all over the place. Dee Anna Justice wasn't
there, anyway. He hadn't seen her or the cowboy since
the two had driven away together. But he was convinced
she would be back, and the ranch was much easier for his
purposes than driving back into the narrow canyon
to get to the private investigator/cowboy's house. He assumed the cowboy would take her to his place.

As he ate, he knew that after last night this would
be the perfect time for him to just leave, put all of this
behind him.

But his pride wasn't going to let that happen.

"The man's throat was cut," a woman whispered to another at the next table. She shuddered and then leaned closer to the other woman. "I heard from my friend at the marshal's office that the dead man was a professional killer."

That caught his interest. His heart began to pound, making it hard to hear what else the woman was saying. So, there had been another contract. He swore under his breath. Things were getting so damned complicated.

"Do they know who did it?" the other woman whispered back.

"Well…you know Burt Olsen?"

"The *mailman*?"

Out of the corner of his eye, he saw her nod. "I heard he's been taken in for questioning. He had gotten into a fight with the man earlier that night."

"Burt Olsen? I just find that hard to believe. That he would…cut a man's throat." She shivered. "Burt always seems so nice."

"You know what they say about deep water."

Poor Burt, he thought. Common sense told him that he'd been given the perfect way out. The cops would think they had their man. Dee Anna Justice would let her guard down. So would her cowboy. He could still finish this job, collect his money and leave the country before his birthday. That's how he had to play this while his luck held.

Beau stood up the Christmas tree in the living room and stepped back to consider it. "Wow, it looks better than I thought it would. Pushed against the wall like that, it really isn't bad." He turned to see DJ smiling at the tree.

"It's beautiful. It doesn't even need ornaments."

He laughed. "That's good, because I don't own any. I thought we could string some popcorn. I'll pick up some lights when I go to town."

His gaze met hers. That kiss earlier had almost had him making love to her in the snow up on the mountain. He stepped to her now. She moved into his arms as naturally as a sunrise. He held her close, breathing in the fresh-air scent of her.

"DJ," he breathed against her hair.

She pulled back to look up at him. What he saw in her eyes sent a trail of heat racing through his veins. She stood on tiptoes to kiss him. Her lips brushed against his. Her gaze held his as the tip of her tongue touched his lower lip.

He felt a shudder of desire. Taking her hand, he led her over to the fireplace. "Are you sure about this?"

"I've never been more sure of anything in my life."

Golden light flickered over them as they began to undress each other. He could feel her trembling as he brushed his lips across hers.

He trailed kisses from the corner of her mouth down to her round breasts. He found her nipple and teased the hard tip with his tongue, then his teeth. She arched against him as they slowly slid down to the rug in front of the fire. The flames rose. The fire crackled and sighed.

On the rug, the two made love as if neither of them ever had before.

Bianca and Ester landed at Gallatin Field outside Bozeman and rode the shuttle to the car rental agency.

While they waited, Bianca looked out at the snow-covered mountains. She'd never driven on snow and ice before. For a moment she questioned her impulsiveness at jumping on a plane and coming here.

Wasn't her grandmother always telling her to slow down, to think things out before she acted? Just the thought of her grandmother made her more determined to get to Cardwell Ranch—and her sister.

"Here's your key," said the man behind the desk. "Your car is right out there. Do you know where you're going?" he asked, holding up a map.

"Big Sky," she said and watched as he drew arrows on the map and handed it to her.

"Maybe we should call," Ester said as they left. "Just showing up at their door... Maybe we should warn them not only that we're coming but that maybe your grandmother did something she regrets."

Bianca shook her head. "I'd rather take my chances. Anyway, call and say what? We have no idea what is going on. For all we know..." Her voice broke. "I know she did wrong, but I still can't get her into trouble. I keep telling myself that Grandmama wouldn't...hurt her own grandchild."

"In Marietta's eyes, *you* are her only grandchild."

"I'm furious with her, but I can't throw her under the bus," Bianca said, making Ester smile.

"I've wanted to do just that for years, but I understand what you're saying. You don't want her going to prison. I don't, either. It's why I called you and told you what was going on."

"We are only about forty miles away." Bianca shot her a look as she drove, following the man's directions from the rental agency. "Roger was the one who hired someone. Maybe she didn't stop him, but it wasn't her idea, right?"

Ester looked away. "I doubt the law would see it that way. She saw Walter Justice as a problem." She shrugged. "Now she sees his daughter as one."

"But Walter is still alive."

"Last I heard, but he's also in prison."

Bianca shot her a look. "You can't think she had anything to do with that!"

Ester shrugged. "I wouldn't put anything past your grandmother. Let's just hope that phone call she made was...real and that she has stopped all this foolishness."

Bianca stared at the highway into the canyon and the steep mountains on each side. "Look what she did to my mother. Forcing her to keep Dee Anna a secret from me. I'm not sure if I can forgive her if something has happened to my sister."

DJ felt as if her life couldn't get any better. It was a strange feeling. After years of holding back, of being afraid really to live, she'd given herself to Beau Tanner completely. Her heart felt so full she thought it might burst.

"It is really over?" she asked him the next morning on the way to Cardwell Ranch. Dana had called and invited them over for brunch, saying the crime scene tape was gone and the ranch was back to normal.

Beau squeezed her hand. "You're safe."

Safe. She realized she'd never felt it before. It was a wonderful feeling, she thought as she looked out on the winter landscape. It had snowed again last night, huge flakes that drifted down in the ranch light outside Beau's home. She'd felt as if she was in a snow globe, one with a cozy little house inside. Wrapped in Beau's arms under the down comforter, she'd found paradise.

Last night she hadn't thought about the future, only the present. But this morning as they neared the turnoff to Cardwell Ranch, she couldn't help but think about her mother's family. What now? If it was true that they'd tried to kill her, fearing she wanted their money... The thought made her heart ache.

Beau reached over and took her hand. "It's going to be all right."

She couldn't help but smile at him. Nor could she help but believe him. With Beau in her corner, she felt she could take on the world.

Bianca turned off the highway at Big Sky and stopped a few yards from the Cardwell Ranch sign that hung over the entrance. She glanced at Ester, who quickly took her hand and squeezed it.

"You can do this," Ester said. "She's your sister."

She nodded, smiling in spite of her fear, and drove under the sign and across the bridge spanning the river. She felt as if she'd been waiting for this her whole life. Even with all the lost years, she and DJ still had time to get to know each other. If her sister wanted to.

Bianca felt a stab of fear. What if her grandmother was right and this young woman wanted nothing to do with her family? With her?

A large new barn appeared ahead along with a half-dozen cabins set back in the woods. But it was the rambling old farmhouse that she drove to, with the black Suburban parked in front. She saw a curtain move.

"Tell me I'm not making a mistake," she said to Ester.

"Letting your sister know she's not alone in this can't be a mistake," the older woman said.

Bianca smiled over at her. "I don't know what I would have done without you all these years." She opened her door, Ester following suit.

The steps seemed to go on forever, and then they were on the porch. Bianca was about to knock when the door opened, startling her.

A dark-haired woman in her thirties looked surprised. Was this DJ? Was this her sister?

"I'm Bianca," she said at the same time the woman said, "I'm sorry, I thought you were…someone else."

The woman looked from Bianca to Ester and back. "Did you say Bianca?"

She nodded. "I'm looking for Dee Anna Justice," Bianca said.

"She's not here right now," the woman said excitedly. "But I'm her cousin Dana."

Feeling a surge of relief at the woman's apparent welcome, she said, "I'm her…sister, Bianca."

Dana smiled. "Yes, her sister. What a surprise."

"I hope not too much of a surprise," she said. "This is Ester, a…a friend of mine. Is my sister here?"

"Please, come in," Dana said and ushered them into the warm living room. "I'll call DJ… Dee Anna, and let her know you're here. Please, have a seat. I was expecting her when you drove up."

Bianca sat in a chair by the fire, glancing around at the Western decor. Until this moment, she hadn't felt like she was in Montana. As Ester took a place on the couch next to her, she spotted the Christmas tree.

Dana turned her back, her cell phone at her ear, and

said, "You should come home now," before disconnecting and dialing another number.

When she turned back to them, she saw what they were looking at—and no doubt the expressions on their surprised faces. "That's my orphan Christmas tree," Dana said with a laugh. "It's a long story." She seemed to be waiting for the call to go through, then said, "You aren't going to believe who is sitting in my living room. Your sister! Oh, it's her all right. She looks enough like you that there is no mistake. Okay, I'll tell her." Dana disconnected, smiling. "She's on her way and should be here any minute."

Bianca had never felt so nervous. Ester reached over and patted her hand. "It's going to be fine," the housekeeper whispered.

She nodded, smiling and fighting tears as she heard a vehicle pull up out front. Dana said, "In fact, she's here now."

"Are you sure you heard right?" Beau asked as he pulled up in front of the house.

Earlier DJ had been sitting cross-legged on the floor in front of the fire, stringing popcorn for their Christmas tree. She had been wearing one of his shirts over a pair of jeans. Her face had been flushed, either from the fire or their lovemaking earlier. She'd looked relaxed, content, maybe even happy. He'd lost another piece of his heart at the sight of her.

Now she looked as if she might jump out of her skin. "My sister. That must be her rental car. Why would she be at the ranch?" she asked, turning to meet his gaze.

"Apparently she wants to see you."

She shook her head, relieved after her call earlier to

the hospital that her father was going to make it. "This is crazy. One minute all I have is my father, and now I have cousins and a *sister*?"

"Who might have hired a hit man to take you out." He pulled out his cell phone. "I'm calling Hud."

"No," she said, reaching for her door. "I want to meet her. I don't need the law there. She isn't going to try to kill me."

He hesitated and finally pocketed the phone. "She'll have to go through me first."

"Seriously, I don't think she'd be here now if she was behind this."

"Apparently you haven't dealt with as many criminals as I have."

DJ laughed and leaned over to give him a kiss. "I have a good feeling about this."

He wished he did.

Chapter 18

DJ couldn't believe that she was going to meet her half sister after only recently finding out that she even existed. "How long do you think she's known about me?" she asked Beau as they walked to the porch steps.

He glanced over at her. "I have no idea."

"Sorry, I just have so many questions."

"Ideally she will be able to answer them all for you. Including who hired someone to kill you."

She looked over at him as they reached the door. "I haven't forgotten. But she's here. That makes her look innocent, don't you think?"

"I'd go with less guilty. But you have no idea what this woman wants. Or why she's shown up now. You have to admit, it's suspicious."

"Which is exactly why I don't think she's involved."

She could tell he didn't agree. "Well, you'll be here to protect me," she said as she reached for the doorknob.

"Yes, I will."

But before she could grab the doorknob, the door swung open, and there was Dana, practically jumping up and down in her excitement.

"Easy," he said behind her. "Let's not get carried away until we find out what is going on."

"I'm glad Beau's with you," Dana said as DJ entered the house. "Hud's on his way," she whispered to Beau loud enough that DJ heard it.

"Really, the two of you…" She stepped into the living room and stopped dead. The woman who rose from the chair by the fire looked more like their mother than even DJ did. DJ stared at her half sister. They looked so much alike it was eerie.

"Bianca?" she asked, although there was little doubt this was the half sister she'd been told about.

"Dee Anna. Or is it DJ? Oh, I'm just so glad you're all right," Bianca said, rushing to her to give her a quick hug. "I have wanted a sister my whole life. I can't believe we were kept apart." She stepped back to take in DJ. "We look so much alike. We could be twins." She let out a nervous laugh.

Out of the corner of her eye, DJ had seen Beau start to move. But he stopped short when Bianca merely threw her arms around DJ.

"I am so glad to see you," Bianca said as she stared at DJ. "I was so worried."

"Worried?" Beau asked only feet away.

Her sister hesitated. An older woman, whom DJ had barely noticed, stood then and moved to her. There was kindness in the woman's eyes. "I'm Ester."

"Ester," DJ repeated as Bianca stepped back to let Ester take DJ's hand.

"I made your doll," Ester said. "Your father kept me informed on how you were doing over the years. I wish I could have done more."

Tears welled in DJ's eyes. "Thank you. I named her—"

"Trixie. That's why I sent you Bianca's, so you would know there were two of them. Two of you. I couldn't let you go on believing you had no family or that no one cared other than your father."

DJ looked to her sister. "And my grandmother?"

Both women hesitated. Bianca looked guilty, which sent a sliver of worry burrowing under her skin.

"Grandmama is not well," Bianca said.

Ester let out a snort.

Just then, Marshal Hud Savage arrived. "What's going on?" he asked after Dana introduced him as her husband.

"That's just what I was about to ask," Beau said. "Where does a hit man fit into this happy reunion?"

Roger Douglas's cell phone vibrated in his pocket. It surprised him. All the way to the airport it had been buzzing constantly, but it had finally stopped until now. He'd thought, as he'd waited for his flight, that both Marietta and the accountant had given up.

Now he pulled it out, curious which one had decided to give it one more try. He saw who was calling and hurried to a quieter area before answering.

"You didn't tell me about the private investigator who isn't letting her out of his sight," Andrei Ivankov said.

Roger wasn't sure what to say. He'd taken the call only because he'd thought the hit man had finished the job. "I take it you haven't—"

"You take it right."

"It's just as well. The client wants to call off the—"

"I'm sorry, I must have misunderstood you."

"She doesn't want you to finish the job." Roger knew the man was born in Russia or some such place, but his English was better than Roger's own.

"I have been out here freezing my ass off and now she wants me to forget it? I had my doubts about dealing with you. I get paid no matter what, plus extra for my inconvenience, and if I don't get paid, I will track you down and make you wish you'd never—"

"Don't threaten me. There is nothing you can do to me. I really don't give a damn if you kill her or not." He'd raised his voice, and several people had turned to look in his direction. He disconnected the call, then tossed the phone to the floor and stomped it to death. Now a lot of people were staring at him.

Roger felt heat rise up his neck. He'd always prided himself on never losing his temper. But he wasn't that man anymore, he reminded himself. He wasn't the meek lawyer who had to kiss Marietta Pisani's feet.

He'd picked up what he could of the cell phone, tossed it in the trash and started back to his seat when he heard his flight called. Clutching the bag full of Marietta's money, he smiled as he got in line.

It wasn't until he was sitting down in first class, drinking a vodka tonic and dreaming of his new life, the bag shoved under the seat in front of him, that he relaxed. Just a few more minutes.

Glancing out the window, he felt his heart drop like a stone. Two security guards were headed for the plane along with several police officers. He downed his drink, figuring it was the last one he'd get for a while.

* * *

"It was a misunderstanding," Bianca assured the marshal. They had all gathered in the dining room around the large old oak table. She turned to her sister. She couldn't believe how much they looked alike. They really could have been twins. "You have to forgive Grandmama. It was her attorney, Roger Douglas. When she found out what he'd done...she was beside herself and demanded he put a stop to it."

Hud and Beau exchanged a glance. "I called the power company. They didn't have any men in our area."

"So the man who was seen on the power pole?" Beau asked.

Hud nodded. "It must have been the shooter."

"Shooter?" Bianca asked.

Dana filled them in on what had happened, first someone taking a shot at DJ, then a man found dead near one of the old barns. "He apparently had been hired to kill DJ."

Bianca's eyes welled with tears. "I'm so sorry. I had no idea. My grandmother had no idea. I'm just so thankful that he missed and that he is no longer a problem."

Hud's cell phone rang. He stepped away to take the call. The room went silent. Bianca prayed that it wouldn't be bad news. She was worried about her grandmother and what would happen now.

"That was the police in San Diego," Hud said as he came back to the table. "They've arrested Roger Douglas. Apparently he made a deal and told them everything, including that he had hired a hit man through another man to kill Dee Anna Justice. He was carrying a large sum of money that he admitted had been stolen from your grandmother, Bianca."

Bianca let out a relieved breath. "I never liked Roger."

"Me, either," Ester said. "He certainly pulled the wool over your grandmother's eyes for years."

"Where is your grandmother now?" Hud asked. "The police said they'd tried to reach her…"

Ester saw her alarm and quickly waved it off. "I got a text from my sister a few moments ago. May was looking after Marietta. She said the fool woman packed a bag and took the first flight out, headed this way."

There were surprised looks around the table. Then Dana got to her feet and announced, "I've made brunch. I think we should all have something to eat while we wait for our new arrival."

Hud said, "I'll have someone pick her up at the airport and bring her here. But the police in San Diego will still have a few questions for her."

DJ felt as if she was in shock. She kept wanting to pinch herself. She'd gone from having only her father to having this family that kept getting bigger and bigger.

Dana told Bianca and Ester that they could stay in one of the cabins on the mountain as long as they wanted. "I know you and DJ have a lot to talk about. But first you have to share this brunch I've made."

"Are you sure there is enough?" Bianca asked. "We don't want to intrude."

Dana laughed. "I'm used to cooking for ranch hands. I always make too much. Anyway, you're family. There is always room at my table for family." She motioned DJ into the kitchen. "Are you all right?"

"I don't think I've ever been this all right," DJ said, smiling. She felt exhausted from everything that had happened. The Cardwells. Beau. Her near death. And finally meeting her sister and the woman who'd made her Trixie and had watched out for her from a distance. It felt as if it was all too much. And yet she'd never felt happier.

She hugged her cousin. "Thank you so much."

"It's just a little brunch," Dana said with a laugh.

"That and you, this ranch, everything you've done. Somehow I feel as if it all had to come together here where it began."

"Have you heard how your father is doing?" Dana asked.

"He's going to make it. His sentence is about up. He's getting out of prison soon." DJ wasn't sure how she felt about that. She could understand now why he'd been afraid of her mother's family finding out about her. The fact that he hadn't taken their money made her almost proud of him. Maybe there was more to her father than she'd originally thought. Maybe when he got out they could spend some time together, really get to know each other.

From the window, DJ could see Beau outside talking to Hud. Both looked worried. "They aren't going to arrest my grandmother, are they?" DJ asked as Dana followed her gaze to the two.

"No, I'm sure it is just as your sister said, a mistake, since that man has confessed to everything."

DJ hoped so. The marshal and Beau turned back toward the house. DJ stuck her head out the kitchen door to see Beau and Hud enter the house. Beau caught her eye and smiled reassuringly.

She felt a shaft of heat fall over her like the warm rays of the sun and almost blushed at the memory of their lovemaking. Beau was so tender and yet so strong and virile. Her heart beat a little faster just at the sight of him.

Marietta had assumed she was being arrested when she landed at the airport and saw the two deputies waiting for her. She was pleasantly surprised to hear that she was being taken to the Cardwell Ranch, where her granddaughters were waiting for her.

On the drive up the canyon, she stared out at the snowy landscape, rough rocky cliffs and glazed-over green river. She'd never seen mountains like these, let alone this much snow, in her life. It kept her mind off what might be waiting for her once she reached the ranch.

Whatever was waiting, she deserved it, she told herself. She'd been a fool. The police had left a message that Roger Douglas had been arrested at the airport carrying a large amount of money on him. Her money. She shook her head. Who knew how much he had squandered? She would deal with that when she got home. If she got home.

Her chest ached. It was as if she could feel her old heart giving out. *Just stay with me a little longer. Let me try to fix this before I die.*

She was relieved when the deputy driving finally turned off the highway, crossed a bridge spanning the iced-over river and pulled down into a ranch yard. She stared at the large two-story house and took a breath. One of the deputies offered to help her out, but she waved him off.

This was something she had to do herself. It very well might be the last thing she ever did.

Chapter 19

They had just sat down to eat Dana's brunch when they heard a patrol car drive up.

Everyone looked toward the front door expectantly. DJ wasn't sure she was ready to meet her grandmother. This was all happening too fast, and yet she couldn't help being curious. This was the woman who thankfully hadn't put a hit out on her. But she was the woman who'd apparently planned to buy her off.

Standing up, DJ prepared to meet her grandmother. Everyone else rose as well and moved into the living room. Hud went to open the door for the elderly woman who'd just climbed the steps and pounded forcibly on the door. She remembered Bianca saying the woman wasn't well, a bad heart. Now she wondered if that was true or if that was just what her grandmother wanted her to believe.

Like Beau, she hated always being suspicious. Wasn't there a chance that they could change? That love could make them more trusting?

Love? Where had that come from? She glanced over at Beau and felt her heart do that little jump it did when she saw him. She did love him.

The realization surprised her. She'd cared about some of the men she'd dated, but she'd never felt as if she was in love. Until this moment.

What a moment to realize it, she thought as an elderly woman with salt-and-pepper hair and intense brown eyes stepped into the room.

DJ felt Bianca take her hand. Beau was watching the older woman as if waiting for her to do something that would force him to take her down.

She almost laughed. He was so protective. He shot her a look that said, *You can do this.* She smiled. He had no idea how strange all this was for her. She'd dreamed of family, and now she had all the complications that came with one.

When the door opened, Marietta almost fell in with it. "I want to see my granddaughter before you arrest me!" she said to the man in the marshal's uniform. It was just like them to have someone here to arrest her the moment she arrived at the house. But she wasn't leaving without a fight, she thought as the man stepped back and she barged in, more determined than ever.

What she saw made her stagger to a stop. Bianca standing next to a young woman who could have been her twin. Their resemblance to each other gave her a shock that almost stopped her old heart dead. This was the child Carlotta had given birth to? This beautiful thing?

"What are you doing here?" Ester demanded. The accusation in her housekeeper's tone shocked her. Clearly their relationship had changed.

"You're starting to remind me of your sister," she snapped. "I came to see my granddaughter."

"*Which* granddaughter?" Bianca asked. She was holding DJ's hand, the two of them looking so formidable, so strong, so defiant. Her heart lodged in her throat as she looked at the two of them. She couldn't have been more proud or filled with shame. If she hadn't been the way she was, these two would have gotten to grow up together.

She could see her daughter in both of the women, but especially in DJ. The woman was more beautiful than even she knew. Marietta thought of that Bible verse about not hiding your light under a bushel basket. DJ was just coming into her own. Marietta wondered what had turned on that light inside her, then noticed the cowboy standing near her, looking just as fierce. Of course it had been a man.

"I came to see *both* granddaughters," she said and had to clear her voice. "But especially you, Dee Anna. I can't tell you how sorry I am that this is the first time we have ever met."

Carlotta was right. All she'd thought about was the family fortune and some ingrate of Walter Justice's trying to steal it. Staring at these two beautiful women, she felt a mountain of regret. She hadn't thought of Dee Anna as anything more than a mistake. She'd simply acted as she'd done all those years ago when she'd had

Carlotta's marriage to Walter annulled. Both times she'd listened to Roger.

"DJ," Bianca said. "She goes by DJ."

Marietta smiled at her other granddaughter. She could see that the two women had already bonded. "DJ," she amended, her voice breaking as she held out her wrinkled hands to her granddaughter. "Can you ever forgive me?"

There were tears in her grandmother's eyes as DJ stepped to her and took both her hands in hers. Marietta pulled her into a hug. The older woman felt frail in her arms, and she was truly sorry that she hadn't known her before now.

"We should all sit down and have something to eat," Dana said. "Food and family go together."

"I need to ask Mrs. Pisani some questions," her marshal husband said.

"Not now. We are going to eat this brunch I made," Dana said in a no-nonsense tone as they gathered around the table again. "DJ, sit here by Beau and your grandmother. Ester and Bianca, would you mind sitting across from them? Hud—"

"Yep, I'm sitting down right where you tell me," he said.

A smattering of laughter moved through the room.

"I married a smart man," Dana said and introduced her husband and herself.

DJ didn't think she could eat a bite but was pleasantly surprised to find she could. "This is all so delicious," she told her cousin.

Everyone seemed to relax, commenting on how good the food was. Ester asked for one of the recipes. They talked about Montana, life on the ranch, Christmas and finally how they had come to know about each other. Marietta said little, picking at her food, her gaze on DJ.

Ester informed Marietta that Roger Douglas had been arrested. "He confessed not only to stealing your money but also to being behind hiring a hit man, so it looks like you're off the hook."

Her grandmother shook her head, smiling sadly. "We both know better than that. So much of this is my fault. Carlotta was right." She teared up again but quickly wiped her eyes. "I'm just so happy that my granddaughters have found each other."

When the meal was over, DJ was sorry to see it end. Dana had offered the cabins on the mountainside to Bianca, Ester and Marietta, but Bianca had declined, saying she was worried about her grandmother.

"She looks too pale," her sister had said confidentially to DJ. "She shouldn't have flown. I think all this might have been too much for her. I want to take her to the hospital to make sure she is all right."

"I'm not sure what good that will do," Ester said, not unkindly. "The doctors have told her there is nothing they can do for her. We've all known she doesn't have much longer."

"I know," Bianca said.

"Do you mind if I come with you to the hospital?" DJ asked.

"No, not at all," her sister said and smiled.

As Hud left to head back to work and they prepared to leave, snow began to fall as another storm came through. The clouds were low. So was the light. "I know you need this time with your family," Beau said as they all headed out onto the porch. "But if you need me…"

That was just it. She needed him too much. He crowded her thoughts and made her ache for the closeness they had shared.

"I'd like to finish helping you decorate the tree," she said.

"I'd like that, too. But we have time. Christmas is still days away."

"Yes," she said. "It's a date, then." She bit her tongue. "You know what I mean."

He nodded. "We kind of skipped that part. Maybe… well, depending on what you have planned after Christmas…"

They left it at that as he started toward his vehicle.

The crime scene tape was gone. Everything seemed to be back to normal around Cardwell Ranch, Andrei thought as he watched the goings-on through the crosshairs of his rifle.

There'd been a lot of company today. He'd watched them come and go, the man with Dee Anna Justice giving her a little more space.

Several times he could have taken a shot, but it hadn't been perfect.

Now everyone seemed to be leaving. His birthday was only days away. He had to make his move. His leg was better. Good enough.

He adjusted the high-powered rifle and scope. It didn't take him long to get Dee Anna Justice in the crosshairs. A head shot was the most effective, but at this distance he didn't want to take the chance.

For days he'd been conflicted. But now he felt nothing but calm. His reputation was at stake. He would finish this.

Shooting into a crowd was always risky, but the confusion would give him his chance to make a clean getaway. Now it felt almost too easy. Was this the shot he'd been waiting for?

He aimed for DJ's heart and gently pulled the trigger.

DJ and her newfound family stood on the porch, saying their goodbyes to Dana. Her grandmother stood a few feet away. DJ heard Bianca ask her if she was feeling all right.

Beau had stopped near his pickup. She could feel his gaze on her. Something in his expression made her ache to be in this arms. He was dressed in jeans, boots and that red-and-black wool coat. His black Stetson was pulled low, but those blue eyes were on her. Her skin warmed at the thought of his hands on her.

"You're my granddaughter in every sense of the word," Marietta said as she stepped to DJ and took both of her hands again. "If I have any money left—"

"I don't want your money. I never have."

Her grandmother nodded. "I am such a foolish old woman."

DJ shook her head and hugged the woman. Marietta hugged her hard for a woman who looked so frail. As she stepped back, DJ heard Beau let out a curse.

She looked past her grandmother to see him running toward her. He was yelling, "Shooter! Everyone get down!"

DJ couldn't move, the words not making any sense at first. Then she reached for her grandmother. But Marietta pushed away her hand. As she looked up into the older woman's face, she found it filled with love and something else, a plea for forgiveness, in the instant before the woman stepped in front of her as if to shield her.

The next thing she knew, Beau slammed into her, knocking her to the porch floor. "Everyone down!"

In the distance came the roar of an engine. Beau was pushing her to move toward the door of the house. "Get inside! Hurry! DJ, are you hit?"

She couldn't do more than shake her head. "My grandmother?"

That's when she looked over and saw the woman lying beside her. Blood bloomed from her chest. DJ began to cry as Beau ushered them all inside the house, then carried Marietta in.

"Put her down here," Dana ordered, pointing to the couch near the Christmas tree. She had the phone in her hand. DJ knew she was already calling Hud and an ambulance.

She and her sister rushed to their grandmother's side.

"Stay here! No one leaves until I get back!" With that, Beau was gone.

Beau drew his own weapon from his shoulder holster. The sound of a vehicle engine turning over filled the icy winter air as he raced to his pickup. He could make out the silhouette of a vehicle roaring down the road toward Highway 191.

He started his engine, fishtailing as he punched the gas and went after it. By the time they reached the highway, he'd gained a little on what appeared to be an SUV.

The driver took off down the icy highway. Beau followed the two red taillights. He quickly got on his cell and called in the direction the man was headed, then tossed his cell aside to put all his attention on driving.

The highway was empty as the driver ahead of him left Big Sky behind and headed deeper into the canyon, going south toward West Yellowstone. But it was also icy. The last thing Beau wanted to do was end up in a ditch—or worse, the river. But he wasn't going to let the man get away.

As he raced after the vehicle, his mind raced, as well. Hud had been so sure that they had the hit man and that a local man had killed him. Was it possible another hit man had been hired when the first failed? Or had there always been two?

This would be how it ended. Andrei could see that now. For so long he'd had trouble envisioning his life after his forty-fifth birthday. Now he knew why.

He'd just killed some old woman. It was worse than he could have imagined. Shame made him burn. He had failed to kill his target and he wasn't going to get away, he thought as he looked back to see the pickup right behind him.

It was that cowboy. What was his story, anyway? The PI had been suspicious and jumpy from the start. Otherwise he wouldn't have spotted him just before he'd fired. The cowboy had probably caught the reflection off the rifle scope. Just Andrei's luck.

Ahead all he could see was snow. He hated snow. He hated cold. He hated this contract. All his instincts had told him to let it go. Stubbornness had made him determined to finish it no matter what. And all because of the coin toss. It had never let him down before. Not that it mattered now.

He felt his tires lose traction on the icy road. He touched his brakes as he felt the back of the car begin to slide and knew immediately that had been a mistake. But it was just another mistake, he thought as he cranked the wheel, trying to get the car to come out of the slide. Instead, it spun the other way. He was going too fast to save himself. He saw the guardrail coming up and closed his eyes.

Beau's heart was pounding. He still couldn't believe how close DJ had come to being killed. If he hadn't lunged for her. If her grandmother hadn't stepped in front of the bullet. So many *if*s.

The taillights ahead of him grew brighter as he closed the distance. He knew this road. He suspected the would-be assassin did not. He could see that the vehicle was a white SUV. Probably a rental.

The canyon followed the river, winding through the mountains in tighter turns. He pressed harder, getting closer. His headlights shone into the vehicle, silhouetting the driver. A single male.

Just then, he saw that the driver had taken the curve too fast. He'd lost control. Beau watched the SUV go into a slide. He let up off his gas as best he could. He knew better than to hit his brakes. They would both end up in the river.

The SUV began a slow circle in the middle of the road. He could see that the driver was fighting like hell to keep it on the road, no doubt overcorrecting. The front of the SUV hit the guardrail and spun crazily toward the rock wall on the other side, where it crashed into the rocks, then shot back out, ping-ponging from the guardrail to the cliffs on the slick road until it finally came to rest against the rocks.

Beau managed to get stopped a few yards shy of the SUV. He turned on his flashers and jumped out, glad there wasn't any traffic. Drawing his weapon, he moved to the vehicle.

The driver was slumped to one side, his deflated air bag in his lap and blood smeared on what was left of the side window. Beau tried to open the driver's-side door, but it was too badly dented. He could hear sirens in the distance as he reached through the broken glass to put a finger to the man's throat. He was still breathing, but for how long?

"Grandmama," Bianca cried and fell to her knees beside the couch. DJ, taking the towel Dana handed her, pressed it to the bleeding wound in Marietta's chest.

"An ambulance is on the way," Dana assured her, sounding scared. The towel was quickly soaked with blood.

DJ joined her sister, her heart breaking. "You saved my life," she said to her grandmother. "Why would you do that?"

Marietta smiled through her pain. "It still can't make up for what I've done. If I had time…"

"You have time," Bianca said. "You can't leave us now."

Her grandmother patted her hand weakly. "My old heart was going to play out soon, anyway. I didn't want you to know how bad it was or how little time I had." She looked from Bianca to DJ and back. "Seeing the two of you together… I'm happy for you. You have a sister now."

She looked to DJ, reached for her hand and squeezed it. "Forgive me?" she whispered.

"Of course," DJ said, and her grandmother squeezed her fingers. "Take care of each other." Her gaze shifted to Ester. "Take care of my girls."

Ester nodded, tears in her eyes.

Marietta smiled and mouthed "Thank you" as her eyes slowly closed. Her hands went slack in theirs. She smiled then as if seeing someone she recognized on the other side.

Bianca began to cry. DJ put her arm around her, and the two hugged as the sound of sirens grew louder and louder.

Epilogue

Beau looked out his office window, watching the snowstorm and feeling restless. It was over. DJ was safe. The bad guys were either dead or in jail. It hadn't taken Marshal Hud Savage long to put all the pieces together with Beau's help. The man Roger Douglas had hired was arrested and quickly made a deal, naming not one but two hit men. Andrei Ivankov, a professional hit man, died before reaching the hospital in Bozeman. Jimmy Ryan, a thug for hire, was also dead, killed, according to lab results, by Ivankov.

Mailman Burt Olsen was in the clear. According to Dana, Burt and her sister, Stacy, had a date for New Year's. Dana figured they'd be planning a wedding by Valentine's Day. Apparently Stacy hadn't waited for Burt to ask her out. She'd invited him to the movies and they'd hit it off, making Dana say, "I told you so."

Meanwhile, Dana's best friend, Hilde, went into labor Christmas Eve. She had a beautiful eight-pound, nine-ounce baby boy. Dana had called earlier to ask if Beau had heard from DJ. He'd said he'd been busy and now wished he'd asked how DJ was doing, since he was sure Dana had talked to her.

"You going to spend the whole day looking out that window?" demanded a deep female voice behind him.

Beau turned to look guiltily at his assistant, Marge. She stood, hands on hips, giving him one of those looks. "What do you want me to do?"

"You should never have let her leave in the first place."

"She was going to her grandmother's funeral in Palm Desert."

"You could have gone along."

He shook his head. "She needed time."

Marge scoffed at that and shook her head as if disappointed in him. "You mean *you* needed time. Apparently you haven't had enough time in your life."

"I hardly know the woman."

Marge merely mugged a face at him.

"It was too soon," he said, turning back to the window. "She had too much going on right then." He glanced over his shoulder. Marge was gone, but she'd left the door open.

He walked out into the reception area of the office to find her standing at her desk. "What? You aren't going to keep nagging me?"

"Would it do any good?" She sounded sad. Almost as sad as he felt.

New Year's Day, Dana listened to the racket coming from her living room and smiled to herself. There were children laughing and playing, brothers arguing good-naturedly, sister and sisters-in-law talking food and fabrics, cousins discussing barbecue, since they had a batch of ribs going outside on the large grill. The house smelled of pine, fresh-brewed coffee and cocoa, and gingersnap cookies decorated by the children.

She wished her mother were here. How happy Mary Justice Cardwell would have been to see her family all together—finally. It was what Dana had hoped for all her life. It was one reason she would never leave this old house. Her children would grow up here—just as she had. She hoped that someday it would be her grandchildren she would hear playing in the next room.

"Do you need any help?" her cousin DJ asked from the kitchen doorway.

Dana stepped to her and pulled her into a hug. "Having you here means more than you can ever know." She drew back to look at her cousin. She'd seen how much Beau and DJ had loved each other. But for whatever reason, they'd parted. It broke her heart.

She'd had to twist DJ's arm to get her to fly up for the New Year. "You wouldn't consider staying longer, would you?"

"I have to return to California. My editor has a list of assignments she wants me to consider."

"I have to ask about your grandmother's funeral," Dana said.

"It was quite beautiful. As misguided as she was in the past, she saved my life. I'll never forget that. Also, I've been spending time with my sister and my father, actually. He's trying to figure out what he wants to do with the rest of his life. That was nice of you to offer him a place here on the ranch."

"I hope he takes me up on it," Dana said. "After all, this is where he belongs. Zinnia would love to see him again. You know, she's a widow."

DJ laughed. "You just can't help matchmaking, can you?"

"I have no idea what you're talking about," Dana said, smiling. "Bianca is also always welcome here on the ranch. I spoke with her about coming up and spending a few weeks. She wants to learn to ride horses. So you have to come back. There really is no place like Montana in the summer."

"You sound like Beau." DJ seemed to catch herself. "He mentioned how nice it is up here once the snow melts."

"Yes, Beau," Dana said, unable to hold back a grin. "The night I saw the two of you dancing down at The Corral, I knew you were perfect for each other."

DJ shook her head. "I'm afraid you're wrong about that. I haven't heard from him since I left."

Dana laughed. "Trust me. I'm never wrong."

It was almost midnight when there was a knock at the door. The old ranch house on Cardwell Ranch was full of family. Dana had just passed out the noisemakers. DJ had seen her watching the door as if she was expecting more guests, but everyone was already there, including DJ's cousins—Jordan and his wife, Stacy and Burt, and even Clay and his partner.

Dana ran to the door and threw it open. A gust of cold air rushed in. DJ saw her cousin reach out, grab Beau and pull him in. They shared a few words before both looked in her direction.

She groaned, afraid of what Dana had done to get

Beau over here tonight. Her cousin was so certain she wasn't wrong making this match. DJ almost felt sorry for her. As much as she and Beau had enjoyed their time together, as much as DJ felt for him, sometimes things just didn't work out, she told herself as he walked toward her.

If anything, he was more handsome than the first time she'd seen him standing in the airport. His blue eyes were on her, and in them she saw what almost looked like pain. Her heart lodged in her throat. Tears burned her eyes.

"We need to talk," he said as he took her hand. She was reminded of the night at The Corral when he'd said the same words. Only that night, he'd dragged her from the dance floor, out into the snowy night.

Tonight he led her into the kitchen and closed the door. When he turned to her, she looked into his handsome face and felt her pulse pound.

"I'm a damned fool," he said. "I should never have let you go. Or at least, I should have gone with you. Since the day you left, I've thought about nothing but you. I would have called, but I was afraid that once you got back to your life…"

"Are you just going to talk, or are you going to kiss me?" DJ managed to say, her heart in her throat.

He pulled her to him. His mouth dropped to hers. He smelled of snow and pine and male. She breathed him in as he deepened the kiss and held her tighter.

"I never want to let you go," he said when he drew back. "If that means leaving Montana—"

"I would never ask you to leave a place you love so much."

He looked into her eyes. "Then what are we going

to do? Because I don't want to spend another day without you."

"With my job, I can work anywhere."

He smiled, his blue eyes sparkling. "You'd move to Montana if I were to...ask you?"

"What are you saying, cowboy?"

He looked down at his boots for a moment, then met her gaze again. "I never saw you coming. This was the last thing I expected, but now that you've come into my life... Come back. Come back to me. I know it probably seems like we haven't known each other that long, but..." His hand went into his pocket. He seemed to hesitate as he studied her face for a moment.

DJ held her breath as he pulled his hand from his pocket and opened it. Sitting in the middle of his large palm, something caught the light.

She felt her eyes widen at the sight of the diamond ring lying there.

"It was my mother's. She left it with her sister so my father didn't pawn it."

DJ couldn't help but smile knowingly. She and Beau. Their connection, as odd as it was, ran deep.

"Would you consider marrying me? Not right away. We could have as long an engagement as you need." He seemed to catch himself and dropped to one knee. "I know this should have been more romantic—"

She shook her head. "It's perfect," she said, seeing his discomfort. She held out her left hand. "And yes, I will marry you. And no, I don't need a long engagement. Leaving here, leaving you, was one of the hardest things I've ever done. It was breaking my heart." Her eyes filled with tears. "Montana feels like the home I've never had. Somehow, I've never felt that I deserved to be happy. But with you…"

He slipped the ring on her finger, rose and pulled her into his arms. "That's exactly how I feel. As if I deserve this if I'm smart enough not to let you get away."

She smiled as he lowered his mouth to hers. "I love you, DJ," he whispered against her lips. In the next room, a cheer arose. It was a new day, a new year.

* * * * *

SECRET OF DEADMAN'S COULEE

This is for Rob Myers, former coroner and always a mystery lover. Thanks, Rob, for all your help over the years. You are one of the few people I can call and ask about dead bodies, poisons and cool scary stuff.

Chapter 1

A grouse burst from the sagebrush in an explosion of wings. Eve Bailey brought her horse up short, heart jammed in her throat and, for the first time, was aware of just how far she'd ridden from the ranch.

The wind had kicked up, the horizon to the west dark with thunderheads. She could smell the rain in the air.

She'd ridden into the badlands, leaving behind the prairie with its deep grasses to ride through sage and cactus, to find herself in no-man's-land with a storm coming.

Below her lay a deep gorge the Missouri River had carved centuries ago through the harsh eastern Montana landscape. Erosion had left hundreds of ravines in the unstable soil, and the country was now badlands for miles, without a road, let alone another person in sight.

Eve stared at the unforgiving land, her heart just as desolate. She should never have come home.

The wind whirled dust around her, the horizon blackening with clouds that now swept toward her.

She had to turn back. She'd been foolish to ride this far out so late in the day, let alone with a storm coming.

Even if she took off now she would never reach the ranch before the weather hit. Yet she still didn't move.

She couldn't get the image of what she'd seen out of her mind. Her mother and another man. She felt sick at the memory of the man she'd seen leaving her mother's house by the back door.

She shivered. The temperature was dropping rapidly. She had to turn back now. She'd been so upset that she'd ridden off dressed only in jeans and a T-shirt, and there was no shelter between here and the ranch.

A storm this time of year could be deadly for anyone without shelter. Turning her horse, she bent her head against the wind as the rainstorm moved in.

A low moan filled the air. She brought her horse up short again and listened. Another low, agonizing moan rose on the wind. She turned back to listen. The sound seemed to be coming from the ravine below her.

A gust of wind kicked up dust, whirling it around her. She bent her head against the grit that burned her eyes as she swung down from her horse and stepped to the edge of the steep ravine.

Shielding her eyes, she peered down. Far below, along a wide rocky ledge, stood a thick stand of giant junipers. As the wind whipped down the steep slope, the branches parted and—

There was something there, deep in the trees. She saw the glint of metal in the dull light and what could have been a scrap of clothing.

Goose bumps rose on her arms as she heard the low moan again. Someone was down there.

The first few drops of rain slashed down, cold and wet as they soaked instantly into her clothing. She barely noticed as the air filled with another moan. She caught sight of movement. From behind the thick nest of junipers, a scrap of faded red fabric flapped in the wind.

"Hello!" she called, the wind picking up her words and hurling them across the wide ravine.

No answer.

Common sense told her to head toward the ranch before the weather got any worse. Eve Bailey was no stranger to the risk of living in such an isolated, unpopulated part of the state. She'd been born and raised only miles from here. She knew how quickly a storm could come in.

This part of Montana was famous for extreme temperature changes that could occur from within hours to a matter of minutes. It was hard country in which to survive. Five generations of Baileys would attest to that.

But if there was someone down there, someone injured, she couldn't just leave them.

"Hello!" she called again, and was answered by that same low, agonizing moan. Below her, the scrap of red cloth fluttered in the wind and, beside it, what definitely appeared to be metal glittered. What was down there?

A gust of wind howled past, and another low moan rose from the trees. She glanced back at the ominous clouds, then down into the vertical-sided ravine as she debated what to do.

She was going to have to go down there—and on foot. It was one thing to risk her own neck, but there was no way she was going to risk her horse's.

The ravine was a sheer drop at the top, widening as it fell to the ledge and growing steeper again as it dropped to the old riverbed far below. This end of Fort Peck Reservoir was dry from years of drought, the water having receded miles down this canyon.

Across the chasm the mountains were dark with pines. This side was nothing but eroded earth and a few stands of wind-warped junipers hanging on for dear life.

Eve loosely tied her horse to a tall sage. If she didn't get back before the storm hit, she didn't want her mare being struck by lightning. Better to let the horse get to lower ground just in case, even though it meant she'd have to find the mare to get home.

From experience she knew the soil into the ravine would be soft and unstable. But she hadn't expected it to give under her weight the way it did. The top layer of dirt and shale began to avalanche downward, taking it with her from her first step off.

She slid, descending too fast, first on her feet, then on her jean-clad bottom. She dug in her heels, but it didn't slow her down, let alone stop her. As she barreled toward the ledge, she realized with growing concern that if the junipers didn't stop her, then she was headed for the bottom of the ravine.

The eerie sound again filled the air. The wind and rain chilled her to the bone as she slid at breakneck speed toward the sound. She swept past an outcropping of rock and grabbed hold of a jutting rock. But she couldn't hold on.

The rough rock scraped off her skin, now painful and bleeding, but the attempt had slowed her down a little. Now if the junipers would just stop her—

That's when she saw the break in the rock ledge.

While the ledge ran across the ravine, a part of it had slid out and was now funnel shaped. Eve was heading right for the break in the rocks.

Just before the ledge, she grabbed for the thickest juniper limb she could reach and hung on. The bark tore off more skin from her already bloody palm as her hand slid along it and finally caught. The pain was excruciating.

Worse, her momentum swung her around the branch and smacked her hard into another thick trunk, but she was finally stopped. She took a ragged breath, exhaling on a sob of pain, relief and fear as she crouched on the ledge and tried to get herself under control.

Trembling from the cold and the fall down the ravine, she pulled herself up by one of the branches. She'd banged her ankle on a loose rock at the base of the junipers. It ached, but she was just thankful that it wasn't broken as she stood, clinging to the branch, and looked down.

She'd never liked heights. She swayed, sick to her stomach as she saw how the ground dropped vertically to a huge pile of rocks in the river bottom far below.

Her legs were trembling, her body aching, hands bleeding and scraped, but her feet were on solid ground.

A jagged flash of lightning split the sky overhead, followed quickly by a reverberating boom of thunder.

Through the now-pouring rain, Eve looked back up the steep slope she'd just plunged down. No chance of getting out that way. She felt sick to her stomach because she had no idea how she was going to get herself out of here, let alone anyone else.

"Hello?" she called out.

No answer.

"Is anyone down here?" she called again.

She listened. Nothing but the sound of the rain on the rocks at her feet.

She couldn't see the scrap of red cloth. Nor whatever had appeared to glint like metal from the top of the ravine. The junipers grew so thick she couldn't see into them or around them. Nor was she sure she could get past them the way they crowded the ledge.

The wind howled down the ravine as the sky darkened and the brunt of the storm settled in, the rain turning to sleet. From deep in the trees came the eerie low moan.

Chilled to the bone, Eve edged along the rock ledge, clinging to branches to keep from falling as she moved toward the sound. The sleet fell harder, the wind blowing it horizontally across the ravine.

She hadn't gone but a few yards when she heard a faint flapping sound—the cloth she'd seen from the top of the ravine! She moved toward the sound and saw the strap of faded red fabric, the edges frayed and ragged. Past the cloth, dented and dusty metal gleamed dully in the cloud-obscured light.

Her mouth went dry, her pulse its own thunder in her ears, as she saw what was left of a small single-engine airplane. With a shock, she realized the crashed plane had to have been there for years. One wing was buried in the soft dirt of the ravine, the rest of the plane completely hidden by the junipers as if the trees had conspired to conceal it.

The moan startled her as the wind rushed over the weathered metal surface of the plane.

It had only been the wind.

She clung to a juniper branch as the storm increased

in intensity, lightning slicing down through the canyon, thunder echoing in earsplitting explosions over her head. Water streamed over the rock ledge, dark and slick with muddy soil.

She let out a sob of despair. She wouldn't be getting out of here anytime soon. Even if she could find a way off the rock ledge, it would be slippery now, the soil even more unstable.

Holding a branch back out of her way, she moved to the edge of the cockpit and used her sleeve to wipe the dirty wet film from the side of the glass canopy.

Cupping her hand over her eyes, she peered inside.

Eve reared back, flailing to keep from falling off the ledge, as her startled shriek echoed across the ravine.

She was shaking so hard she could hardly hold on to the juniper branch as rain and sleet thumped the canopy and the wind wailed over what was left of the plane.

She closed her eyes, fighting to erase the image from her mind, the macabre scene inside the plane chilling her more than the storm.

The pilot's seat was empty, and the strip of torn red cloth caught in the canopy was now flapping in the growing wind. The seat next to it was also empty, but there was a dark stain on the fabric.

The passenger in the back hadn't been so lucky. Time and the elements had turned the corpse to little more than a mummified skeleton, the dried skin shrunken down over the facial bones, the eyes hollow sockets staring out at her.

Not even that was as shocking as what she'd seen sticking out of the corpse's chest—the handle of a hunting knife, grayed from the years, the blade wedged between the dead man's ribs.

Chapter 2

Sheriff Carter Jackson had a theory about bad luck. He'd decided that some men attracted it like stink on a dog. At least that had been the case with him.

His luck had gone straight south the day he found Deena Turner curled up and waiting for him in his bed. He'd been more than flattered. Hell, Deena had been the most popular girl in high school, sexy and beautiful, the girl every red-blooded male in Whitehorse, Montana, wanted to find waiting for him in his bed.

So Carter had done what any dumb nineteen-year-old would do. He'd thanked his lucky stars, never suspecting that the woman was about to take him to hell and back.

Finding Deena in his bed had only been the beginning of a string of mistakes over the next twelve years that culminated in Deena lying about being pregnant and the two of them running off and getting married.

It had been hard at first to admit he'd made a mistake marrying her. He'd seen marriage as forever and divorce as failure. So he'd hung in. Right up until he caught Deena in bed with his best friend.

That had been two years ago. Since then he'd gone through a long, drawn-out, painful divorce. Painful because he felt guilty that it hurt more losing his best friend than it did ending it for good with Deena.

But that was the problem. It hadn't ended for good with Deena. Two weeks ago, she'd decided she wanted him back and that she would do anything to make that happen.

And she meant anything.

He pulled up in front of the house he and Deena had shared during their marriage. It was too early in the morning for this, but he just wanted to get it over with. Weighed down with dread, he climbed out of his patrol car, trying to remember a time when he'd looked forward to seeing Deena in the morning.

As he walked up the cracked sidewalk, he told himself this would be the last time. No matter what.

He grimaced at the thought, remembering how many times he'd left during their twelve years of marriage only to go back out of guilt or a sense of obligation. No wonder Deena just assumed he would always come back to her. He always had.

She opened the door to his knock almost as if she'd been expecting him. After what she'd left at his office for him, he didn't doubt she was.

She was wearing one of his old T-shirts and, from what he could tell, little else. His once-favorite scent floated around her. Her blond hair was pulled up, loose tendrils framing her pretty face.

"Hello, Carter," she said in that sultry voice, the one that had once been his undoing. "I had a feeling you'd be by this morning." She shoved open the door a little wider and gave him "the look." Boy, did he know that look.

Without a word, he reached into his pocket and took out the plain white envelope with her name and address neatly typed on it and handed it to her.

She took it, her smile slipping a little. "Something for me? You shouldn't have."

No, he thought, you shouldn't have. All the surprise visits at work and at his house, the presents, the constant phone calls, the urgent messages. The more he'd tried to get her to stop, the worse she had become.

He waited as she opened the envelope, resting his hand on the butt of the weapon at his hip.

Her eyes widened as she took out the legal form and read enough that, when she spoke, her sultry voice was long gone. "What the hell is this?"

"It's a restraining order. From this time forward you are not to contact me, send me any more letters or packages or come within one-hundred-and-fifty feet of me."

She narrowed her eyes at him. "We live in White-horse, Montana, you dumb bastard. The whole town is only a hundred and fifty feet long."

"If you break the restraining order you will be arrested," he said, hating that it had come to this.

He tipped his hat and turned his back to her as he headed for his vehicle, hoping she didn't have a gun, because he was pretty sure she'd have no compunction about shooting him in the back.

"You just made the biggest mistake of your life, Carter Jackson!" she yelled after him. "You're going to regret this as long as you live, you smug son of a bitch. If you think you can just walk away from me—"

The slamming of his patrol-car door thankfully cut off the rest of her words. This was not the morning to tempt him into arresting her for threatening an officer of the law.

It had taken him years, but he finally understood Deena. She only wanted what she couldn't have. His allure was that he hadn't been available. Just before he found her in his bed, he'd begun dating a neighboring ranch girl he'd known all his life, a girl he was getting serious with.

And that, he knew now, was why Deena had thrown herself at him. Deena had always been jealous of Eve Bailey and became worse after he and Deena married. Even the mention of Eve's name would set Deena off. He'd never understood her jealousy, especially since Eve had left the area right after high school and hadn't come back.

Until two weeks ago. Just about the time Deena decided she was going to get him back, come hell or high water.

As Carter drove away, he didn't look in his ex's direction, although out of the corner of his eye he saw that she'd come down the sidewalk in her bare feet and was now waving the restraining order and yelling obscenities at him.

"Good-bye, Deena," he said, hoping his luck was about to change. Maybe she would meet an unavailable long-haul trucker who'd take her far, far away.

As he drove back toward his office in the large three-story brick county courthouse, his radio squawked.

"Lila Bailey just called," the dispatcher told him.

"She's worried about her daughter. Says they had a big storm down that way last night. Her daughter apparently went for a horseback ride yesterday evening and didn't return home last night."

"Which daughter?" Carter asked, his heart kicking up a beat.

"Eve Bailey."

The way his luck was going, of course it would be Eve. He'd grown up around the Bailey girls. Eve was hands-down the most headstrong of the three. And that was saying a lot. But she was also the most capable. She knew that country south of town. If anyone could survive a night out there, even in a bad storm, it was Eve.

"Lila said one of Eve's sisters saw her ride out yesterday evening toward the Breaks. Eve is staying in her grandmother's old house down the road from her folks' place so no one knew she hadn't returned until her horse came back this morning without her."

Carter rubbed the back of his neck. There was nothing south of the Bailey ranch but miles and miles of Missouri Breaks badlands. Searching for Eve would be like looking for a needle in a haystack. "Tell Lila I'm on my way."

It was a slow news day at the Milk River Examiner office. Glen Whitaker had come in early to work on a feature story he was writing about the couple who'd just bought the hardware store. This was news, since the population of the county had been dropping steadily for years now. While parts of Montana were growing like crazy, the towns along the Hi-Line were losing residents to more prosperous places.

Glen ran a hand over his buzz-cut blond hair and glanced out his office window past the park to the railroad tracks. A coal train was rumbling past. His phone rang. He let it ring a couple more times as he waited for the train to pass and the noise level to drop. "Hello."

"One of the Bailey girls is missing."

Glen groaned to himself as he recognized the voice of the worst gossip in the county. From the moment he took the job as reporter at the Milk River Examiner, Arlene Evans had been feeding him information as if she was Deep Throat.

"Missing?" Most of Arlene's "leads" turned out to either be erroneous or the type of news he wasn't allowed to print. He'd ended up at Whitehorse after working for several larger papers where he'd made the mistake of printing things he shouldn't have.

He didn't want to lose his job over some small-town gossip. But then again, he had printer's ink in his veins. Working for a weekly newspaper, all he wrote about were church socials and town-council meetings.

Glen Whitaker was ready for a good story. "Which Bailey girl?"

"Eve Bailey. I just talked to Lila, her mother, and she said Eve rode out yesterday afternoon," Arlene said with her usual relish. "Her horse came back this morning without her."

Like the Baileys, Arlene lived south of Whitehorse.

The first settlement of Whitehorse had been nearer the Missouri River. But when the railroad came through, the town migrated five miles north, taking the name with it.

The original settlement of Whitehorse was now little more than a ghost town except for a handful of ranches and a few of the original remaining buildings. It was locally referred to as Old Town.

The people who lived there were a close-knit bunch to the point of being clannish. They did for their own, seldom needing any help and definitely not interested in any publicity when something bad happened.

But this could turn out to be just the story Glen had been waiting for—if Eve Bailey didn't turn up alive and well.

Glen already had a headline in mind: Whitehorse Woman Lost In The Breaks, No Body Found.

"Her horse came back without her, so she's stranded out there?"

Arlene clucked her tongue, her voice dropping conspiratorially. "Little chance of surviving that storm on foot. No shelter out there. And it got really cold last night."

Whitehorse Woman's Body Found Frozen.

Unfortunately, it was June and while it could snow in the Breaks any month of the year, the chances were good she hadn't frozen to death. But hypothermia was a real possibility.

The problem was Glen knew about the Bailey girls, as they were called, although they were now young women. Attractive, but headstrong and capable. With his luck, Eve Bailey would survive. No heartrending story here.

He could picture Eve Bailey, so different from her sisters, who were blond with blue eyes. Eve had long dark hair and the blackest eyes he'd ever seen. But then he'd always been attracted to brunettes rather than blondes.

"Everyone is meeting over at the community center," Arlene was saying in her excited high voice. "The women are putting together a potluck for the search party. It's sewing day. We have to finish a quilt for Maddie Cavanaugh's engagement to my son. With Pearl in the hospital with pneumonia we're behind on the quilting. You know quilts are a tradition down here."

He groaned inwardly. "I know." Arlene had tried to get him to do a story on the Whitehorse Sewing Circle ever since he'd taken the reporter job. The group of women met most mornings at the community center and had for years. He suspected it was where Arlene picked up most of her gossip.

"I have to go. My pies are ready to come out of the oven," Arlene said.

"Are you making one of your coconut-custard pies?" Glen asked hopefully. Arlene had taken a blue ribbon last year at the Phillips County Fair with her coconut-custard pie—and he'd been one of the judges.

"I always make the coconut-custard when there's trouble," Arlene said. "This could be your biggest story of the year."

Arlene was forever hoping to be the source of his biggest story of the year. "My daughter Violet is helping me," she said, shifting gears. "Did I tell you she's quite the cook?"

Along with dispensing gossip, quilting and pie baking, Arlene Evans also worked at matchmaking, although she'd had little luck getting her thirtysomething daughter, Violet, married off. From what Glen had heard Arlene had been trying to marry off Violet since she was a teenager.

The older Violet got, the more desperate Arlene had become. She considered it a flaw in her if her daughter was husbandless.

"Save me a piece of pie," he said as he grabbed his camera and notebook, figuring it would probably be a waste of gas, time and energy. He was sure that by the time he reached Whitehorse, Eve Bailey would have been found and there would be nothing more than a brief story about her harrowing night out in the storm.

For a piece of Arlene's coconut-custard pie he could even feign interest in her daughter.

By the time Sheriff Carter Jackson picked up his roping horse and trailer from his brother's place and reached the Old Town Whitehorse Community Center, there were a dozen pickups and horse trailers parked in front.

He pulled into the lot, noticing that all of the trucks and horse trailers were covered in the gray gumbo mud that made unpaved roads in this part of the state impassable after a rainstorm.

Fortunately, the sun had come out this morning and had dried at least the top layer of soil because it appeared everyone had made it.

He'd always been proud that he was from Old Town and was sorry his family was no longer part of this isolated community. No matter how they were getting along at the time, the residents pulled together when there was trouble like a large extended family.

As he pushed open the door of the community center, he spotted Titus Cavanaugh at the center of a group of men. Titus had a topographical map stretched out on one of the women's sewing tables and was going over it with the other male residents.

"Here's the sheriff now," resident Errol Wilson announced as Carter walked toward them.

"We're putting together a search party," said the elderly Cavanaugh, who was unmistakably in charge. If Old Town had been an incorporated town, Titus would have been mayor. He led the church services at the community center every Sunday, organized the Fourth of July picnic and somehow managed to be the most liked and respected man in the county, hell, most of the state.

His was one of the first families in the area. His grandmother had started the Whitehorse Sewing Circle and never missed a day until her death. Titus's wife Pearl was just as dedicated to the group, although Carter didn't see her. He'd heard Pearl was in the hospital with pneumonia. She'd always made sure that every newborn got a quilt, as well as every newlywed. It had been an Old Town tradition for as long as anyone could remember.

"Give me a minute," Carter said to Titus. "I'd like to talk to Eve's family before we head out."

He gathered the Bailey women in a small room at the back of the community center and closed the door. Lila Bailey was a tall, stern-looking woman with long gray-blond hair she kept in a knot at the nape of her neck. At one time, she'd been beautiful. There was still a ghost of that beauty in her face.

With her were her daughters, McKenna and Faith, both home from college. Chester Bailey, Lila's husband, was living in Whitehorse, working for the Dehy in Saco. Apparently, he hadn't arrived yet.

"Any idea where Eve was headed?" Carter asked. The women looked to McKenna, the second oldest Bailey sister.

"I was just coming home when I saw her ride out late yesterday afternoon," McKenna said, and glanced toward her mother.

Carter couldn't miss the look that passed between the two women. "Was that unusual for her? To take a horseback ride late in the afternoon with a storm coming in?"

"Eve is a strong-minded woman," Lila said. "More

than capable of taking care of herself. Usually." The last word was said quietly as Lila looked to the floor.

"Where does she generally ride?" he asked the sisters.

Both shrugged. "Depending what kind of mood she's in, she rides toward the Breaks," McKenna said.

"What kind of mood was she in yesterday afternoon?" Carter asked, watching Lila's face.

Faith made a derisive sound. "Eve's often in a lousy mood." Lila shot her a warning look. "Well, it's true."

Faith and McKenna were in their early twenties. Eve was the oldest at thirty-two.

Lila apparently hadn't expected to have any more children after Eve. Both McKenna and Faith had been surprises—at least according to Old Whitehorse gossip. The local scuttlebutt was that Lila's husband, Chester, had been heartbroken they'd never had a son and their marriage strained to the point of breaking.

But Chester had only recently moved out of the house, taking a job in Saco. While as far as Carter knew the couple was still married, word was that Chester hardly ever came home. His daughters visited him up in Whitehorse.

One of the joys of small-town living: everyone knew everyone else's business, Carter thought.

"You should tell him," McKenna said to her mother in a hushed whisper.

The look Lila gave her daughter could have cut glass. "He's not interested in family matters, McKenna."

"On the contrary, I'm interested in Eve's state of mind when she took off yesterday," Carter said, looking from McKenna to her mother.

"It was nothing," Lila said. "Just a disagreement. Why are we standing around talking? Eve could be injured.

You should be out looking for her." She shot Carter a look that said she wasn't saying anything more about her disagreement with her oldest daughter. "Now if you'll excuse me I have to see to the potluck. Everything needs to be ready for when the men return with my daughter."

She left the room, Faith looking after her, plainly curious about what was going on between her mother and sister.

"If you wouldn't mind," Carter said. "I'd like a word with McKenna alone."

Faith shrugged and left, but with obvious reluctance. When the door closed behind her, Carter asked McKenna, "Why don't you tell me about the disagreement your mother and sister had yesterday and let me decide if it's relevant."

"You mean what they were arguing about? I don't know. I heard them yelling at each other when I came home. Eve stormed out to the barn, riding off a few minutes later. When I asked Mother what was going on, she said it was just Eve being dramatic."

He'd seen Eve angry on more than one occasion, but he'd never thought of her as the dramatic type. Deena on the other hand... "The last time you saw your sister, how was she dressed?"

McKenna shrugged. "Jeans, boots, a T-shirt. I don't think she took a jacket. It was pretty hot when she left."

"What color T-shirt?" he asked, attempting to keep his growing concern from his voice. Eve hadn't been dressed for a night out in the weather—especially last night with that storm that had blown through. For some reason, she'd taken off upset, without even a jacket, and that alone he knew could have cost her her life.

"Light blue T-shirt," McKenna said, sounding close

to tears as if realizing that her sister might be in serious trouble.

"Don't worry, we'll find her," Carter said, shocked to think that after all these years he would be seeing Eve Bailey again. He just hoped to hell he'd find her alive. But as he joined the search party, he feared they were now looking for a body.

Chapter 3

Lila Bailey busied herself arranging the food as it arrived from local residents. She had to keep busy or she knew she would lose her mind. The thought shook her, considering that her mother, Nina Mae, had literally lost hers and was now in the nursing home in Whitehorse.

The only way Lila could cope was not to allow herself even the thought that her oldest daughter wasn't coming back. Eve could take care of herself. Eve was the strong one. Eve was a survivor. Even as upset as she'd been yesterday.

Lila had to believe that. If she gave in to doubts, she knew she wouldn't be able to hold herself together and for Lila, losing control had always been her greatest fear.

More food arrived. She arranged it on the extra tables the men had set up for her. Everyone pitched in when needed. She recalled with shame how the town had offered help when they heard Chester had left her.

Her face flamed at the pity she'd seen in their faces. No one believed Chester would be back. And she was sure they'd all speculated on why Chester had left her.

Well, let their tongues wag. She had turned down their help. She'd pay hell before she'd take their pity. She'd show them all. Lila Cross Bailey didn't need anyone. Never had.

Tears sprang to her eyes. She furtively wiped them away. The last thing she'd do was let one person in this community see her cry.

Not that there was much left. There were only a half-dozen houses still standing, most of them empty, in what had once been a thriving homestead town a hundred years ago.

Amid the weeds, abandoned houses and what was left of the foundations of homes long gone was Titus and Pearl Cavanaugh's big white three-story house at the far end of the street. Next to it was the smaller house where Titus's mother, Bertie, had lived before she'd become so sick she had to go into Whitehorse to the nursing home.

A couple of blocks behind the community center and near the creek stood the old abandoned Cherry house, which kids still said was haunted. Lila was eleven when she heard what sounded like a baby crying in the empty old Victorian house. She still got goose bumps when she thought about it.

At the opposite end of town was Geraldine Shaw's clapboard house, a large red barn behind it.

Overlooking the town was the Whitehorse Cemetery, where residents had been buried from the time the original homesteaders settled here. The most recent grave belonged to Abigail Ames, Pearl Cavanaugh's mother.

Next to the cemetery was the fairgrounds where community summer events took place.

As Lila looked up, a tumbleweed cartwheeled across Main Street. Like many small towns across eastern Montana, both Old Town and Whitehorse were dying, the young people leaving, the old people heading for the cemetery on the hill.

The young people left for better jobs or to go to school and never return, glad to have escaped the hard life of farming or ranching such austere county.

Lila knew that Faith and McKenna had only come home for the summer because they'd heard that their father had moved out. She'd insisted they take jobs in Whitehorse to keep them out of her hair and make it clear that she didn't need their help.

Not that there was much in Whitehorse to the north. It had a grocery, a newspaper, several banks, a handful of churches and a hardware store and lumberyard. The bowling alley had burned down but the old-timey theater was still open, showing one new movie three days a week.

Like other ranchers from around the county, Lila went into Whitehorse for supplies and to stop by the nursing home to see her mother.

Why Eve had come back was a mystery to most everyone but Lila. Eve moved into her grandmother's house up the road and, from all appearances, seemed to be staying, which frightened Lila more than she wanted to admit.

As she gazed out the window, Lila knew it was just a matter of time before she'd be all alone in that big old rambling house with nothing but memories. And regrets.

"They'll find her," a deep male voice said behind her, making her jump.

She felt the skin on her neck prickle as she recognized the voice and realized he had her trapped in the corner between the long potluck table and the window.

Her back stiffened and she had to fix her expression before she turned around to face Errol Wilson.

"I know you must be worried, but we all know how strong Eve is," Errol said. He was a short, broad man with small dark eyes and a receding hairline of salt-and-pepper hair that stuck out from under his Western hat.

As his eyes locked with hers, Lila felt her skin crawl. She nodded, unable to speak, barely able to breathe. Normally, she made sure she kept her distance from Errol at these community gatherings, never letting him get her alone, even with other people around. But nothing about the past few days had been normal.

"Eve's a survivor," Errol continued, standing next to Lila but not looking at her. So close she knew that no one else in the room could hear him. If anyone looked this way, they would think he was inspecting the dishes that had been set out for the potluck.

"Like her mother," Errol added.

"Ready?" Frank Ross called to Errol. "You're going with Floyd Evans and the sheriff," Frank told Errol, and gave Lila a comforting nod before heading for the door.

Lila turned her back to Errol, but she could still feel him behind her, the scent of his aftershave making her stomach roil.

"Don't worry, Lila," Errol said. "We'll find your daughter and bring her back to you. Wouldn't let anything ever happen to her. Just like I'd hate to see anything happen to you."

She gripped the edge of the table, shaking violently with anger and fear and enough regret that she thought she might drown in it.

Please, God, let Eve be all right. Don't punish her for my mistakes. Give me a chance to make things right with her.

But even as she prayed it, Lila Bailey knew there was no way she could make any of this right with Eve.

Carter saddled up with the search party. After the storm, there would be no passable roads to the south. There were few roads to begin with. A couple of Jeep trails when the weather was good. One road that petered out a couple of miles out near his family's old place.

His father had sold out a while back. Carter's brother Cade hadn't had any interest in ranching and Deena had flat out refused to live on a ranch. She thought White-horse was the end of the earth as it was.

So his father had sold the homestead. Not that Loren Jackson had ever had any interest in ranching. He'd always leased the land. No, Loren had wanted to be a commercial pilot, but for some reason hadn't left Phillips County so he'd ended up crop dusting with his father, Ace Jackson.

That was until he'd up and decided to move to Florida.

Carter had never understood his father. Loren Jackson had always seemed...unfulfilled.

So it felt odd to be here and realize that the old place stood empty just up the road. The Cavanaughs had bought the land, but no one had a use for the house, so it had been boarded up.

Carter rode east to avoid seeing the place, going past Bailey property and the house where he'd heard Eve was

staying. One of the search party checked to make sure
Eve hadn't returned.

She hadn't. And McKenna had come along to get a
change of clothing for Eve to wear when they found her.
Then they all rode south, leaving behind farm and ranch
land for cactus and sagebrush.

Titus had divided the men into groups, each armed
with a two-way radio. Ward Shaw had brought along
a saddled extra horse for Eve to ride when they found
her. Everyone was optimistic they would find her alive.

Or at least they pretended to be.

The thunderstorm the night before had wiped out any
trace of her tracks, but her horse had returned this morning, leaving deep gouges in the wet gumbolike mud that
were easy to follow.

The sheriff rode with Errol Wilson and Floyd Evans.
The others fanned out, hoping to catch sight of Eve's
footprints since she would be on foot.

Although Carter had grown up here and known Errol
and Floyd all his life, the three rode in silence with little
to say to one another. Both men were older by at least
twenty-five years and while Errol and Floyd lived within
miles of each other, Carter had never known them to
be friends.

In fact, few people in and around Old Town partic-
ularly liked Errol Wilson. There was something about
the man that put Carter off, as well. Something behind
the man's dark eyes that seemed almost predatory. Errol
radiated a bitterness for which Carter had never known
the source.

As a boy, Carter remembered overhearing some of
the men talking about Errol. There was some concern
that Errol might be a Peeping Tom. Carter hadn't known

what that was at the time. And he'd never heard any more about it. He just figured that men like Errol Wilson generated those kind of stories because they didn't fit in.

Carter gave no more thought to either man as he rode. His mind was on Eve and the argument she'd had with her mother. What had sent Eve riding deep into the Breaks without food or water or proper clothing? Her horse coming back without her was a very bad sign. He was worried what they would find. If they managed to find her at all.

The sun moved across Montana's big sky, drying the mud, heating the air to dragon's breath. No breeze moved the air. Nothing stirred, but an occasional cricket in a clump of brush.

An hour later, Carter reined in as he lost Eve's horse's tracks in a rocky area. "Let's spread out. Holler when you pick up the tracks again," he told the two men.

Errol rode off to the west while Floyd went east, kicking up a bunch of antelope. Carter watched the antelope run across the horizon, disappearing as the land began to drop, funneling forward to the riverbed.

To the west Carter saw one of the other groups from the search party had stopped to clean the mud from their horses' hooves. A hawk soared overheard, picking up a thermal, and nearby a mule deer spooked, rising up from a rocky coulee, all big ears as it took off, kicking up clumps of dried earth. No sign of Eve Bailey.

Carter rode straight south to where the flat, high prairie broke into eroded fingers of land that dropped precariously to the river bottom. He kept to the higher ridges in hopes of seeing Eve's blue T-shirt. The problem was that too much of this land looked exactly the same. That made it extremely easy to get lost. During the storm, Eve could have gotten turned around. If she'd tried to walk out on foot last night she might be anywhere.

At one point, he stopped and realized he could no longer see either Errol or Floyd. He hoped to hell the search party didn't have to find them before the day was over.

He'd just reined in his horse on a narrow ridge, the sides falling dangerously toward the old river bottom when he caught sight of something light blue in the rocks far below him.

Reporter Glen Whitaker couldn't believe his timing. He made it to the Whitehorse Community Center just as Arlene Evans was unloading the pies from the front seat of her pickup.

"Let me help you with those," he said.

Arlene was a gangly woman with an elongated horsy face and laugh that was more donkey's bray. That alone would have put off most people, but there was also a nervous energy that at best made him jittery and at worse made the hair stand up on his arms.

"Violet, say hello to Glen," Arlene ordered.

"Hi, Glen," said a shy and bored voice behind him.

He turned to see Arlene's daughter, Violet.

While better looking than her mother, Violet was still plain to the point of pitiful. Next to her mother, Violet seemed almost catatonic. "Hey," he said.

He'd always suspected that Arlene fed off other people's energy because, like her daughter, Glen found that after a matter of minutes around Arlene he barely had enough energy to escape. And right now escape was exactly what he wanted to do.

"Violet and I can get the pies if you'll open the front door," Arlene said, handing off a pie to her daughter then picking up another before kicking the pickup door shut in one smooth movement.

He had to almost run to get the community center door open before Arlene. They both had to wait for Violet, who moved like sludge.

"Violet, why don't you get Glen a piece of the coconut-custard right away," Arlene said. "He looks like he could use it."

Violet nodded as she wandered off to do as she'd been told. Already trained to obey, she'd make someone the perfect wife, Glen thought. Just not him. At forty, he'd never married. His mother said it was because she'd spoiled him.

"Any news on Eve Bailey?" he asked.

"Apparently not," Arlene said, as she shot a look at the somber group of women waiting in the community center.

All the women looked in his direction, then went back to visiting among themselves or occupying themselves with the needlework in their laps. Glen had never understood it. He was nice enough looking, but for some reason people didn't seem to pay any attention to him.

Feeling like the invisible man, he drew out his notebook and pen as he and Arlene took a seat in a quiet corner and waited for Violet to bring the pie.

"It's a shame," Arlene was saying in a hushed voice so the others couldn't hear. "She has been through so much and now this."

"Eve?" Glen asked, wondering what was keeping Violet.

"Lila," Arlene whispered, glancing in the woman's direction. Lila was cleaning the sink near the back door, stopping periodically to look out, as if she hoped to see her daughter.

Glen wasn't interested in Lila Bailey. No story there.

"Her husband left her, you know. Oh, she tells everyone he moved into Whitehorse to be closer to his job, but we all know the truth."

Arlene took a breath and Glen jumped in, hoping to get some background material, "So what brought Eve Bailey back here?" He watched Arlene shift gears. Apparently she was just getting warmed up on the Lila and Chester Bailey story.

"A man," Arlene said flatly. "It's the only thing that brings a woman her age back to the ranch. You know she's thirty-two. Just two years younger than my Violet."

An old maid in Arlene's eyes.

"I heard she became an interior designer." Arlene lifted a brow as if to say what a waste of time and education that was. "You can bet some man broke her heart and she came running home with her tail tucked between her legs."

Glen wrote on his notepad a new headline: Jilted, Whitehorse Woman Returns Home Only To Die Alone In Missouri Breaks.

Violet slid a plate with a large piece of coconut-custard pie in front of him and sank into a chair as if the chore had spent all of her energy.

He glanced at her as he picked up the fork. "Thanks." She stared back with large, liquid, colorless eyes, but with just enough expectation in them to make him nervous. It hit him then that she would want to get married even more than her mother wanted her to. Marriage would be the only way to make her mother stop trying to hoist her off on men. Any man.

As he took a bite of pie, he noticed Arlene had stopped talking and was staring toward the front door.

A man in his early thirties who Glen had never seen before stood in the doorway as if looking for someone but not seeing them, turned and left, letting the door close behind him.

"Who was that?" Glen asked, seeing Arlene's obvious interest.

"The fella who's renting the old McAllister place," Arlene whispered. "Bridger Duvall. Sounds like the name of an actor. Or a name he just made up. No one knows anything about him. Or why he rented that old farmhouse, since he hasn't shown any interest in raising a thing. He was downright rude when Violet and I went out there to welcome him to the area."

Glen could well imagine what Arlene's welcome visit was all about—and no doubt the man had, as well, the moment he laid eyes on Violet.

"I wonder," Arlene said slowly. "You know he showed up about the same time Eve returned to town." Her eyes widened. "What if he's the man who broke Eve Bailey's heart?"

And this, Glen thought, was how rumors got started.

Sheriff Carter Jackson felt his breath catch in his throat as he stared down into the ravine. The spot of light blue hadn't moved and, from this angle, he couldn't tell what it was but he had a bad feeling it was Eve Bailey.

He raised his binoculars. The light blue moved. He felt his heart lift like helium. Eve Bailey rose from where she'd been almost hidden in the rocks. He watched her work her way slowly up the slope head down, oblivious to him standing high above her. She climbed the rocks with fluid if exhausted movements.

Carter found himself grinning, overjoyed that she was all right, glad he would be able to take good news back to the Whitehorse Community Center.

Now that he knew she was alive, though, he wanted to wring her neck. What the hell had she been thinking riding out like that yesterday afternoon? Maybe more to the point, what was she doing down in that ravine to begin with?

"I've found her," he said into the two-way radio. "She looks like she's all right. I'm going down to get her out. Bring the horse to the top of the ravine." He gave a reading from his GPS.

Titus Cavanaugh came back over the radio an instant later, sounding equally relieved. "We're not far from you. Glad to hear the good news."

Carter dismounted and, taking his pack with his rescue gear, started to work his way down the rocky slope. His earlier exhilaration at seeing that she was alive was dampened at the thought of what her reaction would be to seeing him. It had been years, but he doubted she would have forgotten the way things had ended between them.

Eve had taken off for college right after high school graduation and he hadn't seen her since. He knew she'd come back for holidays to see her parents and sisters, but she'd made a point of avoiding him. And since he lived in Whitehorse, he'd had no reason to go out of his way to see her.

In fact, the way even the mention of Eve set Deena off, he'd stayed as far away as he could from Old Town—and Eve Bailey.

He was pretty sure Eve hated him. Not that he could blame her. Or maybe she hadn't given him a thought since the day she left.

He wished he could say the same.

As he cut off her ascent up the rocky ravine, he realized he was nervous about seeing her. This was crazy. Hell, it had been years. She'd probably forgotten that night in the front seat of his old Chevy pickup behind her parents' barn.

Just then she looked up and he knew Eve hadn't forgotten—or forgiven him.

Chapter 4

Eve Bailey looked up at the sound of small loose rocks cascading down the side of the ravine. For a moment, she was blinded by the sun and thought she had imagined the dark silhouette of a man working his way down the slope toward her.

But she would have recognized Sheriff Carter Jackson just by the way he moved even if she hadn't seen the glint of the star on his uniform shirt. Her breath caught at the sight of him. Surprise, then that old chest-aching pain kicked in before she could vanquish it with anger.

"Stay there," he called down to her in a deep voice that had once done more than made her poor heart pitter-patter.

She defied her heart to beat even a second faster at the sound of his voice as she stopped to get control of herself. Wasn't that just her luck? Rescued by the one person on earth she'd never wanted to lay eyes on again.

She leaned against one of the large rocks, not wanting to admit how glad she was to see another human being, though. She felt weak with relief. That and hunger and dehydration and exhaustion. She hadn't let herself even consider what she would do once she reached the top of the ravine. She'd have had miles more to walk and, the truth was, she would have never made it, and she knew it.

She wanted to sit down and cry, she was so relieved. But why did her rescuer have to be Carter Jackson? When she'd come home, she'd known she would see him eventually. Whitehorse was too small for her not to run into him.

But the last thing she wanted was for him to see her like this, at her most vulnerable. With Carter, she needed all her defenses, and right now she couldn't have felt more defenseless.

She pushed off the rock, determined not to show any weakness as she started to climb again.

Moving had kept her alive. She was cold and hurt and barely able to keep going. But she'd known that with her clothing still damp, if she'd stopped she would have died. It had been a realistic fear given the temperature earlier this morning and the fact that even with the sun now blazing down, she couldn't seem to get warm.

But there was another reason she'd kept moving. She didn't want to think about what she'd discovered down in the ravine. She shivered at the memory of what she'd had to do to survive. That was her, Eve Bailey, the survivor. Isn't that what she'd heard her whole life? Just like her mother, she thought bitterly.

The climb down the cliff from the plane had been harrowing. She'd fallen more than once, her hands raw, her left ankle killing her.

All she'd known was that she had to find a way down, then back up out of the Breaks no matter how long it took. Given that the crashed plane had apparently never been discovered, she'd figured there was little chance of anyone finding her unless she got off that rock ledge.

She'd been sure it would be days before anyone even realized she was missing, since she lived alone and doubted anyone had seen her ride out yesterday afternoon. Mostly, she worried about her horse. The mare would have gotten out of the storm, but where was she now? Eve loved that horse and couldn't bear it if something had happened to her.

A shadow fell over her. She stopped climbing and looked up, having lost track of time again.

Sheriff Carter Jackson stood on the rocks just above her, his hand outstretched. She didn't look at his face as she reluctantly took his hand and let him pull her up onto a large flat rock, too tired to protest. Her legs gave out and she sat down hard, no longer strong enough to even pretend she was tougher than she was.

Without a word, Carter slipped off his backpack and, opening it, handed her a bottle of water.

"Have you seen my horse? Is she all right?" Eve asked before taking a drink, a catch in her throat.

"Your horse is fine. She returned to the ranch this morning. That's what started the search for you."

"Just like Lassie," she said, near tears, and took a long gulp of the water to hide her relief.

"Just like Lassie," he said with a smile. "Her tracks led us to you."

She kept her focus on the water bottle, furious that all it took to transport her back to their senior year in high school was his smile. She could feel him studying her, his look gentle, concerned. Just as he'd been the night he took her virginity in his old pickup behind her family's barn.

Her hands were shaking, legs trembling, the past twenty-four hours taking their toll. Behind her eyes, she could feel tears welling up. She hurt all over, some of those bruises from years ago and her last encounter with Carter Jackson.

She bit her lip and took another drink as she heard him dig in his pack again. Was he thinking about that night in his pickup? More than likely he was thinking what a fool she'd been to ride so far without water or food, let alone proper clothing.

"Here," he said, and handed her a candy bar.

She took the candy, struggling with the wrapper, her fingers refusing to work properly.

Covering her with his shadow, Carter leaned down to take the candy bar from her, ripped the paper open and handed the bar back to her without a word.

"Thanks." She'd known Carter Jackson all of her life. They'd gone to the same one-room schoolhouse through elementary school before being bused into Whitehorse for high school.

There'd been something between them from the moment she'd punched him in the nose in grade-school recess to the first time he'd kissed her, something she'd mistaken for love long before she'd given herself to him in his old Chevy pickup.

She brushed a lock of hair back from her face, knowing she must look a mess. "Go on and say it. I know you're dying to. I was an idiot for riding this far out yesterday without any provisions."

"You don't need a lecture," he said quietly. "You've been through enough."

So true, she thought, studying him. Problem was he had no idea what she'd been through. Not years ago when he dumped her for Deena Turner—certainly not last night.

Carter said nothing as he reached into the pack again and this time took out a pair of rolled-up jeans, a flannel shirt and jacket. "McKenna got these for you from your house."

She stared at his handsome face for a moment, the devoured candy bar like a lump in her stomach. Tears burned her eyes. She'd been so scared, so afraid she'd never get back to the ranch, never see the people she cared about again that she hadn't realized how much she'd scared her family and neighbors. Of course, they would be worried sick about her.

If it had been anyone but Carter who'd found her, she would have wept with joy at being rescued. But she couldn't break down, not with Carter—and trying not to cry had left her raw with emotion.

She took the dry clothing, desperately needing to get moving before she couldn't anymore. The sugar from the candy bar was trying to jump-start her dog-tired body, but knowing that she no longer had to push herself to get home again all she wanted to do was curl up on a warm rock and sleep for a week.

"The…underwear is in the jacket pocket," Carter said, sounding almost shy as he turned his back to let her change.

She couldn't help but remember the last time he'd handed her her clothes. She'd been naked then, though, and even more vulnerable than she was now.

The warm, dry clothing felt wonderful, although it took her a while to get her wet clothes off, her movements awkward and slow. She realized how close she'd been to hypothermia, how close she'd been to dying if she'd stopped even to rest too long earlier.

As she pulled on the jacket, she hugged herself, feeling warmer for the first time in what seemed like days.

With a start she remembered what she'd left in the pocket of her wet jeans. Quickly she checked to make sure Carter's back was still turned before she reached into the front pocket of her dirty torn jeans and, with shaking fingers, transferred the rhinestone pin she'd found in the plane to her clean jeans pocket before saying, "All done."

He turned to look at her. "Better?"

She nodded, fearing he could see the guilt written all over her face. But maybe he didn't know her as well as she knew him. Maybe he never had.

He handed her another bottle of water, picking up the empty one from where she'd placed it on a rock and putting it back into his pack.

She opened the cap and took a long drink, trying to get control of her emotions. She could feel the weight of her old feelings for him heavy in her stomach. Just as she could feel the sharp edges of the rhinestones poking her upper thigh, prodding her conscience.

She dug for anger to steady herself, recalling the morning she reached school to find out that after being with her, Carter had been with Deena Turner. Deena had told everyone at school and announced that they were going steady. Nothing hurt like high school, she thought, but even the memory couldn't provide enough anger to balance out her guilt.

She had to tell Carter about the plane.

Even if it meant betraying her own family.

Carter studied Eve, worried. He knew her too well, he realized, even after all these years. One of the things he'd always liked about her was her directness. She said what was on her mind.

But he could see that she was fighting more than exhaustion, as if trying too hard not to let him know just how bad last night had been. The fact that she hadn't said anything made him fear she was in more trouble than being caught without her horse in a storm in the Breaks.

"I am curious how you lost your horse, though," he said as he stuffed the dirty clothing she'd rolled up into his pack. "You get bucked off?"

Her head jerked up, her dark eyes hot with indignation. "You know darned well I haven't been thrown from a horse since I was—"

"Nine," he said. "I remember." He remembered a lot of things about her, including her stubborn pride—and the moonlight on her face their last night together.

Her eyes narrowed as if she, too, remembered only too well things she would prefer to forget.

"McKenna told me that you and your mom had words just before you rode out yesterday," he said.

"McKenna," Eve said like a curse. "Did she also fill you in on what it was about?"

He shook his head. "Apparently she didn't hear that part."

Eve gave him a wan smile. Nothing more.

"How'd you come to be way down there? It's not like you to end up without your horse in the bottom of a ravine."

"You don't know what I'm like anymore," she snapped, looking back down the steep rocky slope.

"Okay, if you don't want to tell me..." he said as he slung the pack over his shoulder.

"I found something." She said it grudgingly.

He looked down at her, hearing something in her voice that instantly set his heart racing. She was biting down on her lower lip, looking scared. "What?"

"Hey down there!" Errol Wilson called from the top of the gulch. "Everything all right?" A shower of small rocks cascaded down just feet from them.

"She's fine," Carter called back, irritated at the interruption. "Make sure everyone stays back. The ground is unstable and breaking off up there."

"Sure." Errol sounded disappointed, either that the rescue adventure was over already or that Carter had shooed him away.

When Errol stepped away, disappearing from the edge, Carter turned again to Eve. He'd seen Eve Bailey vulnerable only once before. He shoved aside the memory of her in his arms, her bare skin pressed to his, the windows steaming up on his old Chevy pickup....

"You found something?" he repeated.

She rubbed her ankle, wincing as if it hurt. "I found a body."

He felt his stomach clench even as he told himself she had to be mistaken. He'd had his share of calls from residents who'd uncovered bones and erroneously thought they'd found human remains.

Eve shook her head as if she still couldn't believe it herself. She drained the contents of the second water bottle before she spoke. "It was in a plane that had crashed in the ravine."

"An airplane?" he echoed as he looked down into the deep gorge and saw nothing. If there'd been a plane crash out here, he'd have heard about it.

"It was a small one, a four-seater," she said, her voice sounding hollow. "It's been there for a long time."

"Where?"

She glanced to the west. "Back that way. I'm not sure how far. I lost track trying to find a way out of there. But I'll know the ravine when I see it."

He hoped so, but the ravines all looked alike and in the state she was in… "The pilot was still in the plane?" he asked, thinking about the body she'd said she found.

"Not the pilot," she said without looking at him. "One of the passengers." She raised her eyes, locking with his for just an instant before she looked away again.

She'd found a crashed airplane in a ravine with the body of one of the passengers still in it and she hadn't said anything about it until now? The old Eve Bailey would have blurted it out the moment she saw him.

But then he and the old Eve Bailey had been friends. Lovers. The old Eve Bailey would have trusted him.

Maybe she was right. Maybe he didn't know her anymore. But he knew that wasn't the case. Because just looking into her face, he'd seen that she hadn't wanted to tell him about the plane.

The realization shocked him. Why would she keep something like that to herself?

He took a breath and let it out slowly. "You say the plane looked as if it had been there for a while?"

"Thirty-two years."

He sat down on a rock across from her so they were eye to eye. "What makes you think it's been there for thirty-two years?"

She continued rubbing her ankle for a moment before looking up at him. "There was a logbook in the cockpit. The last entry was February seven, 1975."

Carter couldn't believe this. His grandfather and father, both crop dusters, lived and breathed airplanes. They would have known about a missing plane. There would have been a search for the plane and, when found, the body removed even if it was impossible to get the plane out.

Unless the plane had never been reported missing.

He looked at Eve and felt a jolt. There was more.

"The passenger in the plane," she said, her voice almost a whisper. Her gaze met his. "He has a knife sticking out of his chest. At least I think it was a man."

From above them came the sound of more voices, the whinny of horses and more small rocks showering down.

Carter rose, shaken. "I'm going to ask you not to say anything about this to anyone," he said to her.

She looked up at him and nodded slowly.

"Do you think you can tell me where you found the plane?" he asked.

She shook her head. "It's hidden. If not for the storm, I wouldn't have seen anything down there. I'll have to take you to it."

"No, you need to go back with the search party so you can get medical treatment, food, rest."

"I'm fine." She rose to her feet with obvious difficulty. "I assume you brought me a horse?"

"Titus has one up on top for you, but Eve—"

"I told you, I'm fine." She glanced toward the canyon far below them, then at him as if she could read his mind. "Don't worry, I can find the plane again. Maybe you've forgotten, but I grew up here. I know this country."

Unlike Deena, the woman he'd dumped her for. The woman he'd stupidly married, divorced and was still trying to get out of his life. Deena didn't know one end of a horse from the other and she could get lost in the city park. Deena would never have survived five minutes out here last night.

"Eve—"

"I really need to get moving."

He nodded, not even sure what he'd planned to say. Whatever it was, this wasn't the time or the place to talk about the past. "I'll be right behind you."

They climbed out of the ravine, using the exposed rocks like steps. He could see that Eve was dead on her feet. She needed sleep, a hot shower, real food.

But she seemed to draw on some inner strength that the dry clothing and candy bar and water had little to do with. Eve was a strong woman. Isn't that what he'd told himself so many years ago, that Eve Bailey was strong. She'd get over any pain he'd caused her.

He'd lied to himself because he couldn't face the fact that he'd hurt Eve.

It took the last of her resources to get to the top of the ravine, but Eve was bound and determined. She reached the top to cheers of the search party, making her feel even more foolish, as she apologized for wasting their time, although they all insisted it had been no trouble.

"So what happened?" Errol Wilson asked.

Whenever Eve saw Errol, she thought of Halloween night when she was five. Her father had taken her to a party at the community center. Her mother had stayed home, complaining of a headache.

In Eve's excitement to tell her mother about the party,

she'd been the first out of the truck and racing up the steps to the house when she thought she saw Errol Wilson hiding in the dark at the edge of the porch.

Startled, Eve had let out a bloodcurdling scream and tripped and fell, skinning her knees. Her father had come running, but when Eve looked toward the end of the porch, there wasn't anyone there.

She'd tried to tell her parents that she'd seen a scary man, but they hadn't believed her, saying she'd just imagined it.

All Eve knew was that every time she saw Errol Wilson after that he seemed to have a smug look on his face, as if the two of them shared a secret. The smugness had only intensified after he'd seen her yesterday when he was coming out of her mother's back door.

"Eve was thrown from her horse and ended up at the bottom of a ravine," Carter said before Eve could answer.

She shot him a withering look. "I'd prefer that story not get back to my sisters, if you don't mind. I will never live it down."

Everyone laughed. Except Errol.

"Eve, you should know how hard it is to keep a secret in Whitehorse," he said.

"Eve and I are going to take it slow on the way back," Carter said, and looked over at Eve as if wondering what Errol had meant by that. "I'd appreciate it if the rest of you would go back and let everyone know that Eve is fine."

"I know your mother will be relieved," Errol said. "She worries about you. I'm glad I can relieve her mind."

Eve couldn't suppress a shudder as she saw him look back at her as he rode off with the others.

Apparently she and Errol Wilson now shared another secret. One he worried she would tell?

Carter frowned as he saw Eve's reaction to Errol. What had that odd exchange been about, he wondered.

As Eve reached for the reins of the horse Titus had brought her, Carter saw her wince with pain.

"Here," he said, drawing her attention away from Errol. "Let me put something on your hands."

"I'm fine," she snapped.

"You're not fine," he said, hooking her elbow and pulling her over to a rock. "Sit down. You're limping. You need that ankle wrapped. I can tell from here that it's swollen. You also need something on your hands."

Evidently she didn't want him to touch her. He couldn't blame her. In fact, he was still surprised she hadn't laid into him, telling him off good. He knew she wanted to, so why was she holding back? Did she think he didn't know he'd hurt her?

Finding the plane and the dead man inside must have shaken her up more than he could imagine. Or was something else bothering her, he wondered, as he looked to where Errol Wilson and the rest of the search party had ridden off.

Eve closed her eyes and leaned back as if soaking up the sun—and ignoring him as he gently wrapped her ankle.

Her hands were bruised and scraped raw. They had to be killing her. "This is going to burn," he said as he turned up her palms and applied the spray.

She didn't make a sound, her eyes closed tight. If it hadn't been for the one lone tear that escaped her lashes, he would have believed it didn't faze her.

"I'm sorry," he said quietly. "I didn't mean to hurt you."

Her eyes blinked open. He looked into that moist deep darkness and saw the pain and anger. "You didn't hurt me." She pulled back her hands. "Can we please get this over with?"

He nodded and put everything back into his pack. He didn't kid himself. He'd pay hell before ever getting back in Eve's good graces. It would be a waste of time to even try. She'd never forgive him and he couldn't blame her.

But as he swung up onto his horse, knowing better than to offer Eve any help getting on hers, he vowed to move heaven and earth, if that's what it took, for the chance.

Light-headed and beyond exhaustion, Eve found she also ached all over as she swung up into the saddle.

She'd seen Carter's worried look and suspected she looked like a woman who'd fallen down a mountainside. She had.

But none of that was as painful as having to sit there while Carter Jackson saw to her injuries. It was the gentle way he touched her, reminding her of their lovemaking the one and only time they'd been together. It was his concerned expression. For an awful moment, he sounded as if he was about to apologize for breaking her heart.

Eve Bailey could take a lot, but she couldn't take that.

They rode west, working their way along the top of the ridges, the land dropping precariously to the old river bottom. She could feel the piece of costume jewelry in her pocket biting into her flesh as if mocking her for feeling so righteous when it came to Carter.

She argued that the way he'd betrayed her—and her

keeping the pin in her pocket from him—weren't the same thing at all.

The lie caught in her throat like dust. But to admit she'd recognized the pin and knew who it belonged to would be to consider that her family had something to do with that plane and—worse—the dead man inside it. It was easier to lie and pray it was a coincidence that the plane had gone down just miles from the Bailey ranch.

Eve still felt chilled in the dry clothing, although the day was warm as the sun dipped toward the western horizon. Hours had passed without her even noticing it. As she rode, she watched for the ravine where she'd found the plane.

In the distance, she recognized an outcropping of rocks and knew they weren't far now. She glanced over at Carter.

How easy it would have been to keep riding, to pretend she'd gotten turned around, to leave the plane and its secrets buried where she'd found it.

"We getting close?" he asked, as if he'd caught her indecision.

She'd been wrong about him not knowing her anymore. He knew she couldn't pretend to have lost the location of the plane. Any more than she could pretend he hadn't broken her heart.

Carter reined in his horse next to Eve's. Below them was another steep ravine much like the others they'd passed.

He glanced over at Eve. What had her running scared? Eve wasn't squeamish when it came to dead animals. True, seeing a body would have upset her, but it wouldn't have her scared. So what was going on with her?

"Is it down there?" he asked. All he could see was a thick stand of junipers growing out of a rock ledge at least halfway down the steep ravine.

She nodded, looking ill.

"You went down there?" He couldn't see anything that would have tempted him into sliding down that slope.

"I heard a moan. I thought there was someone down there." Her voice broke. "It was just the wind blowing over the metal of the plane."

"The plane is in the junipers?" He couldn't help sounding skeptical.

She looked down into the ravine. "That's why it's never been found I would imagine."

He couldn't believe the chance she'd taken going down there. But Eve wouldn't have thought about her own safety if she thought there was someone down there injured.

He had to see the plane and body for himself and that meant going down there. He'd have to be quick. He needed to get her back to her house. He felt badly about putting her through this. But he feared if he had waited until tomorrow, Eve might have changed her mind about showing him where the plane was. Although he couldn't imagine why.

"Will you be all right up here?" he asked, worried about her.

She slid off her horse, practically collapsing as her boot soles hit the ground. "Leave me some water and your hat. I lost mine. I'll just rest while you're gone."

He dismounted and, pulling down his pack, reached inside for his rain jacket. Rolling it up, he handed it to her. "Put your head on this," he said, clearing a spot for her on the soft sun-dried earth.

She did as he said without even an argument. He knew she was simply too exhausted to put up a fight today. Eve hadn't changed. And that's what made this so painful. He'd been such a fool to throw her over for a woman like Deena.

Her eyes opened and narrowed as if she knew what he was thinking. "You still here?"

"I'll be right back," he said.

She nodded and closed her eyes again.

Leaving her water and the rest of the candy bars he'd brought, he stepped to the edge of the ravine. He could see faint tracks where she'd slid down and where the rain had eroded the earth even more during the storm last night.

He glanced back at her, amazed she wasn't worse off given what she had to have been through. A thought struck him. It had stormed all night. How had she…

Her lashes fluttered as she opened them again just enough to squint at him.

And he knew how she'd managed to survive the night in the storm. She'd spent it in the plane with a corpse.

Chapter 5

By early afternoon, word had spread throughout the county that Eve Bailey had been found safe and sound.

It had been all Lila could do not to break down, her relief had been so great. She'd insisted on staying at the center and cleaning up before the sewing group, not wanting to be alone. Also not ready to face her daughter.

Most of the food had been eaten, but she helped put the rest in the refrigerator for when the sheriff and Eve returned. If they didn't stop by the community center she would take some over to Eve later.

Lila knew her daughter. She hated having a fuss made over her, especially concerning something like this where the whole town was involved.

Eve would send her thanks and go straight home. She'd always been a willful girl, stubborn to the core. Chester used to say she was just like Lila.

The men from the search party had all gone back to their work and McKenna and Faith had gone on into Whitehorse to their summer jobs.

This morning there'd been a sense of purpose, everyone busy doing what they could to help. But now things had returned to normal. Well, as normal as this part of Montana could be, Lila thought.

Now the Whitehorse Sewing Circle could get back to its latest project, making a quilt for Maddie Cavanaugh's upcoming marriage. A community tradition, every newlywed and every newborn had a quilt made by the women who sat around the center quilting by hand.

There were the usual members in attendance today: Wanda Wilson—Errol's wife, Alice White, Ella Cavanaugh, Geraldine Shaw, Arlene Evans and Lila. Carly Matthews was visiting her sister in Great Falls.

Pearl Cavanaugh was the only one of the longstanding quilters missing. She had been admitted last night with walking pneumonia. She'd sent word, though, that she was feeling better. Lila worried that her visit yesterday evening with Pearl had caused her to get sicker. Lila felt sick herself.

There wasn't much talk as the women pulled their chairs up to the quilting frame and busied themselves threading their needles.

Lila went right to work, hating that her fingers were trembling as she made her first stitch. Relief had left her weak and worn-out, worry had made her queasy.

She knew the other women must wonder why she didn't go home to wait for her daughter. Wasn't that what a mother would do after having such a scare? But Lila Bailcy had had many scares in her life. A life of tedious day-to-day routine with moments of sheer panic.

That was how it was when your life was built on lies.

Her fingers shook as she made neat, careful stitches in the colorful cloth. If only she could stitch her life back together as easily.

"You're especially quiet today," Arlene commented.

Lila's head shot up only to find that Arlene wasn't talking to her. Instead, Arlene was staring at Geraldine Shaw.

"Geraldine?" Arlene said as she inspected the size of the stitches Alice was putting into the quilt. "Are you all right?"

Geraldine looked up and blinked as if she'd been miles away. She was a sturdy middle-aged woman, born of Scandinavian stock, thick of body with watery blue eyes and a plain round face. Her graying hair was cut as if a bowl had been placed on her head, the ends chopped just above her slack jaw.

"I'm fine," Geraldine said, forcing her down-turned mouth into a smile before her face went slack again.

For an instant, Lila met the woman's gaze across the quilting frame. She thought she saw something in Geraldine's eyes. Something she recognized. Fear.

"How are the wedding plans coming along?" Lila asked, turning back to her quilting.

"Fine," Arlene said and seemed a little too intent on her quilting.

"Your son getting cold feet?" Ella asked Arlene.

"I just think they're too young to be getting married, if you must know," Arlene said.

Lila noticed that no one disagreed. Maddie, who had just turned eighteen, had given up a scholarship to the university in Missoula to marry Bo. And as far as Lila could tell, Bo, who still lived at home at twenty, didn't have any means of employment.

"I got married young," Alice said. "It all worked out just fine." Alice was nearly ninety and was married almost sixty years when her husband passed away.

"I heard Maddie's been helping over at your place, Geraldine," Arlene said with an edge to her voice that made Lila look up.

Geraldine Shaw let out a cry as she stabbed her finger with her needle. She dropped the needle to suck the blood from her finger, her eyes downcast and bright with tears.

"Did you stick yourself, Geraldine?" Arlene asked.

"It's nothing," Geraldine replied, and picked up her needle again, all her attention on her work.

"I think it's wonderful that Maddie helps you out around the place now that Ollie is gone," Ella said.

Geraldine only nodded and kept quilting.

Arlene looked as if she had something more to say but fortunately Alice jumped in and told a story about her granddaughter.

Lila hated the undercurrents she felt at the table and wished sometimes that she could just gag Arlene Evans to shut her up.

"Did you see that man who's renting the old McAllister place?" Arlene asked, moving on to greener pastures. "Bridger Duvall. That can't really be his name. He stopped in earlier as if looking for someone." She raised her eyes, taking in each woman at the table, stopping on Lila.

"I heard he's writing a book about Whitehorse," Alice said. "Including Old Town."

"Really?" Arlene sounded skeptical. "I don't know why, but I got the impression he was looking for Eve."

Lila stared at Arlene, too dumbstruck for a moment to speak. "You're obviously mistaken," she said, jamming her needle through the cloth. "He was probably just wondering what was going on with all the vehicles parked outside."

Arlene lifted a brow. "All he had to do was ask."

"Well, if he was looking for Eve he would have been with the search party, now wouldn't he," Lila said logically.

Logic always stumped Arlene, who thrived on gossip. Unfortunately, she often got it wrong. Why would the man be writing a book on Whitehorse? Or looking for Eve?

Carter took the rope from his pack and tied it to the saddle. His brother, Cade, had bought some land north of Whitehorse with a rodeo grounds on it. When Carter wasn't acting as sheriff, he calf roped at the arena. He liked being on the back of the horse the way his father apparently liked being in a plane high in the air.

"I should warn you," Eve said without opening her eyes. "That first step into the ravine is a lulu."

Well, he couldn't take the time to find a better way down. He tightened his gloved hands around the rope, pulling on it until he felt resistance from the horse and stepped off the edge of the ravine.

Just as he'd known it would, the top level of the steep incline began to avalanche downward with him.

The horse, trained for roping cattle, kept the line taut as he rappelled down the steep slope. He tried to imagine Eve doing this without a rope. Without a net. The woman was fearless. Crazy, too.

When he reached the rock ledge, he tied off the rope, then worked his way cautiously along the junipers, imagining Eve doing the same. The woman really was something else, he thought as he peered back over the rim of the ledge. Eve had always been afraid of heights, but that hadn't stopped her when she thought there was someone in the junipers who needed her help.

He was beginning to suspect that Eve had been mistaken about this being the ravine when he caught the glint of sun off metal. It shocked him how well hidden the plane was. It was conceivable that the craft wouldn't have been found even if it had been reported missing. Not that he believed it had, given what Eve said was inside the cockpit.

One wing had plowed into the side of the ravine, completely burying it. The other was lost in the juniper branches and, after all these years, woven into the new growth to make the plane impossible to see from above.

It still amazed him that Eve had seen it.

As he moved closer, he saw that she was right. The plane had been there for a long while.

"It's a Navion," he said out loud in surprise as he moved closer. A friend of his father's had one down in Florida. Only about two thousand were built, most back in the 1940s, and none had been built since. They were now popular with collectors because they had held up well, being one of the first metal private planes from that era.

"Wow, it's in fantastic shape given where it ended up." He realized he was talking to himself, something he'd been doing a lot of lately.

As he moved to the cockpit, he held his breath. It was just as Eve had described it. The plane had been well preserved. The sliding canopy—the only way into the cockpit—had remained intact, the windows unbroken but dirty. A strip of torn red cloth was caught in the edge of the canopy. The fabric hung down the side, still wet from the storm.

He could see where Eve had wiped away some of the grime to look inside. He bent closer.

The pilot seat and front passenger seats were empty, but stained as if the occupants might have been injured in the crash. The corpse was strapped in the rear seat, the body mummified over the years. The skin was dried and brown, shrunk to the skeleton, the eye sockets hollow. The shirt was threadbare, even the bloodstain from the wound faded, the jeans in surprisingly good shape, the boots looking like new.

Carter had heard of bodies mummifying under certain conditions but this was the first he'd seen. Eve had said the last entry in the logbook was February. The body would have frozen, then thawed slowly as the months warmed and not decomposed like it would have if the plane had gone down in the summer.

Stuck between two ribs, just as Eve had said, was a hunting knife, the handle grayed with age.

"Damn," Carter said under his breath.

He could see where Eve had climbed into the cockpit. He swore again, imagining her spending the night in there, the storm raging around her, a mummified body in the seat behind her.

He stared at the plane, then at the only way out of here, down a minefield of boulders. Had anyone from the plane gotten out alive?

Carter felt the air around him change. A storm was blowing in again. He had to see to Eve. The last thing he wanted was for her to get caught in another storm, and storms came up so fast out here.

He didn't want to leave the crime scene, but he had no choice. After all, the plane had apparently been here for thirty-two years. What was another day?

As soon as he could get to a landline, he would call the crime lab in Missoula. His cell wouldn't work out here. He could barely get service in Whitehorse.

It was all he could do not to slide back the plane's canopy and have a look around in the cockpit. But the crime scene had been disturbed enough.

He tried to imagine himself spending the night in the close quarters of the cockpit with the mummified murdered man. Eve was more resilient than he'd ever imagined. But then the survival instinct was a strong one. Just like the killer instinct.

Carter worked his way along the junipers, careful with his footing, too aware of the long drop to the bottom of the canyon below him.

He untied the rope from the juniper branch, gave it a tug, then another before he felt tension on the line as the horse responded. Slowly, he began to climb out of the deep ravine. He could smell the promise of rain in the air. June in Montana was like spring most other places. Squalls would blow through, biting cold rain and sleet drenching everything, taking the heat and sun with them.

By the time he reached flat land at the top of the ravine, he was winded, his palms burning from the rope even through his gloves. Just as he suspected, thunderheads loomed on the horizon. A breeze had come up and in the distance he could see a dust devil whirling through the sagebrush.

Eve was sitting up, watching him as he unhooked the rope from his saddle. The breeze whipped her long dark hair around her face. She squinted at him as if trying to gauge his reaction to what he'd found in the plane. "Well?"

"The plane is right where you said it was."

She nodded. "Any idea who he is?"

"None."

"What happens now?" she asked.

"I get the techs from the crime lab to come down and retrieve the body and any evidence. Let's get you back to your house before this storm hits," he said as he coiled up the rope, worried about her.

She still had a scared look as she glanced toward home and slowly rose from the ground, clearly hesitant. "You think we'll ever know who he is?"

The murdered man in the plane? "Forensics can do amazing things nowadays. I wouldn't be surprised if they were able to get some DNA on him." He didn't add, though, that it would be worthless unless they had a suspect's DNA to compare it to. "If anyone else in the plane got out alive…"

Eve looked over at him, as if she'd already considered that. If anyone had gotten out alive, they would have walked to the closest place—her family's ranch.

Eve felt his focus on her as she swung up into the saddle. Carter made her uncomfortable. Because she felt guilty? Or because just a look from him still made her a little weak in the knees? It infuriated her that she could feel anything for him.

"I need you not to mention the plane to anyone until I can get the crime lab in there," he said.

She nodded.

"Eve, about this fight you had with your mother yesterday…"

She blinked, surprised by his sudden change of subject. For a moment, she'd been so intent on the man that she'd forgotten Carter was also the sheriff. "What does that have to do with anything?"

"I don't know. I'm asking you."

She shook her head. "If you're asking if I knew about the plane, I didn't. I told you. I wouldn't even have seen it if the storm hadn't kicked up."

He nodded and glanced toward the horizon. She could see the clouds building up again. They'd be lucky to get back to her place before it hit. She spurred her horse, riding past him and toward home.

"Do you remember what you might have touched in the plane?" he asked, catching her and riding along beside her.

"No, I…" Her voice trailed off. It had been a nightmare climbing into the plane and closing the canopy to keep out the cold and sleet. She'd huddled in the seat, the body directly behind her. She could feel his sightless eye sockets fixed on her. Every sound convinced her the body had come alive and was intent on vengeance, starting with her.

Worse than those nightmares was the fear that it hadn't been just her bad luck that she'd stumbled across the plane.

"I don't remember what I might have touched," she said finally. "I was cold and scared. I saw the logbook on the floor and picked it up. I think that's all." The pin in her pocket bit into her flesh. Liar.

"Okay." Carter couldn't shake the feeling that Eve was keeping something from him. Yet he had no choice but to take her word for it. At least for now.

The lab would find her fingerprints. Soon enough he'd know. He stole a glance at her as they rode toward Old Town. She was worrying her lower lip with her teeth, frowning. He wondered what she was worried about. Not that she would ever tell him.

Cursing himself, he rode in silence. Even if he'd known what to say to her, he doubted she'd want to hear it. And what was there to say? He'd been a damn fool. He'd made the mistake of his life sleeping with Deena, let alone marrying her.

Hell, everyone already knew that—the divorce had made that obvious. And everyone had probably heard about the stunts Deena had pulled, including sleeping with his best friend.

He'd blown any chance he ever had with Eve. Why couldn't he accept that?

She had him worried, though. Something was troubling her. Maybe, like him, she feared about the repercussions news of the plane—and the murdered man inside—were going to have on Old Town and Whitehorse.

Word would get out once the crime lab showed up with its vans and helicopter. The news would travel like a grass fire. There was no getting around it.

He just hoped to hell that none of the occupants of that plane were tied to the town. Unfortunately, his family had lived just this side of Old Town thirty-two years ago and he doubted it would slip anyone's mind that both his father and grandfather had been pilots.

In fact, there'd been a grass airstrip on the Jackson ranch not that far from where the Navion had gone down.

Chapter 6

Eve couldn't wait for Carter to leave. He'd come into her grandmother's house to use the phone, stepping around the ladder and cans of paint. "So you're fixing up the place," he'd said as he glanced at the variety of paint colors she'd tried on the living room wall so far. His eyes had widened a little.

He hadn't commented on her bright color choices.

Just as well, since she was in no mood for his opinion.

He'd made a couple of calls. She'd done her best not to listen. He'd called the crime lab in Missoula, then his office to let them know he wouldn't be back the rest of the day. While he'd told whomever he spoke to at the crime lab about the plane, he hadn't mentioned it to whoever he'd talked to at his office.

All she'd wanted was for him to leave so she could finally have a hot shower and forget for a while about the plane—and the rhinestone pin and murdered man. Forget about Carter.

She hugged herself against the wind that whipped her hair around her face as she walked him out to the porch. Any minute it would start raining again.

He didn't seem to want to leave her. "You should have Doc take a look at that ankle. And you won't forget about not mentioning the plane to anyone. At least until you hear from me. You will hear from me."

It sounded like a promise. Or, in her state of mind, a threat.

"Fine," she said, and went inside. When she peeked out just before she closed the door, he was still standing on her porch. She waited until she heard him ride off before she headed upstairs.

Once in her bathroom, she turned on the shower, stripped down and stepped under the steaming water. But not even the hot shower could chase away the chill that had settled in her bones. She ached all over and was scraped and bruised in places she hadn't even realized.

Exhaustion dragged at her, but she forced herself to shampoo her hair, standing under the spray to let the water run over her long dark hair.

As she shut off the shower and stepped out, she caught her reflection in the mirror across the large bathroom. The glass had steamed up, but she could still see the dark-haired child she'd been. Her sisters and parents were fair, blond and blue eyed. She, on the other hand, had hair the color of walnut and dark brown eyes. She was the duckling in a family of swans.

She had hated being different as a child.

As an adult, her dissimilarity just made her suspicious.

* * *

Carter rode his horse back to the truck to get what he'd need to spend the night in the Breaks. Growing up in this isolated country he'd learned a long time ago to carry survival gear in any kind of weather and enough food and water to last for at least a few days.

There was always the likelihood of going off the road and being stranded for days until someone came along or the county got the road open. Each year someone would go off the road or get stuck and think they could walk out for help instead of staying with the vehicle. A fatal decision more times than not. Out here, you did what you had to survive. Just like Eve had done.

He was tying his sleeping bag onto his horse when Lila Bailey came out of the community center. From her dour expression, he thought she hadn't heard the news that Eve had been found.

"Eve's fine. She's at her house. Her grandmother's house," he added, curious if she was fixing the place up because she planned to stay. "She's exhausted. I doubt she'll be coming down to the community center."

Lila nodded as if that was no surprise to her and he noticed then that she carried two foil-wrapped bundles in her hands. "You're going back out?"

"I saw some mountain lion tracks. Just want to check it out," he said.

Her face was expressionless, but still he suspected she knew he was lying. "You'll want to take some food with you." She handed him one of the wrapped items. It felt heavy. "I saw you loading your supplies on your horse so I assumed you weren't done for the day."

"Thanks."

Without another word, she walked to her pickup

parked in front of the center, her back straight as a steel rod. As she drove away, he noticed there were still a couple of rigs left, including Glen Whitaker's, the reporter from the Whitehorse local newspaper.

Carter hurried, not in the mood for an interview. Glen would be beating down his door soon enough for the story once he heard about the plane—and the body inside.

As the sheriff swung up into the saddle, wind whipped the tall grass, keeling it over, and the first drops of rain began to fall. He hunkered down in his slicker, noticing that the women still inside the community center were watching him from the window as he rode away.

He wondered if any of them knew about the plane. Or all of them. They were old enough. And as close-knit as this community was he could see the whole town keeping the plane a secret—if they had good reason. He couldn't imagine what that reason would be, though. Not when it involved murder.

But maybe it depended on who was dead in that plane.

If the survivors had managed to walk away from the plane crash, they would have needed help. And help was only a few miles north at one of the ranches—the closest being the Baileys' ranch. Unless they had gone more to the northwest, then it would have been his family's.

Carter realized it might all depend on what the plane was doing flying this way in the first place. There was more than a remote possibility the pilot had been planning to land on Carter's family's airstrip. It was far enough from the ranch house and Whitehorse. Remote, but it had been February if Eve was right about the logbook entry being the last one.

More than likely the pilot had just gotten lost in the storm and his destination was Glasgow.

At least that's what Carter wanted to believe. Just as he wanted the passengers and pilot to be total strangers. Much better to believe that they couldn't have survived after the crash, the blizzard, the climb out of that ravine.

That way no one in Old Town would have been involved. That people he'd known his whole life wouldn't have been keeping the secret about the plane. Or the murder. And that this had nothing to do with his family. Or Eve's.

Eve had just gotten dressed when she heard her mother's pickup coming along the lane. From her upstairs window, she watched Lila pull into the yard and cut the engine. Eve waited. She couldn't see her mother's face through the rain-streaked windshield of the pickup, but she could sense her indecision.

It was late afternoon. The worst of the storm had blown through. Eve could see a sliver of clear sky peeking through the clouds to the west, the sun long gone. A light rain still fell, dimpling the puddles left in her yard, leaving a chill in the air.

The pickup door finally opened. Her mother stepped out, avoiding the puddles as she ran through the drizzle toward the house.

Eve turned from the window, and with dread, headed down the stairs. She wasn't up to continuing their argument. And what was there to say, anyway? Her mother was cheating on her father. And with Errol Wilson, if that wasn't bad enough.

When Eve opened the door, she found her mother standing on the porch looking off toward the Breaks.

The doorbell hadn't rung. Nor had her mother knocked. In fact, Eve had the impression that Lila Bailey might have left had Eve not opened the door when she had.

Lila turned toward her, appearing startled out of her thoughts and looking confused, as if she'd forgotten why she'd stopped by. She held something foil wrapped. Food, no doubt. Her mother's idea of love was cooking something for her family. Eve suspected it was avoidance.

"I wanted to make sure you were all right," her mother said. "I can't stay. I just brought you some of Arlene's casserole that you like." She held it out to Eve, but Eve didn't take it.

"Mother, please, come in," Eve said, stepping back. "I was going to come see you anyway."

Lila didn't look happy about either prospect. She had to know that their discussion from yesterday wasn't finished. Her mother was the kind of woman who stuck her head in the sand, hoping that when she came up for air the problem would be gone and forgotten.

It amazed Eve that her mother seemed to be taking the same attitude with her husband, pretending that Chester had moved out just to be closer to his job. The same attitude she'd taken when Eve returned wanting answers.

Wind whirled cold, damp air through the open doorway. "You can take a few minutes, I'm sure," she said. "I need to show you something."

Her mother hesitated, surveying the paint cans and ladder. Clearly she hadn't expected the conversation to take this turn and was curious about what Eve wanted to show her.

"I see you're changing the place," she said, sounding

disapproving as she gingerly stepped around the paint cloths on the hardwood floor and Eve closed the door behind her.

"I really need to get back to the center. Pearl is in the hospital and if we're going to get this quilt done before Maddie and Bo get married…" Lila stopped just inside the living room.

Yes, Eve thought. Her mother always had somewhere she had to be when Eve wanted answers.

"So which color do you like best?" Eve asked, as if that was her only reason for wanting her mother to come in.

Lila glanced at the bright paint smears on the wall and seemed to be trying to think of something nice to say. "They're all fine."

Eve chuckled. The walls at the farmhouse where Eve was raised had had the original wallpaper—until her father moved out. Eve noticed Lila had painted over them. Everything was now white.

Had her mother done that as a fresh start? Or had she been dying to paint over the wallpaper for years? Eve had no idea. Her mother kept her feelings, as well as her own counsel, to herself.

"Pick the one you like. You're the one who's going to be staying here for a while. I really need to get back." Lila started to turn toward the front door.

"That isn't what I wanted to show you," Eve said as she reached into the shoulder bag hanging over the stairs banister and pulled out the rhinestone pin. She'd taken it out of her pocket because it kept biting into her flesh. Even dulled by years in the plane, the stones flashed, making her mother stop at the sight of the pin.

It was old-fashioned in its flower design and at least

thirty-two years old, although Eve suspected it was much older than that. When she'd seen the pin in photographs, she'd always been fascinated by both the pin and the story her grandmother told with it.

As Eve held out the pin now, her mother seemed to shrink away. "What is that?"

"Don't you recognize it?" Eve asked, even though she could see her mother's shock at seeing the pin again.

Lila Bailey had recognized the piece of jewelry—just as Eve had done when she'd found it in the plane. "It's Grandma Nina Mae's. The brooch Charley Cross gave her on their wedding day."

Her mother dragged her attention away from the pin and looked at Eve. "You're mistaken. It can't possibly be your grandmother's. She lost hers years ago, in Canada, I think she said. Anyway, there must be hundreds of pins around like it."

"Actually, I doubt hundreds of them have a replaced stone that doesn't quite match," Eve said. "I'm sure you remember the story."

Lila said nothing. She stood as if waiting for the next blow.

Eve wasn't sure why, but she suddenly felt sorry for her mother. Worse, she realized that she'd been angry with her for years and had blamed her mother for Chester moving out. She thought her mother cold, uncaring. And yet the woman standing before her looked sad and hurt.

Pocketing the rhinestone pin, Eve looked into her mother's eyes. She wanted to demand to know what her mother could possibly see in a man like Errol Wilson, but she couldn't bring herself to do it. She felt too weary.

"If that's all, I need to get back to my quilting," her mother said, and turned toward the door, walking quickly, seemingly afraid Eve would stop her. "We're working late tonight since…well, since we didn't get a lot done earlier."

Eve's fault. Eve always had been a problem, her mother's tone said. Now she was just making trouble again.

Eve couldn't help herself. "Don't you want to know where I found Grandma Nina Mae's pin?" she demanded as her mother opened the door.

Lila stopped in midstep, the door open, the chill of the rain wafting in. "Charley Cross broke your grandmother's heart. I doubt she would want a pin that would only remind her of him, do you?"

"Is that why there aren't any photographs of Dad in your house? Because he broke your heart?" she asked facetiously.

Her mother's fingers whitened as she gripped the doorknob. "I'm not having an affair with Errol Wilson. I'm sorry you misunderstood."

"Just as I misunderstood the letters I found under the floorboards in your sewing room?" Eve shot back.

"If you want to know why your father left, why don't you ask him." With that, her mother left, back ramrod straight, head high. But as Lila Bailey descended the porch stairs, her shoulders drooped. Eve saw her mother grab the railing to steady herself, stopping on the bottom step as if to catch her breath, head bowed.

That show of weakness lasted only moments. Quickly straightening, her mother walked briskly to her pickup through the rain, determination and resignation in her bearing.

As had constantly been the case, Eve felt drained from the exchange with her mother. She also felt sick to her stomach. Her mother had recognized the pin. And she hadn't even asked where Eve had found it.

Didn't it follow that her mother knew about the plane crash south of the ranch in the Breaks—and the murdered man inside?

Glen Whitaker had tried to hide his disappointment when the search party returned with the good news that Eve Bailey had been found alive and well.

Just as he'd suspected, no story here.

What a waste of time. Except for the pie. He'd stuffed himself on Arlene's pie and sampled all the other dishes as well. The only downside was Violet. She'd sat still as a stone, those watery eyes on him like a toad's on a fly.

Violet's younger sister Charlotte had joined them. The teenager smelled of artificial fingernail remover and had complained about being on her feet all day at one of the beauty shops in Whitehorse where she worked.

As Glen polished off the last of the pineapple upside-down cake that Alice White had brought, Arlene said, "Glen, you and Violet should get together sometime."

Glen squirmed in his seat, trying to smile, wanting to run. "I'm pretty busy this time of year." A lie.

"Oh, you have time to take in a show or dinner out," Arlene pressed.

Glen scraped crumbs from his plate, eyes cast down. He couldn't bear to look at Violet, who'd made a pained sound at her mother's audacious efforts to pawn her off.

Charlotte was busy checking her long blond hair for split ends and obviously bored by the conversation.

"I'm busy, too," Violet said.

"I think the two of you would be perfect together," Arlene said, refusing to let it drop.

"Mama," Violet said on a breath.

The tension at the table was palpable. Glen felt a bad case of indigestion coming on. He'd stayed too long. He hadn't even noticed that it was getting dark outside. While skinny as a beanpole, he did love his food and he had to admit, the Old Town women were great cooks. But clearly, he'd worn out his welcome.

"Well, I really should get back," he said, rising from his chair. Violet had her head down, her neck flushed with embarrassment. Arlene looked disappointed and a little upset.

Glen felt guilty for eating most of the coconut-custard pie. "Violet, it was nice seeing you," he said, feeling he had to say something. "I'll give you a call." Another lie.

Violet lifted her head slowly. He felt a start when her eyes reached his. Fury. She knew he was lying. He thought her flush had been embarrassment, but now he realized it had been anger. And it was directed at him.

He hurried out, hating that he'd have to drive back in the dark. On top of that, it was raining.

Once he reached the car, he knew he was in no shape to drive home. He'd parked under a tree a ways from the center and now he laid back the seat and closed his eyes, just planning to let all that food settle before he headed home.

A sound woke him. He sat up, surprised to see that it was pitch dark and had stopped raining. A pickup pulled in and parked. He saw Lila Bailey get out. He'd seen her take food out to the sheriff earlier and then leave.

As late as it was, he was surprised she'd come back. But the lights were still on in the center and most of the old biddies' cars were still parked out front.

Just as Lila got out of her pickup, Errol Wilson materialized from the blackness along the side of the building. Glen, a born voyeur, watched with interest. It was clear they were arguing about something and that Errol had startled her.

Glen slid down a little, taking advantage of the darkness and the fact that they hadn't seen him sitting in his car. Surreptitiously inserting the key in the ignition, he lowered his electric window a little on the side closest to Lila's truck so he could hear.

Lila was keeping her voice down, but he could tell by her tone she was trying to persuade Errol Wilson of something.

A light breeze carried snatches of her voice on the chilly night air. Glen tried to imagine what the two could be arguing about and came up empty. After a moment, Errol grabbed Lila's arm, but she jerked free.

"You'd better do something about your daughter," Errol said angrily.

"I'm not putting up with you threatening me or my family anymore," Lila shot back with venom, advancing on him as she did.

Errol retreated a few steps, his movement awkward, as if he'd been drinking. Errol must have sensed they weren't alone. He glanced in Glen's direction.

Glen made a play of reaching into his pockets, as if looking for his keys. When he glanced back, the man was gone and the door of the community center was closing behind Lila Bailey.

What had that been about, Glen wondered as he reached for the key in the ignition. It was time to go home.

As he turned to look behind him before he pulled out, the driver's-side door of his car swung open. He felt the cold along with droplets of rain from off the car roof as he twisted around in surprise.

From out of the darkness came what felt like a bolt of lightning. Lights flashed behind his eyes. A thunderous sound echoed in his cranium. He felt the pain as he was struck in the head a second time.

The last thing he remembered was someone pushing him over, then the sound of his car engine, the crunch of the tires on the gravel and, as crazy as it seemed, the cloying scent of Violet Evans's perfume.

Chapter 7

After her mother left, Eve sat down with the rhinestone pin cupped in her palms. The stones were cool to the touch. The metal was discolored. As many times as her grandmother had told her the story of the pin, Eve felt as if she was holding something priceless.

Grandma Nina Mae would pull Eve up on her lap and open her old photo album to the day she got married and say, "This is your grandfather, Charley Cross. He was a fine man, no matter what you hear about him. He never stopped loving me. This is the day we got married."

Nina's voice would soften. She would gently touch Grandfather Charley Cross's face and say nothing for a long time.

Then her grandmother would tell her about the pin that she always wore on her brown coat. "Your grandfather gave it to me. It meant everything to me."

"What happened to it?" Eve would always ask.

"Lost. It got lost. That's why you must always keep what you value close." And then her grandmother hugged her tightly.

As Eve studied the pin, she turned it over and saw something that she'd missed before. Several brown threads were caught in the backing of the pin.

She got up and found a sharp knife and worked the threads out of the base of the pin. The threads were frayed at the ends, indicating that the pin might have been torn off an article of clothing.

Her heart began to pound like a drum in her chest. They were threads from her grandmother's favorite old brown coat. If she'd had any doubt about whom the pin belonged to, she didn't anymore. If she had her grandmother's brown coat, she could prove it.

When her Grandmother Nina had gone into the nursing home, Eve had helped pack up all of her things. Her grandmother had saved everything. But Eve remembered the old brown wool coat her grandmother had worn until it was threadbare. Lila had tried to talk Nina Mae into getting rid of it, but her grandmother would have none of it.

"You throw out my favorite coat, Lila, and I swear I will curse you until the day you die," Nina Mae had cried. "You know how much that old coat means to me."

"Mother, it's threadbare. I doubt it even fits you anymore," Lila had argued.

"It's mine," her grandmother had said, angry and hurt. "You of all people should know how much it means to me. I want to be buried in it. Eve, you make sure she buries me in that coat."

"I will, Grandma," Eve had promised.

Her mother had rolled her eyes at them both, but given up and stuffed the old coat deep in one of the trunks.

Eve felt her heart race. Grabbing a piece of clean tape, she carefully attached the threads of fabric to a scrap of paper, which she folded and put in her pocket along with the pin.

Now all she had to do was find the trunk her mother had put the coat in. The attic upstairs was empty. Eve had checked out the whole house when she'd moved in.

Was it possible her father had taken the trunks to the attic at the ranch? Or had Eve's mother gotten rid of them?

It wouldn't have been the first time. Eve Bailey had been eleven when she found the love letters hidden under the floorboards of her mother's sewing room.

She'd found them quite by accident. She'd gone in to use her mother's good sewing scissors even though she knew she would get in trouble if she got caught.

She'd dropped the scissors, heard the odd sound they made as they struck the floor and, when she'd knelt down to retrieve them, she'd felt the floorboard move.

The letters were all addressed to "My Love" and signed simply "Your Love." It was in one of them that the man had asked whether Lila was ever planning to tell "the child" the truth. And Eve had known the truth had something to do with her—the duckling of the family.

And this man, Eve surmised, must be her mother's mystery lover—and probably Eve's real father. He would have dark hair and eyes and look like her. She had hungered for someone who resembled her.

She'd heard her mother coming and had quickly put the letters back under the floorboards, too shaken to confront her mother until she'd had time to think about what it all meant. Finding the letters had been a delicious secret that had kept Eve awake most of the night. She didn't want to give up that secret and she was positive that no one else but her mother and lover knew about the letters under the floorboards.

The next day, Eve had returned to the sewing room, intent on reading all the letters to see if she could figure out who the man was and what truth her mother hadn't told "the child." She fantasized that the man wasn't just her father but that for some mysterious honorable reason he had to remain a secret.

But the letters were gone, the space empty.

She'd confronted her mother only to have Lila tell her that she knew nothing about any old letters but if there had been some, they'd probably been in the house long before either of them was born.

Eve had cried and told her she knew Chester wasn't her real father. Lila had sent her to her room, saying she would hear no more of this foolishness and how she was never to say that ever again for it would deeply hurt Chester.

Without the letters, there was no proof. And Eve hadn't wanted to hurt Chester.

Nor could Eve ever be sure the letters really had been her mother's. Maybe there was no mystery father. Maybe Eve Bailey was just who her mother said she was, the firstborn of Lila and Chester Bailey. And the reason Eve had felt as if she didn't belong was because…well, because she was foolish, just like her mother had said.

Or maybe, Eve thought as she looked at the piece of costume jewelry, Lila Bailey had lied to her. Just as she had about the pin.

But then how much of the other had been lies as well?

Had she lied about an affair with Errol Wilson? About the love letters under the floorboards? About Chester being Eve's father?

The pin was proof.

But proof of what?

It got dark fast out in the Breaks. Carter had found a spot out of the wind, pitching his small one-man tent. The storm had moved on, but low clouds still hung over the stark landscape and the air was damp and cool.

He crawled into the tent fully clothed, leaving the door open. Night fell like a blanket when it came. There was no sign of a light, the darkness complete. No sound, either, other than the occasional rustle of his horse pastured off to the east or the cry of a hawk searching the canyons for food.

Carter lay on his back staring out through the open tent door at the sky, wishing at least for stars or even a sliver of moon to break free of the clouds. He'd spent many nights in the Breaks hunting. But tonight felt oddly different.

Probably because he knew he'd pay hell getting to sleep after everything that had happened today—seeing Eve Bailey again at the top of his list.

He was still amazed she'd come back. When he heard she'd been buying paint at the local hardware store and was living in her grandmother's house, he'd felt elated. Maybe she was staying.

Before that, he thought he'd never see her again except maybe at her wedding—if she had it in White-horse. Now, after seeing what she was doing with her grandmother's house, he wondered if she hadn't come home to stay.

Of course that begged the question why?

Was it just bad luck that she'd been home a couple weeks and discovered an airplane that had crashed in a ravine deep in the Breaks years ago?

He hated being suspicious. Especially of Eve. Deena had made him leery of women in general, but never Eve Bailey. Yet he couldn't explain the way Eve had been acting. Acting almost as if she was hiding something.

A sound. He stopped to listen hard, telling himself he was jumpy because he knew there was a body just over the lip of the ravine. Why else would he feel so vulnerable out here tonight? Hell, he had a weapon and no one knew he was out here.

Or did they?

He couldn't overlook the chance that whoever killed the passenger in the plane was still alive, still living close by. But Carter wondered if the killer must not have known where the plane was. If the craft had gone down in a blizzard in the middle of winter as he suspected, then if anyone had survived, they might not have been able to find the airplane again.

But the killer would know the plane was out here somewhere. After thirty-two years, though, he wouldn't expect anyone to find it. He'd—

This time the sound Carter had heard earlier was closer and he recognized it for what it was, the ring of a horse's hoof on a stone.

He slipped out of the tent, taking his flashlight and his weapon as he did. The night was so dark it was like being in a cave, but he didn't turn on the flashlight.

He'd been so sure that no one could have survived the plane crash, that the murderer had died trying to get to shelter, his bones scattered to the wind over the past thirty-two years.

But Carter knew if the killer had reached one of the ranch houses, then someone from this community would have had to have taken him in. And kept it a secret all these years.

The question was: how far would they go to keep that secret?

Another clink of a horseshoe against stone. The horse whinnied as the rider approached slowly, almost tentatively, and he realized the rider had to be tracking him using some sort of night glasses.

Carter moved to crouch just below the hill. Even with night goggles, the rider wouldn't be able to see him or his tent. With his horse a rise over, the approaching rider would be practically on top of Carter before he realized he was there.

He held his breath. There was always the chance it was just someone curious about what the sheriff was doing out here. Friend or foe? Wouldn't a friend have called out by now? But then the rider didn't know exactly where he was, right?

As Carter waited, the only sound was the slow click of the horse's hooves along the rocky terrain as the rider grew closer and closer.

Still, Carter couldn't see the horse or the rider. The night was too black. But he could hear both. He shifted the flashlight into his right hand, put his finger over the switch and silently urged the rider to come just a little closer. Carter wanted to see who'd tracked him out here.

The interloper's horse whinnied again. The sheriff's horse answered. All sound stopped.

Carter held his breath as he readied the flashlight. Just

a little closer. He knew the moment he raised up to look over the crest of the hill, he would be a target. He'd be an even better target once he flipped on the flashlight to get a look at the rider.

The weapon felt awkward in his left hand, but he wasn't about to fire it unless forced to. If only the clouds would part. Even a little starlight might silhouette the rider—

Just a little closer.

The rider's horse whinnied and Carter's answered it again. The interloper quickly turned his horse and took off at a gallop the way he'd come.

Carter swore as he rose and flicked on the flashlight. The beam caught nothing but dust as the horse and rider raced away into the night. He swore as he stood listening to the sound of the horse's hooves die away in the distance.

If the rider was who Carter feared it was, then the murderer now knew that his secret was no longer safe.

Valley Nursing Home was just outside of Whitehorse in a single-story red-brick building.

As Eve entered the next morning, she heard two women having an argument at the nurses' station. Both strident voices were easily recognizable, given that the two were usually arguing when Eve visited.

The large nurse had her hands on her hips, her face and voice calm as she stood between the two elderly women, trying to make peace.

One of the elderly women was tall and thick with slightly stooped shoulders, cropped gray hair and intense brown eyes.

The other was petite and ramrod straight with a gray

braid down her slim back, startling blue eyes and an attitude that radiated around her like a high-voltage electrical field.

"Grandma Nina Mae," Eve said as she approached the latter woman's back.

"You're in for it now," Nina Mae said, without turning around. "My daughter is here and she'll settle this right as rain."

The nurse shot Eve a compassionate look. "It's your granddaughter Eve, Nina Mae."

"Don't you think I know my own daughter?" Nina Mae snapped, still not looking at Eve.

Eve reached for her grandmother's elbow, hoping to distract her. Nina Mae had her good days and bad. Today was obviously one of her bad ones.

Nina Mae jerked free to glare around the nurse at the other elderly woman, her once best friend—before a man had come into the picture. And long before old age and dementia had set in.

"You sneaky, underhanded—"

Eve got a better hold on her grandmother and steered her down the hall as the nurse took an irate Bertie Cavanaugh in the opposite direction.

"What's going on, Grandma?" Eve asked as Nina mumbled unintelligibly under her breath.

"Tried to steal him again. Thinks I don't know. A woman's husband isn't safe around here." She glanced at Eve and frowned. "You aren't my daughter."

"I'm your granddaughter Eve."

Nina didn't look as if she believed that, but clearly had other things on her mind. "That woman always wanted him, you know."

Eve knew. She'd heard the story enough times over

the years to recite it verbatim. Bertie and Nina Mae had been in love with the same man, Charley Cross. Nina had gotten him for more than thirty years of marriage, although he'd turned out to be no prize. And while Charley had taken off before Eve was born—and not with Bertie Cavanaugh—Nina Mae had never forgiven her friend for trying to steal Charley.

It amazed Eve that even at eighty-six, her grandmother still carried all the old grudges. Clearly time and advanced age didn't heal all wounds. And while her grandmother couldn't remember what had happened two seconds ago, parts of her past were as alive and real for her as if it were yesterday.

"That woman would steal the gold out of your teeth," Nina Mae grumbled as Eve steered her grandmother down the hall to her room and helped her into a chair.

Eve glanced around the room. "Where is your photo album?"

"You sound just like my daughter, Lila, but you don't look a thing like her."

"Isn't that the truth," Eve said, spying the photo album tucked under her grandmother's bed. She pulled it out, sat down on the bed and, her fingers trembling, began to leaf through it, looking for the photograph taken on her grandmother's wedding day.

Eve saw at once that some of the photographs were missing. "Where are your wedding pictures?" she asked her grandmother, who was fidgeting in her chair by the window. "Did you put them away somewhere?" It would be just like her to hide them.

Her grandmother raised her head and for a moment Eve thought she saw understanding in the older woman's eyes. "Who are you?"

"I'm Eve, Grandmother."

"Eve?" The name meant nothing to her. Just like the face. Eve couldn't imagine what it must be like to have chunks of your life, as well as people, erased as if they never existed—and yet her grandmother couldn't seem to forget that Bertie Cavanaugh had wronged her years ago.

Eve had wished for that kind of memory loss when Carter had broken her heart. Unfortunately...or maybe fortunately, she could remember quite well.

"She and that other one steals things."

"What other one?" Eve asked. But her grandmother's mind had moved on to a loose thread on the sleeve of her blouse.

Bereft, Eve watched her grandmother, remembering when she smelled of lilac and would envelop Eve in her arms, holding her in a cocoon of warmth and safety. Her house had smelled of warm bread and she would lift Eve up on the counter and slather butter onto a thick, rich piece and together they would eat the freshly baked bread and Grandma Nina would tell stories between bites as sunlight streamed in the window.

"Grandma?" Eve said, closing the photo album. The photos she remembered were gone. Either someone had taken them. Or her grandmother had hidden or, worse, destroyed them.

Eve reached into her pocket. "Have you ever seen this before?" She cradled the pin in the palm of her hand as she closely watched the elderly woman's expression.

Was there a flicker of recognition?

Nina Mae reached for the pin and took it in her arthritic fingers, turning it to brush her fingertips across each rhinestone, stopping on the one Charley Cross had replaced after her grandmother had lost the stone.

"You remember it," Eve said, her voice wavering.

Grandma Nina Mae's eyes filled with tears as she shoved the pin at Eve. "Get it away from me!" she screamed. "Get it away. Charley. Oh, my precious Charley."

Eve dropped the pin into her shoulder bag and tried to calm her grandmother, but Nina Mae was hysterical now, wailing and wringing her hands.

The nurse came running, demanding to know what had happened.

All Eve could do was shake her head. "Grandma. Grandma, I'm so sorry. I—"

"Please leave," the nurse said irritably. "Let me get her calmed down."

As Eve left the room, she was close to tears. The last thing she'd wanted to do was upset her grandmother. Her mother had been right. Grandma wanted to forget Charley. But did she also want to forget what had happened in that airplane? Because Eve had no doubt that her grandmother had not only recognized the pin—she'd been in that plane.

As Eve was leaving the building, she spied Bertie, both hands in her pockets, hunched protectively over the smock she wore as if hiding something.

Eve was reminded of her grandmother's accusation against Bertie. Was it possible Bertie had taken the photographs? The ones Eve remembered of her grandmother's wedding and the rhinestone pin she was wearing that day?

Or could it have been the other person her grandmother had referred to?

An alarm went off. Eve turned to see the nurse chase down one of the patients who was trying to escape through the side door. When Eve looked down the hall again, Bertie was gone.

Once outside, Eve headed for her pickup, upset with herself. She shouldn't have taken the pin from the plane. She should have told the sheriff about it. It was evidence in a murder investigation.

But Eve knew that was exactly why she'd taken it. For some unknown reason her grandmother's pin had been in that plane. Because her grandmother had been wearing it and her favorite brown coat? Thirty-two years ago her grandmother would have been young and healthy enough to walk away from the crash.

But where did the murdered man fit in?

Eve couldn't explain it but she had a feeling that the truth would force other secrets to come out. Ones she would wish had stayed buried.

Chapter 8

Carter heard the whoop-whoop of the helicopter just moments before it rose up out of the Breaks.

He'd finally dropped off to sleep last night. It had taken a while. He hadn't been able to shake the feeling that the murderer had been out there in the dark last night. That he'd tracked Carter into the Breaks, afraid the sheriff had found the plane.

If the murderer had known where the plane had crashed, then he would have come back and disposed of the body years ago. But it made sense that if the plane had crashed in a blizzard in the middle of winter and the pilot and maybe one of two of the passengers, depending how many had been in the plane, had escaped, they would not necessarily have been able to find the plane again.

The plane had been too well hidden, the area remote.

Few people ever went into this side of the river gorge. Hunters preferred the side with the pines. So did the elk and the large mule deer.

What scared him was that if he was right, the murderer now knew the plane had been found and would cover his tracks, if not disappear entirely.

Then again if it was someone who lived around here, that disappearance would be like a red flag. So there was a good chance that if the killer was local, he might stay put, blend in just as he had for the past thirty-two years, which would only make him harder to find. But none the less dangerous when cornered.

The chopper set down, the motor dying, blades slowing. The doors opened and three crime-lab techs jumped out.

"Mornin'," Carter said, extending a hand. He'd worked with one of the men, a man his age named Maximilian Roswell. Max shook hands with Carter and gave orders to the other men to get the gear ready.

"So what do we have?" Max asked, glancing down in the ravine.

Carter told him about the plane and the body inside. "The last entry in the logbook was February seven, 1975."

Max let out a low whistle and nodded. "You said the body in the plane mummified? That's consistent with the entry in the logbook. If the plane went down in the middle of winter, the body would have kept well, drying out in the cockpit slowly as the weather eventually warmed. And you say the man inside the plane is a passenger. No sign of the pilot?"

"There's a chance the pilot didn't make it out of the Breaks."

"Would be hard to find any remains outside the plane after this long," Max said. "But then, too, he could have made it to one of the ranches."

"If he knew which direction to go," Carter agreed.

"Which could mean he was local. Or that he'd seen the ranches when he'd flown over before the storm hit."

Carter glanced down into the ravine. "What are the chances of identifying the victim?"

"You didn't find a wallet or any other identification?"

"No. I didn't want to disturb the crime scene any more than it had been," Carter said. "What about prints? The person who found the plane climbed inside to get out of a storm."

Max pulled out his notebook. "And this person who found the plane?"

"Her name is Eve Bailey. She just moved back."

Max lifted a brow. "You know her then."

"Yeah," Carter said. "I know her."

After Eve left the nursing home, she stopped by the grocery store as was her usual routine. She never spent much time in Whitehorse, just in and out for supplies and back to the ranch. It had worked well since she'd been home. She hadn't run into Carter. No, that had taken her spending the night in the Breaks, she thought with a groan.

As she came out, a figure stepped from the shadows directly into her path. Startled, she hugged the paper sack of groceries to her and stopped so abruptly she turned her sore ankle again.

"Eve."

Her mind had been on Sheriff Carter Jackson, so she

was even more startled to find his ex-wife, Deena Turner Jackson, standing in front of her, blocking her way.

"Deena." This was something else Eve had tried to avoid—an encounter with Deena.

"I see you found your way out of the Breaks," Deena said, an edge to her voice. "Didn't really need Carter to save you after all."

For the life of her, Eve had never understood the animosity Deena had toward her. Deena had gotten Carter. No contest. Eve hadn't even been in the running. So what was the woman's problem?

Just the sight of Deena brought it all back, though— the hurt, the heartbreak, the betrayal. This was the woman Carter had chosen over her. It was that simple in her mind, that painful to admit.

It didn't help that Deena was so beautiful. Eve had never seen her without makeup or with a hair out of place or wearing something that didn't flatter her.

Eve lived in jeans and always had. Unlike Deena, who had been born and raised in a city, Eve grew up on a ranch. Dresses were something to be worn to weddings, funerals and church.

Also, Eve usually had to pick up feed or fertilizer or some other ranch supply. It would have been pretty silly to dress in anything other than jeans and boots when she came to town.

And that was exactly what she was wearing today— jeans, boots, a Western shirt, her long dark hair in a ponytail, a straw hat pulled down to shade her eyes.

Deena Turner Jackson wore a sundress, sandals and had her blond hair swept up in the latest fashion.

"Is there something you wanted?" Eve asked, realizing that it was no accident their paths had crossed today. Deena must have seen her pickup and been waiting for her.

Around her neck Deena wore a gold chain with what appeared to be her wedding ring hanging from it. She touched the ring now as if it were a talisman, her eyes maybe a little too bright as she smiled at Eve.

Now what? Eve had heard about the divorce, just as she'd heard about the fights and the reconciliations over the years. For whatever reason, Carter and Deena just couldn't seem to stay together any more than they could stay apart.

"Don't get the wrong idea about me and Carter," Deena said.

Eve had no idea what the woman was talking about and said as much.

"There are things you don't know about him."

Eve was sure there were. "Nor do I care." She started to step past, but Deena blocked her way again.

"He isn't the man you think he is."

Eve laughed at that. "You have no idea what kind of man I think he is. Look, Deena, why would I care about Carter Jackson? Remember? He dumped me for you."

Deena brightened a little. "Yes, he did, didn't he?"

"Now if that's all," Eve said, not sure what she would do if Deena tried to block her way again. After all, she was a Bailey and if she hadn't had an armful of groceries…

"You will never have Carter."

Eve bristled. There was nothing she hated more than being told she couldn't have something. She would die trying to prove that person wrong.

Except that one time years ago. Deena had told everyone the very next day that she'd been with Carter. Once

Eve had heard that, she wanted nothing to do with him. Carter had tried to call her a few times. She hadn't taken the calls and avoided him. She'd hidden her heartbreak, graduated and left town as fast as she could. Carter had betrayed her. She had wanted nothing to do with him.

But that was all water under the bridge now. And while she might regret that she hadn't given Deena the fight of her life for Carter, she wasn't going back down that road.

"I repeat, I don't want Carter Jackson," Eve said. "Now get out of my way."

Deena hesitated, but only a second before stepping back. "He will always be in love with me," she called after Eve. "He just used you."

Eve did her best to ignore the woman as she climbed into her pickup. She couldn't imagine anything worse than brawling over Carter Jackson in front of the grocery store, especially at this late date.

But at the same time, Eve had no intention of being that nice to Deena next time. And she was certain there would be a next time.

Carter made a few calls on his way home to shower and change. He called in the identification numbers on the downed plane to the Federal Aviation Administration and was waiting to find out who it had belonged to.

He'd forgotten all about Deena until he pulled up in front of his place and saw the package waiting for him on his doorstep.

He hesitated as he started up the walk. The large box was brown cardboard, with some kind of manufacturing printing on the side. He tried to remember if he'd ordered anything, wishing that was the case.

But he knew better. He'd married a woman he hadn't really known, brought her into his life with a wedding ring and a vow to love her until death parted them. He'd even given her his name—something he'd never get back. Just like the years he'd tried to make the marriage work.

Deena didn't love him. He doubted she ever had. Deena just didn't want anyone else to have him. It was crazy. Completely crazy. And scary. To have someone want you so much that they'd do anything to have you. It scared the hell out of him to even think how far she would go.

It reminded him of the time he'd seen a fox corner a mouse at the edge of a fence. The fox would give the mouse an escape route and even a head start before pouncing on it again.

He'd felt sorry for the mouse. Even as the mouse tired, it seemed to hold out hope that the next time it would get away. The fox finally accidentally killed the mouse. He watched the fox bat the dead mouse around. Clearly, the fox was sorry he'd killed it, the game spoiled.

That's how he felt it would be with Deena. He'd thought he'd gotten away when he'd divorced her. But he knew that the only way she'd ever let him go was feetfirst.

Had he really thought that a legal piece of paper would deter Deena? So what was next? Having her arrested? He groaned at the thought.

She'd pulled on every heartstring she could think of on this quest to get him back, to revive the chase. Over the weeks, he'd found a lot of things on his doorstep, on his desk at work, even once before he'd changed the locks, inside his rented house.

Each time, he'd made the mistake of calling her to demand she stop. As a trained officer of the law, he knew about stalkers, knew that the worst thing you could do was respond, because that only encouraged them. It was just hard to see someone you'd loved become a stalker.

He'd known that if she hadn't stopped after being warned a half-dozen times, then a restraining order wasn't going to faze her.

He didn't know what it was going to take.

He stepped closer to the box, half-expecting to find it ticking. The top of the box hadn't been taped, the corners tucked under with only a dark hole at the center.

He considered what to do with it. He thought about calling one of his deputies to dispose of it. But he was so tired of Deena's pranks and presents.

Giving the box a wide berth, he opened his front door, glad to see that nothing seemed amiss. Not that this was any palace. He'd rented it after moving out of the house he'd bought when he and Deena had gotten married.

It was hard to believe that it had been almost two years and he was still living out of boxes.

He recalled Eve's place. She was trying to make the place her own. His house didn't even look lived-in, the walls a faded white just like they'd been when he'd moved in. He thought about the warm colors Eve had tried on the walls. Even with paint cans and cloths on the floor, the feel of her place had made him want to sit down in one of the overstuffed chairs by the window and stay.

He'd been tired for too long.

He stood for a moment, disgusted with himself. For months he had been stalled, unable to move forward, unable to go back.

But after seeing Eve today, he was ready to move on.

He showered, shaved, changed clothes and went to work, avoiding the box on his doorstep.

There were a half-dozen messages on his desk from the newspaper. Glen Whitaker probably wanted a quote. Carter balled up the slips and was about to toss them in the trash can when the dispatcher appeared in his doorway.

"It's Mark Sanders from the newspaper again," she said. "He's trying to find Glen Whitaker. No one has seen him since yesterday evening at the Whitehorse Community Center."

"He's probably just running late," Carter said, making a face. "You know Glen."

She nodded. "What do you want me to tell Mark?"

"That I'm checking into it," Carter said. "Thanks." He had no doubt that Glen Whitaker would show up and, meanwhile, Carter had something he needed to take care of first—a call he'd wanted to make the moment he saw the Navion plane in the ravine.

Loren Jackson answered his cell phone on the third ring. "Carter," his father said, his greeting more jovial than usual, which meant his father must be in his plane, although Carter couldn't hear the engine.

But high in the air seemed to be where Loren was the happiest. That certainly hadn't been the case when he was on the ground in Montana.

"How's Florida?" Carter asked. It was part of their usual ritual. Next they'd discuss the weather and fishing and after that Carter would hang up.

"I wouldn't know."

Carter frowned. Florida weather was either hot or

wet or both. The fishing was either excellent or damned good. "What do you mean, you don't know?"

"Actually, I'm headed your way," Loren Jackson said.

His father hadn't mentioned a visit the last time they'd talked, which hadn't been more than a couple of weeks ago. In fact, the last time they'd talked, Carter had made a point of asking his father to come up to Whitehorse. It had been years since Loren had been back and Carter had only visited his father in Florida once and that was several years ago.

His father had seemed content enough in Florida, but Carter still thought it odd how quickly his father had left after losing his wife to cancer. Also strange was that there were no pictures of Carter's mother in the small beach house his father had bought. There were no pictures of any kind to document Loren Jackson's past except for his first airplane—a Cessna 172.

Apparently, his father hadn't just started over in Florida; he'd completely erased his past as if there was nothing about it he wanted to remember.

Why the sudden change of attitude now? A sliver of worry worked its way under Carter's skin at the thought of the person who'd ridden out to his campsite last night. He'd thought then that the secret was out. Was it possible the horseback rider had warned others?

"Is something wrong?" Carter asked his father now. "You're all right, aren't you?"

"I'm fine. Can't I just want to come visit you and your brother?"

Yeah, sure, maybe. Carter's suspicious mind was wondering if his father had heard about the plane being found. If that was the case, then his father's sudden appearance in Montana would mean that his father had some connection to that plane crash and the dead man inside.

Feeling scared at the thought, he asked, "Dad, did you know anyone around Whitehorse who owned a Navion about thirty years ago?"

"A Navion?" his father repeated. "Listen, son, my cell phone battery is running low. Let me call you back when I get to town."

And just like that, his father was gone.

Carter swore under his breath. Just before Loren Jackson had disconnected Carter thought he heard a meadowlark in the background. But if true, then his father wasn't in his plane. He was already in town.

Either way, Carter felt his mistrust growing at an alarming rate. He wished Eve had never found that damn plane. But then, he suspected she wished the same thing.

Chapter 9

Lila Bailey stood in her kitchen, staring into the refrigerator trying to remember why she'd opened the door to begin with. She was losing her mind. Just like her mother.

It had been like this ever since Eve had disappeared only to return with that ugly rhinestone pin, and now there was a story circulating that a crime-lab helicopter had been seen heading into the Breaks just south of the ranch, the same area Eve had been found yesterday.

Lila stared into the fridge, telling herself she should eat something because she had to get over to the community center and help finish Maddie Cavanaugh's quilt.

And yet she didn't move. She wasn't hungry. She felt numb and scared, and knew her problems with her oldest daughter had started almost from the time Eve was a baby.

Eve had always been difficult. Chester said it was because she was too smart for her britches. Lila suspected it was because Eve had a way of reading people. From the first time Lila held Eve in her arms and offered her a bottle, Eve had looked up at her with suspicion.

Lila had raised all three girls the same, loving them, caring for them, protecting them. If anything, she'd given Eve more love because she'd seemed to need it more than McKenna and Faith.

But maybe it hadn't been love Eve needed most. Lila could still remember the day she went upstairs to put some of the girls' clothing away and found Eve standing in front of the mirror, frowning. Eve couldn't have been more than five at the time.

"I look funny," Eve had said.

"Don't be silly. You're beautiful."

"Why isn't my hair the same color as yours and Daddy's?" she'd asked stubbornly.

Lila had turned away, busying herself with putting the clothing into the dresser drawers. "Because God blessed you with dark hair and eyes. He wanted you to be special."

Eve hadn't bought it. "I don't want to be special."

Lila had turned then to look at Eve. "We're all special. Like snowflakes, no two the same."

Eve's intent eyes had bored into her. "Violet Evans said I didn't belong to you and Daddy. She said I was adopted. What's adopted?"

"Violet Evans is a…silly goose. I don't want you listening to a thing she says." Lila wanted to wring Violet's neck. The girl must have overheard her mother spreading gossip.

It wounded Lila that Violet could do something so

mean. Lila intended to have a word with Violet's mother. She knew Arlene was just jealous. Eve was such a beautiful child. Violet was plain and gangly like her mother.

"Now go outside and play," Lila had ordered Eve, and walked out of the room.

But Eve being Eve, it hadn't ended there.

"Lila?"

She whirled around at the sound of her name, at the familiar and yet painful sound of it on his tongue and stared in shock at the man standing in her kitchen.

It had been so many years and yet it felt as if it had only been yesterday.

He stepped past her to close the fridge door, brushing her shoulder as he did.

She felt a jolt of electricity shoot through her, leaving her weak and trembling. "Loren."

"I knocked but no one answered," he said, studying her now. He looked so large in her big roomy kitchen. But then Loren Jackson had always taken up too much space around her. "I came right from the airport."

"What are you doing here?" Her voice was raspy, sounding like she felt. Close to tears.

She wanted to throw herself into his arms, remembering the feel of being wrapped up in him, needing him now more than he could imagine.

"I just heard that Chester moved out," he said. "I'm sorry. Are you all right?"

Sometimes she forgot Chester was still alive, still her husband. For her, he was neither.

"I'm fine," she said, the worst kind of lie.

She stared at the man she'd once loved more than life. Loren Jackson had changed. He was tan, his hair completely gray but cut short, making him look distinguished. He was still a large man, broad in the shoulders. Still devastatingly handsome.

She thought of his son, Carter. Handsome like his father. In fact, Carter resembled Loren when Loren was that age. She felt a flush of shame remembering the day she had caught Carter and Eve kissing. The jealousy she'd felt. Lila had been relieved when they'd broken up. It was better for her not seeing Carter, not remembering his father.

"You shouldn't have come," she said, turning away from Loren now.

"You had to know I would."

She grabbed the edge of the kitchen counter. No, she hadn't known he would. A part of her believed she would never see him again, hoped she wouldn't.

"Lila, why didn't you let me know the moment Chester left?" he asked behind her.

She shook her head. Because it was too late. It had been too late the moment Loren married Rachel Hanson.

Loren came around until he stood so close she could feel goose bumps rise on her arms. Her heart threatened to burst at even the thought that he might touch her.

And then he did, his hands cupping her shoulders. She felt the shock, then the warmth, then the comfort that she'd craved since the first time Loren Jackson had brushed his lips over hers, the first time he'd made love to her. She leaned into him as if coming home.

"Lila, you need me. Don't send me away again."

"Mother?"

Lila jerked back at the sound of Faith's voice. At the shocked, reproachful tone of it.

"Mr. Jackson?" Faith said as Loren let go of Lila and turned around. Faith sounded both surprised and upset to see him, but then she'd always been Chester's favorite. Of the three girls, Faith had taken it the hardest when Chester moved out.

"Mr. Jackson stopped by looking for Carter," Lila said.

Faith's gaze narrowed. "I didn't see the sheriff's patrol car when I pulled in."

"Carter is probably down at Eve's," Lila said.

"I should go," Loren said, obviously feeling the same chill in the room that Lila now did. He stepped past Faith, giving her a nod just as he'd done Lila and then he was gone. Again.

Lila stared after him, trembling inside, intensely aware of the gnawing ache that seemed to be eating away the last of her sanity.

Faith gave her a disgusted look as she passed. "I would expect better of you, Mother."

Lila couldn't imagine why, as her daughter stomped up the stairs just as she'd done as a child. Chester would have gone after her, tried to soothe her.

But Lila moved to the window to watch Loren Jackson drive away, her emptiness so complete she felt as if she were weightless. Like this morning's rumors about the body found in a plane in the Breaks. Nothing left but a mummified skeleton. Everything that had made it human lost long ago.

Upset over the phone call to his father, Carter drove down to the Milk River. The sun lolled high in a cloudless blue sky, making the air hot and dry. Crickets chirped from the bushes as Carter pulled up. His radio squawked. It was the call from the FAA.

"I have that information you asked for on the Navion," the man said.

Carter listened, then thanked him and got out of the patrol car. Opening the door to the bait shop, he found his brother in the back filling the minnow tank.

Cade Jackson looked up but didn't say anything as he continued working. Cade was the older, taller and more pigheaded of the two brothers. But he was also the most solid, both of his feet firmly planted in Montana, stable as granite.

Like Carter, his hair was dark, his eyes a deep brown. Women had always flirted abashedly with Cade.

But there had been only one woman for his brother. Carter wondered if it ran in the family.

"Well?" Cade asked, without turning around. "I wondered how long it would take before you came by."

"You heard Dad's coming to town?" Maybe already in town.

"Yep. He called earlier. He said he'd see me later today."

That was so like their father to call Cade, but not him. "He say what he's doing here? I mean don't you think it's a little strange?"

"Didn't say and no I don't think it's any stranger than Eve Bailey getting lost in the Breaks and you having to rescue her," Cade said, humor in his voice.

It had never dawned on Carter that anyone might think Eve had spent the night in the Breaks just to get his attention. "Eve wouldn't do that." Deena would, if she'd have thought of it.

"She's a woman and so far it isn't apparent why she's back in town," Cade joked.

Carter groaned. "Trust me, I'm the last guy on earth she wanted to find her."

Cade turned from the tank to look at him. "So it's true? You never got over her."

"I didn't come in here to talk about Eve Bailey," Carter snapped, making his brother laugh. "I need to ask you something."

Cade turned off the water, wiped his wet hands on a towel and gave his brother his undivided attention.

"Did you ever hear Dad or Gramps talk about a four-seater Navion going down in the Breaks?"

Cade blinked. "That's what you have to ask me? You sounded so serious, I thought—" He stopped abruptly. "Damn, did you find the plane?"

"Eve did, but it's under investigation, so I need you to keep it under your hat for the time being," Carter said, knowing he could trust his brother. Also knowing the news was probably already spreading faster than a wildfire, with the crime-scene helicopter flying over White-horse and Old Town this morning.

"I remember a few planes, but none that weren't found." Cade was watching him. "What kind of investigation?"

"Criminal. There's a body still in the plane. Looks like the guy was murdered."

Cade swore. "But what does this have to do with Dad? He hasn't even lived here for—"

"The plane's been there for thirty-two years apparently," Carter said. "You got to admit, it's odd. The plane is found and not twenty-four hours later Dad flies in."

"You're not thinking Dad was the pilot," Cade said.

"There weren't that many pilots around this area

thirty-two years ago. Especially ones who had their own airstrip—the closest airstrip to the crash."

"The pilot probably wasn't local."

"The plane was. I just got the call from FAA. It belonged to a guy from Glasgow."

"So how could that have anything to do with Dad or Gramps?" Cade demanded.

"Thirty-two years ago, the owner had been dead for two years," Carter said. "The plane had been stored in a hangar at the airport. The man's wife went to sell the plane only to find out it was gone."

Cade shook his head. "Come on, you think Dad or Gramps stole some guy's plane? Why would they do that? They both had their own planes."

Carter could think of several reasons they would do that. "Dad and Gramps would have known about a Navion sitting in a hangar in Glasgow. They would also have heard that the guy was dead and the plane wasn't being used."

Cade rolled his eyes. "Circumstantial evidence at best."

"Come on, you know as well as I do that their crop dusters didn't go as fast and weren't as durable as an aluminum plane. Not to mention their planes were too well-known in the area."

"You're saying they had some reason not to want to be recognized?" Cade swore. "You think the plane was carrying some sort of contraband?" He scoffed. "If they didn't want to attract attention, they'd have used their own planes. No one would think anything of one of the Jacksons' planes landing on the Jackson ranch airstrip."

He had a point.

"But then I'd have to believe that Dad or Gramps were killers," Cade scoffed.

Carter had been a sheriff long enough to know that anyone could kill under certain circumstances.

"This is crazy."

Carter agreed. This was crazy. "We'll know more when we find out who the victim was. The crime-lab techs are getting the body out now. With Dad probably already in town, I just have a bad feeling about this."

"Like Dad could keep some deep dark secret all these years." Cade turned back to his minnows. "You really should take up fishing again. You need an outlet other than cops and robbers."

And murderers.

Back in his patrol car, Carter reached for his squawking radio.

"Mark Sanders is on the phone again," the dispatcher said, and Carter groaned inwardly. "Glen Whitaker didn't show for his interview. His car isn't at his apartment and no one has seen him since he left the Whitehorse Community Center yesterday evening."

Carter cursed under his breath. "Tell Mark I'm on my way out to Old Town. I'll keep an eye out for him." As he started the patrol SUV, he told himself he needed to go down there anyway. He had to see Eve.

Eve Bailey glanced at her watch, relieved to see it was the time her mother left to go to the community center to quilt. McKenna and Faith were at work in town and had plans to go to the play in Fort Peck. They wouldn't be home until late tonight.

In the barn, Eve saddled her horse, more than grateful to the mare. She credited the horse with saving her life.

If the mare hadn't returned to the ranch, no one would have known she was missing and Eve was pretty sure she would have never made it back to the ranch on foot yesterday. Last night, she'd been so exhausted, she'd fallen to sleep the moment her head touched the pillow.

As she worked, she grudgingly gave some of the credit for her rescue to Carter Jackson. She hated to think what would have happened if he hadn't found her yesterday. If no one had. That was big country. They could have missed her easily enough.

She tried to tell herself that Carter had just been doing his job. Thoughts of him turned to thoughts of Deena and the run-in with her. Eve wanted nothing to do with either of them.

Carter and Deena had broken up more times than Eve had even heard about, she was sure. But they always got back together. No reason to think they wouldn't this time. Even with the divorce. Eve planned to give them both a wide berth, just as she'd been doing since she'd been home.

As she finished cinching up the saddle, she suddenly had the strangest sensation that she was being watched. Turning, she looked toward the road. Something flashed like sunlight on glass. She blinked. Whatever it had been it was gone. Odd.

She swung up into the saddle, anxious to go for a ride—even only as far as her mother's house. Carter crowded her thoughts again like an unwelcome conscience and she knew as long as she had the rhinestone pin she'd taken from the plane, she wouldn't be able not to think of him.

Heading east, she rode out across the prairie. She made a wide circle, enjoying the ride, and came out behind the ranch house in a stand of trees. As she reined in, she saw her mother leaving in her pickup.

Eve waited until the dust had died down before she dismounted and headed for the house. No one would be back for a long while, but she felt the need to hurry. She knew it was foolish, but she didn't want to get caught up in the old attic searching for her grandmother's favorite brown coat. If the coat was even still there.

Mostly, she hadn't made up her mind what she would do with the coat if she found it and if the threads from the pin matched. Getting caught would only force her into a decision.

She feared her mother would have already gotten rid of the coat—right after Eve had showed her the pin. Unless her mother had forgotten where the coat was stored.

Eve slipped in the side door of the house that had been her home the first eighteen years of her life. The smell alone brought back good memories. She felt guilty for her suspicions as she moved quickly toward the back stairs.

The old wooden stairs creaked under her step. The house felt strange. Too empty. Even the air had an odd feel to it, as if the house had been abandoned and no one lived here anymore.

Once on the second floor, Eve opened the small door to the attic. It groaned loudly, startling her. She thought she heard a vehicle approaching, froze to listen, but then heard nothing.

Why was she so spooked? But she knew the answer to that. She'd been scared ever since she'd seen that body in the plane, seen the knife sticking out of the man's chest and found her grandmother's rhinestone pin on the floor at the man's feet.

Eve left the door open to let out the musty air of the attic and climbed up the narrow creaking stairs. At the top, she felt around until she found the light switch and snapped it on. Hurriedly she looked around the attic for the old wooden trunk her mother had put the coat in.

The trunk had been at Grandma's house, but Eve's father must have moved it up here after Nina Mae went into the nursing home.

The attic was full of furniture, lamps, even an old crib that Eve and her sisters had slept in. Her mother hadn't thrown anything away apparently.

Eve spied the big wooden trunk in a back corner and worked her way to it. Brushing off cobwebs, she bent down and lifted the lid. The trunk hinges groaned loudly. Eve stopped again to listen. No sound but the pounding of her heart.

Hurriedly, she searched the trunk. The coat wasn't there. She rummaged through the old clothing a second time and realized she'd missed the coat because she'd remembered it as being more substantial than it was.

The coat was just as her mother had said: threadbare. It had been rolled up in a bottom corner—right where her mother had put it.

Eve drew it out with trembling fingers, praying she was wrong as she spread the coat over her lap. She checked one lapel, then the other. In the dim light of the attic, she missed the hole the first time.

The threads had been broken from the spot on the lapel where the pin had been in the photograph Eve remembered. The hole was jagged—as if the pin had been torn from the lapel. She pulled out the threads she'd taken from the pin and compared them. They were a perfect match!

Tears rushed Eve's eyes as she gripped the coat in her hands, fear washing over her. Didn't this prove her grandmother had been in that plane?

A door opened and closed downstairs. Eve rushed to the small dirty window and looked out. She couldn't see a vehicle nor had she heard one since earlier, but she knew someone was here.

Her mother? Had Lila returned for some reason? Or one of her sisters? Eve felt a chill as she remembered that her grandmother hadn't been the only one in the crashed plane. Along with the dead man, there'd been a pilot. Maybe even another passenger. And one of them was a murderer who could still be alive.

Eve's heart raced as she looked around for a place to hide her and the coat. She heard footfalls on the stairs. No time. Someone was headed upstairs.

The light. Belatedly, she reached for the pull cord and turned it off. Had her mother returned and seen the light on in the attic from the road?

She remembered she'd left the attic door open. Whoever was coming up would see that it was open.

She was trapped.

She quickly stuffed her grandmother's coat behind a chest of drawers, then looked around for a place to hide herself. The tall highboy. She could hear footfalls on the attic stairs, the tread too heavy to be her mother's or one of her sister's. The killer? She recalled that feeling of being watched earlier and knew even before she heard him stop, the top stair creaking, that he'd followed her here and knew she was alone.

Chapter 10

Carter heard a soft rustle deep in the attic. "Hello? Eve?"

She let out a groan that sounded both relieved and angry as her head appeared from behind a tall bureau.

"You scared me half to death," she snapped.

"I scared you? Why didn't you answer when I called from downstairs?"

"I didn't hear you."

"What are you doing up here?" he asked as he glanced past her to where she'd been hiding.

"Looking for a lamp for my house," she said a little too quickly. "Not that it's any of your business."

He raised a brow. "Really? In the dark? And I would have thought you'd have driven your pickup over if you were planning to pick up a lamp instead of riding your horse."

"Are you spying on me?" she demanded as he snapped on the light.

"As a matter of fact, I drove down to make sure you were all right. I was worried when I saw you ride off again so I followed you on foot. This lamp you're after, it must be valuable. Otherwise, why wait for your mother to leave before you sneaked up here to get it?"

"I didn't sneak."

It was clear to him that she hadn't wanted anyone to know she was here. Now why was that, he wondered as he noticed a large old wooden trunk, the lid up, the clothes inside it appearing recently rummaged through.

"What's going on, Eve?" he asked seriously. "After everything you went through yesterday, why the urgency to get a lamp out of—" He stopped as he heard a vehicle engine followed shortly by the slamming of a car door.

Eve heard it, too. He saw the fear in her eyes. What the hell was going on?

Her attention darted to the old trunk with the lid standing open.

As he heard the front door open and close and foot-falls cross the hardwood floor, he reached over and closed the trunk lid and saw relief in Eve's expression.

She hurried to snap off the light an instant before he pulled her back behind the high bureau where she'd been hiding before and whispered, "Did I mention I saw your mother head for your house? I think she was looking for you."

He felt rather than saw her reaction. She seemed to hold her breath and listen, just as he was doing as they hunkered behind the highboy.

The footsteps seemed to hesitate at the bottom of the

attic stairs. Whoever it was had seen the open attic door, just as he had. A moment later, the attic steps groaned.

He waited. He could feel Eve doing the same.

The last stair creaked, then the light snapped on and footfalls moved across the floor.

Carter peered around the end of the highboy to see Lila Bailey drop to her knees in front of the old wooden trunk, the same one that he'd just closed.

He glanced over at Eve. She had leaned to the edge of the highboy and was now watching her mother. She didn't seem surprised as the trunk lid groaned open.

Lila began to dig frantically through the trunk, then slammed the lid with a curse. "Oh, Eve, what have you done?" she cried. Then she did the last thing Carter expected. Lila put her head down on her arms on the top of the trunk and began to sob.

Carter felt Eve's hand on his arm as if she wanted to go to her mother. But then she removed it and stayed behind the bureau with him until her mother's sobs subsided. Lila dried her eyes, turned out the light and went back down the stairs, shutting the attic door behind her.

It wasn't until Carter heard Lila drive away that he stepped out from behind the bureau and turned on the light, his focus going to Eve. "What have you done, Eve?" He could see that she was shaken after what she'd witnessed. "Eve, talk to me."

It was his soft tone that was Eve's undoing. She couldn't pretend that he didn't know her. Or she, him. Nor could she go on carrying this burden alone.

Slowly, she reached into her pocket. She'd wrapped the pin in a flowered handkerchief that she'd found in her grandmother's house. It smelled of lavender.

She could feel Carter watching with interest as she carefully pulled back the tatted edges of the kerchief to expose the rhinestone pin.

"It belonged to my grandmother," she said.

Carter held out his hand and frowned as she dropped it into his palm.

"It was a present from my grandfather, Charley Cross," Eve said. "Grandma Nina Mae wore it on her brown coat at her wedding. She never took it off the coat. She told me that when she lost it, just like when she lost Charley, she never got over it."

"Eve, what does this have to do with—"

"Her pin…" Eve's throat tightened, her heart aching at even the thought of what she was about to do. She wished she'd never found the plane. Never found the pin. Never recognized it. She swallowed, thinking about her grandmother. "I found her pin on the plane."

He stared down at the piece of jewelry in surprise. "You found this on the downed plane in the Breaks?"

She nodded, close to tears.

"How can you be sure it's your grandmother's?" he asked, the ramifications of what she was saying obviously finally hitting home.

"A few days before my grandparents got married, Grandma lost one of the rhinestones out of the pin." Eve had heard the story a thousand times so she knew it by heart, but she stumbled over the words. "Nina Mae was just sick about it. So my grandfather took the pin and, even though it was only costume jewelry, had a jeweler in Great Falls put another stone in. If you look closely you can tell which one it was. The stone never quite matched because it's a diamond."

"Eve, slow down. This doesn't prove…" His eyes widened. "There's more." He let out a curse. "Of course there's more."

She brushed at an errant tear, miserable. "Grandma always wore the pin on her favorite brown coat. Both were in all the old wedding photographs. I found brown fibers on the back of the pin. I checked them. They match. There's also a hole in the lapel where the pin had been torn free."

He glanced at the trunk. "That's what your mother was looking for?"

She nodded.

Carter took a breath and let it out slowly. "Eve, do you know what you're saying here?"

She chewed at her cheek, feeling as if she'd just betrayed not only her grandmother, but her entire family. Her grandmother would never know, but her mother...

Eve was still shaken after seeing her mother cry the way she had. It had taken everything in Eve not to go to her. But she knew that Lila would be horrified to know there had been witnesses to her breakdown.

Her mother's reaction to not finding the coat in the trunk pretty much told the rest of the story. Lila Bailey, the queen of secret-keepers.

Yes, Eve thought, she knew exactly what she was saying. Not only was her grandmother on that plane, but her mother knew about it and had kept Grandma Nina Mae's secret all these years.

That's why Eve hadn't told Carter about the pin the morning he found her in the Breaks. Because she'd feared that if her grandmother had been on that plane, then someone in her family had to have known. And her grandmother knew not only the victim, but also the killer.

"Eve, a man was murdered," Carter said. "There is no statute of limitations on murder. Also, there is a law, as you well know, about withholding evidence."

"I had to be sure it was Grandma's."

"You said there are photographs of your grandmother wearing the coat and pin?"

She hated to tell him. "The photos seem to have disappeared."

He swore. "And you don't know anything about what happened to them."

"No, I don't," she snapped. Not that she could blame him for not believing her. She'd kept the information about the pin from him. And might have kept the coat from him as well. Just as she hadn't told him about showing the pin to her mother.

One betrayal per day was enough.

Carter was stunned. He had suspected Eve was withholding information from him, but he'd never dreamed it might be something like this.

To make matters worse, if she was right and her grandmother had been on that plane, then they might never know the truth—at least not from Nina Mae Cross.

Nina Mae had Alzheimer's. Whatever her role was in all this, it was lost somewhere in her deteriorating mind.

"Who knew you'd found the pin in the plane?" he asked.

Eve hesitated, but only for a moment. "I didn't tell anyone about the plane."

"But you showed your grandmother the pin."

She nodded, looking contrite. "At first she just seemed so happy to see it again, but then she became hysterical and wanted nothing to do with it."

Carter shook his head. "I wish you'd told me about this."

The answer was in her eyes. She hadn't trusted him. Given their history, he couldn't blame her.

And yet she had told him about the pin. True, he had her cornered in an attic, but maybe she was starting to trust him again.

"So the coat was in the trunk," he said, recalling Lila Bailey's reaction to not finding what she was looking for. So Lila knew about the pin as well. Did it follow that she knew about the plane? And the murdered man?

How many others around here knew and had kept the secret? He hated to think.

He looked at Eve and wanted to take her in his arms and hold her. He would do anything to protect her from what he feared would come out of this investigation. She looked pale and scared. He knew the feeling.

"Even if your grandmother was on the plane, she didn't kill that man and we both know it. Where is the coat?"

Eve stepped behind a chest of drawers and pulled out the rolled-up brown cloth. With obvious reluctance, she handed it to him.

"The coat is threadbare, but my grandmother's wish was to be buried in it—"

"I'll make sure you get it and the pin back," he said.

"What happens now?"

"I'll have to hang on to both as evidence, Eve," he said, not any happier about that than she was. He'd known Nina Mae Cross and her daughter Lila Bailey all his life.

"I'd like to be alone now," she said.

He didn't want to leave her, but he had no choice.

As far as he knew, the reporter Glen Whitaker was still missing and he needed to talk to Lila Bailey.

"Eve, be careful. Whoever killed that man in the plane...well, the murderer might not have gone very far thirty-two years ago. Not very far at all."

Sick at heart, Eve rode her horse home only to find a note from her mother.

Eve,
I have to attend a funeral in Great Falls. I'm not sure when I'll be back. Please don't do anything until I return. We need to talk,
Mom.

A funeral in Great Falls. Eve didn't believe it for a moment. Her mother had taken off knowing questions would be demanded of her.

Eve opened all the windows as if fresh air would chase away the fear, the anger, the concern for both her grandmother and her mother.

The curtains billowed in the breeze. The day smelled of new grass and sunshine and, soon, the usual—paint.

She had changed into her paint clothes, needing to do physical labor, needing to forget everything that had happened since she'd come home.

But as she stood in the middle of the room, paint brush in hand, she had that odd sense again of being watched.

She moved to the edge of the window and looked down the dirt road. The grass grew tall on both sides. She could hear crickets chirping, smell fresh-cut hay, see birds teetering on the phone lines overhead.

There was no sign of anyone spying on her, and yet she couldn't shake the feeling.

Worse, as she turned her attention back to the mess in the living room, she couldn't remember why she'd even started this project. She hadn't planned to stay. She'd only intended to remain here until she had satisfied the questions she had in her mind. Fixing up her grandmother's house had been just something to keep her busy until she could get to her real reason for coming home.

And that reason had been to find herself. For as long as she could remember, she'd been restless. Isn't that why she'd believed there was some secret involving her?

It had been a series of things that made her still believe that. How different she looked from the rest of her family. Finding those mysterious letters under her mother's sewing room floorboards that mentioned "the child." The feeling that she had another family somewhere.

She'd come home convinced that the answer was here and that she'd never be happy until she found out the truth.

Now all she wanted to do was leave. To run. She was good at running. Bad at staying and fighting for what she wanted. Only she'd never wanted to run as badly as she did right now.

She picked up the can of paint and climbed the ladder. She couldn't run. Not this time. She'd come home to put some matters to rest, including what was going on with her parents. Finding the crashed plane in the Breaks, well, she'd gotten more than she'd bargained for, because that had brought Carter Jackson into her life again— and left her with even more questions about her family.

She shivered and opened the can of paint. After dipping in the brush, she made a wide swipe of color across the wall, then leaned back a little to consider it.

The paint was a warm orange shade that complemented the woodwork. It reminded her of sunsets down in the Breaks, when the horizon appeared to be on fire. Color would shoot up into the sky. Pinks and reds and pale yellows.

Her mother would hate the orange. That alone should have made it perfect. Eve just couldn't make up her mind. She was edgy, worried, afraid. All the things she'd been that had forced her to come back here.

She leaned against the ladder, thinking about her mother slumped over the trunk sobbing as if her heart were breaking. But it was her mother's words she heard now echoing in her thoughts: "Eve, what have you done?"

What had she done?

The phone rang. She put down her paintbrush and went into the kitchen, brushing an errant lock of her hair back from her face as she picked up the phone. "Hello?"

"Eve?"

"Dad." She couldn't believe how glad she was to hear his voice right now.

"I was wondering if you wanted to come up to White-horse for dinner?" Chester Bailey asked, sounding shy and unsure. "I have the day off and I thought…"

Eve felt a drowning wave of guilt. She hadn't seen him since she'd come back, although she had talked to him a couple of times on the phone. "Sure, I'd love to," she said, even though driving to Whitehorse was the last thing she wanted to do.

She looked down at her paint clothes. "It could take me a while."

"No problem. I'll meet you at the Hi-Line Café."

* * *

After driving a few back roads, but having no luck finding the missing reporter, Carter returned to his office hoping there would have been word.

While Glen Whitaker hadn't turned up, Carter did find his father waiting for him in his office.

Loren Jackson fidgeted in one of the chairs opposite his son's desk. He didn't seem to hear the door open, giving Carter a moment to study his father.

Loren Jackson was television-rancher handsome. He was a man who'd always been larger than life, tanned and looking healthy as a horse.

But there was also something about him that made Carter uneasy. His father was clearly nervous. What had made him fly in so unexpectedly and right after a crashed plane had been found in the Breaks? Something was up with Loren Jackson and Carter had a bad feeling he knew what it was.

"Dad," he said, stepping the rest of the way into the room. "Just couldn't stay away any longer, huh?"

Loren Jackson stood as Carter held out his hand. The two clasped hands for a moment before Loren pulled him into a quick hug. "It's good to see you, son."

"You, too, Dad." Carter stepped behind his desk, wishing he hadn't noticed that the notes on his desk that he'd taken regarding the plane in the Breaks had been moved. "You just get homesick for Montana?"

His father nodded, but gave no explanation for what he was doing here. "You look good. They keeping you busy?"

Idle chitchat?

Carter leaned back in his chair. "What's going on, Dad?"

His father gave him a confused look and shook his head. "Can't I come see my favorite son?"

"Cade is your favorite son," Carter said, only half joking. "Find anything interesting in my notes?" he asked.

Loren shook his head slowly, giving up all pretense. "Why the interest?"

"You know me and planes."

"Yeah, I do. I also know there's more than a good chance that you knew the pilot."

"Oh? You've found him, then?" Loren asked, sounding surprised.

"Not yet, but I will."

"After all this time, does it really matter?"

Carter stared at his father in surprise. "Yeah. As I'm sure you read in my notes, a murdered man was found in the plane."

Loren Jackson said nothing.

"Why don't you tell me what you know about it," Carter suggested.

"Me?"

"You going to also tell me you didn't know a pilot from Glasgow who owned a Navion?" Carter pressed. "Couldn't have been many Navions within an hour's drive from Whitehorse."

"What was the pilot's name?"

"Herman 'Buzz' Westlake," Carter said patiently, knowing his father probably knew far more than he did about this whole affair.

"Buzz, sure, I knew him," Loren said.

"You ever fly his plane?"

Loren thought about that for a few moments as if deciding what answer might be best. "You know I think

I did. Buzz took me up once. Let me take the controls. Nice plane."

Carter could see he was getting nowhere. "Dad, if you know something—"

"Son," Loren said, getting to his feet. "I just came home to see you and your brother. It had been too long. This plane being found...well, it's just too bad. You'll have everyone looking at their neighbors, suspecting each other. No good can come from this. Hell, boy, it was years ago. Who cares?"

"I do. Someone got away with murder. That someone might still be living around here."

His father frowned. "Not very dangerous, since apparently he hasn't killed anyone since." Loren Jackson moved to the door and stopped, turning back to face his son. "You've seldom listened to any advice I've given you. This is the one time you really should. What's past is past. Let this one slide. It's best for everyone involved."

Carter couldn't believe what he was hearing. "In case it's slipped your mind, I'm the sheriff. I'm paid to uphold the law. I don't let some murders slide. No matter how old they are. Or who's involved."

"That's too bad, son. Because I'm afraid you'll end up hurting the people you care about the most." With that, he turned and left, leaving Carter fearing the same thing.

Chester Bailey looked up as Eve walked into the café, his face instantly lighting up at the sight of her and making her feel all the more guilty for not making a point of seeing him sooner.

"Eve," he said, getting to his feet to fold her in his arms. "It's so good to see you." He held her tight for a moment, then stepped back to look into her face and saw her tears. "Is something wrong?"

She shook her head. "It's just so great to see you." For years her only visits had been quick ones, little more than overnight and she was gone again.

Eve had come home, against her mother's protests, and moved into her Grandma's little house since it was sitting empty.

"What would you want with that old house?" her mother had demanded.

"The house has a lot of possibilities."

"Oh, Eve, you have no business back here. There are no possibilities for a woman your age," her mother had said.

"What is it you're so afraid of?" Eve had asked. "Why would my coming back threaten you so much, Mother?"

"Don't be ridiculous," Lila had snapped. "I just don't want this life for you. Your sisters are only home for the summer. I can't imagine what would bring you back here."

"Can't you?" Eve had asked.

"You settling into your grandmother's house all right?" her father asked now, as he motioned to the booth.

"Yes, thank you," she said as she slid into the booth across from her father. He seemed smaller than she remembered, his shoulders a little more stooped, his hair much grayer and yet as he smiled across the table at her, he looked incredibly boylike.

"It's what your grandmother would have wanted," Chester said, then frowned as if wondering why she'd wanted the house, why she'd come back. "I'm glad you came home."

"I thought Mother might need me," she said, stumbling a little over the lie. "And you. How are you?"

"Just fine." He picked up his menu. "The special is chicken-fried steak, but have anything you want. Susie makes a fine fried boneless trout."

Susie? Just then a blond woman came out of the kitchen. She was small and slim, her face tanned and lined. Eve realized Susie had to be about her father's age.

"This is my daughter, Eve," Chester said.

Susie smiled at once. "Eve. I've heard so much about you. Your father is so proud of you. Maybe you could give me some tips on how to make this place look better," she said with a laugh.

"Susie just bought the café," Chester said. "I told her how you majored in interior design."

Eve nodded, sensing how close her father and Susie had become. "The place looks great," was all she managed to say. "I'll take some iced tea and the special," she said, without looking at the menu.

"I'll take the same," he said, smiling up at Susie as he handed her both menus.

The door tinkled behind them and Hugh Arneson from the lumberyard came in. "Eve," he called, "glad to hear you made it out all right."

Chester's smile faded a little as he waved to Hugh and asked Eve what that was about.

"I spent the night in the Breaks," she said. "A storm came in. It was just stupid on my part."

Her father's eyes widened. "When the hell did that happen?"

"Night before last. But I'm fine, really."

"I can't believe this is the first I'm hearing about this." He sighed. "I've been putting in a lot of hours at work.

I didn't even get down to Whitehorse until today so I guess that explains it. But I would have thought your mother would have tried to reach me."

"It wasn't necessary," Eve said, covering for her mother and wondering why. She lowered her voice. "Dad, what happened between you and Mom?"

He looked immediately uncomfortable. "Nothing happened. It's just easier living up here with me working in Saco."

Eve shook her head and looked out the café window. A half-dozen dirty pickups were parked along Main Street from the hardware store to the newspaper office.

"Honey," her dad said, reaching over to cover her hand with his. "Your mother and I just need a little time alone."

"Then you aren't getting a divorce," Eve asked in a whisper, her voice cracking with emotion. She hadn't realized until that moment how much she didn't want them to divorce.

"No, of course we aren't getting divorced," Chester said, then looked even more uncomfortable as Susie appeared to place two tall glasses of iced tea on the table. Susie had heard what he'd said. Her cheeks flamed with color and she quickly excused herself.

Eve had trouble catching her breath. Clearly her father was seeing Susie and at least Susie had thought Chester and Lila were getting a divorce. Eve took a long drink of the iced tea, knowing she wouldn't be able to eat a bite of her dinner.

Some more locals entered the café, all coming over to tell Eve how glad they were that she was all right. She thanked them, seeing that her father was getting more upset by the moment.

"I still can't understand why your mother didn't call me," he said.

Well, she's been kind of busy with another man. That and running off to funerals in Great Falls.

Did her father know about Errol Wilson? Is that why he'd moved out?

It dawned on Eve that she hadn't seen her mother take any clothing when she left the house earlier. Had her mother just come up with the funeral in Great Falls after she'd found the brown coat missing? Or had she gone to the Whitehorse Sewing Circle, then planned to pick up clothing for the funeral and leave? And was Errol Wilson going with her?

Their dinners came and they ate, making small talk about Old Town and Whitehorse. Eve managed to choke down some of her meal. The rest she moved around her plate until her father was through with his.

"I should get going," Eve said. "I want to stop by and see Grandma before I go home. Thank you for dinner."

"Let's do it again. Soon."

She nodded and rose to leave. "Take care of yourself," she said as he rose and gave her a hug.

He nodded, his attention following Susie as she went to a table of some local men.

"If you get down to the ranch, you should come see what I'm doing with the house," she said.

He nodded distractedly. "I don't get down that way much anymore."

After his father left, Carter sat in his office wondering if a child ever knew his parent. It was late, but he wasn't ready to go home. He'd never thought of his old man as someone who harbored secrets. But now Carter felt he'd only touched the tip of the iceberg when it came to Loren Jackson.

The thought scared him more than he wanted to admit.

Had his father tried to warn him off this case because he was the pilot of that plane? Thirty-two years ago his father would have only been twenty-four. Loren Jackson could have been flying that plane.

But so could his father, Martin "Ace" Jackson, who'd flown in WWII. So who was his father trying to protect? Himself? Or Ace?

Carter swore. Did he really believe that his father or grandfather could be murderers?

He picked up the phone and called to see if either of the deputies had had any luck finding Glen Whitaker. Neither had. Carter just hoped that nothing had happened to the newspaper reporter.

At the sound of a footfall, he looked up to find Maximilian Roswell standing in his doorway holding a large plastic container.

"Evidence from the plane," Max said, and stepped in, kicking the door closed behind him as he set the container on one of the chairs across from Carter's desk.

Carter felt a moment of panic as he stood and watched Max slide open the container, revealing at least a dozen evidence bags. "You might want to sit down, Sheriff. What I have to show you could come as a shock."

Chapter 11

Glen Whitaker came to in a barrow pit with the taste of coconut in his mouth. He was cold and confused, his legs weak, his head aching.

He managed to stumble to his feet. The landscape was flat and went on forever. He had no idea where he was.

But he could see his car in the opposite ditch, the front fender crumpled around a wood fence post.

He swore and tried to remember wrecking his car and couldn't. He took a step, surprised by how feeble he felt. His hand went to his forehead and he touched the double goose egg where he must have smacked his head on something when he hit the fence post. His body ached all over as if he'd been beaten.

Is that why he couldn't remember anything?

He stood, dizzy and dazed, and realized the last thing he remembered was waking up in his bed and wanting pancakes. When was that? This morning? Or yesterday morning? He stared at the horizon. If the sunset was any indication, he'd lost an entire day. Maybe more.

As he headed for his car, hoping it would at least get him to the nearest ranch house, he grimaced at the taste of coconut in his mouth and the smell of too-sweet perfume on his shirt.

What had happened to him?

The nurse stopped Eve as she entered the rest home. "It took us an hour to calm your grandmother down after you left. Whatever the problem was, let's not have a repeat of it this evening."

Eve promised she wouldn't upset her. But as she started down the hallway to Nina Mae's room, she wondered if she could keep that promise. Maybe just the sight of her would set her grandmother off again.

As she came around the corner of the hallway, she saw a man coming out of Nina Mae's room. He had a photograph in his hand and was looking at it. He must have heard Eve's approach, because he quickly turned, pocketing the photograph as he did and went out the side door, setting off the alarm.

Several of the nurses came running. Eve realized she hadn't moved. She'd been too caught up in wondering why he was in her grandmother's room—and trying to place him.

He was tall, nice looking with dark hair and eyes. She'd seen him before, but she couldn't recall where.

And then it came to her.

Bridger Duvall. He was the man who was renting the McAllister Place in Old Town. The mystery man.

At her grandmother's door, Eve stopped and looked

in. Nina Mae's photo album was open on her lap and, even from the doorway, Eve could see a white spot on the page where another one of the photos was missing.

Did Bridger Duvall know her grandmother? Would Nina Mae have given him a photograph?

Her grandmother closed her eyes, the photo album sliding off her lap and hitting the floor. Nina Mae didn't stir.

Eve stepped in and picked up the album, studying the photos on the page where the latest one was missing. With a start she saw that the other three snapshots on the page were of her grandmother and her when she was a baby.

What would Bridger Duvall want with a photo of her and Nina Mae? As far as she knew he didn't know anyone in the area. But then why had he rented a house here?

Nina Mae opened her eyes.

"Grandma Nina Mae," Eve said, closing the album and kneeling down beside her grandmother's chair. She felt horrible for upsetting her earlier. "How are you doing?"

"Who are you?" she demanded peevishly.

This was so hard. Eve put her head down, bone weary. What had made her think coming home would give her peace? She ached all over and wished she was anywhere but here right now.

"I'm Eve, your granddaughter. I know, I don't look anything like you," she said, before Nina Mae could.

"Of course you don't look like me," her grandmother snapped. "You're adopted."

Eve froze. "What did you say?"

Her grandmother didn't answer.

Eve raised her head slowly. Nina Mae's expression

had softened. She reached out with a hand and gently touched Eve's cheek, her fingers cool and smooth. Tears sprang to Eve's eyes. "You remember me, don't you?" she whispered.

Nina Mae smiled, then closed her eyes and leaned back in the chair again. "Of course I remember you."

Her sisters had told her that Grandma Nina Mae sometimes had lucid moments. Was it possible this was one of them? "I was adopted. That's why I don't look like any of you, why I feel so restless and incomplete, isn't it, Grandma."

"How should I know?" her grandmother answered without opening her eyes.

"Because you're my grandmother."

"You have me mixed up with someone else. Don't you think I'd know my own grandmother?"

She'd said grandmother. Not granddaughter.

Eve rested her head against the arm of Nina Mae's chair, fighting tears. Her grandmother didn't know what she was talking about.

"She called earlier, you know," Nina Mae said.

"Who?" Eve asked.

"Grandmother. She asked when I was coming to see her. I told her I couldn't come for a while. I'm needed here."

Eve felt goose bumps dimple her skin. The nurses said elderly patients often discussed talking to deceased relatives about going home just before they died. Eve didn't want to lose her grandmother. But then she'd already lost her, hadn't she?

She patted Nina Mae's hand until she fell back to sleep and began to snore softly. Rising, Eve looked down at her grandmother and felt a chill, although the room was uncomfortably hot. Eve had been convinced moments ago that her grandmother knew her, knew what she was saying.

Just like those few moments when Nina Mae had held the rhinestone pin her husband Charley Cross had given her so many years ago. Eve had seen the look on her face. She'd recognized the pin and had been remembering the good times connected with it. At least for a while.

Of course the pin would also come with bad memories, given that Charley had run off and left her.

She had so many questions, and now Grandma Nina Mae could no longer provide the answers. Eve had waited too long.

Wasn't it possible that Nina Mae spoke the truth without even realizing it? As a young girl, Eve had been convinced she was adopted. But, according to her birth certificate, she was born on February 5, 1975, at home. The local doctor, Dr. Holloway, had driven down from Whitehorse in a blizzard to deliver her.

With a start she remembered the date she'd found in the logbook from the crashed airplane. February 7, 1975. Just two days later.

On the way home, Eve got behind a rancher moving his tractor down the road to another field. She'd forgotten what it was like having farm implements on the highways, as well as ranchers often moving livestock in the middle of the road. But she hadn't forgotten this slower-paced life or that she'd missed it. She'd missed home, and that surprised her. Missed the people, the place.

She thought of Carter. His divorce from Deena had nothing to do with her coming home. Nothing. He'd go back to Deena. He always had. She shoved him out of her thoughts.

Too bad she couldn't do the same with the airplane she'd discovered in the gulch. Or the rhinestone pin. Or the fact that she believed her grandmother had been in that plane.

She thought of Bridger Duvall. She'd have to tell Carter about seeing him at the rest home. She was positive he'd taken the photo from Nina Mae's album.

But why would he want a photograph of Grandma and her? It creeped her out that if she was right, Bridger Duvall had a photo of her as a baby.

Her head hurt from trying to understand what was going on. She'd planned to ask her father some questions, but the café had gotten too crowded and her father had been so...different.

She had a flash of the way he'd smiled up at Susie. Her heart spasmed at the realization that her father might be happier where he was now than on the ranch with her mother.

Had he found out about Lila and Errol? Is that why he'd left? Eve hadn't been able to bring herself to ask. She didn't want to be the one to tell him if he didn't know. Maybe, more to the point, she knew her father wouldn't feel comfortable discussing it with her. He was a private man who kept things to himself.

Like her mother. And her grandmother.

Carter took the small evidence bag Max Roswell handed him, his gaze locked on what was inside. "This was in the plane?"

The hairbrush was small. A baby's. The handle was yellow, the hair caught in the soft white bristles dark and resembling goose down.

Carter looked from the brush to Max. "You aren't trying to tell me that…"

"There was a baby on board," Max said as he took a seat across from Carter. "We also found what was left of a cloth diaper, a dirty cloth diaper."

Carter groaned. "The baby couldn't have survived the crash."

"Depends on if the baby was strapped in some kind of carrying device. From the way the backseat belt was hooked up, I'd say the baby just might have been." Max pulled another evidence bag from the plastic container and handed it across the desk to him.

The small tube inside the bag was tarnished, but as Carter turned the bag in his fingers, he could still read what was printed on the bottom of the tube: Scarlet Red.

"Lipstick?" he said, his attention shooting from the tarnished tube to Max. "You think there was a woman on board as well?" He tried to sound surprised, but all he could think about was the rhinestone pin and the story Eve had told him about finding it in the plane.

"A woman and a baby," Max said.

Was it possible Eve was right about her grandmother being on the plane. But a baby? "You really think they could have survived? It was the middle of the winter, the closest ranch house miles away."

"I would imagine someone was meeting the plane," Max said.

"But there is no place to land in the Breaks—" Carter stopped, aware of Max's focus on him.

"The supposition is that the aircraft got off course," Max said. "But not ten miles off course. This plane wasn't headed for the Whitehorse airport."

Carter knew where Max was going with this and

decided to beat him to the punch. "You think he was headed for the airstrip south of my family's ranch? But in February?"

"I checked. It was a mild winter. There wouldn't have been much snow and when I flew over that old airstrip on the way here, I noticed that it's along a ridgeline. Snow would probably blow off anyway. I would imagine that's why your father and grandfather put the airstrip there to begin with, don't you think?"

Carter could say nothing as he recalled his conversation earlier with his father.

"A snowstorm blew in late on the afternoon of February seven, 1975, a real blizzard," Max was saying. "I think that's when the plane went down. Missed the airstrip and ended up in that ravine."

"You're sure it was February seven, 1975?"

Max nodded. "I found a gas receipt stamped with that date. It was faded, but still legible."

Carter was having trouble breathing. He waited, afraid Max was about to tell him a Jackson had been flying that plane.

"We found something else in the plane," Max said, not sounding pleased to have to tell Carter this. "Evidence that drugs were being transported on the plane."

Drugs? Carter stared at Max, uncomprehending. A woman and baby and drugs were on the plane? No way was Eve's grandmother involved in drugs. Nina Mae had always been outspoken, opinionated and danced to her own drummer, but she was straight-as-an-arrow moral. She wouldn't abide drugs, let alone help transport and sell them.

Nor would his father or grandfather be involved in running drugs.

"Just because the plane might have been headed for my family's airstrip doesn't mean they were involved," Carter said with more heat than needed.

"No," Max said. "It doesn't. But it's a good bet someone in your family knew the plane was planning to land there. I'm not saying they knew anything about the drugs. The woman and baby would have made good cover for bringing in the marijuana." Max rose to his feet. "So it's just a matter of finding out if the pilot and the woman and baby survived and where they are now."

Carter stared at the investigator. "You can't seriously expect me to continue with this case. I'm too personally involved."

"Are you?" Max asked. "As you pointed out, we don't know that your family knew anything about it."

"But even if that's the case, there's a good chance I know the people who are involved. If you're right and someone was meeting the plane, the chances are it was someone local."

Max rubbed the back of his neck. "That's any small town. I know you, Sheriff Jackson, by reputation. You're not going to let personal feelings keep you from getting justice for that murdered man."

Carter wished he could be as sure of that as Max.

"There's some other evidence in the box you might want to take a look at," Max said. "I'll let you know what we find out about your victim once we get him to the lab."

Eve went home and changed into her paint clothes, determined to decide on a color for the living room. Right now she had three walls painted three different colors. The problem was, she couldn't quit thinking about what her grandmother had said about her being adopted. It had been so strange to hear her grandmother say something that Eve had suspected since she was old enough to notice that she didn't look like she belonged to this family.

She opened the orange paint can and stared down at the semigloss. This house was never going to get painted. She had to know the truth. It's why she'd come home. She'd had this stupid idea that her mother would be honest with her now that she was no longer a child.

But her mother hadn't been honest with her about anything. Not about Chester. Or Errol. Or the rhinestone pin.

No, if Eve wanted to learn the truth, she'd have to do it on her own. She picked up the lid to the paint can, and hammered it back on. Changing out of her paint clothes, she dressed in the darkest clothing she had as the little voice in the back of her head tried unsuccessfully to talk her out of what she planned to do.

What she needed was proof one way or the other—and not a birth certificate from her mother's doctor. If Eve had been lied to all her life, then her mother wasn't the only one who'd been in on it, she thought, as she drove back toward Whitehorse.

It was late by the time she reached the city limits and late enough that there was hardly any traffic. The usual pickups in front of the bars along the main drag, but no cars near the small building that housed Dr. Holloway's office.

Eve made a pass through town. The sheriff's patrol SUV was still parked in front of his office. She just hoped Dr. Holloway wasn't working late as well.

As she neared the doctor's office building, she slowed.

No lights on. There were no other lights on in the buildings around it. Everyone had gone home for the day.

She parked three blocks away, picked up the cloth bag with the tools she would need and walked back to the doctor's office building using the dark alleys. Whitehorse was only about ten blocks square to begin with, so it was a short walk.

Dr. Holloway's office was the only one in the small building. There were no outside lights in the rear. The alley was pitch-black and a minefield of mud puddles and toe-stubbing rocks. She couldn't see her hand in front of her face as she stumbled toward the rear of the building, feeling like the criminal she was about to become.

She knew from all the times she'd come to Dr. Holloway's as a child that the files were stored in the basement. Doc, as he was commonly known, had to be hugging seventy by now and hated computers so refused to have one in his office.

Eve was surprised he hadn't retired. But since he often took vegetables in lieu of cash for his services, maybe he couldn't afford to retire.

The back door was old, just like the lock. Eve stuck the crowbar between the jamb and the door and put her weight into it. The weathered wood cracked so loudly Eve feared the sheriff could hear it in his office blocks away.

The door's edge finally splintered, exposing the interior of the lock. All she had to do was stick the screwdriver into the lock and turn.

The door opened and she stepped inside, closing it behind her, tallying in her head the cost of a new door and lock, restitution for breaking and entering. Doc had always told her she was his favorite Bailey girl, although Eve suspected he said the same thing to each of her sisters.

If she found what she suspected she would, there was more than a good chance Dr. Holloway wouldn't press charges. Otherwise, she'd have to throw herself on the mercy of the court.

Turning on the small penlight from her bag, she shone it down the stairs toward the basement door.

She wasn't surprised to find that the door to the basement was unlocked, but she was thankful.

In the basement, she swung the small penlight beam around the room, looking for a window. There didn't appear to be one so she turned on the light. The large room was full of boxes of nondrug medical supplies and boxes of who knows what. Doc got his drugs from the hospital so he kept little in the office. What few he did, he kept locked up in his safe upstairs.

Eve didn't see any medical records and for a moment feared he stored them elsewhere.

At the back of the room she spotted another door, this one marked Archives.

Hurrying to it, she tried the knob. Locked. She swore under her breath, that feeling of getting in deeper making her hesitate. In for a penny, in for a pound. Wasn't that how it went?

The lock on the archives room was a little harder to get open, but she finally managed to break it. She glanced at her watch, surprised twenty minutes had gone by.

The archives room was musty and claustrophobic. As she stepped in, the door closed behind her, making her jump. She shoved at the door, terrified she'd just locked herself in.

But the door swung open without any trouble. She gulped the not-great basement air, then propped the archives-room door open with one of the boxes and searched for a light. The moment she flipped the switch, the lightbulb made a popping sound and the room went dark.

"Great." Eve turned on her penlight again.

The ceiling was low in there, the shelves and boxes stacked to the top. There were numerous rows of shelves with only a narrow walkway between each.

As Eve moved deeper into the room, she noticed that there didn't seem to be any rhyme or reason for the way the boxes had been arranged. "Would have been too easy to have filed them by last name," she muttered to herself as she moved down the stacks.

Apparently a number had been assigned to each patient. Eve swore again. Unless she had the codes, she'd never be able to find anything down here.

But then she realized that at the very back, the patient files had been stored by year. She found the year of her birth, then narrowed it down to the month. February 1975.

There was one huge box on the top shelf marked February 1975. She shone the light around, looking for something to stand on, and saw a small stool.

Dragging it over, she put the end of the penlight between her teeth and climbed up to pull down the box.

The box was heavier than it looked and she almost toppled off the stool. She dropped it. The box hit the floor hard, tipped and dumped a dozen files onto the cold concrete.

She thought she heard a sound overhead and froze, listening. She could hear the steady drip of a faucet somewhere overhead, but nothing else.

Hurry.

She scurried to pick up the files, using the penlight to search for her name or her mother's among them.

No Eve Bailey. But she saw one for Nina Mae Cross. Treatment for a broken leg. Her grandmother had broken her leg? Eve had never heard anything about that. Then Eve saw the date on her grandmother's medical record. February 7, 1975. The same date the plane had crashed in the Breaks? The time on the report was eleven at night! She scanned Doc's scrawl. Apparently it had been a hairline fracture. He'd splinted the leg at her grandmother's house.

Eve stared at the report. Did this mean what she thought it did? That her grandmother had broken her leg in the plane crash? But then Nina Mae wouldn't have been able to get out. Unless she'd broken it later, after she'd gotten out of the plane and the ravine.

Eve put the file aside, determined to find one of her own. That's when she saw a file for Mrs. Chester Bailey.

Eve opened the file and scanned it. The word "infertility" leaped out at her. She slowed to read as best she could what Dr. Holloway had written in his illegible scrawl. Apparently Lila and Chester had been trying to get pregnant, but with no luck. Doc had suggested infertility testing. Lila said she would talk to Chester.

Eve double-checked the date on the box, her heart pounding. Maybe the doctor's visit had been misfiled. If her mother had given birth to her February 5, 1975, then she wouldn't have been talking to the doctor about infertility tests any time in February of that year.

The office visit was February 2, 1975. She stared at it, knowing she shouldn't have been surprised, let alone stunned.

Her mother had lied. Eve didn't want to believe that her mother had lied to her again. How many secrets did her mother have, anyway?

Eve clutched the file to her. She finally had proof. With this staring her in the face, her mother would have to tell her the truth now.

Eve thought she would feel more elated than she did. She'd been right. But instead of elation, she felt numb. She really wasn't the child of Chester and Lila Bailey. No wonder she'd always felt different. Incomplete. Never felt as if she belonged. So who did she belong to?

She set the file down on the floor and reached to pick up the box to put it back. It was too heavy. She was going to have to leave it. It wasn't as if the doctor wouldn't know someone had been here, given that she'd destroyed two of his locks. She planned to call him in the morning, anyway. With the file, she thought she finally might be able to get the truth one way or another. It hadn't slipped her mind that Dr. Holloway had signed her birth certificate which attested that she'd been born to Lila and Chester Bailey on February 5, 1975. Doc had been in on the cover-up. But why? Why hadn't they just told her she was adopted? It made no sense.

Eve couldn't wait to show her mother the doctor's file. Too bad her mother was at a funeral in Great Falls. Eve would have to wait until Lila Bailey returned.

She had started out the archives door when she heard a thud overhead. No mistaking it for a leaky faucet. Someone was up there.

Eve hurriedly turned off the light and tiptoed up the

stairs to the back door. She could hear someone headed toward the back of the building. Any moment the door from upstairs would open and she would be seen.

She couldn't get caught. Not with the file. There was no way whoever was coming would let her take this confidential file. And she feared the file might disappear. Her first real evidence.

She ran for the back door just as the door from upstairs opened in a rush. All she saw was a large dark shape. He lunged for her. Without thinking of the consequences, she swung her sack of tools, catching him in the jaw. He missed the bottom step, thrown off by the blow, and tumbled down the short stretch of basement stairs to crash into a stack of cardboard boxes. She caught the smell of aftershave.

Eve flipped on the light, afraid she'd killed Doc Holloway, although it wasn't his usual brand of aftershave. But it wasn't Doc who looked up at her from where he'd landed on the floor.

Bridger Duvall. The same man she'd seen coming out of her grandmother's room at the nursing home.

Chapter 12

Lila Bailey had planned to be gone long before this. She stood at the window, staring out into the darkness. She'd only returned to the house to get some clothing. Unfortunately, her daughters' plans had changed and both McKenna and Faith were there.

Both girls had viewed her announcement with skepticism. Lila knew that they had discussed Loren Jackson's earlier visit and didn't believe her story about a funeral in Great Falls.

"Mom, it's too late to drive to Great Falls tonight," McKenna said as Faith came downstairs dressed for the dance they'd decided to go to in Whitehorse.

"Whose funeral is it, anyway?" Faith asked.

"A woman doctor friend," she said noncommittally. "You don't know her. And I prefer driving at night. It's cooler," she said to McKenna. "I'll be fine. You know when you girls are away at college I manage just fine on my own."

"Only because you choose to," Faith said.

"You don't have to go to Great Falls alone," McKenna said. "I could talk to Dad—"

"No," Lila said too sharply. "Thank you," she said, softening her words. "But your father didn't even know the woman and he has to work tomorrow." She knew her daughters worried about her. She wished they wouldn't. It only made it harder.

"I know Dad would come back if you asked him," McKenna said.

Even if true, it was the last thing she wanted. "This is between me and Chester."

McKenna looked disappointed, maybe even a little hurt. Lila squeezed her hand and looked past her at Faith. Her youngest daughter's expression chilled her to the bone.

"She doesn't want him back," Faith said angrily. "She's glad to be rid of him." With that, Faith went out the front door, slamming it behind her.

McKenna looked at her mother. "Is that true?"

"Of course not. He's your father. The last thing I want is a divorce." Not even that was true.

McKenna gave her a hug. "I know he loves you."

Lila could only nod.

She stood for a long time after the girls left, listening to the emptiness of the house to the beat of her own heart like a drum. Or a ticking time bomb.

She was just tired, she told herself as she headed for her bedroom to pack. Eve would show up next. She had to leave before that. She couldn't face Eve. Not tonight.

A warm wind billowed the curtains and she could

smell the flowers the girls had planted outside her window. Tonight the sweet scent made her a little sick.

The house was two stories, a huge rambling thing that had belonged to Chester's family and been added on each generation. She'd loved the history in the worn wood floors, in the china that had been passed down for generations. All she'd ever wanted was to live in Old Town with the man she loved and have his children.

Lila scoffed at how foolish she'd been to think that could have ever happened. Life was full of disappointments. She'd planned to fill this house with children, male children who would someday take over the place.

Chester had been even more disappointed and disappointing. But she couldn't blame him. He'd known he wasn't her first choice any more than she'd been his.

She turned on the light in her bedroom, surprised how dark it had gotten. Time seemed to slip away from her, minutes lost in thought, hours gone as if stolen.

She heard the front door open. Maybe the girls had forgotten something and had come back. She reminded herself that they weren't girls anymore. "McKenna?"

No answer.

"Eve?" She knew Faith wouldn't have come back, as angry as she'd been.

Loren? He would have knocked. Or said something by now.

Lila turned and listened, her bedroom door open, the faint wash of light spilling across the floor from the small light she always left on in the hallway for when her daughters returned.

The front door closed with a soft click.

Lila froze, her heart lodging in her throat. She couldn't have screamed even if she'd tried. Even if it would have done any good. The closest house was Eve's and it was a half mile up the road. No one would hear her.

She heard the creak of a floorboard, then another before the groan of a heavy tread on the stairs. She willed her body to move. Across the carpet to the bed. Her hand trembled as she quietly opened the bedside-table drawer where Chester kept the .22 pistol.

"One shot wouldn't stop much of anything," Chester had said. "So you'll have to keep firing. Aim for the body. The main thing to remember is that if someone were to break in, if you don't stop him, he'll end up using your gun on you. That's why most men would never tell their wives to go for the gun." He had hesitated. "But you're not most wives."

No, she thought, she'd definitely proved that.

She flipped off the safety and raised the gun, her focus on the open bedroom doorway. She knew there would be that split second when the doorway filled and she would have to make the decision whether to fire.

It could be a neighbor. Or one of the girls. Or Chester. Someone who either hadn't heard her call to them. Or didn't care to answer.

Or it could be a drifter like the one who'd come through back in the 1970s, killed Margaret O'Dell in her bed and stolen her car to make a run for Canada.

A shadow fell over the doorway an instant before the bulk of a man filled the space.

Her finger tightened on the trigger as Errol Wilson stepped in.

He smiled when he saw the gun. "That's what I love about you, Lila. You have such a sense for the dramatic."

She itched to pull the trigger and wondered why she

hadn't the first time he'd come into her house with his threats.

But she knew the answer to that.

"Get out."

Errol leaned suggestively against the doorjamb and grinned at her.

"I said get out."

He arched a brow at her. "Don't make a mistake you'll regret the rest of your life, Lila. I've waited long enough."

"I told Chester."

"Chester?" He laughed as he stepped toward her. "Even if I believed you, I know Chester isn't the person you've been hiding the truth from all these years."

"My girls are women now. They'll understand."

Errol must have heard the fear in her voice. He chuckled. He was now within feet of her. Her heart pounded so hard she barely heard him, but the gun never wavered in her hand.

"We both know who you're protecting, Lila, and just how far you will go to keep your secret," he said. He was close enough now that she could see the lust in his eyes.

"If you don't leave now, I'll pull the trigger."

"Yeah, right," Errol said, grinning. "Explain my dead body to your family and friends."

She caught her breath as he snatched the gun from her and snapped the safety on before tossing it onto the bed.

"Come on, Lila, you know this day has been coming for a long time. I would hate to have to force you, but I will."

Lila Bailey clamped her mouth closed to keep from screaming as she felt Errol Wilson's wet lips on her neck. She caught sight of the gun lying on the bed.

He shoved her down on the bed, grinning as he began to unbutton his shirt. She'd run him off last time when Eve had seen him leaving. Just as she'd run him off before. But she knew nothing would stop him tonight.

He opened his shirt. She stared at his bare chest as he started to lower himself onto her, his belt buckle cutting into her stomach. Reaching up to the corner of the bed, she found the gun. It would be so easy to kill him.

She thought of her daughters, especially Eve, as her fingers tightened around the barrel of the gun. Errol was kissing her neck, so sure she would have to give into him now that Chester was gone, now that Eve was home again. He never saw it coming as she swung the gun as hard as she could at his balding head.

The base of the grip connected with the back of his skull, the sound like dropping a cantaloupe on concrete. He'd known she wouldn't shoot him. But she saw that he hadn't expected this. He drew back to look at her in both surprise and pain.

She shoved him off. He tumbled off the bed, landing hard in a sitting position staring up at her, breathing hard.

"I told you to get out," Lila said.

He blinked at her, having a hard time focusing while he reached to gingerly touch the back of his head. He winced, his fingers coming away covered in blood.

"You bitch," he said, without much rancor, too stunned to work up a good mad yet.

"You're getting blood on my floor, Errol Wilson," Lila said as she snapped off the safety and pointed the gun at his head. "If you think I won't kill you right now you are sadly mistaken. Imagine what your wife will say when the sheriff has to tell her that I killed you to keep you from raping me."

"You're going to regret this," he said, but made no move to come at her again as he got to his feet. He wobbled a little as he attempted to button up his shirt. She followed him to the door, the gun on him.

"It won't be my first regret," she said as she watched him drive away.

Carter had been so lost in thought he hadn't realized just how late it was. He'd gone through the items in the evidence bags. A piece of leather, an old notebook, whatever had been written on it faded beyond recognition over the years, a candy wrapper, a package of chewing gum, an assortment of photos of the victim and what he'd been wearing.

The jeans were in good shape. The shirt was so faded it would have been hard to know the exact color. What caught Carter's attention were the man's boots. They were a common brand. The only thing that distinguished them was the color: blue. Dress boots. Same with the man's belt.

Carter inspected the bag containing the marijuana seeds that had been found in the plane, agreeing with Max's drug-smuggling conclusion. Maybe Max was also right that the woman and baby were just cover. Carter couldn't see Nina Mae Cross in that plane, let alone her and a baby. Whose baby? And what about the victim? How did he fit in?

Carter rubbed his eyes and put the photographs back into the evidence bag before locking everything up and heading home.

The box that had been there on his steps was gone.

Nor was there any new surprise package waiting for him as he stopped in front of his house. No sign of Deena. But then he never knew what he might find inside. It wouldn't be the first time she'd gotten in.

He didn't know whether to be relieved or worried. His instincts told him that Deena wouldn't let this go. If anything, she was plotting something big, planning an attack that he wouldn't see coming.

Weary and exhausted, he just wanted to go to bed. He hadn't had dinner, but he didn't care. He wasn't hungry, just tired.

He glanced toward the house again, not in the mood for surprises tonight and unsure whether even the new locks could keep Deena out.

As he started to get out of the SUV, his radio squawked.

"Break-in at Dr. Holloway's," the dispatcher said.

Dr. Holloway's? "I'm on it."

Another squawk. "Deputy Samuelson is on his way as well," the dispatcher said.

Eve heard a siren blare in the distance, the sound growing as if the vehicle was headed for the doctor's office building.

She didn't take the time to find out what Bridger Duvall had been doing there. She stumbled out the back door and ran.

It wasn't until she reached her pickup that she dared look back. She couldn't see anyone following her. She didn't stop to make sure. She opened her pickup door, tossed the file onto the seat and slid behind the wheel. Unfortunately, when she'd swung her bag of tools at

Bridger Duvall, she'd lost her grip. The last she'd seen the bag it had landed somewhere back in archives.

As she pulled out, she saw a woman at the pay phone down the street and recognized her. Deena Turner Jackson. Eve frowned. Was it possible Deena didn't own a cell phone?

Deena exited the booth without looking her way, climbed into an SUV and drove south, probably headed for the country club. There was usually a live band and Eve had heard that Deena was partying it up, trying to make Carter jealous.

Disgusted with that particular love affair, Eve waited to make sure she and Deena Turner Jackson didn't cross paths again before she, too, headed south, toward Old Town.

Her mind was racing. What had Bridger Duvall been doing in the doctor's office and how did he get in? Was it possible he'd broken in through the front door?

She felt almost virtuous about the fact that she hadn't been the only one breaking into Doc's tonight. Also she'd gotten away from Duvall. Both thoughts shocked her. She'd struck the man, knocked him down the stairs, possibly even hurt him. How far was she willing to go to learn the truth? Obviously further than the law allowed.

Carter headed down the street toward the doctor's office building, but at Central he passed a pickup truck he recognized.

Eve Bailey.

She didn't seem to notice him as she drove out of Whitehorse, headed no doubt home.

A break-in at Doc's and Eve Bailey just happens by

this late? But why would Eve break into the doctor's office? She wouldn't. Or would she?

He drove to Doc's. Deputy Samuelson was already there. "What's up?"

"Looks like someone broke in not just through the back door but the front," Samuelson said.

"Any idea what they were after?"

"There's a box of files on the floor in the archives room. I'd assume that was what they were looking for."

Carter followed him downstairs to where a large box sat in the middle of one of the aisles, a stool nearby and a crowbar, hammer and screwdriver in a shopping bag next to it.

"Not exactly a professional job," he commented after seeing the broken locks.

He knelt down to take a look at the date on the box on the floor. February 1975.

The year and month Eve was born and which the plane had crashed in the Breaks.

"Anything else disturbed?" he asked.

Samuelson shook his head. "Looks like whatever was in the box is what the burglar came in for."

Carter nodded. "Give Doc a call, then secure the building as best you can."

Outside, he climbed into his patrol SUV and headed south. It was time to have another heart-to-heart with Eve Bailey.

Eve took a back road home. As she drove, she watched her rearview mirror. No car came racing after her. But she still had the feeling she was being followed. Didn't most criminals think that?

She was so busy watching her rearview mirror that

she was shocked to look up and see a set of headlights coming at her. She swerved back to her side of the road as a pickup blew past going in the direction of town. Eve only got a glimpse of it, but she would have sworn it was Errol Wilson behind the wheel of his old blue rattletrap.

So he hadn't gone to Great Falls with her mother. But that didn't mean he wasn't headed that way now.

She shoved him out of her mind, still shaking from what she'd done tonight. What had she been thinking?

She reminded herself that she'd found what she'd been looking for. She was adopted, just as she'd suspected. The file proved it. And that, while maybe not making her actions right, allowed her to feel somewhat justified.

Everyone had lied to her. Not that it made any sense. There was no stigma connected to adoption. Why not just tell Eve the truth when she was young? Or when she'd asked?

Because there were other people involved in the deception. The thought made her heart race. Doc, for sure, since he'd signed her birth certificate. But were there others? There would have to be. Like her grandmother and other people in Whitehorse and Old Town who would have noticed Lila Bailey wasn't pregnant, but then had a baby.

Unless her mother had pretended to be pregnant.

Eve rubbed her temple as she drove, her head aching.

Whatever the circumstance of her birth, it had obviously been a well-kept secret. And that worried Eve more than she wanted to admit as she noticed a set of headlights behind her.

The night was pitch-black, the road narrow and dark. Eve watched the headlights behind her, surprised to find anyone else on the road tonight, given the hour.

She told herself that it couldn't be anyone after her. Not this long after the break-in. But still she felt a little spooked. Just nerves. Given what she'd learned lately, who could blame her?

She'd driven this same five miles hundreds of times, but tonight seemed different. Tonight she knew the truth. She was adopted. There was no other explanation. And once she showed her mother the medical file, Lila Bailey couldn't deny it any longer. Eve finally had proof, she thought, glancing over at the file on the seat next to her, then at the headlights behind her.

Eve pressed down on the gas, driving faster, anxious to reach the ranch.

The vehicle behind her stayed back some distance. She could see the headlights in the cloud of dust her tires were kicking up. What had made her think it had been chasing her? Guilt, no doubt.

She tried to relax, but she knew she wouldn't be able to until she'd talked to her mother. And Dr. Holloway.

If she'd known where her mother might be staying in Great Falls, Eve would have gone there. As it was, she'd have to wait until her mother returned from the funeral. If there was even a funeral.

Her mother couldn't stay away forever.

Ahead, the road made a sharp turn to the left, then back to the right. Just a little farther and the back road would connect with the smoother and wider main gravel road into Old Town.

Eve came around the corner as the moon peeked out of the clouds, illuminating the landscape. She caught the glint of something up on the hill ahead of her just an instant before she heard a loud crack, then another. The front tire on the pickup blew.

Eve fought to keep control of the truck, but it was impossible. The rear end came around, the tires burying down into the loose earth at the edge of the road. The pickup keeled hard to the right and rolled, skidding on its top before coming to a stop in the ditch below the road.

Dazed, Eve hung upside down, the seat belt cutting into her. The airbag had deployed, but was now hanging slack in her face.

At first she couldn't move, could barely breathe. Was she all right? She wasn't sure.

She reached for the seat-belt release as the cab suddenly filled with light from the car that had been behind her. She heard the vehicle's engine as it roared toward her.

Where had the shots come from? She couldn't be sure. She'd thought it was someone on the hillside in front of her but it could have been from the vehicle behind her.

Frantically, she hit the seat-belt button, tumbling onto the headliner as the belt suddenly released. She fumbled for the door handle, still disoriented and shaken, confused over what had happened. Had those even really been gunshots?

The door wouldn't open. She swung around and tried the other one, aware that the vehicle had stopped. She heard a door open and close. The slim bright beam of a flashlight flickered across the landscape, headed in her direction.

Was he coming to finish the job?

She grabbed the other door handle but, like the first, it was jammed. Part of the windshield lay on the ground. Panicked, she kicked the rest of it out, her pulse deafening in her ears, and scrambled out ready to run for her life.

"Eve!"

She stumbled and fell. The beam of the flashlight splashed over her.

"Oh, my God, Eve," Carter said as he dropped to his knees beside her. From up the road came the sound of an engine revving as it raced away, disappearing into the darkness. "You're bleeding. Don't move."

Chapter 13

As Carter brought the patrol car to a skidding halt out-side the emergency entrance to the hospital, Eve sat up a little. Her head ached and so did her arm from holding a cloth on the cut over her left eye to stop the bleeding.

Dr. Holloway's big black car was parked in the nearly empty lot. Next to it was Errol Wilson's beat-up blue pickup.

Carter rushed around to her side of the car as she got out and shoved open the emergency entrance door to help her inside.

She saw Errol sitting on one of the exam tables, the curtains surrounding it standing open. Doc had Errol holding a thick piece of gauze on the back of his head. The two had been talking. Not talking, Eve amended. Arguing.

Both Doc and Errol glanced over at the sound of the buzzer announcing an E.R. arrival.

"Take her into the empty examining room down there," Doc said, as he finished putting a bandage on the back of Errol's head.

"I'm fine," Eve told Carter as she climbed onto the examination table.

"I'll be the judge of that," Doc said as he stepped in, going to the sink to wash his hands before he turned to look at her. "Kind of banged yourself up pretty good, young lady." He looked at Carter, hovering beside the exam table. "Help yourself to a soda in that fridge down the hall. I'll take care of her now." Doc closed the curtain as Carter stepped out.

Eve heard the buzzer at the E.R. door as Errol must have left. Under the drawn curtain, she watched Carter's boots as he paced back and forth.

"That cut looks like it might need stitches," Doc said, after he gently pulled her arm down and removed the cloth Carter had had her holding on the cut. He hurried on before she could protest. "I know how you feel about needles, so don't go fainting on me. I might be able to get a butterfly bandage to do the trick if you don't mind a small scar. Yeah, that's what I thought."

Her head was throbbing and she hurt all over, but that pain was nothing compared to her feeling of betrayal. She'd known Doc all her life. He'd patched her up more times than she could remember. She'd trusted and admired him and always believed he'd brought her into this world.

Looking into his kind grandfatherly face, she found it nearly impossible to believe that he was part of the deception.

Every instinct warned her not to confront him. Not until she had the file. But the file was in the wreckage of her pickup. At least she hoped it was still there. What if whoever had shot at her had come back and taken it?

She never would have left the evidence behind, but she hadn't been herself when Carter found her and he hadn't given her time to get anything out of the truck before he'd rushed her to Whitehorse and the hospital.

Eve tried to remain calm, to think. She could use this opportunity. If she was careful. "You know my grandmother," she said, grimacing as he cleaned the wound.

He glanced at her as if worried the cut on her head was more serious than he'd thought. "Nina Mae? Of course I know her."

"I mean, you knew her when she was young. Didn't she date your older brother for a while?"

He kept working and, for a few moments, she thought he hadn't heard her. "George was far too tame for your grandmother."

She winced as he put pressure on her cut—and remembered the medical file she'd seen earlier in his office basement regarding her grandmother. She felt ice settle in her chest as she remembered that the file had been dated February 7, 1975, the day the plane presumably crashed in the Breaks.

"She broke her leg once, I heard," Eve said, trying to sound as if she was just chatting to keep her mind off the pain. "Didn't you set it after an accident she had?"

He stopped what he was doing to look at her again. "That leg bothering her?"

She had no idea. "I never heard how she broke it." Eve was shaking. So her grandmother really had broken her leg. Because of the plane crash?

"Hold still," Doc ordered a little less gently. She felt

more pressure over her eye, pain, then he stepped back. "Why the sudden interest?"

She shrugged. "Just curious."

"Sheriff, stop pacing and either sit down or wait outside," Doc snapped irritably.

Eve watched Carter's Western boots disappear from under the curtain, his footfalls disappearing down the hall. "All I remember is Grandma Nina Mae telling me something about a blizzard?"

Doc gave her an impatient look. "Yes, she went out to check one of the animals, I believe, and fell. Are you sure you're all right?" He was studying her, frowning as he looked into her eyes. "How hard did you hit your head?"

"Not hard. She said it was the same night I was born."

He began putting away his supplies, his back to her. "As I recall, Nina Mae fell on the ice. It was only a hairline fracture. Your grandmother was a strong, determined woman. I just splinted it until she could get into my office."

It all sounded so plausible. If Eve hadn't found the file on her mother's infertility, she wouldn't have noticed that his explanation seemed a little too practiced. She would have believed him.

Also, Doc had given himself away. He hadn't corrected her when she'd mentioned being born the same night her grandmother had broken her leg. She might have been born on February 5, 1975, but according to the file she'd seen in Doc's office, her grandmother had broken her leg on February 7—the same date as that in the crashed plane's logbook.

She knew it didn't constitute evidence. How could Doc remember every birth, every broken leg?

But it made her all the more convinced not only was

she adopted but that there was some sort of conspiracy involving her birth and grandmother and the plane crash.

He closed a drawer and turned to look at her. She schooled her expression to one of nothing more than mild interest.

Doc leaned back against the counter, both hands gripping the edge behind him. "Why don't you tell me what this is really about?"

"Sorry, you know me. All this," she said, glancing around the E.R., "makes me nervous."

He studied her. "You should take it easy for a while," he said quietly. "Let your mother see to you."

Let her mother see to her? Eve felt a chill as if the temperature had suddenly dropped in the room. "I'll do that," she lied, shocked by what felt even more like a conspiracy to keep the truth from her.

What had really happened the day the plane crashed in the Breaks? Two days after Eve was allegedly born? One thing was for sure. Her grandmother hadn't been checking animals on the ranch. And a few miles to the south, a man in a small airplane was being murdered. Her grandmother wasn't the only person who'd gotten out of that plane that night. The murderer had been with her.

When Doc led her out of the examination room, Eve realized with a start that he hadn't asked how she'd gotten injured.

Carter noticed that Eve was especially quiet as she came out of the exam room, Doc Holloway behind her, his hand on her shoulder.

"You all right?" Carter asked Eve, worry shooting him to his feet.

"She's going to be fine," Doc said. "She just needs to take it easy."

"We're talking about Eve Bailey, here, Doc," Carter joked, but Eve didn't crack a smile.

"Reminds me of when she was a girl," Doc said. "Always in here for one thing or another. Poison ivy. Broken wrist. Always scraped up and bruised. She just never seems to learn."

Carter saw Eve shiver. He slipped off his jacket and put it around her. She flinched at his touch. He stepped back, giving her space.

"I remember how the two of you used to squabble as kids," Doc said, apparently noticing her reaction. "Didn't she bloody your nose once? Or did she break it?"

"I'd prefer not to go there," Carter joked, but his gaze was on Eve. He was surprised she hadn't jumped into the conversation. It wasn't like her. She was acting strange, no doubt about it. "Thanks for coming down, Doc."

"I had to come down, anyway."

"Yeah, I saw Errol leaving. What happened to him?" Carter asked.

"Working on his tractor, nailed the back of his head good," Doc said. "Glen Whitaker came in before that. Seems he ran off the road. Hit his head. Can't remember what happened."

"He's all right, though?" Carter asked, relieved that Glen had been found and his disappearance apparently solved.

"He'll live," Doc said with a shrug.

Carter noted that Doc hadn't even mentioned the break-in at his office earlier tonight. "Anything missing from your office?"

Doc shook his head. "Probably didn't have time to

steal anything, since your deputy said the dispatcher got an anonymous call right away that someone was breaking in. A woman."

"A woman was breaking in?" Carter didn't dare look at Eve.

Doc shook his head again. "No, the call was from a woman. Said she saw someone trying to break in. Too dark to make out who it was. Probably just kids."

Carter wished he believed that.

Eve moved toward the exit, as if anxious to leave this discussion behind. Or maybe just anxious to get home after everything she'd been through.

The cut over her right eye was covered with a white butterfly bandage. She had a baseball-size bruise on her upper left arm from where she must have hit the pickup door and the knee she'd scraped falling into the ravine only the day earlier was bleeding through her jeans.

On top of that, she was still limping a little from her hurt ankle. The woman was a mess. And yet, he thought, he'd never seen her more beautiful.

Doc's cell phone rang on his hip. He excused himself, saying over his shoulder, "Eve, remember what I told you. No more foolishness."

Carter glanced at Eve. What was that about? He recalled overhearing her ask about her grandmother's broken leg. Seemed strange unless you knew that Eve believed her grandmother had been on the plane that crashed in the Breaks February 7, 1975. Carter took her arm as she started to slump. "Let's get you home."

Eve said nothing as he led her outside.

Once in the car, Carter said, "Okay, what's going on? Is it something to do with your accident?" She'd scared him when he'd seen her pickup's headlights and realized that she'd lost control of her pickup...just as she was scaring him now because she'd acted almost as if she was afraid of Doc.

"It wasn't an accident," she said without looking at him.

"What?"

"Could we get out of here," she said, as Dr. Holloway came out of the building and looked in their direction.

Carter started the engine, backed out and headed south out of town. "What wasn't an accident?"

"Someone shot out the front tire on my pickup."

He darted a look at her. She wasn't serious. If what she was saying was true, wouldn't she have said something on the way into town earlier? He recalled that she'd seemed to be in shock on the way into the hospital.

He'd heard a vehicle taking off up the road but it hadn't registered at the time that the driver might be somehow involved in Eve's wreck.

Once he'd seen how badly Eve was bleeding, all he'd thought about was getting her to the hospital.

And why would anyone want to shoot out her tire? She had to be mistaken.

"Sometimes a blowout can sound like a gunshot," he said, hoping to hell that was all it was.

"Do two gunshots sound like a blowout?" she asked, glaring over at him.

"Why would someone shoot at you?" He was trying to remain calm, trying to be the sheriff and not her former boyfriend—and lover, even if it had only been that one night.

"You tell me, Sheriff. Couldn't have anything to do with what I found on that airplane, right?"

He preferred her sarcasm over the terrified look he'd

seen when she'd come half crawling, half falling, out of her wrecked pickup. Or the odd way she'd been acting around Dr. Holloway.

"Did Doc say something to upset you?" he asked, trying to figure out what was going on with her.

She shook her head and looked away.

"I'm taking you home, then I'll check your pickup."

"No. Stop on the way. There's something I need to get out of the truck."

"Eve, you really need to—"

"I really need to stop at the pickup."

"Fine. I'll stop on the way." He had a bad feeling about what she wanted out of her pickup. The last thing he wanted to do was have to arrest her for breaking and entering before the night was over.

Eve leaned back against the seat, closed her eyes and pretended to sleep. She needed that file. If it was still in the pickup. And she was going to have to tell Carter about it. No getting around that.

As he drove, she considered her actions of the past forty-eight hours and winced inwardly. She'd gone from tampering with a crime scene and withholding evidence to breaking and entering and stealing personal medical records. She'd come home determined to get to the truth. She'd always felt there was a mystery to her birth, but now she suspected it was much more than the fact that she was obviously adopted. A man had been murdered in that plane. And now someone seemed determined to keep her from finding out the truth.

"If there's anything you want to tell me..." Carter said.

She opened one eye to look at him, then closed it.

"Fine."

A thought struck her and she opened her eyes and sat up. Doc said a woman made the anonymous call to the sheriff's department about the break-in. That would explain why the woman hadn't used her cell phone. Everyone had cell phones, even though most of them worked only in a five-mile radius around Whitehorse.

So what had Deena been doing on that pay phone down the block from Doc's office? Calling the sheriff's department? Eve felt a chill. Had Deena been following her?

"Something wrong?" Carter asked.

She shook her head, leaned back and closed her eyes again, not wanting to talk. Her head was reeling. She didn't really believe that Deena had nothing better to do than follow her around, did she?

"Are you sure this item you need to get out of your truck isn't something that could wait until morning?" Carter asked as they neared her wrecked pickup lying in the ditch.

She opened her eyes again to glance over at him. He sounded worried. Almost as if he already suspected what she had to get from the truck.

"How did you just happen to come up on me after my pickup went off the road?" she asked.

He cut a look at her. "You don't think I shot out your tire, do you?"

"I thought you didn't believe that."

He groaned. "I saw you leaving town," he said as he turned off the road. "I'd been worried about you."

The patrol SUV's headlights illuminated her pickup. She was shocked to see how badly the truck had been damaged. To realize how lucky she was to be alive.

* * *

Carter felt a shaft of cold move through him as he saw Eve's wrecked pickup in the headlights. She opened her door and hopped out before he even came to a full stop. He could tell she wasn't steady on her feet. Not that it slowed her.

"Hold on," he called after her. He left the patrol car running, headlights on, and, taking his spare flashlight, went after her.

In the glow of the headlamps, he saw Eve going through the wreckage for something that had apparently been in the cab.

"Here," he said, handing her the spare flashlight.

"Thanks," she said. He saw her shiver as she looked at her destroyed truck.

The way she'd been bleeding, he hated to think what would have happened if he hadn't followed her. Let alone if someone really had shot out her tire.

He reminded himself that the only reason he'd followed her was because he suspected she'd just broken into Doc's office. Actually, he was pretty sure she had. But for the life of him, he couldn't imagine why. Unless it had something to do with her grandmother. Is that why she'd been questioning Doc about Nina Mae's broken leg?

He unhooked his flashlight from his belt and turned it on. "You say the front tire blew?"

"Right front," she said, stooping down to shine her light into the cab. "And it was shot out."

He was still hoping she was wrong as he left her to search for what she was looking for while he went to inspect the right front tire. It definitely had blown. There wasn't much left of it. He was thinking he wouldn't be

able to tell what had caused the blowout when he saw
the dent in the rim.

He let out a curse as he stuck the end of his finger into
the hole a bullet had made. Son of a bitch. Eve was right.
Given the size of the dent, he would guess the shot had
come from a high-powered rifle at some distance away.

When he looked up, he saw Eve crawling out of the
demolished cab of her pickup. She had what appeared
to be a file folder in her hand. Oh, hell.

"Unless you want me to arrest you for breaking and
entering and destroying personal property, you'd better have a good reason for having that file, Eve Bailey."

"I'm adopted," she blurted out, and headed for his
patrol car.

"What are you talking about?" he demanded, following her. She had climbed in and was sitting in the passenger seat, the file folder on her lap, her hands on top
of it as if she thought he'd try to take it from her.

He slid behind the wheel.

She stared straight ahead and said, "My whole life
I've known there was some secret that had to do with
me." He heard the catch in her throat. "Just as I've known
that I didn't fit in with my family. It isn't just that I don't
look like my parents or my sisters. I've always felt…dif-
ferent, incomplete. I know there is a family that I belong
to. People who look like me, who have the same smile,
the same color hair, the same genes." She stopped to take
a ragged breath. "The same medical history."

He could see how upset she was. He'd never dreamed
she felt this way. "Why didn't you tell me this when we
were—" he was going to say dating "—in high school?"

She shook her head. "My mother swore I was just
being silly." She looked over at him. "I couldn't under-

stand where these feelings came from. All I knew was that I felt restless. It's why I came back home. I thought maybe I could come to terms with whatever this was that has haunted me all these years. I have to know who I am, can you understand that?"

He couldn't really. He'd always known who he was, although there'd been plenty of times he wished he wasn't a Jackson. But he could see how much this meant to her, how much she needed the truth. And wanting to get to the truth was definitely something he understood.

"This," she said, holding up the file, "proves that I was right. My mother went to Dr. Holloway to discuss infertility days before I was born. A woman nine months pregnant isn't worried about being infertile. There is no way Lila Bailey gave birth to me on February fifth, 1975, like it says on my birth certificate. Doc Holloway lied and so did my mother and my father and my grandmother."

"Do you hear what you're saying? That there was a conspiracy to keep you from knowing you were adopted?"

"That's why it never made any sense," Eve said excitedly. "Don't you see? The secret wasn't kept because I was adopted. It was because of the murdered man in the plane in the Breaks. I saw a file in Doc's office on my grandmother. Did you know she broke her leg the same day the plane went down? The same day my grandmother was on that plane."

Carter went deathly still as he thought of the baby brush that the crime techs had found in the plane. "Mind if I see that?" he asked, reaching for the file on her lap.

With obvious reluctance she handed it to him. He turned on the dome light and flipped through the doctor's records, stopping on her mother's doctor visit for infertility.

He looked up at her, his mind on the downlike dark hair in the bristles of the baby brush.

It was all supposition. If her grandmother had been onboard that plane, if there really had been a baby on the plane, if they had both survived…

He let out a curse as he handed back the file. February 7, 1975—the night Doc treated Nina Mae Cross for a broken leg. Two days after the night Eve was said to have been born at the ranch.

He hesitated, then reminded himself that someone had shot out the front tire on her pickup. He had to be honest with her. He could see how determined she was to learn the truth and knew her well enough to realize she wasn't going to stop until she did.

"There's something you should know," he said. "There's a good chance that the day the plane went down, there was a baby onboard."

Eve's eyes filled with tears. "Oh, my God, you think I could be that baby?"

"Eve, let's not leap to any conclusions—without evidence," Carter said quickly as he neared her house.

"But there's a way to find out, right?"

He nodded. "The crime lab took some of the hair from the baby brush found in the plane. If we send them some of your DNA—"

"Then let's do it. If you send it right away—"

"First thing in the morning. I'll put a rush on it."

Eve sat back. Her heart was pounding. But the excitement waned quickly. All the DNA test would do was tell her whether or not she'd been on that plane. She still wouldn't know who she was. Worse, she and her grandmother were somehow connected to a murder.

Carter parked in front of her grandmother's house. Her house, she thought protectively. The sky had already begun to lighten to the east. It wouldn't be long before daybreak. He sounded as tired as she felt.

"Are you sure about this?" he asked quietly. "I just don't want to see you get hurt."

"I've already been hurt. I've been lied to and deceived. You don't know what it's like to be betrayed by the people who are supposed to love you." She stopped, realizing what she'd said. "Or maybe you do."

"Deena," he said like a curse. "She deceived me even before we got married."

She'd heard from a friend that Deena had lied about being pregnant to get Carter to marry her, but Eve had thought her friend was just trying to make her feel better about his elopement.

"Once you've done something that you regret," Carter said, "it's often hard to admit how wrong you were. You know you can't undo the damage you've done," he said, looking over at her. "And no matter what you do, someone is going to get hurt."

She saw the pain in his eyes and was surprised at the effect it had on her. She looked away, not wanting to feel any sympathy for him. He'd made love to her for the first time that night, the first time for both of them. Then he'd gone to Deena. If he now lived to regret it, then he'd gotten his just rewards.

"Eve," he said gently. "I've never forgiven myself for what I did to you. I'm sorry. I can't tell you how much I've regretted it and wished—"

She turned toward him, planning to tell him she

hadn't given the past—let alone him—a second thought. It was the look in his eyes that stopped her.

"When I saw your pickup tonight upside down by the road and I thought that I might never get the chance to tell you how I feel, how I've always felt..."

She told herself she didn't want to hear this. That she'd never dreamed of a day he would say these words to her.

He dragged her to him, his mouth dropping to hers. Wrapped in his arms after so many years, she lost herself in his kiss. It felt so right. After everything she'd been through, she just wanted the safety of his arms, to lose herself in his kisses, in his caresses.

Something hit the windshield, making them jump apart. The windshield was covered with what appeared to be dirt and crushed flower petals.

"What the hell?" Carter said, hurriedly getting out of the car.

Eve followed, spotting a dark figure disappearing over the rise in the road. An empty flowerpot lay beside the patrol car. She recognized it as the one that had been on her porch. The porch was empty. Past it, her front door stood open.

She ran toward the house, afraid of what she would find inside. Out of the corner of her eye, she saw Carter hesitate, torn no doubt from going after the person or staying with Eve.

"Eve, wait!" Carter called.

As she rushed to her front door and flicked on a light, she heard a vehicle engine in the distance. She caught her breath as her eyes adjusted to the light. She'd expected the place to be trashed after what the intruder had done with her flowerpot.

To her surprise, nothing looked out of place. She rushed upstairs, Carter hurrying after her, and stopped in the middle of her bedroom. Everything looked the same.

She stepped to a dresser drawer and opened it.

"Someone went through my things," she said, turning to look at him.

"Deena," he said, and swore. "I only got a glimpse of her, but the flowerpot incident is so like her."

Deena had seen the two of them kissing. Eve groaned inwardly. She had enough problems without Deena.

As she started to turn from the bedroom, she caught a familiar scent. Aftershave. She recognized the smell from her close encounter at Doc's office.

"Deena wasn't the only one who's been here." But why would Bridger Duvall have been in her bedroom?

Chapter 14

"Bridger Duvall?" Carter echoed when Eve told him. "Let me guess. There's more to the story."

"I wasn't alone tonight in Doc's office," she said. "I heard someone else breaking in."

Carter recalled that both the front and back doors at the doctor's office had been broken into. "Are you telling me—"

"Bridger Duvall was there."

"The man who's renting the old McAllister place?"

She nodded.

"Did he see you?"

"He tried to stop me from leaving, but I got away. I'd seen him earlier. Coming out of my grandmother's room at the nursing home. I think he might have taken a photograph of me and my grandmother. It was a baby photograph of me."

Carter swore. "What would he want with a baby photograph of you?"

She shook her head.

"I need to talk to Duvall, but I'm not leaving you here alone," he said, reaching for the phone.

"Who are you calling?"

"Deputy Samuelson. I'll have him come out and stay with you until I get back."

"That isn't necessary." She stuffed her hands in the front pockets of her jeans, putting up a fight, but not much of one. She was obviously frightened after everything that had happened. "I'm fine. You scared off Deena and whoever else was here. I really doubt they'd be foolish enough to come back."

"Someone shot out your tire tonight."

"Probably just a case of mistaken identity."

"Right. We have no way of knowing who was behind it at this point since apparently you've been doing some investigating on your own. I should lock you up for breaking into Doc's office."

She held out her hands for him to put the cuffs on.

"I'm serious, Eve. You've apparently got someone running scared."

She nodded as she put her hands back in her pockets. "Which means it has something to do with me and the plane crash."

"Maybe." He worried it was Deena. "You're in danger and until we find out from whom…"

"I'll start locking my doors and being careful," she promised.

"Right." He called the deputy and hung up. "Samuelson's on his way. He was on a call so he's not far from here." Still, Carter didn't like letting Eve out of his sight.

But he knew that wasn't possible, short of arresting her. "Don't give the poor guy a hard time, okay?"

She smiled and he was reminded of their interrupted kiss.

"You should get some sleep."

She nodded, her gaze meeting his, her eyes filling with tears. "What's going on, Carter?" she asked, her voice a hoarse whisper.

"I don't know." He stepped toward her, wanting nothing more than to take her in his arms and comfort her. She'd been through so much.

At first she didn't resist. She felt so right in his arms. She buried her face in his shirt. He pulled her closer. All those old feelings and desires sparked and caught fire.

He remembered their night together in the front seat of his old pickup. He'd never wanted a woman more than he wanted her right now. But he knew that the worst thing he could do was repeat the past. He drew back, holding her at arm's length.

"I can't do this," he said softly.

She shook her head, hurt and anger in her eyes. "What is it you want from me?" she demanded.

"Nothing. That is—"

"No." She stepped away from him. "That's your problem, isn't it, Jackson. You've never known what you wanted."

"You're wrong about that," he said, surprised by her outburst.

"Well, you had your chance. You blew it."

"I know."

"So don't even…" She looked close to tears.

"I want another chance with you, Eve," he said, his heart in his throat. "If you can ever find it in your heart to forgive me. I want your trust. Your love." He took a breath and let it out as he stepped to her, his fingers going to her cheek.

She seemed to hold her breath as he brushed the tip of a finger along her jawline, across her full lips. He heard the small intake of breath she made even over the pounding of his own pulse. "There's always been something between us. Tell me I'm wrong about that."

She said nothing, just looked up at him, her eyes full.

"Only this time, Eve Bailey," he said, drawing back his touch, "I won't be making love to you until our wedding night."

Tears welled to bursting in her eyes. She brushed hastily at them. "You're presuming a lot, Mr. Jackson."

"No, I'm just hoping for a second chance," he said, his voice raw with emotion. "That if you ever need me—"

The sound of a vehicle coming up the driveway drew their attentions. "Samuelson is here," he said.

She nodded.

"Get some rest. I'll be back soon." He headed for the door.

"Carter?"

He turned at the door to look back at her.

"Be careful."

The sun was just cresting the horizon as Eve watched Carter go down her porch steps to talk to Deputy Samuelson.

Earlier, all she'd thought about was lying down. She'd felt dead on her feet, emotionally and physically exhausted from the past forty-eight hours.

But now, as she stood watching Carter from the window, all she could think about was the future and what it might hold. She thought of what he'd said.

If she ever needed him? She'd never needed or wanted anyone but him.

Deena would try to make things impossible for them. But Eve knew it wasn't Deena she worried about. It was her own fear of falling for Carter again that gave her pause.

A second chance? Was it possible for them? Eve hated to even hope and yet it was hope that gave her strength right now.

Her stomach growled. She tried to remember the last time she'd had anything to eat. She knew she needed sleep. But the sun was coming up and she had so much on her mind...

She wandered into the kitchen as she heard Carter's patrol car start up. She opened the refrigerator as she listened to him drive away and felt niggling worry at the thought of him confronting Bridger Duvall.

As she pulled out the ham, cheese and eggs she'd bought at the store, she wondered if Deputy Samuelson would want some breakfast.

She hadn't heard his tread on the porch. As she started to turn to look out through the living room to see if he was still in his car, she heard the creak of a floorboard behind her an instant before a hand cupped her mouth.

The dozen eggs fell to the floor, followed by the package of sliced ham and cheese. Eve struggled to fight off her attacker, but he was larger and stronger, as he dragged her out the back door and across the yard toward the barn.

Carter parked his patrol car in front of the old McAllister place and got out. The large sprawling ranch house sat silent in the early-morning light.

He'd heard the place had been sold to a former stock detective and her husband. Apparently, Bridger Duvall was renting it in the interim. Carter hadn't been able to learn much about Duvall on his way out to the house.

Duvall was single, had lived in Bozeman, about five hours to the southwest, and had been a chef at a couple of restaurants. He was thirty-two and had no warrants or arrests on his record.

Carter didn't see Duvall's black car as he walked up the steps to the front door, rang the bell and waited. A barn cat ambled across the yard, eyeing him distrustfully. In the tall grass crickets chirped. The air was heating up fast, the scents of clover and hay strong. It was going to be another hot one. Which probably meant another afternoon storm.

Carter tried the bell again, then knocked. Still no answer. Walking over to the garage, he cupped his hands over his eyes and peered in. Empty. Either Duvall hadn't come home last night or he'd taken off early this morning.

The sheriff hesitated, then went back to the front door and tried the knob. Few people locked their doors in this part of Montana, but Duvall wasn't from here. To Carter's surprise, the door swung open.

Any evidence he found would be inadmissible in court, he told himself as he stepped inside. But after what Eve had told him about Duvall breaking into Doc's office building last night and possibly being in her house tonight, Carter wasn't about to leave until he looked around.

"Anyone home?" he called.

He wasn't expecting an answer and he didn't get one. He moved through the house. The air was cool and a little stale. He got the impression Bridger Duvall didn't spend much time here. What bothered Carter was what Duvall was doing here in the first place? It certainly was no vacation destination. Few people had ever heard of Whitehorse or Old Town.

Moving through the house, Carter saw that there were no personal items in the living room, kitchen or dining room. Three of the bedrooms were completely empty. The fourth had a bed, the blankets on it crumpled.

Carter stepped in. There was a half-empty water glass next to the bed. He moved around to the other side. A book lay on the floor. A mystery, one Carter had been meaning to read.

Nothing here of any interest. He felt relieved, although he had no idea what he'd expected to find.

As he turned to leave, he saw the back of the bedroom door. A cheap cork bulletin board had been tacked to it. The bulletin board held a half-dozen snapshots.

Carter stepped closer. His heart began to pound. The photographs were of Eve Bailey, all candid shots taken with a wide-angle lens from a distance. And one of her as a baby with her grandmother.

There were photographs of her going into the Whitehorse rest home, ones of her coming out of the grocery store, another of her getting gas at Packy's on the way out of town.

But it was the photograph of Eve saddling up her horse next to the barn and another of her painting late at night inside her grandmother's house that struck like a blade through the heart.

He tried his cell. No service. He rushed out of the house to his patrol car and grabbed his radio. Deputy Samuelson didn't answer. Carter told himself that the deputy was probably in the house with Eve. Knowing her, she was probably making him breakfast.

But he couldn't shake the feeling that Eve was in terrible trouble as he leaped into his car, started the engine and took off in the direction of her house.

A mile up the road, his radio squawked. He snatched it up, praying it was Samuelson. It was the dispatcher with an urgent call from Max Roswell at the crime lab.

"Patch him through." Carter held his breath as he heard Max's voice.

"We've identified your vic from the plane," Max said. "We got lucky. He had a variety of tattoos. One with his military unit number. Another of a heart with two names inside, his and a woman's. Even with the skin mummified we were able to enhance both tattoos by using a computer program. This high-tech stuff is truly amazing."

Carter couldn't have cared less how they'd done it. "Who is he?"

"You might know him," Max said. "He dropped off the radar screen thirty-two years ago. Name's Charley Cross. The woman's name on the tattoo is Nina Mae."

Eve's grandfather was the victim?

"You still with me?" Max asked. "I take it you know him?"

"Yeah," Carter managed to say. "He supposedly ran off thirty-two years ago. To Mexico. At least that was the rumor." He recalled how devastated Nina Mae had been after that.

"He didn't get quite that far," Max said.

Carter's mind was reeling. No wonder Nina Mae had been devastated. If she and Charley had been on that plane...

"By the way," Max was saying. "Those hair samples we took from the baby brush. We ran a couple of DNA tests. The hair was from two different babies. But are you ready for this? They were related."

Eve fought as hard as she could while being dragged into the dark barn. She could tell by his strength that he was a man. The perspiration smell of him made her nauseous.

Swearing as she connected the heel of her boot with his shin, he threw her down hard. It took her breath away, but she scrambled to her feet, ready to run.

Errol Wilson blocked her escape. He had pulled a gun and now held it on her. "I told your mother to do something about you or I would."

She felt the nausea rise in her throat. "What did my mother ever see in you?" she demanded angrily.

"The bitch did this to me," he said, gingerly touching the bandage on the back of his head with his free hand. "I warned her she'd be sorry. She thought she could string me along, paying me off with money, holding back what I really wanted."

A light burned in his eyes. Eve saw both lust and hate. "You weren't lovers." She couldn't believe the sense of relief she felt.

"Your mother is one coldhearted bitch," Errol said angrily. "I told her she'd regret it. But then she never knew what was at stake. She was so busy trying to protect everyone else." He smiled smugly. "Come on." He motioned to the back of the barn. "I have a little present for you."

Eve glanced into the cool darkness, afraid of what he

planned to do. "Why don't you tell me what it was my mother didn't get."

He sneered at her. "You've been watching too many of those shows on television. If you think you can distract me by getting me to talk, think again." He motioned once more with the gun. "I can kill you here if you like, but then you'll never see your surprise. It's waiting for you in the car just outside."

Carter. It was her first thought. "What did you do with the deputy?"

"He won't be saving you. If you know what I mean." Errol laughed. His face quickly turned ugly. "Don't make me tell you again." He pointed toward the back of the barn.

Eve moved slowly, searching the darkness for a weapon. But she saw nothing she could get to fast enough to defend herself before he shot her. She didn't doubt that Errol would shoot her. Probably not to kill. He wanted her to see her surprise first.

Bracing herself, she pushed open the door at the back of the barn and blinked. Bridger Duvall's large black car was parked a few yards away, the trunk open a crack.

Errol shoved her forward, knocking her into the side of the car. He reached into the backseat. "Here," he said, "hold out your hands, wrists together. That's right."

Still holding the gun on her, he awkwardly wrapped the tape around her wrists with his free hand.

"That's too tight. You're cutting off the circulation," she said.

"Boo hoo for you," he said, and ripped the end before tossing the roll into the back again. He lifted the lid of the trunk all the way up.

Eve stared down at Bridger Duvall curled in the large

trunk. His ankles were taped, his wrists taped behind him. He had a gash on his forehead that had bled but stopped. His eyes were wide. Scared. Just like her.

"Get in," Errol ordered.

Eve reared back. She hated cramped spaces. "Please, don't—"

Errol slapped her across the face. "Get in. Lie down. You cause me any trouble and I'll tape your ankles and your mouth."

He shoved her into the back next to Duvall. "You two make yourselves comfortable. We've got a long ride ahead of us." He slammed the trunk lid.

Eve tried not to scream in the total darkness of the trunk. She couldn't catch her breath.

"Breathe normally," Bridger ordered. "There's plenty of air. Your eyes will adjust and you'll see some light. You're all right."

She wasn't all right. Errol had gone mad. Who knew what he'd done with the deputy Carter had left with her. Or what he planned to do with her and Bridger.

The car rocked. The engine roared. The radio came on as the car began to move.

Bridger was right. She could see light, faint, the opening small. At least they wouldn't die of asphyxiation.

"Who is this guy and what does he want with us?" Bridger asked.

"Errol Wilson. I don't know." She could barely make out Bridger's features even though she was only inches away.

"You all right now?"

No. "As all right as I can be under the circumstances."

"So you're not part of this?" he asked.

Obviously not. "You know what this is?"

"Haven't you guessed what you and I have in common? Other than the obvious," he added.

"We're burglars?"

He smiled a little at that, his teeth flashing in the dim light. "We were both looking for files in Dr. Holloway's office. Why is that?"

"You tell me."

"February fifth, 1975." He must have seen her reaction. "The day you were born."

"How do you know that?" The car must have reached the main road. It sped up. Her wrists ached from the tape and her body from the jarring ride.

"I came to Whitehorse looking for you."

His words stunned her. She recalled him coming out of her grandmother's room pocketing a photograph she was sure he'd stolen of her as a baby. Her fear, already off the charts, spiked. "Me?"

"What did you find out the other night in the archives?" he asked. "Come on. We don't have much time."

"I found evidence that I was adopted."

"You didn't already know that?" He sounded surprised.

She shook her head, not wanting to admit her mother had lied to her.

"I always knew," he said. "But it wasn't until my adoptive mother was dying that she told me the rest."

She held her breath. "The rest?"

"It wasn't a legal adoption. They knew someone who knew someone, a woman doctor in Great Falls who found babies for couples that were ineligible to adopt for whatever reason. With my mother, it was poor health."

Eve felt her heart begin to pound as she recalled the

funeral her mother had gone to yesterday. Could it be the same doctor?

"It was all done in secrecy. The couple would get a call in the middle of the night," he continued. "They'd go to the designated spot and would be given a baby and a birth certificate."

She knew even before he spoke what was coming.

"My parents came to the original Whitehorse Cemetery the night of February seven, 1975."

Chapter 15

Carter came roaring up next to Deputy Samuelson's patrol car. Through the curtainless windows, he didn't see Eve or Deputy Flynn Samuelson as he jumped out of the SUV and ran toward the house.

Something was wrong. He could feel it as he pounded up the steps and across the porch. He could see into the house, past the living room, something spilled on the floor in the kitchen.

"Eve! Flynn!" he called, as he raced inside. "Eve!"

The house echoed his cries and his footfalls as he dodged paint cans to reach the kitchen.

A pool of broken eggs lay next to the carton. Near it lay a butcher-wrapped package. His attention flew to the empty kitchen and, beyond it, the open back door.

Eve. He was on his phone as he ran out. No sign of Eve in the yard or the barn. The dispatcher answered on the first ring.

"I need the other deputies out to Old Town White-horse right away," he said into the phone. "Eve Bailey and Flynn Samuelson are missing. Tell the deputies to begin a search of the area."

He disconnected, glancing down the road toward the Bailey ranch. Lila's pickup sat out front. Next to it was a rental car. The same color and make as the one his father had been driving.

Eve felt her heart lodge in her throat as she looked at Bridger Duvall. "You think you were the baby on the plane that crashed in the Breaks?"

"I know I was."

She felt her heart drop. She'd been so sure it was her. "How can you know?"

"My mother told me that they got me from an elderly woman at the old Whitehorse, Montana, cemetery the night of February seven, 1975. These women placed babies. The way it worked was that if you wanted a baby you let someone know. Then you'd get a call, often in the middle of the night. You drove to the cemetery."

"The cemetery?" She remembered stories about strange lights in the cemetery at night, which persisted to this day.

"You waited until someone showed up with a baby and a birth certificate, no questions asked," he continued. "My mother and father desperately wanted a child. They would have done anything." He smiled ruefully at that. "They did. They drove all night to get here and waited in freezing temperatures. And just when they thought they'd been duped, an elderly woman tapped on their window and handed them me and my birth certificate."

Not her grandmother. Someone else. Because Grandma Nina Mae had a broken leg. Was it possible Bridger was wrong about the date? She felt the car slow. Errol turned onto another road, this one paved. The car sped up.

"It was the wrong birth certificate," Bridger said, making Eve start. "The woman had to go back and get the right one. The first one was for a girl, born the same day as me. The name on her birth certificate was Eve Bailey."

Eve began to cry silently. She'd known the moment Carter told her about the possibility of a baby being on that plane that it was her. She'd never imagined, though, that there had been two babies.

"Why didn't you come to me with this information?" she demanded.

"Why would I? I had to assume that you knew, that you were in on it. My mother warned me that I might never know the truth because the whole operation was run by a close-knit group of women who, according to the lady Great Falls doctor, planned to take the information to their graves."

She didn't know what to say.

"We look enough alike and, given the fact that we were both brought in on the same night, there's a chance you're my sister."

"That's not possible." She remembered how much her father had wanted a son. Grandma would have known that. She wouldn't have split up a brother and sister. "They wouldn't have split us up."

"My parents had been on the waiting list for years, but they could only afford one child," he said. "We had a small ranch down by Roundup. My father needed a son if he hoped to hang on to it."

She was angry with whoever had done this, but sympathetic to what Bridger's parents must have gone through knowing there was a sister they couldn't take. "Do they still have the ranch?"

"My parents are buried there. Your grandmother was the woman who met my parents that night in the cemetery, wasn't she?"

"No. She was on the plane. But she broke her leg that night. She couldn't have been the one. She wouldn't have split us up. Not for any reason."

"Then who? You're from here, you must know."

She shook her head. "It was so long ago, if the woman was elderly, she might be dead by now."

"Someone around here knows. If there was a waiting list then someone has to have kept track of the adoptions, the birth mothers, which families got which kid. There has to be a record. Some proof."

She felt numb. Her mind kept telling her none of this was happening. "Where does Errol Wilson come into all this?"

"I don't know. I've just been trying to find out who I am," he said quietly.

Better to worry about how to find his birth mother than what was going to happen when Errol got them wherever he was taking them, she thought, no matter how futile it might be.

Was it possible they were brother and sister? For so long she'd yearned for someone who looked like her. Bridger Duvall definitely did. Her throat tightened, eyes filling again with tears. A brother? One she might never get to know.

"If, when, we get out of this, I'm going to find her," Bridger said. "And I'm going to find where they recorded the names."

"What they were doing was illegal, why would they keep a record?" she said. "It's been such a well-kept secret I doubt there is any way to prove who was behind it."

"Except there's a murdered man in that plane, right?" he said. "And that's why we're in this trunk. Seems pretty obvious that someone's scared we know too much."

"Who told you about the murdered man?" she asked.

"Errol."

Errol slowed, turned and the road got much rougher.

"I don't understand this," she said. But she doubted it would be long before they found out what he had planned for them.

"I suspect it has something to do with the dead man in the plane," Bridger said. "There's no statute of limitation on murder. What's a couple more murders if there's a chance of covering up the first?"

Carter's father looked up in surprise as Carter stormed into the Bailey kitchen. Loren Jackson sat at the kitchen table. Lila Bailey sat across from him. They both had mugs of coffee in front of them and somber expressions on their faces. A stack of photographs had been pushed to one side.

"Carter?" Loren said in surprise.

"I thought you were at a funeral in Great Falls?" Carter said to Lila, hating the accusation he heard in his voice.

"It was a short sunrise funeral. Only close…friends," she said, as if his storming in was nothing out of the ordinary.

"I need to know what the hell is going on and I need to know right now," Carter said. "Eve's missing. And so is the deputy I left with her."

Lila rose halfway out of her chair. "She's probably taken off into the Breaks again—"

"She didn't go for a horseback ride," Carter snapped, voice rising. "She's in trouble because of that damned plane, because of your lies. I just got the ID on the victim in the plane. It was Charley Cross, your father."

She stood, her hand on the back of the chair shaking. "None of that matters. We have to find Eve and—"

"You knew." Carter swore and looked at his father and saw he, too, knew. He swore again. "All these years the two of you have been covering for a murderer?"

"My father wasn't murdered," Lila said. "He was killed in the crash."

"When Eve found the plane, he had a knife sticking out of his chest."

All the blood drained from Lila's face. Loren reached for her, but she shooed him away and lowered herself back into the chair. "Oh, God. I didn't know. I swear I didn't know," Lila said, sounding near tears. "Mother said Daddy died in the plane crash."

"Who was the pilot?" When neither answered, he slammed his fist down on the table, unable to control his anger or his frustration or his fear for Eve. The photographs that had been stacked near the edge started to tumble off. Lila reached for them instinctively. He grabbed them first, spilling them across the table.

"You have to tell me. It's the only hope I have of finding Eve, of stopping this before…" Carter couldn't voice his worst fear. "Who was the pilot?"

Lila shook her head, her eyes filled with fear. "I don't

know. I swear. The fewer people who knew the specifics the better, so Mother never told me."

"Knew what? Damn it. Tell me what the hell your parents were doing on the plane that night."

"They were bringing in babies. Flying them in," Loren said. "I knew about the babies, but I never flew for them, neither did your grandfather."

Carter stared at him. "I don't believe you."

"I had Cade, and your mother was pregnant with you. I didn't want anything to do with it," Loren said more forcefully.

Why didn't that ring true? And then it hit Carter. "You were afraid if you got caught you would lose your pilot's license. That's all you've ever cared about."

"Not all." Loren glanced across the table at Lila.

Carter turned to Lila. "Your mother just left her husband in the plane?"

"She had to protect the babies," Lila said, her voice thick with emotion. "He was dead. If she told anyone, there would be an investigation. She would never betray the babies. Not even for the man she loved."

"Wait a minute," Carter said. "How many babies are we talking here?"

"Dozens," Loren said, looking at Lila for confirmation. "It started back in the 1930s when the CCC was up here building Fort Peck Dam—all those men turned loose on Montana."

Carter had heard about the red-light district outside of Fort Peck. He had a pretty good idea where some of the babies came from.

"Many of the girls were from good families, even distinguished families," Lila said. "They couldn't keep their babies because they were too young or poor or because their parents wouldn't allow it. With other women desperate for children, someone had to find those babies good homes."

"I thought that's what adoption agencies were for," Carter retorted.

"These were Montana women and men, often with little resources. In my mother's case, it was her age, her economic bracket, the fact that she lived so far from a hospital," Lila said.

Carter stared at her in disbelief. "You were one of the babies?"

She nodded. "My mother and father couldn't have children. It was one of the reasons they dedicated their lives to what the circle had started."

"The circle?" he asked, frowning.

"The Whitehorse Sewing Circle," she said. "That's where it began years ago. One of the women heard about a pregnant girl who couldn't keep her baby. The circle decided to help her and made arrangements for the baby to go to a good local family. That's how it started. Later we had the help of several doctors."

Carter stared at her. "That's how you got Eve."

Lila nodded. "And McKenna and Faith."

"They were adopted, too?" He raked a hand through his hair and checked his watch. He had to find Eve. "What about the drugs?"

Lila looked at him in surprise.

"The pilot of the plane was smuggling in marijuana along with babies," Carter said.

"That's not possible. My parents never would have—"

He cut her off. "We don't have time for this now. I need to find out who was piloting that plane the night it crashed in the Breaks." He looked to his father. "You let them use our airstrip on the ranch. Don't tell me you didn't know who was behind the controls."

"That was your grandfather's doing. He allowed them to use the airstrip, but he never flew the planes. He made sure none of us was around when a plane was coming in with a…package," Loren said.

Eve had believed there was a conspiracy to keep the truth from her. She had no idea. And Old Town Whitehorse was perfect for this kind of operation. Isolated and close-knit.

"If my father discovered the plane was carrying drugs and that the pilot…" Lila looked up at Carter. "This pilot, he has my daughter?"

"I think there's a good chance," Carter said. "That's why I have to find him." Before he kills again. "I have no idea even where to look."

The circle could have gotten pilots from out of town. Even out of state or out of the country. Canada was less than fifty miles from here. For all he knew the killer could be transporting Eve across the border at this moment. After all, getting into Canada, if you knew the back roads, was just a matter of opening a barbed wire gate and driving through.

He picked up one of the photographs that had spilled across the tabletop, his mind reeling. It was a picture of his father and Lila. They were both very young and, even in the faded photo, Carter could see that they were in love.

Past it was a snapshot of his father and grandfather standing next to Loren's first plane, under it an older black and white of his grandfather's squadron from WWII.

Carter felt a jolt as he reached for it. "You didn't tell me Dr. Holloway flew with Grandpa in WWII."

"Doc got shot down. He never flew again," Loren said.

"At least not that you know of," Carter said as he stared at the photograph of a much younger Dr. Holloway. "He signed all the birth certificates, right?"

Lila nodded.

Next to Doc in the picture was a kid who didn't even look eighteen. He looked vaguely familiar. "Who is—"

"That's Errol Wilson," Loren said. "He was a mechanic at the end of the war. He loved to hang out with the pilots, Dad said. Loved to fly."

"Errol had a pilot's license?" Carter said, remembering the way Errol had been acting around Eve that day in the Breaks.

"No," Loren said. "That is, he had his license, but he got it taken away because of some mess or another he was involved in. Errol never got over it. Worst thing that can happen to a man who loves to fly."

"Errol and Wanda never had any children," Carter said, his mind racing.

"No, Wanda couldn't conceive," Lila said.

Carter felt his heart rate take off at a gallop. "The circle didn't offer them a child?"

Lila met his gaze, hers hard and cold. "Errol didn't want someone else's bastard. There were enough of them in Whitehorse as it was, he said."

Carter hurriedly got on his radio and put out an APB on Errol Wilson. Then he asked Lila where he could find Doc.

"He came back from Great Falls when I did. He said he had work to do. So I assume he's at his office."

Carter's two-way radio squawked. "Sheriff, we found Samuelson."

Errol brought the car to a stop and killed the engine, filling the trunk with an eerie silence.

Eve looked at Bridger and saw her own fear mirrored in Bridger's eyes as she heard the car door open, felt Errol climb out. The door slammed. A moment later, she heard the key in the trunk lock.

The lid opened. Eve blinked at the sudden light.

"Come on, you two," Errol said. "We don't have all day."

Past him, Eve saw pine trees. She tried to retrace the trip in her mind, remembering the bumpy roads then the paved, then another rough road to here.

The nearest pines would be in the Breaks. But Errol had driven on paved highway for what had seemed like at least an hour. If he'd gone south… Doc Holloway had a cabin in the Little Rockies near Zortman.

Errol helped her out. Her legs were cramped, her wrists aching from the tape, but she found her feet and glanced around. Doc Holloway's old Suburban was parked in the pines nearby.

Drawing a knife, Errol cut the tape on Bridger's ankles. He sheathed the blade to pull the gun again and pointed it at Eve's head.

"Unless you want to see your twin's head blown off, you won't do anything stupid," Errol said, pulling her back a few feet to give Bridger room to get out.

"So we are twins," Bridger said.

"Fraternal, according to Doc," Errol said.

"Doc Holloway? We were born locally?" Eve asked.

"Up north by the border. A home delivery," Errol said.

"What else did Doc tell you about us?" Eve asked. "Do you know who our birth mother was?"

"Doc didn't say, I didn't ask," Errol said. "I had to land on the highway up there. Doc met the plane with the two of you. Whoever your mother was, I'm sure she was just glad to get rid of you."

"You're a real bastard, you know that?" Bridger said.

Errol laughed. "Takes one to know one."

"The sheriff will be looking for us," Eve said.

"Everyone will be looking for you," Errol said. "But they won't find you. Not for a while, anyway. Come on." He shoved her toward a path that led up the hill. "Either of you does anything stupid and I shoot to kill, understand?"

"You're going to kill us, anyway," Bridger said, behind Eve as she started up the trail.

"I can do it now if you keep mouthing off," Errol shot back. "This is your own fault. You just couldn't quit putting your nose into things. You have only yourself to blame."

"Yeah, you keep telling yourself that all the way to hell," Bridger said.

Eve heard Errol hit him from behind. Bridger let out a "whuft" sound. She looked back, afraid of what Errol had done to him, but Bridger motioned for her to keep moving. "I'm fine," he said.

"He tell you that he's been spying on you? I caught him taking pictures of you," Errol said.

Eve turned a little to look back at him.

"Her name was the only one I had. I had to assume she was in on the cover-up," Bridger said.

"Yeah? Well, between the two of you, you've made a real mess for me to have to clean up," Errol said.

As Eve topped a rise in the trail, she saw the cabin. It was small, built of logs, set back against the mountain. There was a porch across the front and an old rocking chair. Next to it, a creek tumbled in a waterfall to drop a good twenty feet into a rocky pool below.

The roar of the creek reminded her of something Doc Holloway had once told her about his cabin. "I have an old rocker on my cabin porch. Someday I'm going up there and I'll just sit and listen to the creek next to my cabin instead of whining patients. Someday soon."

She felt tears rush her eyes. This couldn't be happening. Errol had always scared her. She didn't doubt he planned to kill them. But not Doc. And yet it had been Doc's name on her birth certificate. He was in this up to his neck. But he wouldn't be part of a kidnapping, possibly even murder. She recalled last night at the hospital when she'd seen Errol and Doc arguing. Is this what they'd been arguing about?

As sunlight caught on one of the cabin windows, she told herself Doc wasn't a killer. He was a healer. He had always been kind to her. He wouldn't let Errol kill them. In fact, she was sure Doc would be furious that Errol had brought her and Bridger here. He would fix this, just as he'd fixed her broken wrist when she was eleven.

The cabin door opened.

Just down the road from Eve's house, deputies had found Deputy Flynn Samuelson's body stuffed in a ditch culvert. Samuelson had his throat cut.

Eve was still missing.

Trying not to panic, Carter called for the coroner and

an ambulance and ordered the deputies to keep searching for Eve. He felt his despair growing. Just as he suspected, a killer had Eve. He feared it was the same one
who'd murdered her grandfather thirty-two years ago.

"Sheriff!" one of the deputies called from the barn.
"I found something. Better come take a look."

Carter entered the dark barn, his heart in his throat.
The deputy was standing by the back door, the sunlight
streaming in from outside. Please, don't let it be Eve. He
moved through the barn, bracing himself for the worst.

"I found tire tracks where a vehicle had been parked
back here," the deputy said as he led him outside. "I
found this by the back door." He stepped over to the side
of the barn. "In the grass."

Carter held his breath as he drew back the high grass.
He stared down at the wallet. It was black leather, ex-
pensive looking. As shiny as it was, the wallet hadn't
been there long.

"I didn't touch it," the deputy said.

"Good work." Carter picked up a stick and carefully
opened the wallet to expose a driver's license. Bridger
Duvall. What the hell was his wallet doing here?

"Isn't really a place where a man would drop his wallet," the deputy said. "It's almost as if someone threw it
into the grass there—"

"So we would find it," Carter finished for him. Was
it possible the killer had both Eve and Bridger Duvall?
He recalled what Max Roswell from the crime lab had
said about the baby hair in the brush found in the plane.
Two different individuals. Two babies on the plane. Related to each other.

He checked Bridger Duvall's birth date, knowing
even before he looked that it would be February 5, 1975.

His cell phone rang. He jerked it from his hip. "Jackson."

"More trouble, Sheriff," the dispatcher said. "It's Doc Holloway's office building. It just exploded. They think Doc is trapped inside."

The cabin doorway filled. Eve felt her mouth go dry as she saw that it wasn't Doc Holloway who stepped out.

"Took you long enough," Wanda Wilson said as she moved aside to let her husband and his kidnap victims enter the cabin. She was a wide-bodied, short woman with a round face, close-set eyes and gray hair. For as long as Eve had known her, Wanda had worn a sour expression, as if she'd just eaten something bitter.

Eve glanced from Wanda to the roar of the creek far below the porch. As she looked down and saw the water rushing over the boulders, she felt a wave of vertigo and stumbled.

"What's wrong with you?" Wanda demanded.

"The tape is cutting off my circulation."

"It won't hurt much longer," the older woman shot back.

Errol stopped for a moment, motioning to everyone to be quiet. Eve heard it, too. The sound of a car coming up the cabin road. Then there was nothing but the wind high in the pines and the chatter of squirrels off in the distance.

"I didn't hear anything," Wanda said. "But let's get this over with and get out of here."

"Why are you doing this?" Eve asked, stopping short of the doorway to look back at Errol. She'd definitely heard a vehicle down the road. She was praying it was Carter. All she had to do was buy her and Bridger time.

Errol jammed the barrel of the gun into Bridger's ribs and she thought for a moment he was going to pull the trigger in answer.

"Because of your grandfather, that righteous son of a bitch," Errol snapped.

"Don't," Wanda warned.

"Why not tell them? You want to know why you both have to die? Because you're just like your grandfather, Charley Cross, that's why. He couldn't keep his nose out of other people's business. Him and his high-and-mighty good deeds."

"Errol—"

He didn't seem to hear as he continued his tirade. "Ol' Charley thought I should just fly bastard babies all over the state out of the goodness of my heart. Oh, sure, he'd pay for plane rentals and fuel, then slip me a twenty like I was some servant. He could have over-looked the weed I was running. The bastard was going to turn me in. After everything I'd done for him and your grandmother."

"Oh, my God," Eve said, her knees giving out.

"Damn it, Errol!" Wanda bellowed as she kept Eve from falling all the way to the porch floor. "Shut the hell up."

"What difference does it make now if she knows I killed her grandfather?" Errol demanded. "Your grand-mother thought the plane crash killed him. Charley was unconscious. I waited until your grandmother got out with one of the babies, then I stopped Charley from opening his mouth ever again."

Eve began to cry for the grandfather she'd never got-ten to know. She thought of Grandma Nina Mae letting the world believe that Charley had deserted her, run off to Mexico. She felt sick to her stomach. Her grandmother had had to leave Charley in the plane, to keep the secret. To protect Eve and Bridger and the other children.

"You bastard!" Eve cried, lunging at Errol. Wanda jerked her back.

"Do that again and I kill your brother right here and now," Errol threatened.

Bridger let out a chuckle. "You were running drugs and using the baby operation as a front. Sounds like a pretty good deal to me."

Eve didn't believe Bridger for a moment, but Errol did.

He chuckled. "Maybe I was wrong. I should have taken this kid. The kid and I would have had a great business going. We could have cut Doc out of it entirely."

"Doc wouldn't have gotten involved in selling drugs," Eve said, not so sure about that but wanting to believe it was true. She wondered where Doc Holloway was. What if that had been his car she'd heard and not Carter's? What if Errol knew Doc a whole lot better than she did?

"You always were so naive," Wanda said, grabbing her arm and dragging her into the cabin. It was dark inside, only minimal furnishings. Wanda pulled her over to a trapdoor in the wooden floor and shoved her toward the stairs that dropped down into total blackness.

"Don't do this," Eve said. "No one can prove you killed my grandfather. But if you kill me, Carter won't stop until he finds you." It wasn't much of a threat, but once she said it she knew it was true. "He loves me. He's always loved me. He will track you to the ends of the earth."

Wanda laughed. "Yeah, that's why he married Deena Turner."

"Anyway, this isn't my doing," Errol said. "This is Doc's. His cabin. He's the one who signed all those fraudulent birth certificates. When your sheriff finds the 'retirement' money Doc put away from our drug deals, he won't look any further. He'll believe Doc was flying the plane that night. And there won't be anyone to tell him different."

"Get down there!" Wanda ordered. "Or I'll throw you."

Eve didn't doubt it. She saw no way out. Errol had a gun on Bridger and she suspected it would turn out to be Doc's if Errol had to use it. "At least cut the tape on my wrists. I'm not going to do anything. I know you would shoot my brother if I did."

"Cut the damn tape," Errol snapped. "I'm sick of listening to her whine."

Wanda swore as she took Errol's knife and none too gently cut the tape. "Now get down there."

"What's going on?" asked a voice from the doorway.

Everyone turned at the sound.

Eve stared in disbelief. "Deena?"

Chapter 16

Carter raced into Whitehorse. He could see the smoke from miles away. As he approached Dr. Holloway's office building, he saw that it was a total loss.

"Doc?" he asked the chief fireman.

"We got him out. He was in bad shape, but still alive when the ambulance took him to the hospital."

The deputy had reported back that there was no sign of Errol or Wanda at their house. Carter could feel the clock ticking. What if Errol didn't have Eve? What if he was wrong and the killer wasn't local? Eve could be anywhere.

He refused to even consider that she might not still be alive as he drove to the hospital. An internist met him at the door.

"Doc?" Carter asked.

The intern shook his head. "He was too badly burned.

Even if we could have gotten him airlifted out to Billings or Salt Lake City to the burn center there…"

Carter rubbed a hand over his face. Doc was gone and so were all the medical records. Also gone was any hope of getting answers.

"He was asking for you right before he died," the intern said. "He kept saying Sheriff, and what sounded like cabin? Make any sense?"

"Yeah," Carter said, and ran for his patrol car.

Eve wasn't sure what Deena saw first, the gun in Errol's hand, the tape binding Bridger Duvall's wrists or the shotgun Wanda had grabbed.

"What's going on?" Deena asked again, her voice breaking as her attention settled on Errol's gun, now pointed at her. "Is this some kind of joke?"

"What are you doing here?" Wanda demanded.

Deena seemed to pry her gaze away from the gun to look at the older woman, who had now raised the shotgun, pointing both barrels at Eve and Bridger.

"I was following Bridger's car," Deena said. "I knew he'd been sneaking around Eve…" She glanced at Eve, then Bridger.

Eve saw that Deena held a small digital camera in her left hand and knew at once what Deena was doing here. She'd planned to expose Eve's affair with Bridger to Carter. The woman was so transparent. She'd seen Bridger following Eve and had followed the two of them—right into trouble.

"What are we going to do with her?" Errol demanded.

"What do you think?" Wanda snapped. "We don't have much choice."

Errol started toward the door and Deena. Deena might

be transparent and a whole lot more, but she wasn't completely stupid. Sizing up the situation, she turned and ran.

Carter had never been to Doc's cabin, but he knew the small old mining community south of town. And he'd heard Doc talk about the place enough that he didn't have any trouble finding the road.

He parked the patrol car and, taking his shotgun and extra ammunition, sprinted up the road a way before cutting through the trees. He hadn't gone far when he stumbled on a vehicle he recognized. Deena's SUV. There was a rifle on the floor of the backseat.

"What the hell?" Fear threatened to overtake him. Whatever Deena was doing here it couldn't be good.

He could hear the rush of the waterfall even before he topped a rise and spotted the cabin through the trees in the distance. He saw Doc's car was parked below it. And to his surprise, Bridger Duvall's big black car. No sign of Errol's old blue pickup.

Deena and Bridger Duvall?

Doc definitely wasn't inside the cabin. So what was his car doing here?

Cutting through the trees, he circled the cabin, praying he'd come to the right place. Deena's and Bridger's cars being here had thrown him.

As he drew nearer, he heard a gunshot. He began to run toward the cabin, having no idea what he would find once he got there.

The bullet Errol had fired at Deena burrowed into the door frame, the sound booming through the small cabin.

"Get her," Wanda cried, and Errol took off at a run

after Deena. Another shot, followed by the splintering of wood and Deena's long eerie cry, then silence.

Even Wanda turned to look toward the porch as if she knew Deena had fallen through the old railing and dropped to the creek below.

Eve saw her chance in that moment when Wanda looked through the open doorway toward the porch. Errol would be back any moment. Eve grabbed for the shotgun.

Wanda Wilson was a strong farm woman. Eve's arms were weak from being bound for so long. She wrestled Wanda for the shotgun knowing she would lose.

Out of the corner of her eye, Eve saw Bridger. He had something gripped in both hands, his wrists still bound. He swung a large stuffed northern pike, catching Wanda in the side of the head. Her grip on the shotgun loosened an instant before she slumped to the floor and Errol yelled from the doorway, "I'm going to kill you sons of bitches!"

Eve would always remember the first shot. It whistled past her ear, so close she could feel its power, hear the rush of the air it filled, smell the gunpowder.

Bridger shoved her aside as Errol took aim again.

"No!" she cried as Bridger lunged at Errol. She saw Errol swing the gun toward him, the barrel aimed at his chest. She heard the boom. It reverberated through her skull and she screamed again.

The second shot wasn't as loud. Errol seemed surprised by it. In that instant, before Bridger crashed into him, Errol had stood frowning in the doorway staring at Eve as if he'd thought she'd fire the gun.

Errol fell back on the porch as Bridger hit him.

Eve heard another shot and scrambled to her feet, afraid Bridger had been shot a second time.

But Bridger was up, breathing hard, standing over Errol. Next to him, standing in a shaft of sunlight, was Sheriff Carter Jackson. He was still holding his gun, staring down at the dead Errol.

Carter's eyes filled when he saw her. All he had time to do was open his arms as she flew into them.

Chapter 17

When Lila saw Eve, she broke down, ran out into the afternoon rainstorm and threw her arms around her. "I'm so sorry. I'm so sorry."

Eve leaned into her mother. "I'm all right."

Lila pulled herself together, stepping back to hold her at arm's length to study her. "Yes," she said, smiling through her tears. "You're a Bailey. Bailey women are strong. They're survivors."

Eve's eyes filled with tears as she nodded and let Lila take her into the house, leading her to the kitchen.

"Sit here. I'll make you something to eat. You must be starving."

Eve wasn't hungry, but she knew cooking was how her mother had always dealt with every problem, so she said nothing as she watched her.

Lila made a sandwich and slid it in front of her. She

looked nervous and afraid to sit down, afraid of what came next.

"We have to talk about it," Eve said.

Lila nodded.

"Do you know who my biological mother is?"

"No." Her mother sank into a chair across from Eve, her hands gripped together on the table. "I never wanted to know. You were a gift, Eve, my first child. I loved you more than life. You were my child, my precious child, a true gift from God."

Eve felt her own tears as she saw her mother's eyes flood. "Why didn't you take Bridger, too?"

She shook her head. "He was promised to the other parents. Chester never forgave me. He always wanted a son. He always said that one reason you felt as if something was missing was because of your twin. I'm sorry, Eve. But I couldn't take that little boy from them. There were other chances to get a son, but by then Chester was too angry to care. McKenna and Faith came to us later." She nodded. "They're adopted, as well."

Eve let that sink in. "Are they sisters?"

Lila shook her head. "No blood relation."

"Do you know who their mothers are?"

"I'm their mother," she said, that iron will in her voice. "Just as I'm your mother. I'm sorry I couldn't tell you that you were adopted when you were young. I realize that was a mistake. You were mine. I never thought of you as belonging to anyone else."

It had begun to rain harder, huge drops splattering against the glass.

"I need to go see Grandma," Eve said.

"I can understand if you're angry with her."

Eve smiled. "I'm not angry." It was true. She was

bruised, exhausted, emotionally wrung out, but she wasn't angry or even upset. She'd found out the truth. She didn't want to think at what cost it had come.

She'd discovered a brother she didn't know she had. A deputy had given them a ride back to Old Town Whitehorse while Carter saw that Wanda Wilson was taken into custody and transported to the hospital. Both Deena and Errol would be going to the morgue.

"I want you to know," Bridger had said on the way back. "When I came up here, I wasn't looking to connect with my sister. But I'm glad I found you." He'd sounded as if saying it had come at a cost.

"I'm glad you did, too."

"Even if it almost got us both killed," he'd said with a humorless chuckle. "Would you mind if I stayed around for a while?"

She'd smiled, tears welling in her eyes. "I'd like that."

She knew, though, that part of the reason he was staying in the area was that he hadn't given up on finding their mother. He was convinced that someone here knew the truth. He still hoped to find the woman his parents had met that night in the cemetery.

"I'm all right," Eve told Lila, and smiled as she reached across the table to cover her mother's hand with her own. "Really, Mom."

Tears filled Lila Bailey's eyes. She brushed at them with her free hand. "You'll want milk with your sandwich." She rose to go to the refrigerator.

Eve smiled as she watched her, seeing how hard this was on her, how hard it had been over the years. Lila Bailey was her mother. And they were more alike than Eve had ever noticed before, both afraid of showing their emotions, both in love with men who had broken their hearts a long time ago.

She and Lila would never look alike. They didn't share the same blood or the same DNA, but Eve was a Bailey. And somewhere out there was the woman who'd given her and Bridger birth, given them up in hopes they could have a better life. Eve wanted to find her. Not to find herself, because she'd done that right here.

But to thank her.

The next morning, Carter found his father sitting in the Great Northern Café having breakfast. Loren looked up from a back corner table and smiled, rising to his feet to give his son an awkward hug.

"I don't know how you do it," Loren said, motioning to his son to join him. "You want breakfast?"

"Just coffee. Do what?" Carter asked.

"This sheriff thing. You could have been killed yesterday," his father said, his face pained. "You saved Eve's and that other man's life. Is he really her brother?"

Carter nodded. "Not every day is like yesterday." Thank God.

"How is Eve?"

"She's going to be all right," he said, remembering her in his arms. "She's a strong woman."

"Like her mother. I should tell you—"

"You're in love with Lila," Carter said.

"Yes. Chester has agreed to a divorce. The minute she's free I intend to marry her."

Carter nodded, remembering the strained relationship his parents had for years before his mother's death. "Why didn't you marry Lila if you've always loved her?"

"Our story is a little like yours and Eve's. Lila and I

were young. We had a fight over what her parents were doing. I got drunk and ended up running into Rachel." He paused. "The next thing I knew your mother was pregnant with Cade. Lila married Chester. I married your mother."

"I always thought it was the flying," Carter said.

"It didn't help," Loren admitted. "Your mother knew about Lila, knew how I felt. I loved your mother. I just couldn't love her enough, if you know what I mean."

"Yes, I do," Carter said, thinking of Deena. "Dad, I wish you and Lila the best. I mean that."

"We'll be going to Florida. Lila wants Eve to have the ranch. She's already talked to McKenna and Faith about it. They were fine with it since neither had planned to come back here after college."

"Does Eve know?" he asked.

Loren nodded. "She told her last night. I take it Eve was very happy. She plans to stay."

Carter poured himself a cup of coffee from the carafe on the table and took a drink to hide how relieved he was. Eve was staying. He hadn't been sure, not after everything that had happened.

The real story about the adoptions hadn't come out. The story around town was that Charley Cross had been flying to the hospital in Billings to visit a friend when the plane went down with Errol Wilson at the controls. Unbeknownst to Charley, Errol had been running drugs.

When Charley realized what was going on, Errol killed him and let everyone believe Charley had run off to Mexico.

Wanda Wilson never stood trial. She was killed by an irate inmate in the Great Falls jail before she could tell anyone about the adoptions or the drug running.

Everyone who knew the truth was either dead or not talking.

Earlier, Bridger Duvall had stopped by his office.

"What are you going to do about the Sewing Circle?" Bridger Duvall had demanded.

"You have any proof?" Carter had asked.

Duvall swore. "You know Eve Bailey and I were on that plane."

The sheriff nodded. "But the pilot is dead. So is Charley Cross and Nina Mae has Alzheimers."

"Lila Bailey knows the truth."

Carter nodded. "But she isn't going to bust some old ladies who made it possible for her to adopt her children. If you're looking for vengeance—"

"Not vengeance, answers. I want to know who my birth mother was and someone in the Whitehorse Sewing Circle knows," Duvall had said angrily.

"Well, no one is talking. If anyone knew, it was Pearl Cavanaugh."

Duvall groaned. "You know damned well that she is incapable of talking since her stroke."

Pearl had a stroke after hearing the news about Errol Wilson's drug running and attempt on Eve's and Bridger Duvall's life.

"Does it matter that much, Bridger? You had parents who loved you. Are you sure you really want to know who gave you birth and under what circumstances?"

"Yes. Eve understands. Did you ask her how she feels about this?" Duvall had asked. "She's haunted by this, too. You think she is going to let this go?"

Carter hoped she would find peace now that she knew she was adopted, but he feared she had more in common with Bridger Duvall than just being his twin sister.

"I'm going to be sticking around," Duvall had said.

Carter had nodded. "Eve will like that."

"The answer is here," Duvall had said. "I'm not leaving until I find out the truth."

"Son," Loren said now. "You've never taken my advice." His father laughed to soften his words. "But I'm going to give you some advice I hope you'll take to heart. Don't punish yourself the rest of your life for marrying Deena."

He had thought Deena would do that. But now she was dead. Maybe at peace, since she'd never been able to find peace on earth.

Her parents, who had moved to Arizona some years ago, had taken her body to be buried there. Carter had told them that Deena died trying to save Eve and Bridger. It was a small lie, but one that he knew gave them some comfort.

"Don't put off happiness," Loren continued. "Lila and I intend to enjoy what time we have left. Tell Eve how you feel about her."

"I have. It's going to take time, though."

"You have time," his father said, and smiled. "You have the rest of your lives."

Carter finished his coffee and rose from the table. "Eve's over at the nursing home visiting her grandmother. I thought I'd take her to lunch if she's interested. Will I see you later?"

"You'll see a lot more of me. I won't stay away. Lila and I plan to visit often."

"I'm glad to hear that," Carter said. And he was. He'd never seen his father so happy. It looked good on him.

Carter quickened his step. The rain had stopped and

he could see a little sun peeking through the clouds. He couldn't wait to see Eve again. Today. Tomorrow. And if he had his way, every day after that.

Epilogue

Charley Cross was buried up on the hill overlooking Old Town Whitehorse one windy hot day at the end of July.

Nina Mae stood at the edge of the grave in her favorite brown coat, wearing the pin Charley had given her. Her back was steel straight, her hands clasped in front of her, her eyes as vacant as the blue sky.

Next to her stood Lila Bailey. She wore all black, including the veil that hid her expression. Like her mother, she stood beside the grave, back ramrod straight.

The entire towns of Whitehorse and Old Town, along with half the county, had gathered for the burial. Eve stood with Carter as Titus Cavanaugh, holding his worn Bible, said what a brave man her grandfather had been, how he had done what he believed to be right and died helping others.

Eve searched the crowd gathered under the summer sun, wondering how many of them had been Whitehorse Sewing Circle babies. She felt an odd sense of peace, knowing she wasn't alone. Knowing what it had cost her grandparents so that she and the others would have homes and parents who loved them.

A part of her knew she would always be looking for the mother who had given her away, searching crowds for a familiar face, listening for a laugh like her own.

Carter squeezed her hand as Titus finished with a prayer.

She squeezed back, happier to have him here than he could know. It would take time, but she knew in her heart that one day they would be together.

As Eve placed a single red rose on the casket, Grandma Nina Mae stepped forward. Lila reached for her, as did several of the mourners.

But Nina Mae only rested her pale hand on the casket, her worn wedding ring glinting in the sunlight. Eve saw tears in her grandmother's eyes as Nina Mae patted the casket, then turned to look at the crowd as if searching for someone.

"Have you seen my granddaughter?" she asked in a trembling voice.

"I'm here, Grandma," Eve said, and took the woman's frail arm.

Her grandmother looked over at her, then placed her hand over Eve's and patted it. "Yes," her grandmother said. "You are here, aren't you?"

* * * * *

YOU HAVE
JUST READ A
HARLEQUIN
INTRIGUE
BOOK

If you were **captivated** by the **gripping, page-turning romantic suspense,** be sure to look for all six Harlequin® Intrigue® books every month.

HALOHIINC1012R

❤HARLEQUIN®
INTRIGUE®

SPECIAL EXCERPT FROM

(H) HARLEQUIN®
™

I N T R I G U E

*Former SEAL Pierce Lawrence is looking to rebuild
a family with his five-year-old daughter, but can
Grace Cotton, with her dangerous past,
fit in the picture?*

*Read on for a preview of
RIDING SHOTGUN,
the first book in Joanna Wayne's brand-new trilogy,
THE KAVANAUGHS.*

Pierce was one of the good guys. Brave, a lifesaver with
the medals to prove it. That was the problem. If he knew
the truth, he'd feel he had to save her the way he had to find
justice for Charlie.

Only, trying to save Grace would put him, and possibly
even Jaci and Esther, in danger.

"If you're in trouble, I can help," Pierce said.

Grace took a deep breath and pulled one of her rehearsed
stories from her repertoire. "If you must know, I didn't lose
my job. I had a bad breakup with an ex. I took all of his
possessions he'd left at my place and dumped them into the
nearest trash bin. I decided to take a short vacation while
he cools down."

"Remind me not to make you mad."

"The guy deserved it and he knows it," she quipped. "As
soon as he cools down, he'll be begging me to forgive him
and take him back."

"You have to hang out somewhere until then. What better place than the Double K Ranch? Sounds like a win-win for all of us the way I look at it."

Sounded like she'd backed herself into a corner, and she suspected that Pierce hadn't actually bought her fabricated story.

"I'm really not needed here," she insisted.

"That's not true."

He reached over and took both her hands in his. The touch sent her emotions on a dangerous spiral. She couldn't give in to the desire that sparked inside her. A relationship with Pierce had nowhere to go. It would cause her to make bad decisions. Any kind of relationship would put her and Pierce in danger. It was a risk she could never take.

"We all need you here, Grace."

"I don't see why."

"Then you are underestimating yourself. Esther will likely be hobbling around for another day or two, possibly longer if you're not here to keep her from doing too much."

He inched closer. Her pulse skyrocketed.

"Jaci adores you," he continued. "And you're being here with them while I'm off investigating the murder claim and taking care of some needed repairs around the ranch would make it a lot easier on me."

A few more days. Time with Pierce, Esther and Jaci that would make it all the more painful to go back to her safe little world of emotional isolation when this was over.

Pierce placed a thumb under her chin and tilted her face until his lips were only a hairbreadth away. "I want you to stay, Grace, because I really like having you here."

*Don't miss RIDING SHOTGUN by Joanna Wayne,
available January 2017 wherever
Harlequin® Intrigue books and ebooks are sold.*

www.Harlequin.com

Copyright © 2017 by Jo Ann Vest

HIEXP1216

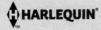

INTRIGUE

EDGE-OF-YOUR-SEAT INTRIGUE, FEARLESS ROMANCE.

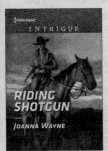

Save $1.00

on the purchase of ANY Harlequin® Intrigue book.

Available wherever books are sold, including most bookstores, supermarkets, drugstores and discount stores.

✂

Save $1.00

on the purchase of any Harlequin Intrigue book.

Coupon valid until March 31, 2017. Redeemable at participating outlets in the U.S. and Canada only. Not redeemable at Barnes & Noble stores.
Limit one coupon per customer.

52614444

Canadian Retailers: Harlequin Enterprises Limited will pay the face value of this coupon plus 10.25¢ if submitted by customer for this product only. Any other use constitutes fraud. Coupon is nonassignable. Void if taxed, prohibited or restricted by law. Consumer must pay any government taxes. Void if copied. Inmar Promotional Services ("IPS") customers submit coupons and proof of sales to Harlequin Enterprises Limited, P.O. Box 3000, Saint John, NB E2L 4L3, Canada. Non-IPS retailer—for reimbursement submit coupons and proof of sales directly to Harlequin Enterprises Limited, Retail Marketing Department, 225 Duncan Mill Rd., Don Mills, ON M3B 3K9, Canada.

5 65373 00076 2   (8100)0 12235

U.S. Retailers: Harlequin Enterprises Limited will pay the face value of this coupon plus 8¢ if submitted by customer for this product only. Any other use constitutes fraud. Coupon is nonassignable. Void if taxed, prohibited or restricted by law. Consumer must pay any government taxes. Void if copied. For reimbursement submit coupons and proof of sales directly to Harlequin Enterprises, Ltd 482, NCH Marketing Services, P.O. Box 880001, El Paso, TX 88588-0001, U.S.A. Cash value 1/100 cents.

® and ™ are trademarks owned and used by the trademark owner and/or its licensee.

© 2016 Harlequin Enterprises Limited

HICOUP01216

New York Times bestselling author

B.J. DANIELS

introduces *The Montana Hamiltons*,
a gripping new series that will leave you
on the edge of your seat...

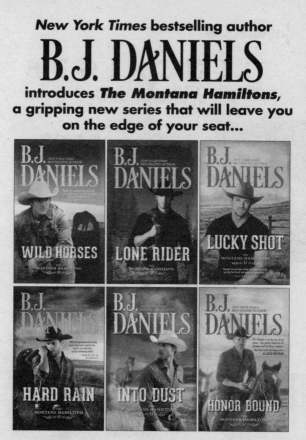

"B.J. Daniels is at the top of her game... The perfect blend
of hot romance and thrilling suspense."
—*New York Times* bestselling author Allison Brennan

Complete your collection!

HQN™

www.HQNBooks.com

PHBJDTMHSR4